P9-AQM-968

A *WASHINGTON POST* CRITIC'S CHOICE

*Please turn the page
for more reviews. . . .*

WAiTiNG iN VAiN

Colin Channer

ONE WORLD

Ballantine Books • New York

A One World Book
Published by The Ballantine Publishing Group
Copyright © 1998 by Colin Channer

www.ballantinebooks.com/one/

ISBN 0-345-43012-3

Manufactured in the United States of America

First Hardcover Edition: July 1998
First Trade Paperback Edition: July 1999
First Mass Market Edition: February 2003

10 9 8 7 6 5 4 3 2 1

For my wife, Bridgitte Fouche, who believed
before she knew.

prologue

On the day he met Sylvia, Fire woke up in Blanche's arms with a numbness in his soul. It was his ninetieth day of celibacy, and the night before had almost been his last for Blanche had tied his wrists in his sleep and pounced on him.

He wanted to talk to her but didn't know how. Couldn't decide how to do it without losing his temper or his pride. He searched the room for answers—the arched windows . . . the rattan chairs . . . the hardwood floors with the swirling grain . . .

The mattress stirred. He heard the strike of her match. Felt the heat. And the tidal pull of her lips. She was naked, and the urgency of smoking did not disturb her breasts, which were hard and still like turtles.

A lizard crawled from the windowsill to the peak of the angled ceiling and slid down the pole of the old brass fan whose blades were sheathed in straw. It flicked its tongue and wagged its head, shaking loose a fold of skin, and puffed a red balloon.

Fire watched it closely, enchanted by its beauty; Blanche sucked her teeth and said it was a nuisance. He didn't answer and she began to taunt it, choked it with rings of smoke till it arched its back and sprang. It fell on her belly with a thwack and did a war dance on her birthmark, a swatch of brown below her navel. She watched it for a while, amused by its bravery, then whipped her body sideways, shimmering the flesh on her hips, and spilled the lizard to the floor.

Fire closed his eyes.

3

Last night he'd dreamed that they'd wallowed in a muddy ditch in a sunflower field. Her belly was wet with almond oil and her nipples were gummed with molasses. A believer in fate and the wisdom of dreams, he'd been dreaming of molasses for months now. And molasses, he knew, as an intuitive man, was the airborne scent of love. Blanche was not the woman though. He was sure. And denial was a way of preparing for her . . . whoever she might be.

Blanche watched as he rose, snatched glances as he dressed. He was tall and rangy and his hair was a cluster of twists and curls. His body looked like a pencil sketch, proportioned but not detailed, except in the chest and upper back.

He went to the terrace and sat in a rocker beneath a brace of ferns, which rustled and fluttered like moody hens. The land cruised away below him, drained through an orchard to an old stone fence, then plunged in an avalanche of crabgrass and buttercups to a terraced farm. Beyond the valley, surreal through the mist, was the broad, flat face of Kingston.

He took a mango from a bowl and peeled it with his teeth. What would he say to her? How would he say it? She was singing in the shower now. He imagined her body—the swell of her thighs, the rise of her ass. And, of course, her breasts. When would he say it? Soon, he thought . . . but not right now.

Resting the fruit on a stack of books, he picked up the poem he'd begun the day before.

> *I dare not love you as you deserve.*
> *It is not that I don't know how.*
> *I do understand the language of love,*
> *and were it a different world*
> *I would write you poems etching you*
> *into the tender cliché of Negril's palmy coast . . .*

He didn't know where he'd take it. He didn't understand poetry really. He'd never studied it. He believed in it as an act of faith.

A flock of birds curled into view. Bird. He began to think of Ian now. They used to call him Bird as a boy for his hawkish nose and pelican legs. What will it be like to see him again? He checked his watch. It was eleven. Air Jamaica was leaving at three; and they were always on time. He would be in New York at seven.

Blanche came out and joined him. She was wearing one of his shirts. It was a soft tangerine with a broad camp collar and flaps on the pleated pockets. A few months short of fifty, she moved with the angular vim of a teenager. She leaned against the banister, a Rothmans between her lips.

Age had refined her beauty, had streaked her hair with silver and added lines and accents to the poetry of her face—commas that made him pause at her eyes, dashes that framed her mouth. She had brows like Frida Kahlo, and lips like Chaka Khan.

"New York," she began. "How long are you going to be there?"

"Just the weekend," he said.

"Then you go to London. And you're coming back when?"

"The end o' August."

"Three months."

She glanced at the old Land Rover beneath the orange tree. Mud encrusted its rusting grill. The windshield was down. The top was off.

"You might need more than a duffel and a knapsack, you know."

He didn't answer. There were footsteps in the kitchen beneath them. What the hell was Miss Gita doing?

"Miss Gita!" he called out as he leaned over the railing. "How much time ah must tell you to rest yourself?"

Miss Gita limped into view with a tray of coffee, dressed in a fading floral shift, her hair a silver line between her face and a red bandanna. An old woman with brown skin like masala, her parents had come from India in the early nineteen hundreds as indentureds—after slavery.

"Ah was only cutting up some tings," she said. "Doan mek nuh fuss over dat. And plus is work ah work here. Is not charity."

"Awright, bring it then."

He settled back in his chair and listened as she shuffled through the creaking house, which was yellow and white with lattice trim and a shingled roof arranged in peaks. The ground floor was made of masonry, and the second floor of wood.

"What ah should bring for you from New York, Miss Gita?"

He wished she'd say, "My son." But she'd given up hope. He stared at her face, which had been thrown off balance by a stroke. It was hard to believe she'd been young once, he thought. Young and beautiful. And wanted by men. Poor Miss Gita. She wasn't a saint; but she'd paid her dues in life. Her blind eye swam out of focus. The good one anchored his gaze.

"Bring a missus," she replied. "The place need a woman. I don't like taking order from people who don't live ere."

"I'll see what I can do," he said awkwardly. Miss Gita left and he took a sip of coffee. It wasn't sweet enough.

Blanche refused to drink hers in protest. She filled her mouth with a cigarette instead. She struck a match. It didn't spark. Her fingers were shaky. Nerves. She fed the Rothmans to the wind.

As she watched him pick up the mango, she marveled anew at his face. Like reggae it was a New World hybrid, a genetic mélange of bloods that carried in their DNA memories of the tribes that fought and fucked on the shores of the Americas—Chinese and Arab, English and Scotch from his father's side; and from his mother's, Dutch and Portuguese Sephardic Jew. But the final combination—brown like sunfired clay, cheeks high and spread apart; nose narrow with a rounded tip; lips wide and fluted—was vibrantly Yoruba and Akan.

Last night was wrong, Blanche said to herself. But she'd

been holding back for months now . . . had even thought she would get through it. But last night, knowing he'd be leaving today just made her desperate. Or was it angry? Three months is a long time for a woman, she thought, especially with a man like this, one who makes love from the inside out—from the core of her soul where she hides her fears, to the taut muscles on the back of her neck. And the way he was eating that mango—the flesh becoming slush and dripping down his arm.

The juice was inking the nib between her legs, making her want to draft an epic on his face. Couldn't he just screw her? She'd take just that. So what if the love was gone? The first time had been just a screw. And she had no regrets. Seeing him nude that first time had made her think of holidays, of turkey legs slathered with gravy. At first she thought he'd be a rammer, a longhorn bedroom bully, which would've been fine. She liked a little roughness at times. But he held her like a dancer, assumed that he would lead, and frigged her with finesse. He understood her needs. Wordplay for him was foreplay. Her thighs were the covers of an open book—a journal lined with fantasies and fears. He read her like a child, slowly, with his nose against the page, using a finger to guide his way. So he knew when to baby her and when to bitch her up.

If he didn't want to screw her, she thought, couldn't they just flirt? Flirting was more than his pastime. It was a condition. He couldn't help himself. He was intelligent and amusing, which was why women fell for him. That's why she had fallen. In the days when he loved her, his words kissed her ears like butterfly wings. Now they stung like wasps: "I don't want you anymore. Leave me alone. I don't care how you feel."

She forced a smile. He didn't respond, but she knew he wanted her. She could feel it. What to do? What to say? She wanted to be the mango so he could suck her down to the seed.

"That looks good," she said. Maybe they would screw if she aroused him. "Would you like to share it?"

He looked at her, looked away, then stretched the mango toward her. She nibbled the tip and licked it carefully, glossed it with her saliva, then, working like a boa constrictor, pulled for a second into her mouth the fruit and his trembling fingers.

A whale began to surface through his deep blue jeans. A voice said, "Suck it." A strange voice, little more than a murmur. Then he gathered it was his and leaned away from her. Licking nectar off her chin, she stared at him. He tried to glare, but couldn't—couldn't even speak.

"Kiss me."

The words were hers. He tried to resist. Thought he had, until his tongue was a honey stick in hot tea. Soon he was melting into memory . . . into their first kiss ten years ago in Cuba.

She was standing on a street corner in Old Havana, a map in her hand, using her own brand of filleted Spanish to explain to a group of curious onlookers that the Yanquis didn't hate them, that the Yanquis in fact pitied them and really hated the French, who they found repugnant and smug. She didn't know how to say "smug" in Spanish.

"Apuesto," he said from the back, *"pulcro."* Their eyes met.

"Excuse me," she said, as the crowd trailed away, "do you speak English?"

"No," he replied. "Do you?" She was wearing a lavender dress and sandals. He was wearing an *Exodus* T-shirt and Red Army boots. He liked her voice. She spoke with a flourish, as if her words were meant to be drawn in calligraphy.

They drifted into a walk, cruised the cobblestoned streets, brushed against each other as they passed under arbors of billowing clothes. She took photographs of the crumbling houses . . . posed on the hoods of vintage cars. It was her first visit to Cuba, she told him. She was forty, and taught English and Near Eastern studies at Columbia. Her father was

Jamaican, her mother from Iran. She'd been raised outside
Toronto.

They had lunch in a *paladar*. Over *gallina vieja* and yellow
rice she learned that he'd been living in Cuba for three years,
had gone there to study with the famous muralist Francisco
Irtubbe after receiving a fine art degree at Yale. He was
twenty-four and Jamaican, and his favorite uncle, I-nelik, had
toured and recorded with The Wailers.

She asked if he was a communist and he told her no. Said
he was a socialist. Then they began to talk about art and she
said there wasn't any money in murals. Money isn't all, he
replied. What is? she asked. Love, he said . . . all you need is
love. She said that was a crock of shit. He liked her directness. It was hard to find that in women his own age.

He offered her a drink when they left the restaurant. She
looked at him . . . cocked her head . . . seemed unsure. He
smiled, as I-nelik had taught him, and led her home without
discussion.

They sipped *mojitos* in the courtyard, a moldering square
of tiles around an almond tree, and shared a *macanudo* and
talked and listened and argued, entangling their minds in a
wrestling match which she won with ease, for she was wiser
and more worldly. She'd lived in five countries, including
Morocco and India, and spoke Arabic, Farsi, French, and
Hindi.

They went inside when the night brought rain. Setting cans
to catch the leaks in the parlor, they talked some more, leaning against each other on the swaybacked sofa with their feet
propped up on a milk crate.

At some point—he could never remember when, because
it had been so unexpected—she pointed to the record
changer, a hefty old thing from Albania, and asked if he had
any jazz. The question felt like a test, a requirement for entry
to her finishing school. He knew this by the way she smiled
when he asked her, like a bartender at a good hotel, "What

can I get for you?" She smiled from the inside, happy for the both of them.

They listened to Johnny Hartman, giggled each time the record changer fell asleep. Then he put on The Wailers— *Kaya*—and the bass began to lick them like a curious tongue . . . and nothing was funny anymore.

"Would you like to dance?" he asked. She said yes, and he held her by the waist, which was soft even then, and sank his hips into the sweet spot. She shook when he started to stir it up, then answered his circumlocutions with inquiries of her own. They continued to dub after the last track had faded like the paint on the wall she was cotched against. Her legs were apart. Her dress hiked up. Her body clammy with their mingled sweat. What to do? They weren't quite sure. Then there was a power cut, and it was inevitable.

"What are you thinking?" she asked.

"That I want you to stay the night."

She slipped a hand down his thigh. "Why?"

"I want to see you naked."

She coaxed his hand into the pulpy split. "See me through your fingers," she said. "Let's pretend to be blind."

"I want to see you," he replied, "to keep a piece of you with me forever. We might have the night and lose the day."

"But I only need today," she whispered.

"But I need tomorrow . . . I'm just that kinda guy. Share a little tomorrow with me."

She kissed him.

"Before I say yes," she said, "I should tell you something. I am woman . . . I am water. You are man . . . you are stone. Water will wear down stone."

They stayed in touch through letters. Phone calls sometimes. But those were harder, requiring a connection through a third country. Then she came to visit three months after leaving and he began to smell molasses. One night, as they biked along the Malecón, she asked if he was dating. She hopped off the handlebars and they sat with their backs to the sea. He told the truth.

"You must get rid of them," she said. "I love you too much to share you."

"And you," he asked, "are you involved?"

"The very question," she replied, "insults me."

They wrote once a week for the next two years—soppy letters that made them laugh—and saw each other twice, each time for three months during her summer break. He wanted to see her more, but couldn't. He was routinely denied U.S. entry because he was labeled a communist.

Then twenty-six months, three weeks, and two days after they met, he got a three-day visa through luck and bribery, and went to New York to surprise her. He found out she was married—with a mortgage, a dog, and three children.

"I'm so sorry," she said, as they cried in her office. "Just give me time . . . I'm just waiting on the right time to leave."

"When will that be?"

"Soon," she said. "Soon as things are right . . . it's all in the timing."

book one

chapter one

Chinatown collides with SoHo and Tribeca at Canal and West Broadway, chucking chi-chi bistros against hardware stores, stereo shops, and purveyors of fake Chanel. As the clock closed in on midnight, Fire stepped out of the subway here and strayed through the gates of love. Dressed in a red T-shirt and slack-fitting jeans, he forded Canal and strode up West Broadway in his tough, scuffed boots past cafés and bars whose faces were pressed together like a Polaroid of friends from prep school. His destination was the Marie Rose Galleries, where his friend Ian Gore was having his first show in five years. By the note in his pocket, the opening had been over for two hours. But this didn't bother him. After twenty-five years, Ian was used to his lateness, and he understood Ian's mood swings.

I wonder how he looks, he thought, as a doorway caught his eye. For all its pretensions, he liked SoHo. The brickwork reminded him of London and the ironwork reminded him of older parts of Kingston. He liked the scale of it. It was low. One could see the sky without trying.

As he walked along Spring Street, contemplating Ian's life, he saw a woman walking toward him in a navy blazer with buttons shaped like sunflowers.

She was tallish and slender, with short, curly hair. And like a dancer, she walked with her toes pointed outward and her neck held loose.

Trailing behind her in the coltish breeze was a light silk

scarf whose flutter he thought was romantic. As she passed, he turned around and sent her a smile, an unsigned thank-you card for having a nice vibe.

He hadn't been to New York in a couple of years. And at Greene it struck him that the gallery had moved. Ian had forgotten to remind him.

From a phone up the block by a parking lot, across from a store named Jekyll & Hyde, he called Information for the new address. But what if they were gone? He glanced at his watch and decided to call, and as he angled to dig for pocket change, he saw the woman in the navy blazer waiting for the phone.

She had lashes like the bristles of a paintbrush and strong, rougeless cheeks.

"Are you through?" she asked. Her voice was warm but girlie—honey mixed with ashes.

"No," he replied. "But you can go if you want."

She accepted politely. A smile hissed across her face—a sparked explosive fuse.

His mouth was suddenly dry. He felt an urge to wet his lips. He didn't, though, unsure of how she'd take it.

She struggled with a shopping bag.

"You want me to hold that?"

She refused politely. Then it slipped. And he grabbed it.

"Are you sure?"

"It's okay," she said. "Thank you." And placed the bag between her feet.

A piece of paper fell to the sidewalk. From where, he wasn't sure. He picked it up and read it as he leaned against a car. It was a shopping list for music: Toni Braxton, Babyface, and Gal Costa. Gal Costa? Tropicalismo . . . nice.

She was his age, he figured, and worked in the arts. Not music though. She would've been more determinedly stylish. Not fashion either—her taste would've had more edge. Design? Maybe. She could be an art director. But for a big firm. Not a boutique. Now where was she from? Her accent was

American, but not from New York. The Midwest maybe, or California. California? Hollywood. She had the trained articulation of an actress.

In the middle of his reverie she grabbed her bag and left, and he walked to the corner, warmed by the encounter. Gal Costa. He thought of Brazil, its pungent food and sensuous music, and turned to smile again. To his surprise she was smiling after him.

"Was that your smile or the reflection of mine?" he asked, slowing down. She was about ten yards away.

She shrugged her shoulders to mean "whatever."

"I hope it was the reflection of mine," he said. "I wouldn't like you to smile at me like that before you get to know me. When you get to know me I'll know what it means. Right now I might have the wrong idea."

She shrugged again.

"If I asked you your name, would you tell me?"

"No."

"I promise not to laugh if it's ugly. I'll just refuse to use it."

She looked at him blankly.

"Go ahead," he said. "Try me."

"No."

He took her coolness as a challenge . . . vowed to make her laugh.

"Try-y-y meeee!" he sang, mimicking James Brown. "You know that song?"

"Yes."

"Oh, you like Bob Marley?"

"That's not Bob Marley," she said. "That's James Brown."

"I knew that," he said, steadying her eyes with a stare. "Just checking."

"Checking what?"

"To see if you're truly monosyllabic or just faking it."

She chuckled, which encouraged him.

"Will you tell me your name now?"

"No."

Her answer did not convince him.

"Well, I won't ask you then. I'll just make one up for you. I'll just call you the woman-with-the-unique-buttons-on-the-navy-blazer-with-the-cute-nose-with-something-hanging-from-it."

She wiped her nose quickly.

"That one hold you!"

She laughed.

"Well, I guess I'm not doing so badly."

"What do you mean by that?"

"I got you to laugh."

"Maybe I'm easy," she countered.

He caught a flash of tongue, a bit of pink against her teeth. He liked her more now. She knew dalliance from harassment. Many women had lost that, had sacrificed good sense for politics.

"I'll flatter myself and say you're not," he said, taking a careful step toward her.

"Why flatter yourself when I could do it for you?"

"If you really want to flatter me, call me."

"I won't."

"Then I won't give you my number."

A smile brewed behind her lips. A chuckle bubbled out. The light changed and he thought he would lose her . . . but she waited . . . stood there staring at him, studying his face . . . his clothes . . . his boots. There was mud on them. On the way to the airport he'd helped to pull a car from a ditch.

"The light changed, y'know, Miss No Name. You coulda crossed."

He took another step toward her. She didn't back away.

"And you have another call to make"—she looked at his shoes again—"Muddy Waters."

"No, I don't," he replied, concocting a story. "I lied to get a chance to talk to you."

"Lying?" she said. "An admirable trait."

"And as we speak," he replied, "I'm composing grand

epics . . . about how you wrestled me to the ground and forced me to take your number."

She laughed like a higgler.

"Is someone waiting for the stuff in that bag?" he asked. "I hope not."

"Unfortunately, yes," she replied.

"Unfortunate for her? For you? For me?"

"Why do you think it's a her?" She smiled awkwardly.

"If a man was waiting for you, you'd be gone already."

"Oh! That is so sexist."

"Sexy?"

She bit her lip and looked away. "Maybe I'm here because he's patient."

"Is he?"

"Not really."

He raised his brows. She laughed again.

"So he's probably missing you, then."

She shifted the bag to her other hand. "I hope so."

"You don't know?"

"I mean . . . I mean . . . you can't swear for people."

He lowered his voice. "Are *you* missing *him*?"

"Not really . . . I mean . . ." She checked her watch. "He should be pulling up around the corner any minute now." She laughed nervously. "Maybe I miss him . . . I don't know. I wasn't thinking about it."

"How long you been together?"

She calculated quickly. "Going on two years."

"Nice," he said.

"I guess," she replied.

"And you don't know if you're missing him? *You know.* You just don't want to tell me."

She suddenly became distant.

"By the way," he said, trying to reconnect, "can I call you to tell you I'd like to see you again?"

"Sure," she said matter-of-factly.

"Who should I ask for?"

"The-woman-with-the-man-she-doesn't-miss. People are waiting for me. I've gotta go."

She began to back away. He asked for her number again and she told him no.

"It was nice to have met you, Miss No Name."

"It was nice to have met you too, Muddy Waters."

He stopped. She stopped as well. A passing car side-lit her face. She was a portrait framed by Gordon Parks.

"It would be nice to see you again."

"I don't feel the same way."

"Why?"

She glanced at his shoes. "I could fall for a man like you."

"What kinda man is that?"

"One who makes me laugh."

"Is that right?"

"That's the point. It's wrong . . . so wrong for me to have these . . ." She aborted the word.

"Feelings," he said.

"Yeah . . . feelings, like I know you from somewhere . . . or that you'd be nice to know."

"Yeah? You like me then?"

"I think that's obvious."

"Why you like me?"

"Because you're smart."

"Actually, I'm retarded." He crossed his eyes . . . made her laugh again.

"And on top of being smart you have nice teeth—a man should have nice teeth. Not necessarily perfect teeth. But nice ones—and you're bow-legged. You remind me of a cowboy. You're my high plains drifter. And I like your nose."

"My nose?"

"It's very sleek . . . like a jaguar."

"The car?"

"The cat," she said, ignoring him. "You're very feline, you know. Your hair is like a lion's. Plus you have really nice skin. I wish I were as dark as you."

"It rubs off, y'know."

"I'll take your word for it."

They stared at each other, unsure what to say.

"So what do we do now?"

"Go about our business," she said, "and wonder, what if?"

"What if what?"

"What if, what if . . . you know . . ."

"It would be really nice to see you again, Miss Sweet Words."

"That would break the rules of flirting. I'm sure you know them. You do it so well."

"No, I don't," he said, trying to stall her.

"Yes, you do."

"Okay . . . take care then."

"Okay, Clint."

She whistled the theme from the *The Good, The Bad, and The Ugly*, smiled, and walked away. He watched as the night consumed her. Then he called the gallery, and headed east to Crosby.

The street was dark and lonely. Grungy. Gloom seeped out of the ground like tar. In the nearground, beneath a scaffold, a red flame bloomed and withered, and a voice cut through: "Yow, faggot."

He trailed it across the cracked sidewalk into the shadows of what he saw was a doorway. His first thought was, He hasn't gone, he's still here. Then he thought about the last time he'd seen him, how badly that had ended, and wondered if this time would be different.

Am I still upset? he asked himself. He thought about the money, forty thousand pounds. He wasn't sure. But it had never been the money. It had always been the treachery and the lies.

He formed the face in his mind, saw its decay, saw the beauty that remained insistent. When Ian was young he'd resembled Haile Selassie, especially in the forehead and the eyes.

"Yow," Fire said as Ian stepped into the light. "Good to see you."

They hugged and parted quickly.

"Tink you miss this," Ian said, glancing into Fire's eyes. He killed the cigarette on the heel of his shoe—his black loafers looked expensive. His pants fit loosely. He'd lost some weight. His hollow cheeks were rutted, and he'd chipped a tooth. Through his shirt, his joints were knots of rope. Miss Gita would be sad to see her boy.

"So how everything?"

"Yuh nuh know . . . cyaah keep a good man down." He held his face low. "Can I ask you something? How it feel to be a six-footer?" He looked up again, his eyes set close like the barrels of a shotgun.

This is shit, Fire thought. Is this all you have to say after all this time? And how should I reply? The opposite of being five-seven?

What about your mother Miss Gita? The one that lives with me now—that works for me as a maid because her son, the famous sculptor who made the cover of *Time* magazine, bought a car with the money I lent him to buy her a house so she could have somewhere to live in case an overdose killed him. And where is the Benz now, Ian? Repossessed . . . like the house in Paris and the Prince Street loft and the beachfront villa in Barbados.

"You want a cigarette?" Ian asked.

"I done smoke eight years now. You know that."

"Yeah . . . I forgot."

They fell into silence.

"So where's Claire?"

Fire began to blame his anger on fatigue. It wasn't fair, he thought, to be mad at him, after all that he'd been through.

"She's inside."

"So what you doing out here? Just come for a smoke?"

"That . . . and waiting for some beer. We was playing some poker upstairs and run out." He glanced at his TAG. "The fuck a-take so long?" He glared at Fire. "And why *you* take so long?" Fire began to answer but he cut him off. "Y'always have a *rassclaat* reason."

Silence reclaimed them. Filled their lungs. Made their breathing uneasy.

"So how's I-nelik?" Ian asked. He lit another Newport. Took a deep drag . . . glanced at his shoes . . . willing Fire to read his mind. Being here isn't easy, he wanted to say. I always feel useless in front of you . . .

"He's awright," Fire said, hoping Ian would ask about Miss Gita, hoping also that he wouldn't ask about his father.

Claire was having a smoke outside the gallery when Fire and Ian arrived.

She started toward them, her form swinging loosely in an A-line dress that draped from a collar of beads. Her skin was black like a seasoned wok, and her dreads were long and crinkled. She was French, from Martinique.

"How are you?" Fire said as he hugged her. Her body had the heft of an upright bass.

"You were right about him, y'know?" Ian said. "The fucker always late but him always show."

Fire stamped kisses on her cheeks.

This is the way it should be, Fire thought, as he remembered Lisbon. The villa they shared in the Alfama and light in the afternoon. Ambition mattered more than fame then . . . and friendship more than money. Fame and money. Ian had come to New York to find them. Mine them, he'd said. But after he found the mother lode the shaft caved in and trapped him.

"I love the both of you," Ian said as he joined their hug. "It should always be this way."

Fire looked at Claire and raised his brows. They were more than Ian's friends. They were mother and father and brother and sister, nurse, teacher, counselor—specialists in seeing and satisfying his needs.

Headlights lurched around the bend.

"Oh, fuck," Ian said. "It's Lewis."

"The prick?" Claire asked with a chuckle.

"He's too fake to be a prick. The man is a fucking dildo. Send him home, nuh Claire. Is your gallery."

She made a funny face at Fire and rubbed Ian's neck.

"So who's Lewis?" Fire asked as the lights grew brighter.

"A collector," Claire said through the crook of a smile. "He's got some money. He's my best client. He made his first million in college—exporting skin-fading to Nigeria. Then he made even more money on Wall Street doing whatever people do there. Then he left that a coupla years ago and started this company that does something with inner city housing . . . some nonprofit development thing . . . I don't know. What I do know, and I guess what I really care about, is that he buys a lot of Ian's work." She turned to Ian. "So you better behave."

Lewis pulled up in a black Range Rover. At first Fire thought he knew him, but soon realized his error. He looked like a model he'd seen in an ad for Duke hairdressing cream.

"Hey, guys," Lewis called, "how are you?" His voice was warm and measured. Ian sucked his teeth. Claire said a bright hello. Fire nodded politely. "I'll be right back. I'm gonna put this in a lot." The engine revved. The big wheels turned. The rear lights faded to black.

He was tall, Fire saw when he returned. And muscled. Very gymned. He could see it through his T-shirt, which was tight and ribbed like a condom. He had a really firm handshake, and had learned in a course, Fire guessed, that it was important to look people directly in the eye when being introduced.

"So what's going on," Lewis said, turning to Ian. "Is Sylvia here?"

"She gone to get some beer," Ian replied. "She's been gone a while though. Maybe she meet a man. Women like men, y'know. Trust me."

"That was funny. But do you know what's funnier? I didn't bring my checkbook tonight."

Claire giggled and Lewis laughed.

"Don't patronize me." Ian's cigarette glowed like a nova.

"Why not?" Lewis said with a laugh. "I'm your biggest patron."

Claire sensed a flare-up and motioned Ian to be quiet. Lewis chuckled and went inside. Ian spat the butt against a car.

"I don't know wha Sylvia see in dat pussy."

Claire rubbed his back. "Love is blind, Ian."

"You see love when you see them?"

She glanced at Fire. "That's not my business."

Ian shrugged his shoulders and went inside.

Fire was curious now. "Why Ian don't like him?"

"Who *does* Ian like? But in all fairness Lewis is an asshole. He's very condescending. Sylvia and Ian have gotten tight, and I think Lewis feels threatened by that. And Ian doesn't think that Sylvia should be with Lewis. He thinks she's settling. But who cares?"

"So who is this Sylvia?"

"Nice girl. You'll meet her soon. She's a frustrated writer who's been working on a novel for the last six years. She's a magazine editor at *Umbra*. She's good people, and a really good poet. She's published two collections." She peered at a figure in the distance. It wasn't who she thought it was. "Ian has a point though. She and Lewis are kinda different."

Fire followed Claire inside and walked himself through the show, a collection of cast-iron tableware with a floral motif. What's this about? he thought. He picked up a vase shaped like a tulip. The work was nice, very detailed, but he wasn't sure if he would call it art. He'd never tell Ian this—not now anyway—but the place looked like a sample sale at Pottery Barn. The work was too—he searched for the word—neutral. It lacked perspective and conviction, subversion and commentary. Where was the wisdom and the humor? Ian's work used to be ironic. Now it was simply iron.

He saw some plates embossed with sunflowers and thought of the woman in the navy blazer. *She* hadn't lost her irony. Muddy Waters.

Water. He had to take a pee. His thoughts were still with her as he stood over the bowl. His cock filled his palm like a fat iguana. He should've asked for her name and number again. No, he shouldn't have. She was involved . . . like Blanche had been, and in any event, pressing her might have turned the sweetness into vinegar. She had a vibe about her, though, that woman . . . and those sunflowers . . . it was all quite interesting . . . the sunflower field in the dream . . . the sunflowers on her blazer and again in Ian's work. Did this mean something? Could she be the one? No, she couldn't. She was involved, and therefore unavailable.

He tried to forget her as he went upstairs to the office, a loft above the gallery floor with ocher walls, a wooden floor, and a pressed-tin ceiling.

Lewis asked him to join the poker game. He told him he didn't know how to play. It was one of his inconsistencies that he didn't like to gamble though he loved to court adventure.

Claire suggested dominoes. But before she could retrieve her set the doorbell rang.

"Are you hungry?" she asked before leaving to answer it.

He said yes and she told him there was food in the kitchen and directed him to follow her.

"It's good to see you," she said at the foot of the stairs.

"It's good to see you too."

Her brows began to rise. She released her lower lip and her mouth began to open, but she changed her mind.

She went to get the door. He passed beneath the office, down a wide hallway to the kitchen, which was tiled in black and what he thought was gray until he adjusted the dimmer and a fine rain of light washed over the stainless steel fixtures and the marble-topped workstation that filled the space like a carrier in dry dock. Rummaging through the fridge, he found and placed on top of this *Intrepid* some grapes, a fruit tart, conch turnovers, a platter of *farofa*, and a bowl of *feijoada*.

He'd given up red meat for six years now, but like most of his actions, had not in fact declared it. With a few exceptions, he was wary of definitions, not because he was indecisive or undisciplined, but because he believed that bearings were more important than boundaries. Instead of definitions he preferred guidelines—points of departure that gave him the confidence to range across borders without losing his way.

Feijoada. He stared into the eyes of the soft black beans and smelled the garlic sweat of cow tongue and salt pork, and thought of the women of Salvador, their skins as smooth as banana leaves, spicing their pots on Sundays with cheap cuts and scrap meat as they've done since the days of slavery. A little pork wouldn't kill him, he thought. But then it might. He replaced the *feijoada* in the fridge. On the edge of his focus, footsteps came closer and a voice called out: "Excuse me, could you give me a hand?"

He straightened up, and turned around. Standing before him with one arm along the door frame and the other weighed down by a shopping bag was the woman in the navy blazer, backlit from the hall, her skin shining like an almond glaze, her lips trembling like beds of earth about to burst with seed.

"I'm sorry," she said. "This is so embarrassing. I didn't expect to see *you* of all people here . . . and I . . . and I'm . . . I'm . . ."

"You are . . . ?"

She leaned backward through the doorway and glanced left and right.

"Sylvia," she said, her brows furrowed deeply. "Sylvia Lucas."

"Adrian. Adrian Heath. But people call me Fire."

She rested the bag on the floor, and gazed at him, slicing wide arcs across his body, trying to dissect him.

"Where'd you get your buttons?" He was thinking now of all that he'd heard about her.

She told him, as she rested the bag on the other side of the room, that they were not the originals but details she'd added on her own.

"I'm sorry to put you through this," he said as she unpacked. "You didn't want to see me again. But we both keep bad company."

"It's okay." She turned her back to him.

"I'd like to give you my number," he said, driven by the momentum of habit, "so you can call to arrange another coincidence." He was sure now that nothing would happen. He'd already met her man.

"I shouldn't take it," she said without looking. "I'm never going to use it."

"That's okay. Paper is cheap. And you won't have to give me yours. We will only be in touch at your convenience."

She turned around, puffed her cheeks, and began to crease the paper bag against her body, working in the deliberate order of measuring, scoring, and folding.

"I think we should go," she said when the bag was the size of a change purse.

He held his number out to her. "Take it," he said softly. "There is nothing to fear." He wagged his head when he said this, and closed his eyes in a languid blink that calmed her like a soothing fan and made her want to trust him with his muddy boots and knotted hair and basic Timex watch. She liked his mouth. It made her think of her clit as a shrimp in butter sauce.

Slowly, she placed her palm on his. He let it rest there. She watched as his eyes changed from suns into moons and his face assumed the gravity of evening. Things were happening inside him that she didn't understand, things that she sus-

pected had to do with her, things that made her nervous—for
they were things she'd like to do with him. In her head she
heard a poem that she'd written the week before, "Dreaming
of Mango":

> *Sunshine on some full-smack lips,*
> *mango dripping on the chest,*
> *sweeter at the raisin tips*
> *that look out darkly from the breasts.*

"I think we should go before we get in trouble," she said.

He smiled. She hoisted herself onto the workstation, and
let the sight of his mouth suck her in.

"Why am I doing this?" she asked. "Getting myself in
trouble. Jeopardizing something I already have. Something . . .
I don't know what to call it. But something . . ."

"That you don't want to lose."

"Right."

"What would you do if it suddenly left you? Would you
chase after it?"

"I don't know. Maybe not," she said slowly.

"Maybe yes?"

"Maybe," she said. She saw his lips now as through a mi-
croscope. The wrinkles and ridges that trapped his saliva.
"One part of me would want to, and the other part would not.
I don't know. I really don't know."

"Think about that before you call me."

He gripped her hand. And she blinked. And when she
opened her eyes, thinking she was about to tell him to let her
go, something rushed from his direction. This thing, this ex-
ploding ball of wetness, shorted for an instant her memory
and will, so that she didn't realize at first that it was she who
had kissed him and not the other way around, and further, that
it was she now—or a stranger who was misusing her body—
who was opening her legs so that the body of this man whom
she was pulling toward her for motives she didn't understand,

but which she realized she must now resist, could press itself against her, reconfirming her as soft by the hard truth of its intent. His waist was at her knees now, rushing toward her dampened groin. His lips were beginning to part now, and she could see their underside, where terra-cotta became wet clay.

She had less than a second to act. And as she jerked her head to the side and closed her eyes, preparing for the adventure of impact, her involvement with Lewis, faced with its mortality, projected its history inside her head. She'd met him on the grass courts at a friend's house in Martha's Vineyard. He was sitting on the sidelines, shirtless, his muscles filmed with sweat, a strikingly handsome man. At first she thought he was a model, but as she learned when they met again at a dinner party, he'd grown up in Baltimore, the son of a shop clerk and a mechanic, and had become a millionaire through hard work, good schools, and a little bit of luck. He was unmarried, without children, respected by his peers and well connected, as evidenced by the people who made it their duty to say hello—filmmakers, congressmen, musicians, and bankers. And at some point in the evening, she asked him to write an investment feature for *Umbra*. The piece, which was never done, because he could never find the time, became the pretext for twice-weekly phone calls, which gave way to long lunches at good restaurants, then dinners and weekends, then . . . this.

What had been the real attraction? It wasn't just his looks. It was more than that. It had to be. It must be. She couldn't remember. Then she thought of something. At some point early on it came up that she'd recently bought a Catlett silkscreen, and they began to talk about art. Was that it? She didn't know. She'd never considered their happiness before. And here she was trembling in fear—her own fear of flying. This must not happen.

As soon as she said this—which may or may not have been aloud—Fire's kiss skidded across her cheek. She ran to the door, straightened herself, and went to join the others.

* * *

Fire returned from the kitchen with the beers, which she'd forgotten, and found her leaning against Lewis on a tasseled sofa that sat across a table from some velvet chairs. Her legs were drawn up, and she was shuffling a deck of cards while Lewis and Claire talked business about a pair of candle-holders. Ian was in a corner muttering into his cell phone.

Fire held the tray in front of Sylvia and she reached out without looking, which pricked him, although he knew her intent was not to snub. At the last second, as her fingers began to curl around a Red Stripe, he tilted the tray, causing a minor chink and splash. He derailed her focus as she helped him, rummaged her eyes for something—something he couldn't describe, something he knew he'd know on sight.

"I see you two have met," Claire said, chuckling with Lewis.

"And I've made a big splash."

Sylvia dabbed her pants with a napkin. Fire held his hand toward her. She took it charily as if it were a fish and said her name, framing her words with a fragile smile. He squeezed her hand secretly, wondered why, and concluded that he was teasing her. She was, after all, teasing him. It couldn't be more than teasing, he told himself. It must never be.

Smiling, he introduced himself. His voice flowed like water over river stones. She creamed warm sweat in his waiting palm.

"Nice to meet you," she said. "Don't worry about the spill."

"There are more to come. I'll be serving the drinks tonight."

They didn't speak for the rest of the evening, but carried on a private intercourse through looks and gestures. A raised eyebrow meant, "Hi again." A stroke down the nose was, "I like you." Smacked lips said, "We're really mad." And a low-ered head urged, "Let's stop this now and get on with our lives"—which he thought would be easy because he lived in

Jamaica to begin with, and would be leaving New York in two days. But also because she was involved.

Late in the evening, after being quiet for a while, Sylvia raised her eyebrow again, triggering in Fire the memory of the first time he'd thought about sex. As he sat on the floor sorting records, he saw again the tenement yard ringed with zinc sheets where he spent as many summers as he could with his uncle I-nelik, a pudgy dread whose features were always hidden behind welding goggles and a beard that hung in clots. He saw the shotgun houses, scrubbed to pastel softness by the heat, and the wandering bands of mongrels—mangy beasts whose teats flip-flopped like paper bags.

He was eight years old, on his way with I-nelik to Harry J's for the first session of what would be Marley's *Natty Dread*. They were driving along Molynes Road in the yellow Alfasud that I-nelik had bought before he left dentistry. As usual, they talked about whatever was on I-nelik's mind. This day it was sex. He wanted to know if Fire had had it. Fire wasn't sure. "Is that like kissing?"

I-nelik laughed and asked if he'd ever woken up in the night and heard his mother breathing like an asthmatic. Fire told him yes.

"That," I-nelik said, "is sex."

"But what if Daddy kill her?"

"Well, in a sense, you daddy kill her every night, but him have a special way of pumping her back to life."

He thought about his mother's gasps, and began to really fear for her. What if his father's pump should fail? Would he, as a male and the only child, be asked to revive her? One time when they went to Walt Disney World—he must've been four then—they all slept in the same room and he'd seen how his father held his mother at night . . . heard the words he breathed into her neck . . . but didn't see anything that looked like pumping.

Pumping. For reasons he didn't understand at the time, the

word made him aware of his body, its different parts and their differing capacities for giving and receiving pleasure.

There was a thing he did in private, with what he called his puppy, a secret thing only he knew about, a thing he'd discovered by accident one day while crawling under I-nelik's house. Sometimes he'd do this thing while a girl from the neighborhood watched.

She'd caught him doing it in a burned-out car in an empty lot behind the primary school, and swore that she would spread the news unless he bought her a pack of Smarties. He didn't think he was doing something wrong. He thought it was natural but private, like a bowel movement. So for the same reason that he wouldn't want to be famous for taking a shit in an old car he went to the shop and bribed her.

After she guzzled the box she confessed that she hadn't come to the car by accident—that she used it for the same purpose. But before he could start a turf war, she told him they should share it. It was nicer when you did it while someone watched, she said. He asked her how she knew this. She said she used to spy on her neighbor, and when he caught her he asked her to watch. Sometimes he would give her a smalls if she helped him.

"Help him how?"

"Help him fingle it."

"How much?"

"Fifty cents."

He couldn't believe what he was hearing. How could anyone do that? he wondered. Nothing would come between him and his puppy, especially another hand. His puppy was the smoothest place on his body. Why should he surrender the pleasure of touching it? The girl's neighbor was a fool, he thought. *He* should charge *her*. Not the other way around.

"You have money?" she asked.

He told her no.

She would only watch then. She wouldn't touch.

They met every day that summer, arranging by coded signals the exact time to arrive. Sharing this secret made him feel both powerful and vulnerable, powerful because he knew something that others didn't know and vulnerable because it took just one person to make everyone know it.

Sylvia made him feel the same way.

He watched her more intently as the night went on, noticed little things about her, that she sucked her tongue, for example, when she was thinking, and cracked her neck when she felt pressured. Sylvia spoke with a subtle lisp, and on her chin was a shallow dimple, the lasting impression of a mother's kiss. Intellectually, she was her man's superior, but she mostly restrained herself. Fire saw it in her eyes, the way she pulled the shades down to make his light shine brighter.

"Oh come on, Lewis, Isabel runs away with Tristão because she wants happiness." They had finished playing poker and were discussing John Updike's *Brazil*, which Lewis was reading in paperback. "Why is that unrealistic? Because she is white and he is black? She is rich and he is poor? You can't judge a novel by real life, Lewis. A novel is its own reality." Sylvia looked at Claire for support. "She runs away with him at first to rebel against her family—because he's forbidden, sexually and otherwise—not because she loves him. The love comes later, and that's what carries the story—the lengths to which they go to preserve this love." She glanced at the others, then settled on Lewis, who was unimpressed—which upset her. Why couldn't he understand? Why was he so literal? "You might understand it better if you read *The Romance of Tristan and Iseult* by Bédier. *Brazil* is essentially the same story set in modern times."

"I can't imagine anyone doing that," Lewis replied. "Have you ever heard of anyone doing that, Sylvia? Anyone you know?" He looked to Fire for reinforcement. "Why can't novels be like real life? I don't think that's asking too much. I'm sure poor people would run away with rich people. But I don't see many rich people sitting around waiting for the pauper with a bag of love." He paused . . . seemed to remember something. "Well, maybe I'm speaking out of turn, because there's this guy I went to Wharton with, Marcus Reid, brilliant guy—a shoo-in for senior vice presidency—until he ups and marries a word processor. I couldn't believe it. He fucked his life in a single stroke."

Ian sucked his teeth and opened another Guinness.

"How did he ruin his life?" Fire asked. He didn't know enough about the business world to see the analogy.

"Well, for one, he stopped getting invited to the right places—where he'd meet the right people and make the right connections. His peers, and more importantly his bosses, considered him a loser. In any event, he might have actually preferred to stay away from certain situations, y'know. I'm sure his wife felt awkward whenever she was introduced to the kind of people she normally worked for. Bottom line: it just doesn't look good."

The room was silent.

"Is there something *wrong* with them being in love?" Fire asked.

He was giving Lewis a chance to redeem himself. He didn't want to think the worst.

"Well, let's just say I wouldn't waste my time falling in love with someone like that."

"So you actually choose who you want to be in love with, just like so?" He snapped his fingers.

"Yes."

"You've never just met somebody and you just felt a spontaneous . . . almost, well . . . like . . . a spark between the both of you?"

"When I was a kid, sure. But I can't afford to do that now. That kinda love isn't practical. I have too much at stake."

Silence fell again. A more intense one.

Ian glared at Lewis. "You're so fulla shit," he said quietly. His eyes were bleary and his speech was slurred. He sneered,

then smiled, then tried to go back to sneering again but lost
his way, inadvertently creating the kind of warped-genius expression perfected on screen by John Malkovich. He tilted his
head and drained the bottle at arm's length, splashing his lips
like a toilet seat. "So if Sylvia was an editorial assistant you
wouldn't deal with her?"

"Well . . . I'm not saying that, but . . . I mean . . . maybe I
wouldn't have met her . . . so I guess I wouldn't . . . I don't
know."

Ian wiped his mouth with the back of his hand and leaned
across the table. "What you mean you don't know?"

"Look, Ian," snapped Lewis, "Sylvia and I have what we
have, and it's none of your business."

"*Why* is it such a big deal to say that you'd be with your
woman no matter what kinda work she did?"

"Why is it your concern?"

"Why you cyaah answer?"

"Why is it your concern?"

"But why you cyaah answer, Lewis?"

"Don't fuck with me, Ian."

Lewis was pointing at him now, and Ian began to laugh. He
glanced at Fire for support. Fire looked at the floor to avoid
embarrassing Lewis—but not before showing Ian the sparkle
in his eyes. Claire, who had grown accustomed to this kind of
catch-up, watched the whole thing in ironic amusement, expecting it to fade any minute. But it continued, gathering volume like a landslide.

Sylvia slammed the book on the table. The men continued
to jabber. So she shouted, "Stop. It's getting out of hand!"

Ian narrowed his eyes. "Sylvia, you're such a *bombo*. You
don't see de man don't love you? Is not you him love—is
what you is. Dat don't bother you?"

Fire kept his head low. He didn't want to see it. Didn't want
to compound the woman's embarrassment.

"It's none of your business, Ian. It's not your business at
all."

"So hol on. You woulda be with him if he was a transit worker or a manager at a McDonald's?"

"It's none of your business. We have what we have and we're happy."

"Let's go, Sylvia," Lewis said. "I don't need this shit. And I don't want these candleholders, either."

Fire looked up. Sylvia was standing on the other side of the table, her hands on her hips—which seemed wider now but also less erotic since being dusted with political fallout. Mix-up was not a good thing.

"Goodbye," he said, extending his hand. "It was nice to have met you. Nice meeting you, Lewis."

Lewis ignored him. Sylvia held his hand and squeezed it. It felt tight. He let go.

As Sylvia began to walk away, Claire pulled her to the side and they spoke quietly. Lewis said he would meet her in the car.

Ian began to laugh. "Fuck you," he screamed, pounding his bottle on the table. "You fucking fake, you."

"I am not a fake," Sylvia shouted. Claire covered Sylvia's mouth and tried to calm her.

"Who the fuck talking to you?" Ian replied. "I was talking to Lewis. Ah, throw me corn, me never call no fowl. Let her go, Claire. She think I fraid for her."

Claire told him to shut up and walked Sylvia downstairs. She came back shortly, unsure of what to say or where to begin.

She turned to Fire. "How can I make a living if he behaves like a shit? He needs to know when to shut his damn mouth. Those candleholders were the only things that sold today. And because of this prick," she pointed at Ian, "Lewis returned them. Luckily, Sylvia wants them." She wiped her face with her palms. "So at least we can say we sold something."

"Fuck Lewis," Ian muttered. "Fuck Sylvia too."

Claire sighed.

Ian began to mutter incoherently.

"Go to sleep," Claire snapped. "Tomorrow we have a date."

"I not going nowhere with nobody."

"Yes, you will. Just get some sleep."

"No way. I'm drunk. I'm sleepy. I'm pissed and . . . I'm beginning to piss."

A wet spot spread on his pants.

"He's not going to make this barbecue tomorrow. I can see that. Fire, why don't you meet me there?"

Sylvia sat with her body against the car door as they crossed the George Washington Bridge, trying to distance herself as much as she could from Lewis. Her hands, tired from being rolled into fists, rested in her lap. In her mind, she was still in the gallery, the argument was still going on, and she kept hearing the question again. *"So if Sylvia was an editorial assistant you wouldn't deal with her?"* What did it mean, she wondered, that he had basically said no? Would she be with Lewis if he were a transit worker or a manager at a McDonald's? She wasn't sure. She asked herself if he would be the same person, if he'd be able to hold the same conversations, if he'd be equipped with the same intelligence and have the same values and opinions.

How much of us is what we do?

And who was she?

Was she a writer with a day gig at a magazine or was she a magazine editor who wrote on the side? There was a part of her that said she was whatever paid her bills. At heart, she was a writer though. She knew that. But writers don't have security . . . and she needed that. Security was important to her. Which is why she'd never managed to take the time off to finish her novel. Would a writer without money be like a word processor? She looked at Lewis, who thought this meant she wanted to speak.

"Do you know how much money I've spent on Ian's work in the last year?" Lewis asked. He was ready to fight again.

He was upset with her for buying the candleholders after he'd returned them. "Close to eighty thousand dollars. If it wasn't for me he woulda starved to death years ago. And *I* need to take *his* shit? Nobody else takes his shit! He should kiss Claire's ass every chance he gets. She's the only one in New York who still shows him."

He glanced at Sylvia. "He needs some cutting down. He punched Victor Aarons—one of the biggest gallery owners in New York—because Victor jokingly called him a 'fartiste.' And don't forget the time he pissed in a bottle of PJ and sent it to a critic who'd given him a bad review. That was years ago, but it still goes to show what kind of person he is. Nobody wants to touch him. I'm one of the few people who supports this little shit, and he tells me, 'Fuck you.' Fuck me? Fuck me? Oh, no, fuck him! Fuck him, and fuck anyone who sides with him."

"Does that include me?"

"Do you side with him?"

"On some things, yes. So what does that mean?"

"It means f—"

"I must have missed that," she replied, smugly.

"You didn't miss a thing," he said through his teeth.

"Oh? Then what *did* you say, Mr. Cole?"

"I said f—"

"Yes?"

"F . . . forget about it."

"That's what I *thought* you said."

"Don't talk to me like that."

"I can speak to you any way I please."

"Delude yourself."

"In a lot of ways, maybe I have been."

"What does that mean?"

"I know what it means, that's all that matters."

"What are you talking about?"

"Nothing."

"Here we go—something suddenly becoming nothing."

"In more ways than one."

She began to think of Fire. What did he think of her? Had the argument changed his view? She began to feel him now, the lines in his palm, the buds on his tongue—and smell him. His scent was comforting . . . like a new book . . . or mown grass after evening rain.

"Lewis," she began slowly, "if I abandoned you, would you chase after me?"

"What is this? Poetic question hour?"

"Just answer me," she said. "If I abandoned you, would you chase after me?"

"Look, Sylvia, I don't want to start another argument with you, and I sense one coming if I don't say the right thing."

"You're avoiding my question. Just like you avoided Ian's."

He drummed his thumbs against the steering wheel. What was her problem tonight?

"Sylvia," he began quietly, "I'm sorry for all this, and I suppose you are too. This is just so . . . so . . . it's just not good. Look at what we're doing. We're fighting over a pair of candleholders. A pair of *stupid* candleholders. You know what? Why should they come between us? Let's turn around right now and take them back to Claire. They'll be out of our lives and we'll be fine again."

"But I want them."

"Why?"

"They're beautiful . . . and . . . it's hard to explain . . . it sounds so hokey." She was thinking of Fire's hair now, how much she wanted to loose her fingers in that palm grove reclaimed by wilderness.

"Go ahead, it's okay—talk to me."

"I have this attraction to fire that I can't explain."

"You've never mentioned this before."

"I know. I didn't know it myself until tonight."

"I see."

"I don't know, Lewis. It was just spontaneous, I guess. It just happened like"—she snapped her fingers—"that."

"Why would anyone be so attracted to something so dangerous?" he asked, suppressing his urge to laugh.

"The warmth. Sometimes a little warmth is worth a burn or two."

He pretended to understand, and slowly pulled out of the conversation. They rode along in silence for a while, until at some point, without notice, she asked to be taken home. Without uttering a word he swung around and drove her to Brooklyn Heights.

"Are we still going to Diego's barbecue tomorrow?" he asked. They were parked in front of her building now, a brownstone on a narrow street lined with trees.

"I think we need some space. I need to figure out some things."

"I guess that means no then. I guess we're headed for another one of those patented Sylvia withdrawals. That shit is just so tiring. So how long is this one gonna last? You know what? I ain't even gonna sweat it. See you when I see you."

"Goodbye, Lewis."

He watched her till she shut the door. She didn't look back. He put his seat back, fumed a bit, then drove home to Englewood.

Sylvia took a shower and lay on top of the sheets. It was the quiet time of morning, close to dawn. The windows were open and the breeze was as soft as powdered skin.

A cinnamon candle, thick and brown, squittered light across the room, dropped some on her belly, where it pooled in her navel and spread down to her pubis, coating the hairs, making them feel like starchy grains of rice when she touched them . . . as she was doing now. Whirling them between her fingers as she rubbed her belly, which the light had filmed with a glaze that made her skin not amber, but caramel, a murky, sticky dark like molasses. It gave her greater confidence in her sensuousness, made her want to know her body in a new way—the old way really, but with a new curiosity. What would he feel if he touched me?

She got up and turned on the fan, switched it to low, angled it to lick her thighs when she lay down again. She brushed herself with feathered strokes from her forehead to her knees, her fingers spread wide, her wrists held loose to accommodate the changing topography—the dunes of her breasts, the drifts of her ribs, the quicksand yield of her hips.

It was nice to have met you. She felt heavy, waterlogged. She squeezed her thighs. She was ready for release. Leisurely, then urgently, she stroked herself to sleep.

chapter two

She woke up knowing that she'd dreamed about Fire. *What,* though, she couldn't recall. But he'd been there. She could feel him in the sweet ache that washed her navel . . . the phantom pain of something that had filled it . . . rubbed it . . . a lubricated pinkie or a tongue perhaps.

Sitting on a side chair, her elbows on her knees, she tried to recall the shadow that the sun had wiped away. Her toes rippled the dhurrie—ruffled it like a sheet on a trysting bed.

Why did he affect her so? She furrowed her brows, setting a trap for the answer. He was handsome, but that wasn't it . . . she'd met more striking men. And he wasn't professional—or didn't seem to be—which for her was a basic requirement.

Had she ever heard of him?

She had. From Ian. But what, though? There was a rumble in her head, a distant one, as the answer lumbered toward her, coughing and wheezing like an old steam train.

She tried to define him in the meantime from the little that she knew.

He was Jamaican, obviously. Educated and middle class from his accent. And had spent some time abroad—at college perhaps—most likely in the States.

Age-wise he was thirty, thirty-two . . . and lived where now? Well, that would depend on what he did. He was involved in the arts somewhat—but not to the point where it paid his bills. If it did she would have heard of him. The black art world was too small. Too inbred. Too incestuous for her to not have known him. Especially in New York.

But which art?

There was a thing about him—a sense that dirt didn't disturb him—that made her think "sculptor" or "painter." He wasn't a dancer, for sure. His posture didn't say that.

Graphic designer was a maybe . . . Web sites and that kind of thing. Those guys often dressed like that. She was sure he always dressed that way. There was nothing contrived about it, like a diving watch or an ostrich belt, that would have marked him as a poseur.

She considered "writer" briefly, then chucked it away. If he were a writer, she reasoned, he would've had a say about *Brazil*. Even if he hadn't read it. Writers were like that. At least the ones that she knew. Arrogant and opinionated.

Then she remembered.

He was a musician . . . or did something related to music. The conversation was like ashes now, finely ground, with glowing shards. He was connected to The Wailers somehow. How, she couldn't remember. But there was a connection. She thought about his hair . . . and it made more sense. But then again it didn't. What did he play? Then she remembered: his *uncle* used to play with The Wailers.

She was back where she'd begun.

Why did he affect her so? The not knowing made her queasy. Made her anxious to clear her mind.

She tried to distract herself with cleaning. It was a roomy apartment, a one-bedroom with cream walls, and a kitchen divided by a breakfast counter from a front room with bay windows.

And yet the place had a feeling of transience. An indifference to design that suggested eclectic taste—a chintz-covered couch paired with steel end tables. Generally, her tastes *were* eclectic, though for her own space she preferred English country. She didn't consider this her own space. It was just an apartment. She would have English country when she bought her house. She'd been living in the apartment for five years now, three years longer than she'd planned, but this didn't discourage her. She was used to setbacks. So many things had happened in her life.

She'd been born in Jamaica but had no memory of the place except that she'd lived in a house near water. It was a wooden house, in a yard with three other houses that, when she was younger, she'd remembered as outhouses or something—a kitchen and a bathroom perhaps. There was a time when she thought the house was big, with concrete walls and a wide lawn. But she knew now that the house had seemed big only because she was small, and that her recollections of concrete walls came from her stay in the sanatorium where she'd been quarantined from four to eight with TB.

She didn't remember very much of her childhood. According to Syd, who raised her for a while, her father was a butcher and her mother was a go-go dancer, the black sheep of a rich Syrian family who ran away to shack up because "she was the lowest dog around."

She could only remember a year with her parents, the year she returned home, when the sounds and smells of the hospital—coughing and Dettol—were replaced by those of animals. The sourness of shit and sweat. Hair being singed from skins to make drumheads. The arcing whoosh of the butcher's knife. The gush of blood and the squeal of death.

Of her parents there were few recollections. Her mother was the color of almond paste and had curly hair down her back. Her father was antenna-thin and hacked and spat a lot. That was it and no more. She still had no idea who they were. What did they believe, she wondered. What had made them laugh? What had been their hopes for her, their only child? Why had they visited her only once a year when she struggled to breathe each day?

Sometimes, less now than during high school, she would wonder how much she was like them, ask which of their traits were hers. Was it her need for order? Her love of the arts? Her aversion to risk? Her strength in academics? There was no way to know. Her father murdered her mother in a jealous rage when she was nine years old. Chopped her up, buried some parts, and minced the rest for dog food.

A week before he closed the case by making a confession, Mr. Lucas sent Sylvia to the last known address of his estranged brother, Syd, a decommissioned sailor who worked at the Brooklyn Navy Yard. His face a shallow engraving of Billy Eckstine—whom he claimed was a distant cousin— Syd lived alone in a rooming house in Bedford-Stuyvesant. He was an alcoholic and had no children—at least none for whom he felt responsible—and didn't know how to raise a child, least of all a girl. He would send her to school with her hair uncombed, and dress her in clothes that were sizes too big, and he never checked her homework, because, he claimed, his eyes got dim in evening light—but really because he was illiterate.

In spite of this she quickly grew to love him. He was different from any adult she'd ever known. In many ways he was a child—he had few rules for himself, and even fewer for her. That and their natural curiosity made them great friends.

That's what he was, her friend, which is why she never called him "Uncle." He would allow her to smoke at jazz clubs if she stayed with him for the second set. And they would go to museums on Sundays, sometimes walking over the Brooklyn Bridge hand in hand, counting cars and reciting whole scenes from westerns.

She would write to her father, but he never replied. When she got older, she began to wonder if he could read or write. Maybe he wanted to reply but couldn't. But by then it didn't matter. She had never really known him, so there was little for her to miss. Her mother, Syd told her, had died in her sleep. She didn't know the truth till she was grown.

Every Friday before he went drinking, Syd would bring her a book and take her for a banana split or cheesecake at Junior's. They would sit in their special booth and talk about whatever was on her mind, which was usually something about the girls who picked on her because she was different. They're just jealous, he would say to her, because they don't have good hair like you. Which would make her happy because she *did* have the longest hair in school, even if she didn't know how to manage it.

On the way home, as they walked along Fulton, they would listen to his pocket radio and sing along with the hit parade. That's the best way to lose an accent, he used to say. Good singers have good diction—my cousin Billy told me that.

As soon as they got in he would make her take a bath, wait until she settled herself, then ask her to read to him from the latest book he'd bought her. At first he would squat on the floor beside her, with his chin on the edge of the bed, then gradually, while smiling and praising her, he would lie down beside her and stroke her face and tell her how nice she looked. He knew, he would say—he could tell these things, he added—that she would grow up to be a TV star like the colored girl on *Star Trek*.

He would call her beautiful. And when she said that she was ugly, that she was too skinny to be pretty, he would run his hand under her nightie and say, "But right here fat . . . and right there fat . . . and behind here fat . . . and in the middle here . . . lemme check it again . . . is *so* fat. Can I kiss it?"

If she said no he would make funny faces and she would indulge him. Not just because it thrilled her—it felt dangerously good, like jiggling a shaky tooth—but because in the hospital no one had wanted to touch her. In school no one wanted to be her friend—she spoke funny and dressed funny and her hair was frizzy, and she couldn't play sports because she was always out of breath.

But Syd said she was beautiful. Why not let him kiss her where she peed? He wasn't hurting anyone.

He would always leave her money when he left for the bar. Five bucks on the pillow beside her face, which like the rest of her would be able to sense a touch before it landed. So sensitive it had become. So connected to itself and the air around it.

Something about the money didn't feel right, and she would ask about it. He would wink and say that it was for emergencies.

Like what?

Like anything, he would tell her as he buttoned his shirt. We all have to pay our way in life.

With menstruation came an awareness, an intuition, that neither she nor Syd was a child—that what they were doing was not a game, but something serious. One evening as he buzzed her blossom she thought about the things that adults had placed inside her—thermometers in her ass, depressors in her throat, air tubes in her nostrils, syringes in her ears. On reflection she concluded that none of them had been pleasant, and that all of them had made her nervous. Why should this thing—she knew the name but was afraid to conjure it—that Syd had begun to coax inside her fairly often now, be any different . . . any more benign . . . any less reason for concern?

Why?

There was no one to ask. No one to speak to. She had no friends or family but Syd. One Thursday afternoon, she edged up to a girl she barely knew and asked if they could talk. As they sat facing each other in the cafeteria, she leaned forward and framed the situation hypothetically, speaking in a whisper. "I have this friend . . ."

When she was through the girl said take the money. They were all getting fucked, she said, pointing around the room. She, she, she, she, she . . . they all be getting fucked. They *wish* they was getting paid.

Fucked. The word braced her. Placed everything in perspective. Getting fucked. She didn't like the sound of it. If she had once thought of Syd as fulfilling her, or of them as fulfilling each other, she felt different now. Used.

They all be getting fucked.

She looked at each in turn. They were all girls she didn't like.

Now that she spoke American and chose her own clothes and knew how to style her hair she resented them. Not for how they'd treated her, but for how easy it was to be them—how easy it was to surpass them. She was the only one who took the exam for Brooklyn Tech. The only one who wanted a career. These girls—the girls getting fucked—didn't want careers. They wanted jobs. No. She would *not* be like them. She wouldn't get fucked anymore. Syd would have to stop.

The next evening she hid a knife beneath the sheet. When Syd began to touch her she told him to stop, but he didn't listen. She ended up in juvenile court and a group home in Harlem. That's where she met Diego Peña, a foul-mouthed boy with a bullet head and bushy brows who would study with her at Columbia and grow up to be a filmmaker.

She took a break from straightening up the apartment and checked her watch. It was time to go to his barbecue.

"So what are you working on these days?" Diego asked, his Buddha belly draped in purple. "Which sistah-mama superstar is gonna be your cover girl?"

"Oh shuddup," she said, tugging one of his chins. "We're doing a twelve-page spread on black New Orleans. That's going pretty well."

He chuckled.

"What's so funny?"

"Black New Orleans. Isn't that like Latino San Juan?" She punched him playfully. *"Umbra* kills me, *mami."*

They snuggled and laughed in the filtered light of the stained glass windows, artifacts that he'd bought on a trip to Cochabamba and installed in his West Street loft. Decorated in what he called "homodecorous," the space was sponge-painted a soft tangerine and divided into rooms by Burmese screens and fabric tents that draped from rings in the ceiling.

Almost a year had passed since he'd seen her. In demand

since winning a jury prize at Sundance, he'd been filming a
courtroom drama in Australia for the last ten months, and had
been back at home for only a week now.

Twice when he'd traveled to New York during the shooting
he'd arranged to have dinner with her, and she'd canceled
each time because of work commitments. Or so she said. He
wasn't completely convinced. He suspected that she was
bearing a grudge from the argument they'd had the week before he left for Sydney, when she'd asked him to critique her
novel.

Be frank, she'd said. Be cruel. Let me really know how
you feel.

And when he told her the story was ridiculous, she said
that fame had turned him into an asshole, to which he replied,
"But you were one from birth."

The fight notwithstanding, it was good to see her. Sylvia
was like his sister. Sometimes his mother. But he sensed her
need to be his daughter now, and this made him feel important. He seemed to matter less in her life since she'd started
dating Lewis. Maybe he was projecting. But still . . . it
seemed that way.

So while the other guests mingled on the roof, he stole
her away for a lie-down in his bedroom, a teepee of translu-
cent silk.

At first they talked easily but carefully, their words assuming the cadence of footsteps falling on narrow stairs. Then
slowly, as they each became aware of the sameness of the
other, their words began to run and skip and race like children
scampering over an open field. And they began to open up to
each other, he about whether he deserved success, and she
about knowing she'd outgrown her job.

"I hate it," she confessed. "It's so boring. It doesn't challenge
me. I mean, it's not just *Umbra*, it's the magazine business—
you cover the same things over and over again . . . y'know . . .
sports and media stars . . . fashion . . . tropical vacations . . .
gadgets for an easy life. Diego, there are so many mornings

when I lie in bed asking God to make me sick so I won't have to go to work."

She rolled her head from side to side, breaking loose the tension that was cocooned in the base of her neck.

"Well, you know what I've always said," Diego replied. "Leave."

"Sure . . . and do what? What else is there? Corporate communications? Teaching? Advertising? P.R.? I'd hate that too. They're all the same. Long hours and people who suck your energy and drown your imagination. Come on, what would I do if I left?"

He reached toward the nightstand for a glass of water, considering what to say and how to say it. There is only one thing to do, he thought, taking a preemptive aspirin.

"You could finish your novel and sell it. Forget what I had to say about it. If you left *Umbra* you could really spend time with it . . . and finesse it . . . and really make it work."

She asked for an aspirin, sat on the edge of the bed, and lowered her head between her knees to stretch her spine, where tension was crawling like a worm along the stem of a leaf.

Absently, she took the pill without water, and was forced to endure its scrawl along her throat, a chalky bitterness as galling as graffiti. Wincing, she drained the glass, then leaned against Diego's belly and stared up at the teepee, whose silken folds faded as her gaze burned through to the past.

"There is one side of me, Diego, that loves to write . . . I mean . . . you know that. But I've given up on getting that novel published. I don't even call my agent anymore. I haven't spoken to her in months. The rejection letters just became too much . . ."

The words trailed off into a hum, which was her way of fighting tears. Hums were better than sighs. One could always pretend they were songs.

They lay together quietly for a while, listening to each

other breathe as music and laughter dripped through the ceiling, balming them like sea spray.

I wish I could just lie here, she thought . . . and fall asleep.

But she was animated by a new thought: "The politeness is the part that's damaging, y'know. They never tell you the truth. They never say, 'Give it up because your work is shit,' or 'Join the right clique and you'll be okay.' So instead of packing it in, you keep hanging on, waiting for your luck to turn, like those guys with their eyes glazed over at the OTB. But it never comes, man. Not for most people at least. And I don't have time anymore. I'll soon be thirty-five, Diego, and I have to get on with my life."

She sat up again and looked around this space that Diego owned, saw all the things he had—the chairs from Java, the Turkish rugs—and thinking of their similar backgrounds asked herself, How is it that we're so different? Why can't I be like him? Why can't I just *be*?

She was thinking now of the day he quit college to work as a gofer at a production house. There she was on the steps of Low Library, begging him to stay. There he was, striding across the quadrangle . . . driven to madness . . . drawn to his calling, he said, after seeing Sidney Lumet's *The Verdict*.

"You can't just go like that," she'd screamed. "How many Dominicans ever make it to Columbia? This is not just about you, Diego. This is about a nation of people."

"I can't live for others," he told her. "I have to live for me. Success or failure will come on my terms."

"But what if you fail?"

"If I think about that," he said, "I'll never try."

That was ten years ago. Ten years and three features, the most recent one with a forty-million-dollar budget.

Angry with herself for being weak, she went over to a window and watched the boats on the Hudson, fiddling as she stood there with the knot in her sheer white blouse, as the pain seeped back into her navel, which she'd funkified with a clip-on hoop.

"I'm not like you, Diego," she said, misting the glass with her breath. "In a lot of ways, I wish I could be. I've rewritten my novel so many times. It's gone from serious fiction to mystery, then back to serious fiction, then somehow it became a thriller at one time . . . and now I think it's a contemporary romance. You know what? I really don't know what the fuck it's about. I don't even know what *I'm* about."

He tried to gather his face in a look that matched his feelings. But it was hard to know which particular combination of his pointy mouth and beady eyes would best convey this thought: We both know what you have to do, so cut the shit and do it. You don't *really* want to write, Sylvia. You want to be a success, and you'll take it however it comes.

But he didn't say this. Instead, he tried to lighten the mood. He walked over to her with his stomach sucked in, and asked, in a Mae West–meets–Eartha Kitt voice, "How's Lewis? Tell that hunk of a man that a certain gay filmmaker would like to invite him for dinner and show him the benefits of the Fat for Life diet."

She laughed out of gratitude.

"What time is he getting here anyway? That trim motherfucker?"

"He isn't coming . . ."

"Oh, yeah? What happened?"

"Let's just say we're taking a break." Her expression began to congeal in a frown. "We got into this fight last night and I didn't like the way he talked to me . . . and a lotta bullshit went flying in both directions and we learned a little about ourselves . . . and I decided that I needed some space."

She told him most of the story.

"You miss him?" he asked.

"Not really . . ."

"You think he's missing you?"

"I really don't care—"

"Oh come on, you can't stop caring like that."

He snapped his fingers, a simple act in its own right. But

she heard in it the echo of another snap. And in her mind she was sitting across the table from Fire asking herself in a fearful tone, What if I were wearing a dress or skirt, how would tonight be different?

The thought unnerved her, and she slid back into the dream from the night before.

She is naked on her bed . . . legs apart . . . and he's outside, watching her through the window, his belly wet with sweat. She shuts her legs. Sits up. Draws up the sheet. Wraps her arms around her knees. "Get away," she screams. "Go . . . or I'll call the police." He grabs her with a stare. "Show me," he says with ragga sangfroid. And she obeys . . . surrenders— not to the words but to the attitude—the arrogance distilled to the flavor of meekness. She unfolds herself slowly, like the answer to an ancient riddle, sliding her palms over her thighs and hips, into the mouth of her essence, where her fingers coax the pouting lips to flash a vampy smile.

"Nice," he says, sweating more now. "I want to come inside."

"No," she says. "Only through the window . . . you'll fuck me if you come in here . . . and I don't want that."

"Why?"

"Because when men fuck you they have power over you."

"So what? You fuck your man or your man fuck you?"

"We make love . . ."

"Nutten wrong if you let a man fuck you, baby . . . as long as he's the right man."

"No, I don't want that," she says. "But we could play though . . ."

His shoulders begin to hunch now.

She opens the window and a soft breeze fills her mouth with the remembrance of sea foam and cane juice.

"Come," she says. "Come here."

He plants his palm on the window frame and leans in toward her face, bearing in his pores the memory of lemongrass and orange blossoms.

Then a sudden wind slams the window shut.

"Hold it," she says, as she rattles the latch. "Don't waste it."

"You want it?" he asks. He is caught in the sweep of a powerful tide. "If you really, really want it then mash the glass." She covers her face and breaks it, cowering as it clatters like a bag of marbles.

When she opens her eyes, though, he is gone. She looks through the window and he has disappeared. She steps out on the fire escape. The wind wipes kisses on her naked ass. Where is he? She peers into the backyard, behind the cherry tree. Then as she lowers her head in disappointment she sees it—a shard of glass in her navel and blood, blood, blood.

"Help," she cries.

But no one hears her.

"Someone help me . . . please . . ."

"Sylvia. Are you okay?"

It was Diego calling her. As she tried to answer him she was asking herself, Is that it? Could I really just want to suck him off? She thought of all the cocks she'd sucked. The number was small—but certainly too many to own. Had she ever wanted to just gulp someone like that? No. And why not? She didn't know. There had been people that she wanted to screw, though . . . but she'd never pursued the impulse . . . at least not all the way. Could I just want to suck him off? She began to consider it now . . . saw herself in the kitchen at Claire's, lips flared out, cheeks sucked in, jawbone trembling beneath the weight.

"Sylvia, are you okay?" Diego insisted.

"Yes," she said.

In her mind she was answering an urgent request for a little more tongue.

"Did you hear a word I said in the last ten minutes?"

"Ssssure."

"So . . . are you willing to do it?"

"Uh-huh."

"What am I asking you about?"

His voice was a mix of grunt and bark, throaty with a machete edge.

"I don't know."

"I'm talking about *Umbra*."

"Oh . . . yeah," she replied, smacking her lips unconsciously. "No . . . I can stick it out if I have to . . . I guess."

"Seriously, *mi hija*," he said, taking her hand. "Are you
sure?"

"Yes . . . I am." Shut up, she wanted to say, you're breaking
my concentration.

"C'mon, tell me the truth."

"Why don't you believe me?" she said, shaking her hand
loose. "I was just venting a few minutes ago. I'm all right.
I'm fine. Some days I'm finer than others, but I'm fine."

He held her face. She stiffened. She didn't want to be
touched right now. She wanted to remain suspended in the
weightlessness of fantasy.

"You're not happy there. Why don't you leave?"

His palms felt like slugs. She pulled away sharply.

"Mi hija—"

She cut him off. "Stop, Diego. Leave it alone."

"You're such a crazy bitch sometimes."

She got up to leave. And he held on to her. She tried to
twist away.

"Okay, *mami,* I'm sorry . . . but stay so we can talk."

Could I really just want to suck him off? The question was
a ball of stress behind her eyes. As soon as she acknowledged
it, it bounced back and forth between her temples, then began
to ricochet around her head at faster and faster speeds.

"Diego . . . let me go."

She had to leave.

"Just listen for just a sec . . ."

Could I really just want to suck him off?

She began to scream. Hyperventilate. "Let . . . me . . . go."
She lost control and slapped Diego, splitting his lip.

"You need to get outta here," he said, heading toward the
kitchen. "I'm about to get a little hostile."

She began to apologize but he waved her away.

"Get the fuck out before I kill you."

chapter three

On the seventh floor of the Fulton Inn, a hotel on the edge of Prospect Park, Fire lay down by a curtained window and wrote a letter to Blanche. Shirtless and barefoot, flowers by his side, he opened a packet of flecked beige paper and swam in a sea of thoughts, his pen skimming the words like a seal moving through scalloped waves.

He glanced outside and thought of why he liked this part of Brooklyn so. He paused and considered the arc within his view—the rambling woods in the rolling park . . . the triumphal arch at the roundabout . . . the grand boulevard with the old shade trees . . . the museum's dome above a stand of trees. It was a little slice of Europe, where beauty was a premise, and form was more revered than function.

Order. Practicality. Efficiency. He'd always thought of these as gates, not goals—filters through which one had to pass to reach the state of nonchalance. But last night's confrontation had made him think again, and this was one of the things he was writing about. The other was the bouquet, oriental lilies pink and aromatic.

Of course he could have called. But the ritual of writing—the choosing of the paper, the finding of the pen, the convening of the thoughts, the drawing of the letters—was an intimate act that sometimes gave him the pleasure of kissing, for a pen could be many things: a finger . . . a tongue . . . a nose . . . a cock. And paper, with its possibilities of color and finish, could easily be a forehead . . . a back . . . a cheek . . . a belly . . . the pumiced sole of a delicate foot.

June—, 19—

Dear B,

Thanks very much for the flowers. That was very generous of you. You really didn't have to—well, of course you know that. I guess this is a part of what makes them special—the indulgence. You have always indulged me, haven't you?

Something happened last night to remind me of how special you are. I went to Ian's opening and there was this couple there that Ian got into a fight with. The argument started because the guy said that this friend of his, some kind of corporate type, had ruined his life because he married a word processor. Ian asked him if he would be with his girlfriend if she were an editorial assistant and he said he wouldn't. He said that he wouldn't be with someone who was a liability.

After putting Ian to bed I went jogging in the park to clear my mind. And out there in the dark alone I began to realize how lucky I am. I had nothing to offer you when we met. I had no money, and I could barely take care of myself.

I love you for that, Blanche. No matter how things turned out or how they are. I will always love you for loving me before you knew I would be me.

—Fire

As he folded the page and licked the stamp he remembered a letter she'd written to him. About three months after he had gone to New York and found out she was married, she'd sent him a pleading missive in which she begged him to meet her in London, where she'd be lecturing at SOAS. She'd thought about things a lot, she said, and was sure he was her man. You must come, she wrote. You're the most important thing in my life. Let's work things out. I'll buy the ticket. You can pick it up in Kingston. Your sperm still clings to my womb.

They worked things out in London, and he left there with a deal—he could see other people until she'd settled her life. After this they'd be together . . . *where* they didn't know . . . but they'd work that out . . . details and things like that. And all was well it seemed; then four months later, he received another letter—a postcard this time—she was pregnant again for her husband. And he moved to Brazil without telling her . . . lived in Salvador for a year . . . painting and teaching English . . . until she tracked him down and begged him for forgiveness. It was an accident, she said. It wasn't planned. Don't shut me out. Even if you don't want me anymore . . . at least say you used to love me. He didn't; and she told him that she'd wait for him in case he changed his mind. A year went by without hearing from her . . . without even knowing how she had been. Then he got a letter from Ian and found out that she was sick with cancer and that her husband had left her and taken the kids when he'd found out about her affair. He went to New York to see her and ended up staying for a while . . . stayed through radiation, two mastectomies and silicone. That's when he started to write . . . at first little captions for the hand-drawn cards he used to make her, then poems, then narrative meditations on love and loss. You must write more, she said one day as they returned from the doctor—they'd just found out that the cancer had spread. Please save the stories that will die with me . . . the love stories I didn't write . . . I should have written more about love. Are you willing to try something different? he asked. She said yes. I know a man in Cuba . . . a Santero . . . I've heard great things . . . but you're in no shape to travel. Right now, she replied, I'll try anything.

During the month they spent in Baracoa he fell in love again. And six months later, she went to her doctor and he told her she'd been cured. Soon after that she went back with her husband . . . for what she said was the last one's sake. But he didn't protest this time. He packed his things and went to live with Ian and Claire in Lisbon and began to really write. After that he and Ian moved to Paris; then he moved to London, where he spent five years. He'd been back in Jamaica for a year now, and so was she—lecturing at the university. She was divorced now, finally, and wanted them to try again. Love had never been the issue, she said: he was twenty-four when they met and she had to be practical, had to think about her children . . . one had to be practical in matters of love.

Why was it so hard to shake her? Fire thought, as he fanned himself with the envelope. She'd even made him late for Ian's opening. As he was about to get ready to leave she asked if they could lie down for a while. He sucked his teeth, and was about to get short with her until she said, Don't worry . . . I just want to hold you. Nothing else. It wasn't so much what she said, but the way in which she said it: as if she really meant it . . . and . . . they went to bed and cuddled; there she pressed her breasts against his heart and milked his swollen guilt. He fell asleep and missed the flight and woke to the rain of her tears. She cried as he arranged his clothes . . . was still crying when Sarge brought the Land Rover around the front. Don't cry, Miss B, the foreman said. His smile was as white as his hair. Daddy soon come back. I can't help it, she said from the verandah. I always cry when he leaves me. But dat's common assault, Miss B. You should use to it. I don't know, Sarge, she said. This time just feels different. Different how? I don't know, she replied. Just different.

Ian stirred and Fire drew the curtains against the light. But it found a way to seep through, lightening the tone of the somber wood that had been exquisitely turned and beveled to furnish the room.

He never felt closer to Ian than when he saw him asleep—when the skin on his face shrank back to his skull, smoothing the wrinkles that began to appear when he started doing coke in art school.

What moved Fire was Ian's vulnerability, the way he wheezed instead of snored, the way he clung to soft objects— a grip that contained the hope that maybe he wasn't a man yet . . . that there was still some time for him to change.

The night before, when Fire had to peel away his sweaty clothes and set Ian in the tub to wash away the piss and grime, his body had felt like a golf bag, the thin bones clanking like driving irons.

He was trying to roll out of bed now, rising and falling like a bat with broken wings. He tried to speak but his mouth gaped like a sore.

"You awright?" Fire asked.

He nodded, then words began to dribble out like pus. "Remember what you ask me bout Lewis last night?"

Fire checked his memory. He remembered now, but he thought he'd been muttering to himself.

"Well, this is it . . ."

Fire threw him a pair of boxers, yellow ones with blue stripes, that he'd bought him that morning. Ian slipped them on and thanked him with a nod.

"Fire, you and me are like brothers, y'understand, so you cyaah repeat anything I gweh tell you right now. Me and Lewis are involved in a slight *bandoolo* business."

Fire leaned against the window. Ian sat on the edge of the bed, bending forward as if the weight of his story was pulling his body off balance.

"Hear me now. Back in the days when I was licking like a granda shit a week I met Lewis through this beef name Margaret. Nobody you know. A Yankee beef from down south . . . as a matter of fact I still slap it now and then.

"She, now, is a beef that know a whole heapa people— she's the program director for CGR. You know them, right? WCGR . . . jazz station? Well, anyway, she introduce me to him at an opening at MOMA and everything was criss, cause I use to see him hanging around the galleries and all that, but I really never knew him. I knew him as a man that used to buy a lot though. But that don't really mean nutten because you have people who buy with other people's money. Which in truth was what he was doing. His company was starting a corporate gallery and they gave him three million to go and spend. And I heard that for every piece he bought for them he bought another one for himself. But that's neither here nor there. Everybody tief when them get the chance.

"Anyway now, we exchanged numbers and he told me he wanted to come and see me because he was interested in looking at some of my work, and I told him plain and straight to fuck off, because him use to fuck Margaret too—Margaret is what you'da call a mattress, if y'know whatta mean—and for me personally, pussy and business don't mix.

"Well, a few months after that I kinda find meself running shorta money due to the lifestyle I was programming." He began to smile now. "Girls and all that. Man . . . this is something they should teach in school: 'If you want to get pussy, stay in school. Cause nutten bring pussy like money.' But anyway, all the pussy programming make me just doan waah do no work. It was just drugs and pussy, pussy and drugs, morning noon and night till the money start run out and I ask my dealer to lend me some dollars.

"This fucker now, Nasser, a vile fucking Sudanese— ex-fucking army staff sergeant—lend me two hundred grand at around forty percent interest and steady me again for like another six months . . . But then is still pussy and drugs so I start fucking up—fucking up bad-bad—and make the man come look for me.

"One day I'm at the dentist getting a root canal and boodoom! the door kick off and is Nasser and around three big-neck man. And before I coulda bawl out, man, them grab me *rass* and throw me in a car trunk and drive me outta one old dock out by Greenpoint and park the car inna the hot-hot sun for half a fucking day.

"Fire, it was some Joe Pesci shit. While me inside the car the Novocain wear off. So check it now—the fucking tooth wide open and me can hardly breathe, cause the only air is a from a little hole where them dig out the lock. So is like I waah bawl out but I don't waah use up all the air. Listen man, there is nothing like when you waah cry and cyaah cry. Is some freaky fucking shit.

"Ever so often, just outta the blue, them woulda just beat pon the car trunk with some baseball bat and iron pipe. The sound me a-tell you is terrifying—like God coming for him world. And then them start with the piss. Remember the little hole in the trunk? The man-dem start piss through that now. So the piss coming in and frying in the heat, so is like now I don't even waah breathe.

"Nightmare, man. It was a *bloodclaat* nightmare. When them let me out, them gimme two weeks fe catch up. As they say in Jamaica, 'Humble calf suck the most milk,' so I humble my fucking self and go to Lewis and we work out something. He would lend me four hundred thousand and I would pay him back over time in art. And this is where it get shady now, because this is not work that pass through Claire. She don't even know this work exist. So she don't get no commission. So that Claire won't find out now, Lewis sell the stuff abroad, to like Latin America and the Far East—cause me name still high in them place deh."

"Fuck," Fire said.

"Lawyers draw up everything."

"So you broke your contract with Claire, then?"

"Not exactly. Legally speaking the stuff I pay Lewis with are gifts. No judge will see anything wrong with that. But yeah." He shrugged his shoulders. "But yeah . . . I broke a contract."

Fire shoved his hands in his pockets. The ruffneck in his heart felt for his fists.

"So the girlfriend," he asked. "She know bout this?"

"Who? Sylvia? Nah. She don't know shit. All of what I telling you go down before she meet him. She'da leave him if she find out though. Definitely. Shit, she wouldn't even cheat on her taxes."

"So tell her then—" He caught himself. "No, don't do that. But don't pay him no more . . . we'll work it out."

"I haven't paid him in a year. That's why things stay the way they stay. Him threatening me with all kinda shit. Lawsuit. Immigration . . . because, as you know, I'm legally a citizen of France, and I've been over here for the last few years on an expired tourist visa. Yow, when I thinka how much work I gi dat pussyhole . . . I mussi pay him like a thousand percent interest over the last five years. From I born outta my mother womb I never see anybody so fucking—"

"So what have you learned from all this?" Fire asked. He was thinking of Miss Gita now. "I notice you're wearing a chronograph. A regular watch wouldn't do?"

Ian looked up at him, his eyes dimming then flaming— bulbs hit by a power surge.

"You know what I love about you?" he said as he picked up his clothes. "You always feel like you can judge me. Like you perfect."

He pointed with an open hand as he dressed with the other.

"You waah know why I wear a TAG and you wear a Timex? Because you used to visit the ghetto on holiday and I used to live there. Because your father is a painter and my ole man was a thief. Because your mother was a pilot and mine is a maid. Because before I went to study in London I'd never been on a plane. For these and other reasons, Fire, I cyaah wear a Timex. I must wear a TAG. You know what your problem is, Fire? You like to be a savior. People don't always need you, man. Trust me on that."

The phone rang. Claire had had to leave Diego's barbecue early and had asked someone to give Fire a number to reach her.

As soon as he got off the phone Ian said he had to go, promising to meet up with Fire later and do something.

"What?" Fire asked.

Ian said he'd figure it out.

"Hello?" A woman's voice in an organ swell, the sound easing up then bearing down on the lick of a guitar. Al Green. "Love and Happiness." One of his favorite songs.

"Hi," he said, dancing with himself. "I'm a friend of Claire's. She left this number for me. Is she there?"

The reply was churned to froth in the reverend's wake.

"Could you repeat that, please?" Fire asked.

"She was here a while ago, but she had to leave."

"Can you do me a favor, darling? Can you tell her, please, that Fire called?" He plugged his ear with a finger. "Tell her that I'm at the Fulton Inn . . . well, if you won't be seeing her then this is probably a waste of your time then . . . aah, if you happen to hear from her, just tell her that Fire called and that I'll probably be leaving here in another coupla minutes— What time is it now? Four and mash. I'm late—and . . . that I'll call her."

He stopped dancing and leaned into the phone. "Are you there?"

Her voice was fainter now . . . even more distant. "Yes . . . you should try her at the gallery. I think . . ."

"I'm sorry . . . I missed—"

"I think she's at the gallery. Call her there." Her voice was sharp.

"Okay, I'll do that . . . and you feel better."

"What do you mean?"

"You sound kinda hoarse, like you getting a cold." He lay on the bed and muffled one ear with a pillow. "You know what's good for that? Lime juice with honey. If you don't like honey use some brown sugar."

"Thanks . . . thank you . . . that was really nice of you."

"You're welcome . . . and remember, if you hear from Claire, ask her to call me . . . please. And if you don't have a lime—you just need *one*, y'know—is awright to use a lemon. Awright?"

"Okay . . . bye."

He called Claire and she told him not to leave, that she was coming over. And suddenly the room felt empty, and he began to wonder how long it would take her to arrive.

Was it Claire? he wondered as he lay in bed. They'd been lovers for a short while, years ago. Was he still attracted? He didn't think so. But he wasn't sure. Blanche would've said yes, though. According to her he was weak for "the dark ones." Which was true. His mother was dark and mellow like Guinness.

The feeling didn't go away when Claire arrived, which made him realize that what he was calling emptiness was a part of him and not the room, because it clung to him like the smell of sweat as he rode on the back of Claire's Kawasaki, his arms around her waist, his crotch up on her battyridered ass. Flatbush Avenue, a broad street, was clogged with shops and traffic—lumbering buses, sharkish livery cabs, and an assortment of coupes, sedans, and four-by-fours displaced by the cabs and buses into each other's way—a clash of greedy metal through which Claire flew like a vulture into the stench of death.

Using the same instinct that allows one to understand the sentiment of a foreign language, Fire began to intuit that his feelings of loneliness were related somehow to that voice on the phone—to the texture more than the text, to the mood. Who was she, that woman whom he could hardly hear, but whom he was feeling now, her words coming soft against his ear? He was still thinking about her as Claire picked her way through a quiet neighborhood of narrow, shaded streets lined with brownstones and carriage houses. She stopped in front of a house, said something that didn't come through his helmet, ran up the steps and rang the bell, and Sylvia came out to greet her.

She was shoeless, a spatula in one hand, the other hand
clasping her waist above the knot that held together a gauzy
blue sarong, a scrim of cloud through which her long legs
shimmered like lightning in a storm. As he stood there beneath an elm, doing his best to steady the bike, the throbbing
shaft of steel between his thighs, he felt her absorbing him,
pulling the wetness out of him, the sweat from his pores, the
spit from his lips, the oil from his wood, the blood—his very
life—which he felt beating against his veins, wanting to spill
itself at the corners of her house to protect her from any spirits that might be sent to harm her.

He realized now—felt it, rather—that *she* was the voice on
the phone. There must be a reason why we're meeting like
this, he said to himself. He set the bike on the kickstand and
walked toward her, his lug soles drumming the pavement like
the hands of a shaman, a masked and feathered juju priest, in-
toning a prayer of thanks to the ancestors. At the top of the
steps, he took her hand, which was smaller than he'd remembered, and thought about what Ian had told him.

"How are you, Sylvia?" he asked.

She replied, "Fine, I think." The spatula was wet with molasses, which had dribbled over her toes, which he wanted to
suck now, as the aroma of cookies wrapped itself around him
like a scarf.

"Anyway," Claire said, edging between them, "we're going
out for a ride. I just came to drop this off." She gave Sylvia the
receipt for the candleholders.

"What are we doing later?" Fire asked. "Should we all get
together? Ian said Gregory Isaacs is playing Club Rio. Does
anyone want to go?"

Sylvia tilted her head and gave him a smile, a subtle one
that preserved the calm of her face. Why is it that I want him
so? she asked herself. She was thinking now of the words that
she'd scribbled on a notepad as soon as she'd gotten off the
phone with him:

It's funny you should have called just now because I was thinking quite intensely about you. It's so hot and I've been wandering around here naked at times, luxuriating in my own sensuality and having all sorts of fantasies about you. Anyway, there I was, lying on the sofa, topless in my sarong, legs open, stroking my inner thighs, enjoying the tingle, wanting to feel your much larger hands there. To be honest, I spent some of this afternoon on my bed imagining you here. Oh, I just want to be with you, eat you, have you lick the salt sweat off my body.

"I think Gregory Isaacs would be nice," she said. She hadn't been to a reggae show in years. "What about you, Claire? Would you like to come?"

"Sure, if I'm welcome." Claire pinched Fire's elbow. "But we have to go."

"And I have to finish my cookies." She waved goodbye and turned toward the door.

"It starts at ten," Fire said. "So we'll meet you there at around nine-thirty, and"—he looked away, caught a smile, and brought it back for her—"I'd like to taste something from your oven . . . bring me a cookie later, nuh?"

His words skipped across her mouth. Her face became a rippling pond.

"Just one?"

"Yeah. Everything has to start somewhere."

He arrived at ten-thirty and immersed himself in the crowd, a flash flood of humanity that had swept through West Forty-ninth Street, voraciously swallowing hydrants, Dumpsters, and mailboxes before stagnating in a pool, fatigued perhaps by the heat. The aroma of marijuana sweetened the air against the pungency of tobacco, boiled corn, jerk chicken, and floral perfumes. Gold was everywhere. Teeth. Bracelets. Hairpins. Necklaces. And rings. If some fabrics were not intended for some outfits, and some outfits not intended for some bodies, one would not have guessed. Gold lamé, crushed velvet, crinoline, satin, and raw silk proudly girdled bellies that had borne too many children too early. And hair? As much as money could buy.

There were a few rastas sprinkled in, steadfast in righteous drabness in the fashion Babylon, their only embellishment being the white girls strung around their necks. The white boys in grunge gear shared joints with their buddies and tripped out on the bass belching from the belly of a black BMW marooned at the entrance of a parking garage. Patois swirled and collided in midair, and burst into sparkles. "Why dem don't let in de people dem? De metal detector business holdin up too much time. Dem have metal detector? Me better go puddown me gun and come back den."

Gripping the straps of his knapsack to settle it, Fire edged through the mob, swiveling left and right, his eyes skimming the horizon like a periscope, his body pressed on all sides. Where were they? Was that Claire there? Before he could look more closely, his view was blocked by an exuberant weave, a fan-shaped piece of gelled hair-sculpture that eclipsed in size and range of color the open tail of a peacock. As the crowd began to evaporate from the narrow, cracked sidewalk, he drifted down the street to the stage door, which was guarded by a surly giant dressed in black, a chain-smoking southerner who seemed to know only four words, *no* and *can't help you*, which he dispensed in a monotone to all who asked for help. Maybe both of them changed their minds, Fire thought as he returned to the entrance, sorry now that he was flying to England in the morning. He stood there waiting. Then left a message with the corn man and went inside to see the show.

Standing under the balcony of the musty old theater, Sylvia, in a lavender sundress, was lonely in the company of four thousand people. Taking a sip of her Campari and orange juice, she tried to flee the melancholy, tried to take her thoughts in a different direction, but they shadowed her, like

the sharks that trailed the schooners west from the coast of
Africa.

Claire, whom she'd summoned by phone as soon as she'd
left Diego's, had predicted this falling away. They'd spent the
afternoon together on her sofa, most of the time in silence, a
silence which became reflection, then later, after Claire had
left, bacchanal—music, baking, dancing, and wanton mas-
turbation, during which she stroked herself and pinched her
nipples and buried into her mound of earth a plantain wet
with olive oil.

She drained the glass, her fourth in the last hour, and began
to feel a comfort with the music that she hadn't felt at first.
And as she stood there, caught in a tidal draft of bass, the
snare smacking wet like a belly flop, the guitar slicing through
like an oar stroke, the horns fine and light as sand in an under-
tow, she began to think of herself as a fish, and the people
around her as blades of sea grass. With the onset of weightlessness she became more aware of her body, of how much of
it she couldn't feel, of how much of it she wanted to touch, to
reexplore, to reassure herself that it was all there, all hers—
all hers to give to whomever she pleased . . .

Gregory was drifting across the stage, in an orange three-
piece suit, his skinny back swayed like a sea horse, his voice a
rippling whinny. She closed her eyes, hugged herself, and listened through her pores.

> They can't get me with silver
> They can't get me with gold
> They wonder why I love you so
> Half the story has never been told
> But they would never understand
> What it means to need someone
> All I need is you . . . only you will do

When she opened her eyes he was there, dressed in rumpled khakis and a blue T-shirt that smelled of laundry soap.

For a second she wasn't sure what to do. Her first thought was to smile. But *his* smile, the one that warmed her face now, was so bright that she feared that hers would not shine through—that it would be swallowed like a village on the edge of a town.

Standing beside each other, feeling the heat of each other's body distinct from the heat around them, they did not speak, their silence an agreement that the music was too loud for them to hear themselves. With smiles and glances, furrowed brows and pouted lips they carried on a dialogue about the people around them, trying to deflect attention from the momentous opportunity that faced them—they were alone in a dark place without supervision. Frightened by this, Sylvia broke the silence, tugging at Fire's shirt so she could lean his ear toward her, but she found herself unable to speak. Cautious as well, he spoke to her from a distance.

After the show, they decided as they covered the half block to Broadway that he would share a cab with her. Why not? they reasoned, as she linked her arm in his. They were both going to Brooklyn. And the cookie? Yes . . . the cookie that she'd promised him. She'd forgotten it at home. At home in Brooklyn where they were both going . . . together . . . in the same car. How convenient. So shouldn't he just stop by and get it, then? Which was not a bad idea, considering that he'd brought her a gift of coffee. Blue Mountain.

Standing at the curb, conspirators in a crowd that did not know them, they felt the electric warmth of newness, of possibility, running through their bones. Below them, in the carnival of Times Square, the lights of the cars hurtled by with a wondrous joy that seemed to say: This is what it would look like if we screwed.

"The next time we're out and there's music, we should dance," he said, leaning toward her. They were standing in the street now, between a Mustang and a Blazer. She was tipping to hail a cab. His languid words were germinated seeds of lust. His voice, strong but weighted, did not ascend above a whisper. "I should've thought of that inside. I should have asked you . . . but I like to ask for what I know I'll get. I don't handle disappointment very well."

"I wouldn't have disappointed you," she said, bolder now than she would have been had she not been drinking. "Here's what I would've done." She wet her lips unconsciously, which signaled him that her mouth was a silken purse that would close itself around his pearls of joy. "I would've danced with you . . . fast or slow . . . however you like it. I hope it would be slow though. You have to be slow to be sexy. You do a lot of things slow, don't you, Fire?" She didn't wait for his reply. "You walk slow . . . you talk slow." She pursed her lips and stroked his face with streams of air. "I've never seen you eat though. I hope you do that slow as well."

"Well, it all depends on what I'm eating," he said, pretending to tie his shoelace. She was leaning back against the Mustang now, her hips thrust forward, her thighs ajar. "It also depends on how hungry I am . . . and how much I like this thing . . . and whether or not I'm eating in public. Because as you know, none of us eats the same way in public as we do in private. In private you don't care if the gravy runs down your chin. Cause if there's enough to dribble then there must be even more to lick. And come on, now," he grazed her shin with his cheek as he slowly rose. "Some things you just can't eat with finesse. Like fried chicken. It doesn't taste good unless your lips get greasy—your whole face, really. Your fingers too." He flipped her hem with his nose. "Y'have a skillet?" he asked, standing erect now.

"Yes," she said, spreading her legs, blind to the stares of passersby. Deaf to their giggles. He slipped a bare foot between her knees.

"And what about skills?" he asked, pinching her thigh with his toes. "Y'have skills? You need skills to skin the chicken, y'know. I don't like mine with the skin on it. D'you know how to skin it and pluck it? I don't like supermarket chicken, y'know. Chicken should be fresh. The meat must still be warm when you cook it."

She smacked his knee and began to laugh. He wiggled his foot into his shoe and laughed with her.

"Are you out of your mind?" she said. "How can you just put your foot beneath my dress like that? So easily?"

"I must admit that pants would've posed a bigger challenge."

"Shush, you know what I mean. How can you just step outside yourself and do things like that? Are you like this with every woman?"

"Only the ones that let me."

"I hate you," she said, with sparkling eyes. Her smirking mouth was drawn in a thin line.

"I hate you too," he said, drawing her close. He rubbed the back of her head as she buried her face in his chest, where his nipple seemed to inject her cheeks with a dye that made them flush.

A cab came. They got inside, she ahead of him because he held the door. And they began to snuggle before the driver had put the Chevy in gear, he leaning against a door, almost horizontally, and she on top of him, sighing as his hand skimmed over her wavy hair, calming her soul like a breeze.

"Is this what it should feel like?" she mumbled, peeling back his T-shirt like a foreskin. As she nuzzled his chest, he pinched a nipple between two fingers and began to suckle her, rocking her, steadying her as the cab bounced out of potholes and swerved to avoid collisions, holding her both hard and soft.

"Should *what* feel this way?" he asked, wincing but not disturbing her as she pulled on him sharply and clenched him between her teeth, lapping at him hungrily, wanting to nourish her spirit with his essence.

"Should you want a man to mother you?"

"You want me to mother you, sweet girl?"

"Right now, I do," she said.

"I'll be your mummy then. Hush, sweetness . . . go to sleep."

By the time they reached her apartment she was snoring.

"I'm sorry," she said when he roused her. "I didn't mean to doze off. I haven't hung out in a while." She yawned. "Oh excuse me." She reached into her purse. "Here's my share—"

He patted her hand. "Just cool. It's okay."

She opened the door. Something in the mood had changed.

"So we'll do cookies another time, then," he told her. He reached into his knapsack for the burlap pouch of coffee.

Sliding across the seat to her he placed one foot on the sidewalk, signaling that he was able if she was willing. She took a step toward him, which raised his hopes, then stumbled, and he grabbed her arm to steady her.

"I think I drank too much," she said as he stood up. She leaned on him. "I think I need to go inside and get some sleep. Can we get together another time? I wouldn't be good company tonight."

She looked up at him, slack-jawed and squinting.

"Okay," he replied, letting her go, "the next time I'm in town I'll tell Claire . . . and we can get together. I wonder what happened to her anyway?"

"What do you mean *in town*?" she asked, suddenly alert. "You don't live in New York?"

"I live in Jamaica," he said, smiling. "And I'm going to London at eight in the morning."

"Well . . . call me . . . whenever . . . you're in town," she replied, trying to hide her disappointment.

"Claire has your number, right?"

He was sitting in the cab now with his feet outside.

"I don't want Claire to know my business," she said.

She was squatting on her heels in front of him. She rested her hands on his knees.

"Tell you what, then, let's make things simpler. So that nobody will have to know anybody's business, why don't I give you my address then so you can write to me when you feel like."

"Let's make it simpler than that. Call me when you get in. I wanna talk to you." She dug into her pocketbook and scribbled on a business card. "Here."

She kissed her palm and patted his face. He watched to make sure she got in safely, then left.

He discovered when he got in that she had written her number—accidentally, he presumed—on one of Lewis's business cards. And as he sat on the edge of the bed beside the phone, spritzed by the scent of Blanche's flowers, he felt relieved that he and Sylvia were in separate rooms. For what would it all have been worth in the morning? She was involved. And in a manner of speaking, so was he.

He did not call her. Instead, he wrote her a letter. On his way to the airport, he stopped at her house, and in the orange light of dawn, slipped it beneath her door.

Hungover despite two cups of coffee, Sylvia found the envelope on her way to work and tossed it in her portfolio without reading it, for she thought it was a letter from her landlord, who lived on the street behind her. He often left her correspondence like that, in plain envelopes inscribed with just her name.

Why? she kept asking herself as she made her way to Clark Street, slouching in her skirt suit through the shaded streets. Her pace slowed with each succeeding step, as if the convoy of fellow professionals that trundled by were tapping her strength. Why? Why? Why? The rest of the question refused to be drawn into her mind until she entered the elevator at the subway station. There, compacted in the steel cage that lowered its passengers through the bedrock like old South African miners, she felt the weight of those around her forcing the thought through her intestines, into her belly, up into her throat, to coat the roof of her mouth. Why didn't he call me? Even just to say goodbye.

She wanted to talk to him. Now. Desperately. About what, she didn't know.

And as she imagined herself together with him, strolling a beach or sitting under a shade tree along a country road, she told herself that she wouldn't care. Then she thought some more and decided that she would, knowing—in a way that she could neither describe nor explain, for she had never felt this way before—that he would want to discuss the same things as she, or would at least know how, which was something that she couldn't say for Lewis, or most of the men she'd been involved with. They were bright men to be sure, but bright in a linear way, like laser beams. Intense. Focused. But Fire's light had the expansive sprawl of a sunset . . . diffuse . . . layered . . . natural and organic. Lewis and the others had the brightness of the mind, which was accessible to anyone with the right life chances. Fire, though, had the brightness of the soul. Which was a grace. He understood her jokes, related to her references, and shadowed her subtlest shifts in mood. This is the way, she thought, that Billy Strayhorn must have felt when Ellington played his music—like, "Shit, this person can read my mind."

Last night, for example. In the taxi. When he nursed her. How did he know that she needed that . . . to be babied . . . at that moment? And what was it in him that made him sacrifice his own need, to give her the security—as momentary as it was—of belonging, and not necessarily to him, but to something outside herself?

Had it been another man—a strip of faces crossed her mind—there would've been a presumption, an insistence even, that the intimacy was about his need and not hers. And as she considered the idea of the laser beam again, she saw that it was related not just to intelligence but to a whole way of being. Which is why the tenderness he showed her was so erotic—it had transcended the needs of the flesh.

As the elevator doors opened and she was swept along the crosswalk and down the steps to the platform, she concluded that Fire had more than the strength of a man. He also had the strength of a woman. A penis as a totem could not fully represent him. For he was more than a giver of pleasure. He was a giver of life. As she thought about this she didn't feel tired anymore. She wanted to sing now. She wanted to dance. With him. To any song. Fast or slow. However he wanted it.

As the train bumped and rattled beneath the river, she ignored the fetid armpits of the fat man beside her and mused on how nice it was to feel at home with a man. She had never felt such ease with Lewis. But then she had never felt such ease with herself either.

If she'd gone to the show with Lewis, it would've been a different experience. His tastes were tethered to jazz and R&B. Everything else, including blues and classical, was intolerable, or at best inoffensive. Which is why they listened to his music more than hers. Her tastes included his. And although she felt guilty, she had to admit it—it was easy for her to step down to his level.

Something had happened at the concert that she hadn't remembered until now. As she and Fire stood next to each other, close but not touching, they shared a joke without speaking. It was quite a silly joke actually, but telling nonetheless: a woman directed a friend to the bar by pointing with her lips and not her fingers. Being Caribbean, she and Fire recognized the archetype, so they laughed. Had she been with Lewis she would've had to explain it. Then the joke would've lost its taste.

As she considered this, she realized that she'd been quietly missing her culture for years. She loved jazz. She loved classical. And the blues and R&B. But she didn't feel them in the same way she felt some Trenchtown bass *bussin* her head or some Lavantille steel pan *racklin* through her bones. She hadn't dated many men from the Caribbean, and this was an issue she'd never come to terms with, but which she suspected had a lot to do with Syd. And in relationships, she'd always found it easier to collapse into the man's head-space than to ask him to expand into hers.

When she got to work, her secretary Boogie Boo brought her breakfast. As usual, carrot juice and a bran muffin. This morning she couldn't have it though. She was in the mood for some cornmeal porridge.

"Syl."

"Yes, Boogie Boo."

"You need to be with Virgil in ten minutes."

She checked her watch. Twelve-fifteen. What had she done all morning? She glanced around her office, a big space with gray carpeting, black cabinets, and stackable chairs piled high with papers. What *had* she done all day? Nothing. Nothing except think about her weekend. Lewis. Ian. And Fire.

Boogie Boo—it was not her real name but she insisted on being called that—knocked on the door and entered.

"Which Virgil do we have today?" Sylvia asked. "The good one or the bad one?"

Boogie Boo twirled one of her orange braids and wrinkled her upturned nose. Slim-hipped and dark, she was twenty-four and counted among her "things" music/dance/performance poetry/acting/modeling and aerobics instructing. This was just her day job.

"Come on, it's a Monday. Whadyou think?" she replied, leaning against the door. She was dressed in thrift store crimplene—a sky blue leisure suit—and white platforms to match her nails. "I heard—and I can't say who told me, so don't ask, cause you know I'll tell and that would just be wrong—that he's really pissed about that New Orleans feature. That whole Congressman DeVeaux thing. Didn't I tell you it wasn't gonna fly? But you don't listen to me. Nobody listens to me around here. Y'all people just don't like to listen. It's the man's magazine. Why argue? He's the founder, publisher, and editor-in-chief, not to mention Führer, Il Duce, and Pope."

Sylvia sucked her teeth and fanned Boogie Boo away before she made her laugh.

Boogie Boo raised her brows and shrugged. "By the way," she said, as she was about to leave, "if you're not gonna have that muffin, can I have it? I have the serious munchies today. I got so fucking blunted this morning, you wouldn't believe."

Sylvia took a minute to relax, then went down the hall to the publisher's office, taking care to announce herself before taking a seat in one of the red leather wing chairs in front of Virgil's giant oak desk.

Virgil was standing by a huge picture window behind his desk, smoking a cigar and looking out on Rockefeller Center, his hands clasped behind his back, black wool crêpe suit draping from his shoulders, his bald pate swelling out of the collar of his white shirt like a bare bulb extruding from the socket of a plastic lamp. Imperious, he let Sylvia's greeting hang in the air a bit before acknowledging it. Then he turned around, sat in his chair, balanced his bifocals on his Roman nose, and trained his icy stare on her.

"Everything looks great about the Black New Orleans feature," he began in his low mumble. Furrows raked his forehead. "Except for one thing—we can't fuck with Congressman DeVeaux like this. If we run this, niggers'll lose their minds."

Niggers. The word made her wince. There were other people who could've said it without unnerving her. But not him. The son of an Italian media baron and an African-American opera singer, Virgil Pucci could pass for white—which he'd done until he was thirty-five. Then he reclaimed his blackness when he learned about a federal program designed to open radio and television ownership to minorities. In two years, with the backing of his father, he was in control of twelve FM and eight VHF stations across the country. Five years later he sold them to a Fortune 500 company for thirty times their original price and used the profits to buy a huge West Coast cable system. Fortyish, bored, and independently wealthy, he launched *Umbra* as the first in a series of magazines aimed at African-Americans, who for him were not a readership but a market—one that was larger and richer than entire countries in Western Europe.

No. It was not cool for him to use the word *nigger*, she thought. With him she couldn't be sure it was coming from a place of love. But what could she do about it? Nothing. And what did she want to do? Nothing. He was paying her ninety grand a year to hate him.

"Close the door, Sylvia," he began, the furrows deepening across his forehead. "We need to talk privately."

Sylvia bit her tongue and did as she was told.

"You supervised the DeVeaux article," he continued. "I left you alone. You used a writer that wasn't one of ours and I left you alone. Now in this article, there's exploration of those embezzlement charges that are being brought up against brother DeVeaux. I know he discussed them on the record, but he changed his mind afterward. I mentioned this to you some time ago. But nothing has been done. Congressman DeVeaux has fought very hard for his people all his life, Sylvia. They love that fool down there. He's brought them more pork than there are pigs in Iowa. *I* know he stole the goddamn money. The government knows. I'm sure the people on Mars know too. But the black folks down in New Orleans don't know. And they don't *wanna* know."

"Virgil, can I interrupt you for a second? When did black people sign a contract saying they wanted to be treated like children? I'm a journalist, Virgil, not a copywriter for the City of New Orleans Visitors Bureau. There are a lot of wonderful things about New Orleans. And we cover a lot of them in the feature. So why can't we show a little of the other side as well?"

"Lemme tell you a little secret," he said, whispering. "Black folks don't need balance right now. They need positive images. White folks can tear down their leaders, Sylvia, but black folks can't afford to. They have too few. I've told you several

times but you don't listen—you need to reorient your thinking. You need to get into the mind-set of the folks in the street.
Black America is not New York. Them niggers out in Detroit
and down in Atlanta are not mature enough to handle the
truth. Black folks are directionless right now. And what they
want are myths, ideals, heroes. Whether or not this is what
they need is another issue."

Was it really worth fighting for? she asked herself. What
would winning this one achieve? He wouldn't change. Neither would the magazine. But, Jesus Christ, if only he would
let her do her job sometimes.

Virgil looked at her appraisingly. She looked away. He
sliced the tip off a Romeo y Julieta.

"I know you think I'm nuts, Sylvia. But I'm telling you
like it is. This isn't *Time* or *Newsweek* or *Emerge*. This is *Umbra*. I wish it didn't have to be this way. But as I've always
said, black folks need dictatorship. For all his faults, Mus-
solini did a lot for Italy. He held that place together . . . And
by the way, accounting says they're missing hundreds of
dollars in expense receipts for this feature. Deal with that
quickly, please. It's already becoming a problem or else
they wouldn't have told me about it. Anyway, that's all I have
to say right now. I need the chair you're sitting on for a
meeting."

Sylvia left the office at the end of the day hating her job
more than ever. To make matters worse, she got drenched on
the way to the subway. When it began to rain, she put up her
umbrella and a freckle-faced kid in a baseball cap grabbed it
and ran away. As she chased him she tripped and fell and her
skirt sailed over her head.

A homeboy with a gold tooth gave her a hand. And as she
stood there thanking him in the pouring rain, he asked her if
he could "fix her drawers for her." She told him to go fuck
himself and hustled underground.

At home she showered and changed into a white T-shirt and

had more coffee with some of her cookies. Folding her legs beneath her, she sorted the wad of bills that she'd been carrying in her portfolio for the last week. Work had been hectic. So she hadn't had a chance to take care of a few things. Which made her angry with herself. She always paid her bills on time. Her credit would have to be perfect if she wanted to buy her house. Banks decline black applicants routinely.

Working through a hierarchy, starting with American Express, she finally came to the envelope that she'd found that morning. By the time she went to bed, she'd read the letter thirty times.

Dear Sylvia,

I should've called you, shouldn't I? I think writing is better though. Certainly in this case, because some things sound so silly when you say them. Actually, writing letters can be silly too. Like right now I feel silly doing this. In fact as I'm writing this I'm having visions of you in the back of a classroom, showing it to the other girls and giggling at my handwriting. No, you strike me as the type who would read it to the class from the top of the teacher's desk.

It was really good to see you tonight. At first I felt guilty for being happy that Claire didn't make it. But being in your company washed guilt away and replaced it with another feeling that shall remain nameless to protect the innocent.

I'm about to do something adolescent, but bear with me. It's hard to behave like a grown-up when a woman is making you feel too giddy for your age.

When we met, I had no idea that we'd ever see each other again. And I walked away from that phone booth filled with so much sweetness—and here's where the adolescent business comes in—like Bob must have felt when he met the person who inspired the song "Waiting in Vain."

I have to go. I'm packing to leave. My things are all over the place. I ransacked my suitcase looking for clothes this evening. And I'm expecting company. (Yes, at this hour. Ian said he's sending a bearer with a package for me. What can I say? Ian is Ian.) I'm going to England for the entire summer, so I won't be seeing you soon, which is both good and bad, if you know what I mean. As I said to you tonight, I don't handle disappointment very well.

I'll always remember you, Sylvia, and the time we shared. Now I know how Dizzy must have felt when he heard Bird play the first time, like, "Yeah, this is the sound I've been searching for inside myself." What more can I say, nice girl? To be or not to bop?

So . . . I must go now. It would be nice if you choose to remember me. Yes, I'd like that. Remember me as the guy who didn't want that cab ride to end, who didn't want you to wake up until whatever was causing you to toss so much had been washed out of your soul, who really wanted to kiss you goodbye. I hope you like the coffee. My friend Sarge grows it on this little farm. Write to me in Jamaica and I'll send you more if you want. Take care, Sylvia. It was nice to have met you.

—Fire

Daggers of lightning ripped the sky. Thunder balls shook the room. And the candles drew scary pictures on the walls. Sylvia fell asleep on her belly. One arm cuddled a pillow beneath her. The other one was glued between her legs.

As she sank deeper into sleep, her face relaxed and the smile began to fade. But it took a very long time.

book two

chapter four

Through his window in the first-class cabin, Fire watched the twilight soaking through the clouds. He was struck once again by the drama of the heavens, by the colors and shapes and textures that throbbed and shifted and eddied there. Leaning back in his seat, he concerned himself with the package in his hands, the one that Ian had sent to him at four o'clock in the morning, stipulating, as the bearer said, that it not be opened till he was over the Atlantic, where he was now, approaching the coast of Wales.

It was a letter he saw when he opened it—attached by a clip to a check drawn on an account at a bank that was based in the Caymans.

Fire—

Don't cash this until two weeks when certain things straighten out. I'm selling the watch. When I do that the check will be good. Right now it will bounce. Please though if you could give mama 2000 pound for me in the meantime then deduct it from when you cash the check which should be soon. Tell her the money is from me. Tell her I look good. Tell her she don't see me cause I shame of my roots. Don't say what you saw.

Waiting to meet Fire at Heathrow was his cousin Courtney. He was short and ginger-haired, with narrow eyes cut into a broad, flat face. He grabbed Fire's bags and hurriedly led the way, babbling on about carburetors, headers, and limited-slip differentials as they moved through crowded passageways and skipped up stairs to the third level of a parking garage, where parked between a yellow Toyota Supra and a black Honda Prelude was his latest restoration project, a '72 Ford Cortina Lotus—a boxy, pearl white coupe zipped from head to tail with the Lotus flash in racing green.

Stepping over the bags, Fire walked around the car, running his palms over the paint job, checking under the wheel wells for rust. Then, satisfied that the exterior had neared perfection—there was a small dent near the driver's door—he asked to see the engine, the legendary twin-cam, push-rod dynamo that spurred a hundred and fifty horses to power the rear wheels. As he checked it, he was thinking about his mother.

It was his mother, not his father, who had taught him about mechanics. Her father, who was a cousin of the Manleys, was a fighter pilot in the RAF during the Second World War, and returned home to introduce crop dusting to the family farm where she was born and raised. By the time she was fourteen Fire's mother had learned to overhaul and operate the biplane.

Backing off so he could look at the Cortina in relation to the cars around it, Fire noted to himself that he would take it over either the Toyota or the Honda, which—with their aerodynamic noses and power-assisted steerings and noise-dampened cabins—in the company of the old Ford were like yuppies in a blue-collar bar. He loved old European cars: Mini Cooper Ss . . . BMW 2002s . . . Volvo P 1800s . . . Alfa Romeo Alfettas. Driving cars in which he could feel the pores of the road through the fingers of the shocks and hear the guttural cussing of the engine as he pushed it toward redline.

"Lemme drive," he said, excited now.

Courtney threw him the keys, admonishing in his South London accent that his baby cousin be careful. "Many have died so I could have this."

Fire laughed at the vocational reference. Courtney was an undertaker. He'd passed only woodwork and bible knowledge at O level. What else, his father had said at the time, was he fit to do?

Settling into the Recaro seat, Fire ran his hand over the burl dashboard and flush door panels, eyeing excitedly the rows of analog gauges and toggle switches.

"Go on," Courtney urged. "Crank it."

When he twisted the key he felt as if he'd tweaked a lion's ear. A roar erupted from the belly of the machine.

"Want some music, Fire?"

Courtney pulled some tapes from the backseat.

"Wha y'have?"

"The Diamonds. *Go Seek Your Rights*; Sugar Minott, *Good Thing Going*; and a dancehall mix tape. Kilamanjaro versus Stone Love."

"Yes, rudie," he said, booming him—pressing fists. "Gimme some o' dat."

The windows down, the engine bawling, they shunted onto the motorway, seduced by the nihilistic ghettocentric rhetoric, urged toward rebellion by the brutish kick drum, which came down on their skulls like a pistol whip, commanding them to mash the gas.

When they reached Brixton, though, a different mood fell over them. To Fire it felt as if the skins from the dead in the Atlantic and in the plantation fields had been sewn into a shawl and draped around his shoulders.

Arriving from America, where black people had so much more—more wealth, more education, more numbers, more influence, more history, and consequently more hope—to this London, this England—where black people have lived in large numbers for only fifty years and had not had a chance to nurture their own Spike Lee or Reginald Lewis or Alexis Herman or Toni Morrison or Henry Louis Gates or Colin Powell or Johnnie Cochran or Carol Mosely Braun—underscored his reason for moving home.

Jamaica, despite its motto, "Out of many, one people," was a black country, and he was a black man, and there, on that island, no matter how hard things were at times, he waited for scraps at no one's table. He was no one's scapegoat. No man's Sambo. No one's recurring nightmare. And people there did not whisper the word *white* in conversation, because they know that in 1833 and 1865 and many times before that and since, the black people of Jamaica have risen up and spilled white blood, licked it off their fingers, swallowed it, burped, and said, "No problem."

On the high street, a doddering bus transformed the car into a front-row seat for the long-running drama of the Brixton tube station, which if it were ever adapted for the stage should be called *Notice Me*. For camped outside, lying in wait to pounce on weary passengers, were scores of predators, some in packs, some alone. A skinny Trinidadian in a tight brown suit and tube socks was waving his bible like a tambourine and screaming for all to repent. A group of Black Israelites in outfits inspired by *Ali Baba and the Forty Thieves* and *Star Wars* were screaming into a microphone, in a fake American accent no less, that the white man would be the black man's slave after the coming Armageddon. To which a Greek chorus of coked-up druggies lounging on a cardboard bed in front of the 7-Eleven were screaming, "Monkeys can't rule anything except bananas." Which made the schizophrenic dread who'd been screaming as he defended himself against invisible stones realize that he wasn't being pelted by the duppy of the last white woman who gave him head but rather the last monkey on which he'd performed cunnilingus. "Monkey pussy taste nice but i wi mad you," he screamed to the preacher. "Doan nyam it." The preacher screamed back in tongues, "Shala-mala, shala-maloo . . . askillapunka . . . I rebuke you." To which the dread screamed, "You suck de same monkey too." And the preacher began to beat him with the bible. "Shala-mala, shala-maloo . . . Lissen, I wi put away

God business and throw licks in you moddacunt, y'know.
Stop dis chupidniss now!"

Further on, they passed the market, a pepperpot of food
and races; and Cold Harbour Lane, the new front line, where
rudebwais in Hilfiger distribute pharmaceuticals to a richer,
more wanly dressed white clientele; and the park around St.
Matthew's, a hulking presence with Doric columns that due
to lack of faith was no longer just a church but also an arts
venue—with a restaurant in the crypt.

Continuing on Effra Road, they passed some terrace
houses in need of love and care; and the Eurolink Business
Centre, a hothouse of local capitalism in the shell of an old
synagogue. Then moving quicker now, as Fire felt the pull of
his house, they cut through Brixton Water Lane and entered
Herne Hill, a scarf of relative affluence on the edge of Brock-
well Park.

"So where's Nan?" Fire asked, as they walked up the steps
of the brick Victorian.

Courtney checked his watch. "On her way home from
classes, I'd fink."

They'd stopped for takeout on the way.

"She won't be hungry when she comes?" Fire asked. "You
didn't pick up anything for her."

Courtney thought for a second, then shrugged his
shoulders.

"Is awright," Fire said as they went inside. "I'll make
something."

Courtney shrugged again.

"So what she doing at the polytech?" Fire asked, noting
that the lawn was shaggy. Come on, he thought. You've living here rent-free, Courtney, you *could* take care of the fucking place.

"Farting around," Courtney said, straightening the For
Sale sign. "She claims she's studying computers . . . she can't
even fucking type."

"So what is she doing, then?"

"I fink it might be word processing. But I'm not really sure."

Fire had purchased the house when he sold film rights to his first novel, *The Rudies,* an epic about the rise and fall of a Jamaican gang in London. At the time, the neighborhood, like a lot of Brixton, was considered marginal. Since then, however, yuppies, priced out of Thatcherite Dulwich, had moved in, increasing property values exponentially. He didn't foresee this when he bought the place, neither did he care. He bought it for the park, an undulating green triangle, with a duck pond and a wonderful lido, where he saw nothing but sky while floating on his back in the summertime, the sun warming his face like a hot copper penny.

To command a view of the park, he kept the top floor for himself. Courtney and Nan lived in a first-floor duplex, and Phil, Fire's first roommate when he moved to London, lived on the floor below him. Phil was away on tour with a chamber ensemble and was expected to return in a month.

"So, did Nan get called for the gig with that design firm?" Fire asked, as he made her a veggie-rice pilaf. He was down in Courtney's kitchen. Some eggplant, which had been tossed in olive oil, was sitting aside on the counter. In a Dutch oven, the rice was simmering in a vegetable stock seasoned with onions, garlic, cinnamon, and allspice.

"No," Courtney replied. He was sitting at the breakfast table, shoveling food into his mouth.

"What about the gig with *The Face*?" Fire asked, chopping the plum tomatoes.

"No."

"I can't see why she doesn't get hired. She's a good photographer." He reached into a cupboard for a bottle of honey.

"She's got problems," Courtney said, flatly.

"I know," Fire replied with a chuckle. "You."

Courtney changed the subject. "How's your dad?" he asked.

"Fine," Fire replied, spilling the box of currants he was opening. "Still at the School of Art. How's yours?"

"All right. Still a cantankerous bugger, but e's all right. E's still fucking around with that twenty-one-year-old Paki girl. I wish I can be like im at is age. E's sixty-seven! D'you realize tha? And e's still able to keep up! E's got the dick of deaf. I'm convinced that's how Mum died. Fuck cancer. He poked er to deaf."

"Where's he living now? The old man told me he moved."

"Wimbledon. Did he also tell you Dad's girlfriend is pregnant?"

"Get the hell outta here!"

He stirred the eggplant, the currants, and the honey into the rice. Only the dill was left.

"Serious as cancer . . . or getting poked to deaf for tha matter. Six months pregnant. Maybe Dad didn't tell your old man because he didn't want to get im jealous. Your dad's not into girls anymore, is e?"

"Whatever."

"So school begins next week," Courtney said, retreating from this sensitive issue. "It's Kings College ain it?"

"Not this year. I'm doing some fiction workshops for emerging writers at the Eurolink Center. Word Star is putting it on."

"Well that's mighty nice of you. From what I've heard they don't have much money to pay a big shot like you. Mr. Somerset Maugham Prize. What's next then, a Booker? Nan says you've been—what—short-listed for *Dangling on the Brink of the Edge*? Maybe that'll be your breakthrough in America. It's a shame you don't do well there."

"Well, if it should be it will be. What is for you cyaah be un-for you, y'know, Courts. The American market is so difficult. So big and so competitive. They have so many of their own writers to admire. Updike. William Kennedy. I have enough money now to do the things I like to do: buy music and books, travel, help people, laze about. And success in

America might ruin that. See, Courts, there is a certain point, with money, where it can become a burden. Where you always feel like you have to be watching it. And you have to hire people to watch it for you. Then you have to start watching them. Then you won't have any time to read books and listen to music and just laze about. And then you don't want to help people because the money becomes an end in itself, and you become so taken up with making it grow, as they say, that you don't want to do anything that might make it stand still even for a little bit. Yeah, I want my money to grow. But not like a tree. Like grass. Spread out."

"So is Word Star paying you then?"

"Of course. If you give away things for free people don't appreciate it. They begin to feel entitled. And that's a bad thing. No one's entitled to anything but a fair chance, kind encouragement, and a kick in the ass when they keep fucking up, Courts. And that's why I'm over here. But should I really have to do this? Where are the black writers who were born here and spent most of their lives here? The ones who've done really well? America. That's where they are. Teaching in the best universities."

"Would you call them sellouts?"

"No. It's quite complex. They're trying to get the biggest market for their work. And that's understandable. There're only a million and a half black people in all of Britain versus thirty-two million in the States. I guess they feel they have to get more before they can start giving back. Labels like 'sellout' are too simple to describe the challenges faced by black people, Courts. Have always been. No, I wouldn't call them sellouts. They've had to take a different route because they haven't been as lucky as I've been. By the way, how are Little J and Kyle and Locksley?"

"They moved to America—Brooklyn, I believe. A lot of people have moved over there. England's getting tougher and tougher every day. Layoffs everywhere. Maybe I should move over there. The funeral business must be better over

there wif all the drive-by killings and disgruntled postal workers. Not to mention cancer and hypertension. Shit! Over ere
I've got to wait for a car to run over somebody or until someone dies of old age or boredom."

Fire and Courtney stayed up chatting about cars and music
until they heard the tinkling of Nan's keys at the door. They
were in the living room now. Fire was flushed with warmth
when he saw her. He'd known her since they were teenagers.

"Oh, you've already got supper," she said, as she walked
toward Courtney to give him a kiss. She spoke with
modulated precision. "I brought you supper, luv—for you
too, Fire—donners." She dug a space between them with
her hips.

"I heard you're going to the polytech, Nan," Fire said.
"What're you taking up?"

"Computer-aided retouching—Adobe Photoshop."

"Courts told me you were doing word processing."

"What does he know about me? He pays me no mind. He's
too busy with his dead bodies. I'm beginning to think he's a
necrophiliac—"

"That explains my attraction to you, Nan."

Nan slapped Courtney playfully, then continued on about
school.

When Fire woke up the next morning, Nan was sitting on
the edge of his futon. Wiping his hair away from his face, he
sat up and gathered the covers around his middle, aware—too
much so, he felt—of the form of her breasts through her light
nightgown.

She'd acquired some lines in her face, he noticed—to her
advantage, for they drew attention to her best features: her
dark eyes and thick lashes, and her slightly crooked Cypriot
nose. Poor Nan. She needed a different kind of man, Fire
thought. She needed a man who encouraged without prompting. For, as bright as she was, Nan was in thrall to self-doubt.
At times he was inclined to believe that Courtney withheld

his support to ensure that she'd never outgrow him. Which began to make more sense now as he considered how Courtney had pressured her to drop out of university in Liverpool, where she'd gone to study math, threatening to leave her if she didn't return to London—where there were lots of lonely black girls. In love and insecure, she obeyed him, promising her parents that she'd finish up at Goldsmith's. But that didn't work out, and she lucked into a job as a photographer's assistant, which she did off and on whenever she could find time. Courtney's ego required a lot of nursing.

"I've got something to show you," she said, handing him her portfolio.

He asked her to get him a T-shirt from his duffel bag, which was sitting on the floor between a steamer trunk and a folding chair. As she turned away he flipped through quickly, preparing himself before she asked his opinion. To his relief, most of the work was good. Good but not brilliant. Solid though. Which is all most people will ever achieve in this life.

"I'm digging it," he said, slipping on a striped gray top. "I can see where you've grown." He pointed to a silver halide print of three black men, all with white hair, sitting on the stoop of a rooming house, their eyes fearless, but their coats drawn tight around them, showing their vulnerability. "Now this here is the boom shot. It's not just about technique. It's about empathy. You've steeped the essence out of these men like they were tea leaves. This is the kind of thing that Cartier-Bresson and Roy DeCarava do so well."

"I like it, but it's not the kind of thing that editors are looking for, I'm afraid." She leaned across him and skipped a few pages. "This is more like it as far as they're concerned." Three naked women seemed to be making love to a draft horse. One had her nipples thrust toward the horse's mouth. One had her face beneath the horse's tail. The third was draped over the animal's back. Adding to the quote unquote complexity was the fact that it was a mare and not a stallion.

"Well, it's up to you to decide who you are, y'know, Nan.

I'd say if this is what you have to do for a while to get through, then do it—bearing in mind, though, that with these kinds of deals with the devil you can easily forget the original intent and end up being a part of the very organism you used to run away from. So, who are you?" He flipped between the images. "This or that?"

"I don't know," she replied.

He put his hand in hers. She played with his fingers, as she used to before she and Courtney started going out. They'd met through their parents, who'd known each other from jet school. Her dad was a pilot for BA; his mum had flown for Air Jamaica.

"You have to decide," he said, pulling away from her. "I hate to sound bullshitically existential, but life really is about the choices we make given our situation. You know your situation, Nan. It's up to you to make the choice."

"I guess." She looked away.

"How've the interviews been going?"

"Not well . . . It's the book, I think. It's not very good."

He felt a twinge of annoyance, but he didn't show it. He resented weakness in the people he loved; that was why he did his best to make them strong. He couldn't count on weak people during the times when he needed to be held, and reassured—which was more often than he led others to believe. This was a part of Blanche's appeal. It hadn't been all about love. She was the only person in the world on whom he could depend, into whose arms he would fall backward with his eyes closed, knowing she would be there to catch him with hands as big and soft as mittens.

Looking at Nan now, he saw not an old friend, but yet another person who needed to draw strength from him.

To whom, he asked himself, would he turn if he needed help right now? He couldn't think of anyone except Blanche. And maybe not even her anymore. For she was a part of another set of problems. He thought about the letter he had written her from Brooklyn and wondered if he'd been right to mail it. Yes, he decided. She deserved it. She'd done so much. Even this house. She'd helped him to pick it out. Explained to him the nuances of down payments and mortgages, things he still didn't know or care that much about.

"Well, Nan," he said with a smiling face, "just put together a new one."

"It's expensive to do and I can't afford it."

"I'll give you the money, Nan."

"I couldn't do that, Fire."

"I'll lend it to you."

"It wouldn't matter. I'd only fail."

"So why're you going to the polytech then?"

"To get out of the house. Sometimes I think I'm going crazy."

She broke down and started to cry.

"I want a steady job, Fire . . . I'm tired of having to ask Courtney for things . . . I want to be my own person."

She fell on top of him and he held her, stroking her hair with one hand, ignoring the discomfort of the other, which was trapped awkwardly beneath her.

Nan was depressed for days after that. There were days when Fire wanted to sit down and talk with her, but that would've been helping her to cheat, he thought. It was her situation. And she had to make the choice—after which, he believed, she'd be stronger.

Soon after his arrival, Fire settled into a daily rhythm anchored by his need to paint, a violent primal urge that would punch him in the belly in the middle of the night and drag him half asleep, half awake to the bathroom, shove his face under a bracing stream, kick him down the stairs to the shed in the back of the house, and jab him even as he worked furiously, in different media on different days, but never the same thing in a row, and never anything that he would have recognized as his own had he not been there to witness the work being released from the tip of his brush, which he maneuvered like a machete, slashing back and forth across the canvas as if its whiteness, its neutrality, were something that had to be destroyed, had to be chopped open and gutted so that its hidden emotions could spew forth, staining its skin with a multicolored stream that shone like blood and was bitter as bile.

This is not me, he said to himself one day after being kidnapped during a lunch break at one of his workshops. He hadn't even bothered to wear an apron. Paint was splattered all over his shirt, his jeans, his boots, all over the floor, even on some of the work that he'd done over the previous days, work that had been left to dry against the moldy brick walls that sucked the life from the one bare bulb that hung from the ceiling by a length of cord.

Why this, and why now? he asked, considering his stylistic evolution. At home he'd been influenced by the work of his father, a master draftsman and composer in the Western realist tradition. At Yale, where he first began to imbibe the ink of Derek Walcott, he was seduced by the light of impressionism. After that was a leap to constructivism and the work of the Mexican muralists, which led him to Cuba, where he was drawn to the vibrant, rhythmic art of the color-intuitive campesinos.

And now he had done *this*, he half-said, half-asked, hearing in his head the feathery tenor of his father's voice. *This.* The impact of the word flung his arms out wide and spun him around, showing him in the swirling abstractions a vision of himself that he recognized as neither past, present, nor future.

Sitting on the dull cement floor in a corner, beneath a tent of cobweb, he tried to remember if he'd ever experienced anything like this, resting his chin on his knees for support as his head filled up with thoughts and memories. After sorting and stacking and counting and filing and cross-referencing for date and subject and characters and ideas, he was as unclear about his compulsion as he'd been at the beginning. He checked his watch. He was fifteen minutes late. Today they would have to wait. Because the feeling was pulling him up now, and shoving him toward a canvas.

You've survived three weeks of this, he said to himself as he mixed some green on a palette. But what is *this*? he asked again. His brush bit into the unknown. What the hell is *this*?

With the ballerina still on her toes, floating across the stage like a mast on the horizon, the applause went up and the curtain came down, and the Dance Theater of Harlem's benefit performance for the United Negro College Fund broke for intermission.

Sylvia, in a black dress, a string of pearls around her neck, took Lewis's hand and walked with him, cutting her steps short, as equally handsome couples who had paid to be seen in the right company poured into the center aisle and streamed into the lobby of the New York State Theater at Lincoln Center.

Patting him on the arm as she spied Boogie Boo, Sylvia asked Lewis where he'd be. He pointed to Virgil and patted her shoulder.

"Oh, Boogie, I feel like I've died and gone to negro hell."

"Oh come on, Syl," Boogie replied. "You know black folks ain't got money till they showing it. And ain't nobody can work an evening gown like a sister who knows her hair's a-yit. After looking at some o' them hairstyles tonight I've got a mind to quit work tomorrow and open me a shop."

"Stop, Boogie, stop," Sylvia whispered through her teeth. "Can't you see I'm being sophisticated in my too-high shoes. Goddamn, girl, if these hooker pumps don't kill me, you will."

"Oh come on, Syl, you know whamtalkin about. Just check it right. On the night before an event like this a stylist is a sister's best friend. See, cause sisters know they can't always vouch for black hair. Cause black hair likes to improvise. Black hair is like fucking jazz. And not swing either. Bebop.

Why d'you think so many sisters are wearing dreads today? Dreads can't do shit but stay nappy."

"So where's your date, by the way?" Sylvia asked.

"The fellas I talk to wouldn't wanna be here."

"They might have if you'd told them it was a Dance Theater of Harlem event."

"Oh, it's not about ballet or anything like that. It's about the people they'd have to deal with. The men I talk to would see right straight through this bullshit. This has nothing to do with ballet or the United Negro College Fund. Come on now, Syl, you're older than me. You know that. If it was all about helping they'd donate the money at the end of the year and claim it on their taxes. Why pay a toll from Jersey to be here, and add to your expenses? But it's all about macking. They make it seem like only ghetto people mack. It's the same thing. This is like Bentley's on a Friday night. But instead of mail room clerks in their one tired suit, you have CPAs in their one tuxedo."

"By the way," Sylvia asked, through a laugh, "how'd you get tickets to this?"

"Well, you only needed two, right? It's not like you have a family or anything."

As she laughed with Boogie Boo, Sylvia asked herself, Is this really how I want to live my life . . . surrounded by these people? She didn't. Then why, she asked, did I telephone Lewis and make up with him two weeks ago?

"Virge."

"Lou."

"How're you doing?"

A photographer for *Jet* magazine was right on cue, documenting this historic occasion for black posterity. Two black men in black tuxedos hugging.

"So how've you been, stranger?" Virgil asked, keeping his arm around Lewis's shoulders.

"Good. Just busy trying to make some money."

"And how's that going?"

"Let's put it this way. If I complained I'd be ungrateful. They believe in me. No one asks any questions."

The lights blinked.

"What're you doing later?" Virgil asked as they headed back to their seats. "Come uptown with me for a private after-party. A little group's getting together."

He whispered the details in Lewis's ear, nibbling a bit on his earlobe.

"You're gonna get yourself in trouble," Lewis said with a chuckle. "You're looking too good tonight."

"Oh, I keep forgetting," Virgil muttered, as Sylvia approached, "that we're not like that anymore."

"And I think it might be best if it stayed that way."

They'd been "like that" as a matter of convenience five years ago. The involvement lasted a few months, then petered out after they both realized that the essence of the attraction had been neither love nor lust, but status—like the feeling of wanting to drive a Rolls but not really wanting to *own* one.

They remained in touch, however, which wasn't difficult, the black bourgeoisie being so small and inbred, and washed each other's back over the years. But it was always conditional. Scrub for scrub. A rule that was never made explicit, seeing that they both accepted recompense as a very basic principle.

The after-party was held at the home of a prominent attorney on Hamilton Terrace, a crescent of limestone houses on a hill above City College. There Sylvia suffered her way through an evening of cocktails and banal conversation with a group of politicians, businessmen, and academics. Where are you, Boogie Boo, when I need you? she thought, as she listened to Lewis drone on about his latest redevelopment plan for central Harlem.

As a leading attorney tried to impress her by reciting Phyllis Wheatley, she asked, "Have you read Rita Dove? Or Yusef

Komunyakaa?" He had not. She asked to be excused and locked herself in the bathroom for ten minutes to renew herself. Her arches were killing her. She wanted to take her shoes off. But it wouldn't look good, now would it?

While she was gone, Lewis and Virgil withdrew to the terrace.

"Did you hear that Sekou's wife is leaving him?" Lewis asked, referring to a Columbia professor whose marriage seemed Kodak-perfect as they spoke.

"No," Virgil said, leaning closer.

"For a white man," Lewis continued. "Brother Africa is *dying*, I hear."

"Actually, I don't think it's because it's a *white* man. He doesn't want her with *any* man. He doesn't want competition. You've heard about him, haven't you?"

"I've heard rumors, but I don't pay them any mind. Niggers talk a lotta shit."

"Speaking of niggers talking . . . I heard the other day that you and Sylvia had broken up."

"Oh. That was a big rumor. Everything's fine."

"Can I tell you something frankly, Lewis?"

"Go ahead. If you've got something to say, don't hold back."

"I never thought you two were a good match. I mean . . . I can't tell you who to choose, but . . . let's see . . . how can I put it? . . . Sylvia is just not grounded enough for you. She lacks a certain aggressiveness. She's talented enough to be a queen bee but she's content with being a worker—does that analogy make any sense? She doesn't place herself in the right contexts to get noticed. I used to think she was lazy. I'm inclined to believe that she's just not ambitious. And her politics are just so bizarre. I don't think she understands the black experience. I couldn't believe it when I saw her résumé: she'd never worked for a black organization in her life. That should've cued me in. Suffice it to say, we have political problems . . ."

"Like what?"

"And I know I don't have to say that this is just between us, but take Congressman DeVeaux . . ."

During his time of great confusion, Fire received several letters from Blanche, and wrote to her in return.

In the beginning it was little more than an expression of obligation. She had responded to the letter that he'd mailed her from Brooklyn, explaining with economy and mature composure that she had used the time away from him to think about their history, and that she had now come to the conclusion that her desire for a relationship was selfish and unreasonable, and that she would simply like to be his friend. Why lose that? she asked. Who knows me better than you do? She didn't mention the flowers; neither did she comment on the story he related. And she completely ignored his mopey expression of love, which had begun to worry him after he'd dropped the letter in the mailbox, for it promised much more than he thought he was capable of giving.

His reply, hastily drafted in pencil on composition paper while he rode the bus to his workshop, was brief, considerate, and sincere. She shouldn't call. They needed distance for the new reality to set in. Writing was fine, but he couldn't promise either long or speedy replies. And although she was under no obligation to agree, he thought it would be best if she immediately returned the house keys to Miss Gita and took any belongings that she might have at the house back to her apartment. Sarge would take care of his things at hers.

He heard from her within a week. A cheery note saying that she'd done all he'd asked, reminding him however that Sarge couldn't locate his set of keys for her apartment. Did he have them in London? And would he, if he did, send them via express mail along with a few books she hungered for.

He went to Foyle's in Charing Cross Road and the next day mailed her five volumes, two collections of poetry and three long novels, along with the keys and a rambling letter of apology that found its purpose in the last line: "There is something unsettlingly final about this."

To which she replied in a postcard delivered via two-day service: "That is not what I want to hear. What I want to hear is, 'Blanche, I don't need you to look after me anymore.' Can you say that, Fire? Can you honestly say that?"

Shortly thereafter he was faced with a second compulsion—exchanging with her, by express post, thick, honest letters examining their history from the beginning till now.

One morning, just before sunrise, five weeks after he arrived, he was drawn from sleep by a sound that seemed to be calling from a distance. A sound as soft as it was beautiful, like moondrops falling on a mountain lake. Still groggy, he opened his eyes and made out through the mist of semi-consciousness a ghostlike figure drifting across the room—shirtless, he gathered, from the flash of pink that leaped from the dark when the man, as he now realized, passed under the trickle of window light.

As he sat up, unsure if he was dreaming or awake, the figure leaned against the back of a chair, revealing its familiar profile—the long neck and narrow shoulders that seemed to have been drawn by Dr. Seuss.

"Phil," Fire said, fully awake now. "How the fuck're you doing?"

Gangly, with buzz-cut sandy hair, Phil held his horn like a baby and slapped him five, taking a seat on the edge of the futon.

"So when'd you get in?" Fire asked.

"Oh, I just got in about a half hour ago," he said, gray eyes bulging. "Fuck, after hearing you snoring from downstairs, I said I'd have to wake you up so I could get some sleep." He began to laugh. Spastically. Which is the way he did everything except play music—as if God felt guilty for giving him so much talent and chose to deny him many other qualities, including shrewdness. As Ian liked to say, Phil was not the sharpest knife in the drawer. Neither was he stylish. His glasses, which were clearly too large, bloomed out of his nose like the wings of a moth.

What he was, though, was loyal and genuine. And giving. Qualities that Fire could not always ascribe to Ian. As a result, there'd been a time when Phil had replaced Ian as the person closest to him.

As he'd recently written to Blanche, second to her, Phil was the person who knew him best. Ian had known him longer, but not as deeply. There were a few reasons for this, he had written. In some ways he and Ian were rivals. Ian was the more gifted artist. And as a result Fire's father had paid him more attention, seemed to encourage him more, and to have higher expectations; that was one reason why he and his father had begun to drift apart. Also, Ian had lived apart from Fire during crucial periods of his life, had not traveled with him on many important journeys and waited with him at crucial junctures. During college and the years immediately following, they had mostly written, and in fact had lived together only as adults in Lisbon—only for about two and a half years. He'd lived with Phil for five. And Phil had seen him through his artistic breakthrough and triumph, and had watched over him during all of Blanche . . . Although Phil couldn't offer any meaningful advice as Fire tried to unravel himself from the memory of Blanche after she'd left him for her husband that very last time, his support was unfailing.

"So when are we going to have a drink, then?" Phil asked when he'd finished telling Fire about his tour.

"Maybe next week," he replied, getting out of bed now, as he heard the urge crunching up the stairs to the landing and stopping at his door.

"Well, you know I'm going to New York on Monday, don't you?"

"No, I didn't. What for?"

"An audition for the New York Philharmonic. Keep your fingers crossed. Hopefully I'll get hired so I can stop living hand to mouth. By the way, has Courtney spoken to you about the rent?"

"No."

"I'm two months behind, but I've got some money coming in. I'll catch up in the autumn. By then a number of things should have straightened out."

"Hey, man," Fire told him. "Come on, Phil, how often did I have my rent that first year when we lived together? Pay it when you have it. Otherwise don't worry about it. If you want something to worry about, worry about your audition. You need a place to stay over there?"

"I'll be staying with Ian."

"Are you sure he knows this?" Fire asked. "He didn't mention anything to me. I'd double-check with him if I were you. Plus you know his situation . . . it's up to you, really. I played it safe and stayed in a hotel."

"Well money's a bit tight at the moment, and I'll only be there for a few days. I guess I could manage it if I had to. The audition is what really matters to me. I just have to do what I need to do to get through it. I need this one bad, man. If I don't get it, I don't know what I'll do."

Fire was up now, pulling on his jeans and heading down the stairs without shirt or shoes. Phil trailed behind him.

"Where you going?" he asked.

"To paint."

"Shit, you haven't done that in years."

"And you should see the stuff I'm doing. It'll blow your mind. It's blowing mine."

"D'you know what I see when I look at this one?" Phil said, biting his lower lip as he picked up one of what were now over a hundred and fifty canvases.

"No," Fire said, working furiously, wondering if this interpretation would be as classic as the last.

"I see a bird, right . . . flying through a forest . . . but like the forest is burning up . . . that's what all this red messy-looking stuff is here." He pointed to something that Fire didn't recognize as anything. "But the bird is flying through these flames—"

"Phil," Fire asked as he mixed some yellow, "so how come the bird isn't getting burnt?"

"Well, cause it's not real flames. It's only a picture, and the bird knows that."

"So it's a real bird, then, flying through a picture?"

"Right. Oh, come on, Fire, it can be anything you want it to be. That's what I want it to be."

Fire began to hack away with the yellow, slicing through a layer of green.

"So, Phil, why would you want to see this particular scenario—a bird flying through fake flames?"

"Well," Phil began, picking up another piece, "I was watching this program on television about a brushfire and there were all these little birds that died. And I began to think of a way to help animals in fires. And so I started thinking that maybe Du Pont or one of those companies could make a spray that would make animals fireproof. Y'know, something that you could spread like insecticide . . . I really can't explain how it would work. But I think it's worth looking into—"

"Right, but where does the fake picture come in?"

"So what? You believe that everything in life is real? How do you know we're not dreaming this right now? Someone asked me that the other day and I couldn't answer."

Fire looked at Phil, looked at the work in progress, and looked back at Phil and began to laugh. "Because," he said, "it would be a fucking nightmare."

"Maybe we're onto something," Phil said. "What did Freud say about dreams? I know you probably know."

Fire spent about thirty minutes trying to explain Freud to him, then gave up after Phil began adding his own theories to anything that didn't make sense to him. The good thing, though, was that talking had somehow made the urge go away.

While Phil locked up the shed, Fire walked to a shaded spot by the back fence and sat on a bench beneath the apple trees, which were heavy with leaves and fruit.

"There might be something in that whole dream thing, you know," Phil said, as he sat next to him. "What have you been dreaming about?"

He couldn't remember. Not just what he dreamed. He couldn't remember dreaming.

"Well, what are you not dreaming about, then?"

"I know you're trying to be helpful, Phil, but maybe this is one of those things that will work itself out over time."

"I think I'm onto something though. Okay, name five things that you're not dreaming about."

"Phil, don't you realize that any five things will do?"

"Okay then, name five."

"Why? It doesn't make any sense."

"Okay then, so name four."

Fire began to laugh at the absurdity of the situation.

"Okay then, three."

"Phil, stop . . . please." He was laughing hysterically now.

Nan came out to her window and shook her head at them.

"Okay, name two."

"I can't think right now."

"Okay, name one then. Name one thing that you haven't been dreaming about because you're scared of dreaming about it."

And Fire heard himself say, "Sylvia."

Then suddenly, as if seized by a falcon, his soul was picked up, yanked up, ripped from his body and taken way into the sky, above the clouds, across the time-and-space divide, and he saw their affair laid out on a timeline, and witnessed the moment when he decided to protect his feelings by trying to forget. As soon as he'd written her that goodbye letter, he saw, he had willed her memory away, putting to use that psychic muscle that adolescent girls often use to will away their periods because they're afraid of becoming women.

Now, sitting on the bench beneath the apple trees, smelling the unctuous aroma of the fallen fruit, he lived again the feeling that washed his body when she appeared at the door in her sarong . . . barefoot . . . molasses dribbling over her toes. Oh, he thought, as the hairs on his body curled over and began to massage his skin, I miss her so. I want her now. I want her here with me, on this bench, so that I can cradle my head in her lap and have her talk to me, about anything, in any language, even if it's one that I don't understand. He began to inhale the smell of her hair, which was strange because there had been no memory of it until now, as he thought of holding her and rocking her in the back of the cab. As he thought about this her sweat began to bead his lips like dew. When he had actually kissed her, he hadn't smelled or tasted anything. Now he was getting a kind of scent like . . . or was it? Each time he tried to name it, it caught a breeze and flew away.

That afternoon, Fire went to the London Graphics Center in Covent Garden and bought some supplies. He stayed up working into the night.

When Phil left for New York, he carried with him a very special gift.

Phil called Sylvia as soon as he checked into the Fulton Inn. He'd taken Fire's advice and decided not to stay with Ian.

"Hello, *Umbra* magazine. How may I help you?"

"Good morning. May I speak to one Sylvia Lucas, please?"

"One moment."

"Sylvia Lucas speaking."

"Hello, Sylvia, my name is Philip Llewellyn," he said, remembering the script that he'd been given. "I'm over here from England for a bit and I've got a little parcel for you from a famous blues singer by the name of Muddy Waters. When do you suppose we could meet up so I can give it to you?"

There was silence on the line.

"Are you there?"

"Yes," she said. "That's . . . awfully nice of him. Oh . . . I didn't think that he remembered me. Oh, wow . . . I don't know what to say. Aah . . . that's a really nice of him thing to do. Oh, sorry, that didn't make much sense, did it? I'm a little disoriented today. What's your schedule like, Phil? How soon can we meet?"

"Well, I've got some auditions coming up, and, to tell the truth, I'm not terribly familiar with New York. It's my first time. Maybe if I told you where I am staying, you could arrange to meet me sometime."

"Okay, Phil, where are you?"

They made arrangements to meet that evening.

The sun was low across the tops of the trees in Prospect Park when Sylvia entered the lobby of the Fulton Inn with a bouquet of cut flowers, hoping that it had really been Fire who called—wishing, as her heart rolled around like a child demanding to be born, that Phil was simply a character that Fire had assumed to make this surprise even more special, and that he would step out from behind one of these columns and smile at her now. Any minute.

This would not happen though. She asked the concierge for Phil and was told that he was out.

"Did he leave a package for anyone?"

She was handed a small burlap sack containing a box wrapped in corrugated brown paper, topped with a sisal bow.

Flushed with curiosity and excitement, Sylvia kept peeking into the bag on the way home, happy not so much that he had sent her a gift, as that he had remembered her.

As soon as she got in, she sat on the bed and opened the box, finding inside a handmade book, twenty-four pages of heavy-gauge paper bound with needle and embroidery thread. Affixed to the cover was a dried rose. Inside was a series of warmly impressionistic streetscapes languorously rendered in ink and gouache—all unified by the presence of a woman in whose form she recognized a bit of herself.

There was a poem done in calligraphy on the inside back cover. Her middle turned to liquid when she read it. She had to lie down. Flopping backward into the pillows she imagined herself as a skydiver—freefalling through the clouds, too thrilled by the feeling of weightlessness to think about hitting the ground.

> *PERSON*
> *"He." I say "he" to construct the fiction*
> *of this thing. I can now call it love*
> *and riddle his passions with old clichés.*
> *He sees her in strange cities, her body*
> *poised in orange light, and he paints*
> *her onto canvases, constant orgasms,*
> *admissions that she haunts him always.*
> *"Him," I say, not "me"—it is all fiction.*
> *—Fire*

She wrote to him that night.

August—, 19—

Dear Fire,

I haven't stopped thinking about you since the time we met. Thank you so much for your package. I received it today, and I was thrilled out of my mind.

When I met you my life wasn't perfect, but I'd grown accustomed to its routine. I apologize for being so apprehensive with you, but I'm sure you can understand why.

I know that you're probably wondering, then, why I seemed so friendly toward you when you and Claire came by that Sunday. It was because when you called my number earlier that afternoon, looking for Claire, you were concerned that I wasn't sounding well without knowing who I was. And that told me that you are kind to people period—

not just to the ones in whom you have a romantic interest. And that small act, that display of basic goodness, elevated you in my estimation.

You may prove yourself to be other than I believe you to be. Maybe you are not bad, but ordinary, like most people, who give to get. And as I survey my own life I realize that at times I have accepted this social currency as being valid, and have traded in it myself.

I don't know much about you, Fire. As a matter of fact, I don't know you at all. But when I met you something happened inside of me, and (since you were allowed to be trite in your letter I should have a chance too) a spark was lit. And every time I've been in touch with you, it has grown brighter.

I'm about to say things, Fire, that I don't want to say, so let me go. Things about needing your nipple so bad right now. Things about touching myself the first night that I met you and falling asleep with you on my mind.

My Jamaican guy—Grace Jones won't mind if I bite a piece of hers.

—Sylvia

Her letter arrived on one of his days off and he immediately called her. He was lounging in bed in yellow boxers, his head propped up against a pillow, a glass of water on the nightstand. A soccer player, Fire had a strong body that suggested torque rather than horsepower. He had a hard, wide chest. A dense middle. And long, sturdy legs that matched his arms.

With each spin of the dial ripples of excitement washed through his body. The excitement, however, was no longer simply romantic. There was a strong undercurrent of eroticism that was threatening to drag him out to sea and drown him. For the first time he experienced the sensuousness of the rotary dial, the slipping of his fingers into the holes, the tight fit, the twisting around, the arcing groan of the spinback. It was ten in the morning for her, three P.M. for him.

"Hello," Sylvia said when she came on the line, "how are you?"

"Fine, and yourself?"

"Good, thank you."

"I have your letter here," he said, "and I'd just like you to know that it's nice to know that you think I'm nice."

"But you are."

"You're at work, right? I can't remember where I called you."

"Yes, I'm at work. What are you doing?"

"I'm in bed," he replied.

"Lucky you."

"Not really . . . I'm alone."

"I was alone in my bed last night, but you don't hear me complaining," she said.

He closed his eyes and pictured her lying next to him . . . in her sarong . . . with a smooth leg thrown over his . . . a warm hand on his chest . . . moist lips foraging along the back of his neck.

"What's your bed like?" he asked, catching her off guard.

"It's a bed . . . rectangular . . . mattress . . . box spring . . . sheets," she replied, slipping through a fissure, falling into his groove.

"Are you in bed right now?" There was a wetness beneath her. She paused awhile to enjoy it.

"Yes," she replied.

Her legs were falling open.

"Are you alone?"

"No."

"Who is there with you?" he asked.

"You."

"And what am I doing?"

She closed her eyes.

"You're lying beside me and rubbing my belly."

"Do you like the way I'm rubbing it?"

"Yes."

"Why?"

"Because you're gentle, and . . ."

"And?"

". . . you have this way of making your strokes stray into the waist of my underwear and up against my breast."

She slipped a hand beneath her skirt.

"And you like that?" he asked.

"Yes . . . Fire . . . I do."

"I'm using my lips now, to do what my hand was doing before. Which do you prefer?"

"Your lips."

"Okay, I'll use my lips then. But what should I do with my hands?"

"Caress my breasts."

"With both of them?"

"No. Use one to caress my breasts and use the other one to play with me."

"Where should I play with you?"

"Inside my underwear."

"My hand is there now, inside your underwear. It's very wet here. And warm."

"I know," she replied, "you have made it that way. Play with me."

Her fingers eased the silk away. And her flesh gave way to her softest touch like mud on the floor of a still lagoon.

"What should I play with?" he asked.

"You know what to play with."

"How do you know that I know?"

"You know."

"Maybe I don't."

"Don't make me say it," she said. She was breathing heavily and her voice was trembling. "Don't make me tell you to play with my clit and finger-fu . . . manipulate me inside with your fingers."

"Why?"

"Because I'm fingering myself as I'm talking to you and I want to come so badly. But someone could come through this door any minute."

Fire felt a coolness near his waist, and looked down to see his cock growing toward his chest from the moist heat inside his boxers. He held it. It was hard and brown like a length of renta yam. At the top, in a nick, a custard-colored sap spilled out in soft eruptions.

"So if you want to come, then come. I'll hug you."

"Don't hug me . . . make love to me."

"Fast or slow?" he asked, rolling over on his belly.

"Slow at first," she said. "Put it a little way in then pull it out, so I can savor the size of the head. Tease me with it."

"There you go."

"Yessss."

"Like that?"

"Yessss. Now push it deeper." She had two fingers inside her now.

"Like this?"

"Yessss. Stroke me deep."

"I'm up against something, what is it?"

"That's my cervix. You're all the way inside me."

"I didn't realize that I was so deep."

"You're very deep. I like to feel you up there, Fire. I like to feel you up there. Now move around inside me and make me wetter. I know you can do that."

"Like this?"

"Yes."

"Faster or slower?"

"Just like that."

"What should I do just like that?"

"Make love to me."

"What?"

"Make love to me, Fire. Make love to me."

"Fast or slow? Hard or soft?"

"Fast and hard."

"Okay, I'm making love to you fast and hard."

"Yes, I'm wet enough that you can make love to me as fast and as hard as you want." She clamped the phone with her neck. "Pump me."

"Can you hear me smacking up against you?"

"Yes."

"Can you feel my perspiration wetting you?"

"Yes."

"Dripping off my chin into your face?"

"Yes."

"Raise your legs for me."

"Oh God!"

"Raise your hips so I can get my hands beneath them."

"Oh God!"

"Move with me."

"Oh God!"

"Now hold still and take me. Take me. Take me however you want."

"Come with me, Fire!" she whispered through clenched teeth. "Come with me! Come . . . with . . . meeeeeeee!"

She leaned back against her chair and pulled her knees toward her chest, struggling to catch her breath.

"Hush, baby, lay on my chest. I have you," he said. "Lay on my chest. I have you."

She composed herself before replying.

"Fire, I can't believe that I just did that . . . I can't believe that . . . Oh God, my skirt is all wet . . . Shit . . . If someone had walked in—"

"When are we going to see each other?" he interrupted. "I think it needs to be soon."

"I don't know," she replied awkwardly. "You're there, I'm here."

"I want to see you, Sylvia."

"I want to see you too . . . Fire," she replied, while considering that she was back with Lewis now.

"Why?" he asked.

"Because . . ." she began.

"Because?" he asked, urging her through her loss of words.

"When I see you I'll tell you," she replied, laughing to ease the tension.

"I'll see you tomorrow then."

"What do you mean?"

"I'm coming to see you."

"You're joking, right? You're always joking."

"No, I'm serious."

"Where are you going to stay?"

"With you."

"That's not . . . very . . . practical . . . right now."

"It doesn't matter where I stay, really, as long as I get a chance to see you."

"You're going to come for how long?"

"The weekend."

"Just to see me?"

"Yeah," he said casually.

"Right."

"You think I'm joking, don't you?"

"Of course you're joking," she said.

"Well, what are you going to do when you see me sitting on your doorstep?"

He was laughing. So was she. Then she suddenly became silent.

"You have company, I gather," Fire said.

"Yes," she replied, trying to sound businesslike. "Can I get back to you on that? . . . Okay, bye."

Virgil had entered her office in a huff. Shit, she thought. That whole thing with the receipts again. She had to get them in tomorrow morning, he said, or there would be trouble.

Unfortunately, she didn't know where to find them.

Sylvia got up the next morning and continued the frantic search that had begun the night before. Her apartment was a mess. Desk drawers were out and their innards scattered widely. Books covered the living room like pebbles on a beach. Sitting on the coffee table in her white pajamas, she covered her face with her hands and tried her best to remember. Where were they? Where could they be?

It was 8:15 and . . . Shit, she realized. She needed the 8:00 A.M. train because she had a meeting at . . . Shit, she needed an earlier train at like quarter of to catch an 8:30 meeting.

Picking her way over the rubble she dashed in and out of the shower and scrambled to get dressed in the bedroom—she slipped on some slacks and jumped into some shoes and hauled on a top without any consideration, then shot out the door.

As she closed it, though, she remembered. She'd left her portfolio inside. She bolted back inside to grab it, but it wasn't where she thought she'd left it. In the hall room. By her computer. Where was it? By the time she'd decided that she had to leave it, it was 8:30. What to do? What to do? Better call the office. But where was the phone? Not where it was supposed to be. Hadn't she just seen it when she was looking for her portfolio? She thought so. But she hadn't been looking for the phone then, so she wasn't quite sure.

She couldn't believe she had allowed herself to come to this—to be so out of control. In the first place she should've filed the receipts a while ago. But to have the place a mess like this was completely unforgivable. A part of her wanted to smile when she thought of the reason, the force that had exploded within her, creating this shambles in which she was standing now, this outward expression of her state of mind.

He made me come, she was thinking . . . with words . . . over the phone . . . from a distance. He made me let go. Made me feel okay to step outside myself. Made me feel feelings that I'd locked away since Syd.

For most of her life she had accepted that it was her, she was thinking now, and her baggage. And although Sylvia had

stopped faking orgasms a few years ago, she still had a sense
of being incomplete, and felt awkward about touching herself
in the presence of a lover. She'd been disappointed every time
that she had tried. A lot of men felt it was a form of castration.
Others thought it was a show and pulled away to watch. Then
there were those like Lewis, who tried but simply didn't
know what to do . . . no matter how many times and in how
many ways she'd tried to show him. So she usually did it
alone. Fire . . . Fire . . . Fire. She was hearing his voice now.
How is it that you just know?

It's so simple. An orgasm, at its core, is a mind thing.

But, yes, she had to call her office. Where was the fucking
phone? In her mind she saw it on the bed and she went to dig
through stacks of paper there. There, under the pillow she
was sure she felt it. Shit, it was the remote. She tossed it in
frustration and heard behind her the crash of glass and the
thud of wood.

She leaped across the bed to investigate, scattering clothes
and paper. One of her favorite pieces of art was a small col-
lage by James Denmark. Now the glass was shattered. The
frame was broken. And the work itself had a two-inch rip.

And as she went for the broom and dustpan, the phone began to ring. Where was it coming from? She listened, cocking
her head. The kitchen. She stumbled through the mess. The
fridge. The *fridge*. The goddamn phone was in the fridge.

"Hello," she said frantically.

"Hi, Sylvia. How are you?" It was Lewis.

She checked her watch. It was almost nine. "I can't talk
now, honey. Ring me at the office."

"What's the hurry?"

"I have a meeting with Virgil and I'm already late. Is it
something urgent?"

"Actually, Virgil asked me to call you to tell you that the
meeting won't be happening till tomorrow."

"Why would he ask you to do that?" she asked, leaning

against the fridge. The closeness of Lewis and Virgil had always bothered her. "I work for him, not you."

"Well . . . he's here at my place. The other night, at Lincoln Center, we started a dialogue that might turn into something big. So we're having a breakfast meeting. It started early and now it's running over."

She toyed with a jar of black pepper as she composed her thoughts. "You're not his messenger boy, Lewis. Let me speak to him."

"Sylvia, calm down." It sounded to her as if he had placed his hand over the receiver. "Virge and I have a friendship that goes back before you. Don't forget that. Don't encroach on it."

"Do you know what, Lewis? Whatever . . . this just shows complete disregard for me as a professional. I hope you know that. To ask you to call me to cancel a meeting."

"Well, if you'd been at the office as you were supposed to I'm sure I wouldn't have to do this."

"First of all, I'm always on time, so there's no need to call me out on that, okay? And second of all . . . I don't have time for this. Look, I'll talk to you whenever."

She hung up.

He called back. "Don't you ever fucking do that again!"

"Leave me alone, Lewis. You are just so small to me right now. Just leave me the fuck alone."

"I did the other day and you came running back."

She threw the jar against the wall. It exploded like a powder keg.

"Are you saying that you don't want this? Just tell me if that's what you're saying. Be big about it," she said.

"All I'm gonna say, and I'm not gonna say any more right now because this is all looking very unprofessional, is this. If we split up I know for sure I can survive."

"Fuck you!"

She hung up again and marched out of the house. Fuck the portfolio. Fuck the receipts. Fuck everything right now.

But somewhere along that short passage from the front door to the stoop, as Sylvia left the safety of her home for a place where she'd lost control, an invisible hand pressed the anger from her and wet her down with fear. For as she stepped out into the bright, hot morning, she was quaking with the primal fear of darkness—a fear grounded in the infinity of fearful possibilities, the fear of not even knowing what she shouldn't be afraid of.

Why does he think he can talk to me like that? she asked herself. What have I done? What am I doing? Why did I go back to him? What was there to prove? What was there to gain?

The questions echoed in her belly like stones dropped down a well. Feeling weighed down, she sat on the stoop in her wrinkled clothes that didn't match, and thought about the mess that was her life. At times like these, she thought, it would be nice to have a father or a brother or a son—a man to reassure her that it was them and not her that was fucked up.

How was it that Lewis couldn't understand her hurt? she wondered. Or was it that he did, but simply didn't care? He said he could survive if they broke up. What was he implying? That she couldn't? By what ludicrous standard was he measuring her? She came into this world alone and she would leave alone. At first this declaration filled her with defiance. Soon after, though, as she considered that she was alone now, and had been for most of her life, she began to feel vulnerable. If she lost her job there was no family to move back to, or any sibling to put her up, or any uncle to arrange a job. Unlike him. Unlike most people. Was that what he'd meant? If so, he was right in a way. Which made her depressed now, made her turn her face from the sun and hide it between her knees.

She began to hum, the monotony of the sound echoing the white noise that filled her head.

A dog barked. She looked up out of reflex, then dropped her head again.

Footsteps went by. Three people, by the sound of it. A man

and a woman, talking to each other. The third person, the one in slippers, did not speak. Those steps trailed the others.

A truck rumbled by and stopped a few doors down. She recognized the driver's voice. UPS. Overhead a plane descended toward La Guardia. Down the street someone was watering their garden. Mr. Jonas, most likely; he was always getting shrubs delivered from *Calyx.*

More footsteps. From the direction of Mr. Jonas. Man. Definitely. The bite of the heel into the pavement said that. And the length of the stride. White man, most likely. A black man around at this time of day was most likely making deliveries. Which most likely meant sneakers.

Other steps from the opposite direction. On the other side of the street. Voices too and the creak of wheels. One voice Hispanic. The other white ethnic . . . Italian maybe . . . and younger. Homemaker out with the nanny and baby. Baby who just cried out. "Put da blanket da baby." The other voice stalled, not knowing if this was question or statement.

A car washed those sounds away and the other footsteps drew closer. Began to slow down.

A helicopter cut through above her, heading for Wall Street across the harbor.

The footsteps were replaced by the silence of a shadow.

She felt the coolness. Felt the darkness on her skin through her clothes. She anticipated the question—directions perhaps. But none was forthcoming. And the shadow was lingering.

He was watching her intensely, she could feel it. Which made her uneasy now. The neighborhood was safe but . . . She was vulnerable with her head down. What if he were a burglar, scoping apartments? Or a rapist?

She had to look. But should she be discreet or brazen? If she saw his face and he was in fact a criminal, that might scare him. But if he was truly dangerous, should she draw attention to herself? Or even allow him to see her face?

She heard the pavement crunch beneath his soles as he

swiveled to move again. Which relieved her. Until the first step came in her direction. Up the steps.

On adrenaline now, she raised her head and wedged her hand across her brows to block the sun and defend herself and saw that it was Fire—freshly shaven, his hair brushed back, dressed in a white linen shirt that was open at the neck, and black dress pants and square-toed shoes that shone like the wheels of a new Mercedes.

Calming her with his shadow, steadying her with his eyes, he smiled at her and called her name softly, and gave her a posy of freshly cut tulips.

"I can't . . . believe . . . you're here," she said, feeling the sweet release of tears. "I can't believe you came. To see me . . . I thought . . . it was a . . . joke."

He lowered himself to his haunches and took her face in his hands, holding it as if it were a porcelain vase.

"No. I wasn't joking," he said, using his thumbs not so much to wipe away the tears as to massage her face. "This is madness between us. And madness is a serious thing. Yes, Sylvia, I'm here. I'm here to see you." He brushed his lips across her brows. "Why're you crying, sweet girl?"

"Just lots of stuff," she replied. "Nothing I'm ready to talk about right now."

"It's okay," he said. "In the fullness of time. Everything happens in the fullness of time."

They walked together to the subway, Sylvia carrying her flowers through these streets that she knew and where she was known, past old houses whose shuttered windows and drawn curtains seemed to turn a blind eye to this indiscretion, no longer feeling fit to judge, having witnessed for over a hundred years this same couple in different incarnations, making this journey toward the blissful possibilities of uncertainty.

They were lovers now. It was clear to anyone who saw them. Clear but not provable. But people can see things, and know them, without being able to explain. What did it mean, for example, that he would sweep back hedges with the fore-arm of his new white shirt for the simple pleasure of being beside her instead of ahead or behind? Or that her smaller, more softly shod feet were falling against the pavement in counterpoint to his longer, heavier stride, forming a single rhythm played by two? It meant that they were lovers. Lovers already in heart and mind . . . and very soon in body.

As they waited to cross a street, she dared to take his arm, tugging him back toward her as he leaned around a truck to check for oncoming traffic. The sensation of touching excited her. The naturalness of it. The way his smile told her it was okay for her to take responsibility for him. Desirable even.

"I didn't tell you before," she said as they neared the sub-way. They were on Henry Street, a thoroughfare flanked with storefront shops and a high-rise condo complex made of pre-fab concrete. "Thank you so much for the flowers. They are really beautiful. I couldn't leave them at home. I have to take them to work with me. I hope you don't think I'm countrified for doing that."

"Would it matter what I think, though?"

"Yes, actually."

"Why is that?"

"Because I really want you to like me right now."

"Right now and not tomorrow?"

"Tomorrow too. But right now more than ever."

"Okay, I like you now more than ever."

When they reached the token booth he asked, "So when will I see you?"

"Call me at the office," she replied. "We could have lunch. Where are you staying?"

"The Fulton Inn."

"I didn't mean to cry when I saw you," she said. "I was just having a very bad morning."

"And here I was, thinking they were tears of joy."

"You've gotten lots of those, I'm sure," she said. "You don't need mine."

"Yes I do. As a matter of fact I think you should cry for me right now to make me feel really wanted."

"Boo-hoo, hoo. There you go."

"Thank you."

This feels so easy, she thought. So natural. She pressed her thumb against his lips, choosing it and not a finger for its softness and dexterity, for its ability to convey to him the impression of a kiss.

"I feel like I could just hold you and smooch you right here, Fire."

"Smooch?"

"Yes, 'smooch,' like white people in those sixties beach movies. Smooch."

"Well, don't let me stop you from"—he made his brows dance—"smooching me," he replied.

"Not here though."

"Why?"

"For me to smooch you to show you how happy I am, I'd have to smooch you too many times . . . and my train is coming any minute now. You have no idea what you've done for me this morning, Fire. You have no idea what it means to me that you've come here . . . to Brooklyn . . . all the way from London . . . overnight . . . for no other reason than to see me. I needed this. But I didn't know I did."

An intense silence fell over them, and they stared at each other for a second, which in their heightened state of attunement felt like a minute. In this suspended flash of clarity, in which the world around him and his swirling thoughts moved slowly, showing their undersides, Fire glimpsed the logic behind the chaos of the universe. He began to understand why he needed her, and why he needed distance from Blanche. Sylvia needed him, showed her vulnerability, which made him feel useful, potent—valuable in the way of a solution to a riddle. And Blanche did not. She was older and—especially when they'd met—more accomplished in many ways, and she refused to surrender control to him even when she was ill . . .

The most she would ask of him in those days was to bring her water, and read to her, and drive her to the doctor. And she only seemed vulnerable while begging him to return to her. After which, things would be the same. He was a child for her. At best an adolescent. But with Sylvia he could be a man . . . whole . . . ranging freely between the roles of giver and receiver.

"I'll walk you down," he said.

He watched her get on the train. She stared at him through the window. He moved his mouth, pretended to say something. She wrinkled her brows, trying to tell him that she didn't understand. He pretended to say something else. She wrinkled her brows even more, transforming her face into a sign that read, "Hurry up and say it slowly. The train is about to leave." He mouthed some more. She gave up. Put her thumb in her ear and her pinkie in her mouth to say, "Call me." He blew her a kiss. She swallowed it, still trying to make sense out of nonsense as the train entered the long black tunnel.

chapter five

He called her in the early afternoon.

"Hello."

She leaned back in her chair and began to rub her belly through her yellow cotton blouse.

"Where are you?"

"Brooklyn," he said. "Outside a Senegalese place named Keur N' Deye. I just left Moshood's. I had to get a few things for my cousin and his girlfriend. Phil and I were supposed to be hooking up, but I haven't seen him. But anyway I'm not here to see him. I'm here to see you. What are *you* doing?"

"Besides thinking about you?"

"Yeah. Besides thinking about me."

"Nothing much. Work."

"I heard a rumor," he said.

"What rumor is that?"

"That you're going to leave work early and spend the rest of the day with me."

"Sure, if you hire me when they fire me."

"They won't fire you. Just tell them that this guy who really likes you has come a long way to see you. They'll understand. D'you know what? Lemme talk to your boss."

She told him to hold on and then did her impersonation of Virgil's mumble. "Hello, Virgil Pucci speaking."

"Hello Virgil, how are you today? Listen, my name is Mr. Likesylvialucasalot, and I'm really and truly infatuated with her, and would really like to see her. And I know that she's a really important member of your team over there, but consider this—there are many people who can do what she does for you, but only one of her who can do what she does for me. So could you be a really nice guy and let her go, please?"

"You are so silly," she said.

"Thank you very much, coming from you that is really high praise. But seriously. Take the day off and come and see me. It's a Friday, they'll understand."

"I can't, Fire," she said, weighing various deadlines and the missing receipts. "Really." She had to be sensible. She was alone. She had to remember that.

"Just tell them you're sick," he said. "Or that your mum died or something like that. But whatever you do . . . just come."

"I think you're insane."

"I *must* be, right? To be doing this."

"Or maybe you're like this with every woman."

"No, just every other one. It's too expensive to be this nice to all of them. Only the top fifty-five get this kinda treatment. The rest get dinner at McDonald's."

She glanced at her bouquet, which was down to ten tulips. Boogie Boo had swiped two. "Thanks for the flowers, they're beautiful, and it was just so nice of you. You know what's so incredible about you? You're like a witchman or something. You just have this way of reaching out to me when I'm feeling most vulnerable. Like that time you called my house looking for Claire and you were concerned about me . . . out of the blue . . . without knowing it was me. And then this morning . . . you don't even want to hear what happened—trust me. I had the worst morning, and then I came outside and you were on my doorstep with flowers. You do realize we have to take you for genetic testing, cause real black men don't do these things according to the news. Honestly, Fire, I didn't take you seriously when you said you were coming. I just thought it was something nice to say."

"Why'd you think I was joking?" he asked.

"Because . . . I mean . . . men just don't do that. At least not unless they're rich, which—don't take it the wrong way—I don't think you are. Or unless they've had sex and they know it's good."

"Which is sorta the case."

"Don't remind me. I'm so embarrassed."

"About what?"

"Our . . . how do you say . . . office phone sex . . . or is it phone office sex?"

"Who knows, maybe you were faking it. You were probably soaking your corns and clipping your nose hairs."

"Okay, lemme come clean. You're right. But I forgot to tell you that I put you on speaker phone. Now the whole office wants to meet you."

He laughed with her.

She liked that Fire could be so zany and self-deprecating then turn around and write a poem like "Person." For the poem was not only passionate. It was good. It showed a clear understanding of form. Of course she'd known men who could have written that and even better. But that was not the point. They hadn't.

"Fire . . . why are you doing this to me?" she asked.

"Doing what?"

"Making me want to leave my job and come and spend the day with you."

"How am I doing that?"

"By talking to me. The longer you talk to me, the more I want to get out of here. You care about me, don't you, Fire?" she half said, half asked. "I know you do. Where are you going to be in a half hour? I have to leave here. I'm feeling very sick."

They arranged to meet on the Brooklyn Bridge, on a bench on the walkway above the road. Sylvia dragged herself there, burdened by the weight of the sky, which had fallen on this humid day from the weight of its own wetness and draped itself across the city. Exiting a cab at Chambers Street, she picked her way through the flowered triangle of City Hall Park, edging behind a press conference on the steps of the neoclassical box that anchored the green. Weaving through a band of demonstrators, she ducked under a barricade, crossed the street, and entered the walkway in front of the Municipal Building, a towering Beaux Arts masterpiece with an awe-inspiring colonnade. There, she reached for her sunglasses and then made her way up the incline, dodging bikers and joggers, alert to the movements of camera-wielding tourists, herds of them in J. Crew, who stopped without warning, obstructing progress with the fuck-you languor of cattle.

He wasn't there when she arrived. Knowing he might be hiding, she wandered around the base of the huge stone columns that support the bridge's arches.

She checked her watch. She was on time. He, of course, was late.

Reminding herself not to sulk, she passed the time by reading poetry—*Midsummer* by Walcott—passing through screens of imagery to another life, a life of razor grass and bougainvillea and rivers that frolicked instead of oozed like the one that slunk beneath her now into a dishwater sea.

Drawn into transcendent verse, she lost track of time. And when she was through she realized that she'd been waiting for an hour, which didn't bother her as much as she'd expected, for it gave her time to think about her actions and their possible consequences. She'd lied to her colleagues and slacked off about the receipts. But more important, she was having an affair. Now, as she sat there, higher than most of the city, she felt his spirit filling her, fading into her marrow. And there, on that bridge, halfway between her home and her office, she began to understand why Aretha trembles that way when she sings "A Natural Woman."

But all this for what? She could lose her job, or her relationship. Or both. For what reason? To spend a day with a man she barely knew.

She looked at her watch again. She should leave, she thought, at least on principle . . . she should walk away right now.

But she made no attempt to go. Because under the ambivalence and apprehension simmered a feeling—and whether it was intuition or hope she wasn't sure—that meeting Fire on this August day would change her life somehow.

She turned her face on the runners and bikers trickling back and forth; she marveled at their stamina in the liquid heat. As she sat there, suffering pasty licks of tongues of breeze, a Japanese man in a Panama hat sat on a stool across from her and began to weave standards on his box guitar. She began to hum along . . . quietly . . . to herself . . . getting up to drop loose change in his collection plate. Did she have a request? She asked if he knew "You Go to My Head."

And as he played it for her she closed her eyes and thought of Fire: saw him standing in the kitchen at Claire's gallery in his red T-shirt and baggy jeans; felt the madness of that first kiss; saw him as she left him at the phone booth, neither of them expecting ever to meet again. What a weird thing, she thought, just meeting a stranger and feeling a charge and then finding yourself in "like."

Suddenly she heard a loud collision, and she opened her eyes to see a wriggling heap of spandex, flesh, and metal. Hands from the gathering crowd picked through the bundle, helped the victims to their feet. The crowd began to grow, pressing sweaty bottoms in her face, wilting her with its collective heat. She'd been waiting for over an hour now. And she really hated to wait. Where the hell was he? He had better come soon.

The crowd was stirring now. People were arguing, maybe even shoving a bit. She couldn't see. Then as a woman grabbed her child and scurried away, the crowd erupted into a helter-skelter. People flying like shrapnel.

Sylvia saw a glimmering knife and a splash of blood, and two men rolling toward her, heaving and throbbing. She lunged away in time and they crashed into the bench. She scrambled to her feet, her knee bruised and her slacks torn, and ran, leaving in her wake a clamor of thumps and bangs and curses.

On the Brooklyn side of the bridge she leaned against a wall to catch her breath, trembling like a severed limb. Sagging from heat and fright, she slumped to the ground, her knee popping like a hot coal, pulling on the thread of air she'd snagged between her teeth as a squad car raced up the walkway, sirens barking, lights ablaze.

After a few minutes she began to walk back to the bench, but stopped when she made the turn to enter the bridge proper and saw that the crowd had remade itself.

This is just too much, she thought. He should've been on time. She turned around and shuffled home.

There was no place to rest in that shambolic place, so she was forced to clear the bed, and this drew her into a larger action of sweeping, dusting, and polishing that was usefully distracting. At minutes after nine, she showered and went to bed, tired, anxious, and disappointed. She'd called him several times without getting an answer.

At five after midnight the telephone jolted her awake. The response to her grunted hello was Fire's voice, recognizable but thinner.

"How are you? Where are you?" she asked anxiously.

"At the hospital."

She gathered the sheets around her. "Are you hurt?"

"No, I'm fine."

"What's the matter?"

"Phil swallowed some pills today."

"Oh, my God. How is he?"

"Not so good."

"Where are you?"

"St. Vincent's Emergency Room."

"Do you need me?" She was out of bed, ready to fling on some clothes.

"No, love, I'm fine. But thanks."

"If you need me, Fire, I'll come for you."

"I'll be okay." His voice cracked. The fissure went right through her.

"If you need me, Fire, I'm there."

"No . . . baby, don't worry yourself."

She didn't know him well enough to know how to convince him. And she didn't want to pressure him. He needed his energy for himself and his friend.

"Okay, but if you need me, call me, okay?" She began to lay out some clothes on the chair.

"I'm sorry about today," he said. "I apologize to you from the bottom of my heart."

"It's okay," she replied. "It's okay."

"I thought about you a lot today," he said. "When I found out what happened to Phil I started to think about some of the things I want to do in this life. And getting a chance to know you was one of them. This thing between us is not ideal, Sylvia. I know that . . . this situation. But there is a certain logic to the chaos of the universe, and I don't think our convergence is random. It has a meaning, Sylvia, and a purpose. And we owe it to ourselves to discover that . . . to find out what it is. Who knows, maybe this is the path through which we'll become good friends. Or maybe we're here to validate our respective involvements . . . to strengthen them in the long run. I . . ." His voice cracked again.

She sat on the edge of the bed. "I thought about you too, Fire. I was really mad at you today. While I was waiting for you a lot of crazy things happened—"

"Like what? Are you okay?"

"Yes, I'm fine. I'll tell you about it some other time. I was so angry . . . but now I'm so sorry, baby . . . so, so sorry. If you don't want to be alone tonight . . . you can stay with me. Okay?"

"Okay . . . but are you sure? I mean, there are other people to consider."

"Yes . . . it's fine . . . no one else will be here. And anyone who wants to be here needs to call before coming."

"Okay."

She slapped her forehead. "I shouldn't have said that . . . about coming to stay with me . . . I'm sorry . . . I didn't mean to jump to conclusions. Oh, God, this is so weird. I'm sorry. I'm sorry. Maybe I'm just tired. I'm like really tripping now."

"Don't apologize. I understand how you feel."

She lay back on the sheets. "So come, then. Don't stay alone. Come stay with me. I'll look after you."

"Thank you so much . . . I really need you right now."

"Will you hold me, Fire, and tell me that it's right to feel this way? Will you tell me I'm not out here on my own?"

"You're right to feel this way."

"I need you to say it while you're holding me though."

"I promise. But now I have to go."

"Okay. But call me."

"I will."

"Promise?"

"I will."

Sitting in the sickly spray of fluorescent light, Fire unbuttoned the neck of his shirt and prepared himself for the worst as the Filipino nurse approached him with the set jaw and blank eyes of a giver of bad news. Shoving his hands in his pockets, he followed her to an adjacent hall, where without preamble she presented the facts. Overdose of sleeping pills. In and out of consciousness. Serious condition. No sense in waiting. Go home and rest.

She turned and walked away, leaving him to stare at her figure being absorbed into the dull gray walls. At the end of the corridor, a pair of double doors opened slowly, admitting to the waiting room another frazzled soul, who would sit in a hard plastic chair under frigid lights and wait for the facts while learning to associate bleach with the odor of death. His hands behind his back, his head held erect, Fire tried to shorten his depth of field like a camera, not wanting to record in sharp detail the scene before him—the knotted faces, the whining children hurriedly dressed in the middle of the night—all of this while a drone streamed in through his spinal cord and up through the base of his skull, filling his head with nothing but the sound of its own nothingness. Then quickly now, as tears filled his eyes, the room began to melt from solid to liquid.

Margaret, who had brought him Ian's letter, was almost upon him before he saw that she was the person who'd come through the door. How was she connected to this? But before he could ask or guess, she flung herself against him.

Phil, she told Fire, was her boyfriend. She and Ian had broken up.

"It was all so sad," she said—her face was pressed into his chest—"because it had all begun so suddenly and was about to end the same way."

The facts marched into his skull, where they shouted down the white noise. Phil and Margaret. Margaret and Phil. How? Why? In what time frame? All this while he held her, absorbing her shudders and convulsions, soaking them up with his body, adding more weight to his soul. He needed to go soon. He needed to be looked after as well. He was sorry, he said, thinking of Sylvia's lap now, but he couldn't give her anything more than facts.

Margaret began to give details about Phil and her, but Fire stopped her politely and gave her yet another fact. He had to go, and the clerks in billing needed to speak with someone. Would she deal with them? He had no idea how these things worked in America.

"It's not that I don't want to," she said, "it's just that I don't . . . y'know . . ."

"Know him?"

"Yes. I don't even know his full name or his address."

"Well, I have to go," he said. "I've been here for thirteen hours now and I need to get away."

He gave her his details and Phil's information, then left.

He didn't realize he was drenched in sweat until he went outside and the wind transformed his body hair to splinters. Standing outside on Seventh Avenue, he sensed what it was like to be a tree in a metropolis—to be a living, breathing thing that was ignored. As he looked around for something to call out to him, to pull him in a direction, he felt his feet being sucked into the earth below the concrete, felt his toes turning into roots.

He'd never known New York to be indifferent. There was always something calling out to the lonely. Good things and bad things, novelties and fixtures, bright lights and dark places, saviors and con men. But tonight, though, the city just went about its business.

Raising his head slowly, he looked up at the sky and couldn't see the stars through the mustard gas of smog. Jesus Christ. This place would deny him now the basic right to wish.

"Whassup?"

He looked over his shoulder and saw a guard—a one-eyed youth with two gold caps.

"Why you looking like that, B? One o' your boys up in here?"

He nodded.

"Whassup? He got shot?"

"He might have tried to kill himself. We're not sure yet."

"He white, right?"

"How'd you know?"

"Cause when niggers get upset they kill another nigger."

Fire shrugged his shoulders.

"But yo, I gotta go finish my shift. I just came out for some air. I don't know how they expect a mofucker to get well with that death smell they got up in there."

Fire shrugged again.

"But yo, don't worry about your boy, man. What's gotta be gotta be. Go home and chill with your lady, man, and don't give a damn about a thing."

He slunk away. Fire found a phone and called her, tapping his feet as he dialed, trying to ignore his stiff chest and trembling jaw. She wasn't picking up. He called again. Same thing.

He didn't know what to do now. Didn't know what to think. Call again now? Call again later? If so, how much later? Don't call and just show up? Go to Brooklyn, then call again from Brooklyn Heights? Go to the hotel and sleep and call her the next morning? Is she sleeping? Is she out? Is she on her way here because she's concerned about me? Is she home but doesn't want to pick up because she's changed her mind about me coming over? Is she okay? If she's not okay, what would I do? Call the cops and send them there? Or would that be a job for EMS? Fuck, maybe Lewis came over and she doesn't want to pick up? Or she wants to pick up but knows that she shouldn't? What if she isn't okay? Is she okay? What if he's there? What are they doing? Are they talking? Are they eating? Are they sleeping? Are they making love? Are they fucking? If they are, is she liking it? Is she on top? Or is she on the bottom? On her back or on her belly? Are they standing up against the fridge? Is she bent over with her head in the fridge and her legs apart? Is she okay? Is she okay? Is she okay? Did she really mean to tell me to come over? Did she mean it then change her mind? What if I went over there now, what the fuck would we do anyway? Talk? Sleep? Eat? Make love with her head in the refrigerator? Or would we start kissing at the door then make love right there—half in, half out, half clothed, half nude, half sane, half mad—and roll down the steps halfway into the street and confuse a drunk driver? Is she okay? Is she okay? Is she okay?

He decided to call her again, but he was out of change. As he stood at the curb to cross the street to get some, a cab discharged a fare in front of him. He stood there looking at the open door, not knowing what to do until the driver, a Russian with limp brown hair, asked him where he was going.

"Brooklyn."

"Where exactly, sir?"

He thought for a minute. Should he go to his or hers? He mumbled directions to the driver, leaned against the door, and went to sleep.

Like a higgler, he stood at the top of the steps with his shoulders straight, his back erect, his body aligned to ease the burden that weighed on his head. Through the door a bunch of keys were tinkling like a kora, and soft feet moved on the floorboards like mallets on the keys of a marimba.

She was home. A sigh curled him over like a bent blue note, giving him release, toppling the basket of woes at her doorway, where she was standing now, in slippers and white pajamas, framed by yellow light, needing only wings to be an angel.

"Come," she said. "Come inside." She led him to the couch and helped him remove his shoes, leaving him to return with a pail of water foamy with bath salts, aloe vera, and mint leaves. Working quickly but with care, she rolled up his trouser legs, exposing his calves, which were round and firm like cantaloupes, and helped him settle his feet in the warmth.

"Are you hungry?" she asked, standing now. She lit two candles and turned off the lights. "I was out at the grocery when you called. I needed some ingredients for something I wanted to make you."

"Thank you so much," he said, as bands of muscle laid down their arms. "You've gone outside yourself tonight."

She went to the kitchen, pulling his eyes like smudged ink on wet paper, and returned from the oven with a saucer of cookies, trailing behind her the scent of almonds.

She slipped a cookie between his lips, allowing her finger to linger there as he licked it clean of crumbs and butter.

"You are too sweet to me," he said, floating off to sleep. She had begun to massage his neck now.

"So you've finally gotten your cookie then."

"Finally . . . after such a long time. Can I have the recipe?"

"No. I want you to come here whenever you need them."

"Don't worry," he said. "I know what makes them special."

"Oh do you?" she said, wrapping his hair around her fists like reins.

"Yes," he said, languorously, lulled even more now by the scalp massage, by the ebb and flow of pulling. "Molasses."

"How'd you know?" she asked. "I only used a drop."

"A man can smell these things."

He woke up on the couch, draped in bedding, blue-gray sheets like rain observed from a distance. The basin was gone, the plate cleared away.

As he rose he heard her breathing, sucking in and heaving out with concentrated effort as if inhaling and exhaling were not instinctive, but skills she'd learned from a teacher who'd told her to practice always—even in her sleep.

He followed the sound, and found her lying in bed, on her side, in a corner, with her spine against the wall, curled back into herself like a fist.

If he'd fallen asleep with her, would she be breathing easier? He felt his own breathing slowing down, changing its pitch, sounding like cassava being grated for a pone. And as he was swallowed by the rhythm of her back and forth, he sensed with his spirit and not his mind that maybe, if he just tried hard enough, he could breathe for her and lighten her slumber.

Pulling the door halfway shut, he took the phone to the kitchen and called the hotel to check his messages. There were three from Margaret. He called her and received good news.

Phil would be fine. The pills were an accident. And he'd be staying in New York for a little while because his audition would have to be rescheduled. This, she said, would give them time to know each other. The story was quite funny, she said, but it was best to hear Phil tell it.

"Phil."

"Fire." He was as happy as a dread with an ounce of weed.

"So how are you? Margaret said you'd be coming out in a few days. So what's happening with the two of you, by the way? This is all quite strange and new. What's going on? What happened with the pills?"

"It was an honest accident. The kind of thing that could happen to anybody. D'you know what *feng xiu* is? It's the extract from the smegma of this rare Chinese deer. And they use it to make a pill called *feng xiu xiang*, which you can get in Chinatown."

"What are these pills good for?"

"Long erections. You can pop one and stay up for twenty minutes. I was having some problems with Margaret and Ian told me what to get and where to get it. You can't get it everywhere. It's sold from this little hole in the wall in a cellar on Mott Street. And they'll only sell it to you if you give them a code word."

"What?"

"It's really potent stuff. It's illegal, actually. It has dangerous side effects."

"Like what?"

"Well, taken without a meal it can shrivel your cock."

"So how is this connected to the sleeping pills?"

"Well Margaret's a hard revver—Ian says she's the town bike but I don't take what he says seriously—and we were supposed to be getting together later, so I figured I'd take an extra dose to make her happy. Well, I thought if I took a lot of them I could make her *really* happy. And I took the wrong pills by accident."

"Whose pills? And where did this happen?"

"Oh, the pills are mine. I haven't been sleeping well in the last couple of months. I'm a bit concerned about my career, actually. Good gigs are hard to come by. I'd just left a program at the New School and—"

"Phil, are you serious about all this? I don't want to laugh then find out that you've got, as they say, issues, you know."

"Fuck, I wish I were joking. But it was kinda cool though. Have you ever had your stomach pumped? Oh, it's really cool. They hook you up to this big machine and they run a tube down your throat. You should try it just for the experience."

"Phil, can I ask you a question? Does anything ever bother you?"

"Sure. Not having a gig. But I'll be fine though."

"So I'll come and check you this evening then. I have to take care of certain things in the day. You need anything from the outside? Food or anything?"

"No, the food here's great."

"Phil, it's hospital food."

"The only thing better is airline food. It's not the food so much. I like the way they separate everything into compartments. Okay, you could bring me something, but make it something that's easy to fix up like that. Don't bring a burrito or anything."

"So by the way, how's Ian taking this thing with you and Margaret?"

"Fine. He's the one who arranged it."

"Whadyou mean?"

"It started as a threesome, actually. Sort of like the black-birds on the wall. Now there's two. I think they've just gotten tired of each other, Ian and Margaret."

"I see . . . Well, she seems quite nice. Very bright."

"She knows a lot about music, too, man. We learn a lot from each other. But what are you doing over here?"

"A little business."

"Give over, Fire. It's Sylvia, isn't it?"

"Just cool, man."

"Come on, Fire. I'm not stupid y'know. I was the one who brought the parcel for you."

"Just cool, man. I can't really talk right now."

"Come on, Fire. I won't tell."

He leaned into the phone. "Okay . . . but this is between me and you."

After washing the dishes from the night before, and sealing the cookies in sandwich bags, he trawled her fridge and cupboards for a sense of her taste and went out to the shops to get ingredients for breakfast, leaving behind a note to say he'd soon return.

On the night when he'd dropped her off at home, he was remembering now, the driver had taken a route past some Middle Eastern shops.

After a few wrong turns he found it, the old Lebanese quarter along Atlantic Avenue near Smith Street—not so much a bazaar as a throwback to the civility of prewar Beirut—where men with dark mustaches and open-necked shirts sipped cardamom coffee at sidewalk cafés and women dressed by Macy's ordered baklava and pistachio cakes in French as well as Arabic as their Segaddicted kids waited outside to make sure the cops didn't ticket the Camry.

Inside Sahadi Importing, a neighborhood suprette whose informality seemed to mock the yuppies who wanted to insist it was gourmet, he edged around barrels of bulgur wheat and fava beans, and squeezed by counters lined with five-gallon jars of dates and figs and nuts and sun-dried fruit, choosing for his basket carefully by using his senses the way his mother had taught him—sniffing for signs of fermentation, squeezing for fitness, even listening. The sign of a good avocado is a rattling seed.

On the way back he picked up a shirt, some socks, and some boxers at a Gap on Montague Street. Once inside the apartment, he checked to see that Sylvia was fine and then went about prepping breakfast. He showered and changed and waited for her to rise, feeling quite at home now after taking a seat on her toilet.

In the living room again, he turned on the telly and switched back and forth between a key contest in Mexican-league soccer and an episode of *Xena*, wondering as he smothered his laughter who was the worse actor, the striker taking a dive in the penalty box or the gladiator trying to sound like Kirk Douglas in *Spartacus*.

Still tired from the night before, he nodded off to sleep, waking up a little after noon. She was still not awake, so he occupied his time by wandering through the apartment. She had a decent collection of art, including Elizabeth Catlett and Romare Bearden originals. But it was clear that she hadn't bought the work just for its investment value. A lot of it, he concluded, she simply liked. Crossing his legs on the floor, he rifled through her music, a collection that was deep and wide, ranging from jazz and classic soul to soukous and qawwali. She particularly liked Al Green and Marvin Gaye, and Cassandra Wilson and Sweet Honey in the Rock. Her library, though, was deep but narrow. Her tastes were decidedly American, and didn't seem to stray beyond the French and Russian must-reads like Camus and Dostoyevsky. It's fascinating, he thought, how difficult it is to predict people's tastes. For judging from the art on her walls and the music in her racks he'd expected to see well represented the work of writers like Naguib Mafouz and Nadine Gordimer and Maryse Condé. But greatness was the dilemma of America, wasn't it? It was a large, rich country with only two neighbors, so one could easily live here in comfort without considering the rest of the world—as the rest of the world has to consider itself in addition to considering America. His novels, for instance, had sold a million and a half copies in the Commonwealth, mainly in Britain, Canada, and Australia, but had done about twenty-five thousand in the States. Which didn't bother him. Success in the States would come—if it did—like most things . . . in the fullness of time.

There were some photo albums on the bottom shelf. He took his time going through them, struck by the absence of childhood pictures or any group shots with family. Why is that? he wondered, adding this to the list of things he wanted to ask her later.

Gaps notwithstanding, the albums gave him a bit of context. And after going through them he felt as if he knew her a little better. He knew where she went to school. And had an idea of her career track. He knew now, as he'd suspected, that she'd traveled fairly widely, and also, as a photo in a carnival costume showed, that her bottom was fuller than it appeared in her clothes.

The scene looked like Trinidad or Barbados. His lashes licked her image from the page. Her body was in profile and her face was turned toward him, smiling, as if she knew, as the shutter sliced away this moment of her life, that one day a man would recognize this as the essential her—a lover of life and its possibilities.

He was pulled out of his thoughts by a rustling, and what he thought was her voice. But he wasn't sure. For he'd heard it across time and space—from within the paper on which the picture was printed, on that layer just below the ink, where the life behind the image really exists, where he'd held her hand and danced with her behind a float, imbibing rum drinks and diesel fumes and salt-laced sweat, dancing on the street in a crowd with the same vitality with which he would shuffle inside her sweaty shabeen as soon as they were alone.

Going to her room, standing by the door, he found her still sleeping, and realized, as he watched her mumbling groggily, that the rustling had been the friction of her clothes against her skin. For she was lying on her belly, naked, her white pajamas crumpled with the sea green sheets, one leg splayed, the other drawn up the way women do when they want to feel a deeper heat.

Moaning from the depths of her unconscious, she rolled onto her back in a settling of shimmering flesh, falling now beneath his shadow, which splashed over her breasts, draining away through her cleavage into her navel.

As he leaned against the doorway of this quiet room whose drawn shades granted privacy, he felt every hair on his blood-hot body filling each pore in hers.

He pulled away. This place was hers. And therefore privacy wasn't theirs until she'd given him permission.

He returned to the couch. There he pondered the possibilities of her body: the lean torso, the full calves, the firm thighs that melted like pitch into soft hips. And her bottom, which he knew now had not been overdramatized by a wide-angle lens. It was tight at the sides without dimples or blemishes, but filigreed, as women's bottoms should always be, with stretch lines.

He channel-surfed, trying to get away from it, but it followed him to talk shows and sports roundups and cartoons and sitcoms and rescue reenactments . . . this big, brown batty on a string.

He heard her stirring again, and her voice calling his name, then a pause, during which, he could tell, she was dressing.

"Oh, it's so late," she said from the bathroom door, a little bit shy before brushing her teeth. "I'm sorry . . . I really didn't mean to oversleep like this and pay you no mind. I'm being such a bad hostess. I hope you found ways to entertain yourself?"

"That you don't have to worry about."

"Good. I'll be with you in a minute. And did I tell you good morning? Good morning."

"Good morning to you too."

"Are you hungry or anything?"

"Yes, but I've started breakfast. I'll finish now that you're up. Go ahead, shower and all that, then we can eat."

"You're making us breakfast. I was wondering what that smell was. Okay, two more points for you. I'll be really quick then."

In the shade of the cherry tree in the small backyard, in a corner by the fence, they spread a blanket and had a simple meal: *buljol,* chips of salt cod tossed in thyme and olive oil with garlic, diced tomatoes, chopped onions, and minced bell peppers; and bake, an unleavened bread made from flour and salt with a pinch of baking powder and butter. On the side they had avocado slices, cubes of feta cheese, and, to cool their lips, sugar and water with crushed ice.

"This is really good," she said, with the first bite. "I never thought of feta cheese with codfish before. But it works. Who taught you to cook?"

"My mother," he said. "I'd say she, mostly, and then there were other people that showed me little things. A lot of it too is just using your mind and trying new things all the time. Then you start creating like a music composer."

"Right," she said. "You can project how certain things will work together and adjust before you commit."

"Yeah . . . exactly."

"So," she asked, smiling, "do you cook all the time or just when you want to impress people you don't really need to impress because they've already fallen into you?"

"Well, for people like that," he said, eyes radiating humor, "I extend myself beyond food."

"Yeah? To where?"

"To drink."

He took a lime from his pocket. "Now, in the hands of an ordinary man this would be a simple green ball," he said with a straight face. "But watch magic happen."

He wiped his knife on a napkin and sliced the lime. He pointed to her glass. "Now I want you to take a sip."

She did.

He squeezed some juice in her glass and stirred it with his finger. "Now taste it."

She giggled as she lifted the glass to her lips.

"Taste different, don't it?"

"Yeah," she said, playing along. "Wow, that magic ball was really impressive."

"But it wasn't the lime," he said, reaching out and stroking her face. "It was the magic finger."

Out on the street now, she in a red summer dress and he in a khaki shirt and pants, they walked along dreamily, holding hands and hugging like they were no longer humans with choice and free will but puppets—marionettes moved by wires to the keyboard of a grand puppeteer.

On the cobblestoned Promenade above the Brooklyn-Queens Expressway they sat on a bench and looked out over New York harbor at the concrete forest of Wall Street. The sun was pinned to the creaseless sky—a medal on a soldier's chest—and the East River was as alive with boats as it used to be with fish, big boats that seemed tiny as they sailed beneath the Brooklyn Bridge, whose cables from this distance were a giant spider's web. In the foreground, right below them, old warehouses were stretched out on the water's edge, basking, like caimans on a jungle embankment.

"Have you read *Brazil*?" she asked, taking his hand.

He had.

"And did you like it?"

He understood this for what it was: her way of saying that he shouldn't think low of her for being here, because she'd been pushed to this . . . for the man—he wouldn't use his name anymore—didn't make her feel like being natural was enough.

"I like Updike's work a lot," he said, being careful not to claim him as an influence. That would've modulated the discussion. Changed its key. Made it about him. Which he didn't want. Not that he was ashamed of being a writer. He just didn't want to be defined by it. For he was many things, with many dimensions—all of which he wanted her to eventually see and know.

"In *Brazil*," he continued, "you really see the things that make Updike great. Imagery and metaphor, and the keenness of detail. One of the things that make the book brilliant is the

setting. In a Latin American literary context, baroquely or-
nate language doesn't feel overwrought. Imagine if *Brazil*
were set in the contemporary American west, and Isabel were
the daughter of a white municipal banker, and Tristao a
homeboy named Tyrone, from Harlem. I mean, Updike got so
deep into the esthetic of writers like Gabriel García Márquez
and Jorge Amado that the book almost reads like it was trans-
lated from Portuguese or Spanish—those eighteen-clause sen-
tences and all that. No, man, that book is sheer brilliance,
man." He thought for a bit. "And then there's the whole weaving in of Brazilian history and politics. And the masterful
control of the time sense—"

"I guess I know who you're casting your Nobel vote for,"
she said, feeling weak now, as though she'd been standing beneath a cataract of words. Literary passions were so seduc-
tive. "Who else do you stalk at readings?"

"Fiction or poetry?"

"Both."

"Well, Updike, as I said. Naipaul. Henry Miller. Márquez.
Carpentier—"

"Who's Carpentier? I don't know him."

"A Cuban writer. He's kinda considered the father of magic
realism. He wrote *Explosion in a Cathedral* and *The King-
dom of This World*."

She laughed inside, wanting to hug him for reading good
books, for being able to share this passion with her.

"Wow, there are so many," he said, faced now with an
embarrassment of riches. "It's hard for me to think—but I'd
have to add Toni Morrison and D. H. Lawrence. In poetry,
now, there's Walcott, Neruda, Guillén, Yeats, Rita Dove,
Philip Larkin . . . Kwame Dawes down in South Carolina . . .
different people for different moods."

"Do you write a lot of poetry?"

"Not anymore. Only when I get the inspiration." She
leaned against him. "Only when I feel the vibes. And you?"
he asked, placing his arm behind her, on the back of the

bench, where it perched in waiting—a jaguar in a tree. "Who do you like?"

"In fiction . . . Toni Morrison, James Baldwin, Zora Neale Hurston, and of course Updike—I'll never forget reading *Couples* the first time—and Margaret Walker. And in poetry, I'd say Maya Angelou, and Margaret Atwood from Canada, and Langston Hughes and Rita Dove and of course Walcott. The funny thing about Rita Dove, though, is that I love her almost as much as a novelist."

"Oh, I didn't know she wrote novels."

"She wrote only one, *Through the Ivory Gate*. It was published in the early nineties. It's about this black woman who grows up very poor in a small town in Ohio. Her parents are migrant workers from the South in this mostly white place. So this woman grows up having her own identity struggles—y'know, northern versus southern, black versus white—and then she goes off to college in Wisconsin where she studies music and theater in this almost completely white environment. She becomes a puppeteer and ends up being the only black person in a traveling puppet troupe, and this group becomes her whole world for a while, so all her relationships are with people in the troupe—which means with white men. Anyway, she ends up leaving the troupe and going back to her hometown, where she takes up an artist's residency at a school. So the whole going home then becomes this process of exploration . . . y'know . . . coming to terms with her past . . . separation . . . identity . . . reconnecting."

"Wow . . . I'll put that on my list of things to read. *Through the Ivory Gate.* That's what it's called, right?" He was circling her with words, suspecting that she saw some of herself in that narrative. He was thinking now of her album . . . the missing pictures of childhood . . . the absence of her parents. And her voice—something he'd noticed the first time they met—it was suspiciously neutral.

"Where's Rita Dove from?" he asked, approaching the subject obliquely.

"I'm not sure."

"Somewhere midwestern, nuh?"

"That sounds right."

"Have you ever been there? To the Midwest?"

"Yeah . . . on business."

"Do you think you could live there?"

"No," she replied. "I don't think so. It's too cold."

If she were midwestern, he thought, she would've added something like "although I spent the first x years of my life there." He had to maneuver some more now. Asking people where they're from, he knew, was sometimes uncomfortable. People carry so much baggage from home.

"What about the West Coast or the South?"

"I like the West Coast a lot. California especially, for the ocean and the sunshine. The south . . . I'm not so sure about. I like a lot of it . . . like New Orleans and Atlanta . . . and the Gulf Coast beaches. But I don't know about living there so much. In many ways I'm a spoilt New Yorker."

"And in other ways?"

"In other ways . . . I don't feel like I belong here."

"How long have you been here?"

"Most of my life."

"From where?"

"Guess."

"I have no idea."

In his mind he was walking through her house, looking for clues. On looks alone she could be many things. Latina. North African. Native American. But none of these were right. He knew that. He could feel it.

But as he pictured her at the phone booth rocking back on one leg and considered her name and her familiarity with the selections at the concert, he began to suspect she was Caribbean, and further, from one of the English-speaking territories.

But from where? It was hard to say on looks alone. The Caribbean islands are flakes of three continents—Asia, Africa, and Europe—ground up and dropped in the ocean like cod-fish cakes in hot oil, becoming in the process something new and exciting that is often hard to define.

"Trinidad?" he asked. She might be part East Indian.

"No," she said. "Let's put it this way, I could've been your next-door neighbor."

"You're Jamaican?"

"Yeah, man."

Her shoulders relaxed, and she smiled.

"From where?" he asked, drawn even closer now.

"Kingston, I think. But I was only eight when I left and haven't been back."

"Oh, I shouldn't even talk to you then."

"Oh, stop," she said, laughing with him.

"Y'is not me frien again," he said, speaking patois now. "You lef de rock at eight and y'is hummuch now?"—thirty-four, she said—"An you doan touch back de rock? Shame o' you."

"Oh, stop, it's a long story."

"Okay, tell me, lemme see f ah fogive yuh."

She wanted him to know, wanted him to connect with her, wanted him to know she was one of his, hoping this would make a difference. To whom? And in what way? She wasn't sure.

"When my mother died my father sent me to live with a relative in the States, and while I was here, we lost touch. I don't know if he's dead or alive. I'm an only child, so I never felt there was anything to return to, really."

"Oh no." He stroked her brow. "Oh, I really didn't mean to make a joke about it."

"Oh, don't be sorry," she said. "If anything, *I* should be sorry for bringing this up now . . . for imposing this on you."

His arm, which had been waiting behind her, slipped around her shoulders now. She leaned over and wiped her face with the tail of her dress and leaned against him, shifting her weight to create her own space between his chest and arm.

"You remind me so much of that place, Fire," she said, her

face turned toward the sky. "You make me think about it in a way that had never been as important to me. I feel like that woman in *Secrets and Lies* felt when the child she'd given away as a baby comes back into her life as an adult. God, man. It's all the luggage that comes with that kind of rediscovery. Fire . . . for the longest time . . . before I met you, I thought all that luggage was at the bottom of the sea, man. And then you—you come along flopping like a frogman in your scuba gear, going, 'Hey, this grip has your name on it.'

"I remember thinking one day, 'God, why do I feel this way about this man?' And I guess the answer has something to do with the fact that, along with all the really wonderful things about you, you remind me of that place. Yeah, I know—*Through the Ivory Gate.*"

"So go home, then," he said. "Go home and see what you might find."

"I think if I knew people there it would be easier. But to go there as a tourist, I think, would make me feel even more alienated. Fire, I don't even know the name of the place I'm from. I know it's in Kingston and fairly close to water, and the people were shit poor, but that's it."

"What about the relative you used to live with? He might be able to tell—"

"He's dead, the fucking bastard. Excuse my French."

"If the people in your area were rich," he asked, "would that make it any easier?"

She thought for a bit.

"I think so. Going home is one thing. Going home to bad news is another. The way I feel is the way a lot of African Americans used to feel about Africa. Before they knew of Africa's greatness they were afraid to embrace it. Now they go there with joy. They sing and dance on the plane. It would be easier for me to go back if I knew I would find something I could be proud of. I know it sounds trifling, but it's true."

"Poverty for most people is an inherited condition, Sylvia.

There is nothing to be ashamed of. Ignoring or taking advantage of poverty—now that's a sin. We can't choose our histories. When we come into this life the greater part of our history is already in place—race, class, gender, religion, sexual preference, wealth, access . . . the things that remain pretty much constant throughout our lives. It's not like the opposite of poor is happy. So why kill up yourself? Come home, sweet girl . . . even for a day . . . to sit by a river and eat a mango and say that God is good."

"I should, shouldn't I?"

"And if you need a family, I can always rent you some o' mine. Some o' them I'd give you free. I'd even pay the shipping."

"Oh, you are so cheesy."

"Is that good or bad?"

"Cheese is fat. Fat is comfort food."

She kissed his nose, trailing a mist of moistness as she pulled away.

"So you know a lot about me, and I know nothing about you," she said, standing in front of him, leaning against the metal railing, which was a few feet away from the bench.

Her life to this point had been a matter of avoiding history; she didn't ask people about their lives because she didn't want them to ask about hers in turn. So most of her involvements, both romantic and platonic, had been rooted in shallow earth. But with Fire she was feeling wet ground beneath her, layers of silt brought down from the hills of her foreparents and laid down over thousands of years in a cycle of flooding and retreat, a pulling away that had left behind a treasure of minerals to nourish her like a tree. Her body was feeling damp now, from sweat, humidity, and the sap on the tip of her bud.

"What do you want to know?" he asked.

"Let's start with your family."

"Well, I'm an only child—"

"Like me."

"Okay . . . and I grew up in Portland, in a little district outside Port Antonio, until high school, then I moved to Kingston. After high school I came to the States to go to college."

"And your parents, what are they like?"

"Nice people," he answered, thinking now of what he should say, wondering how much he wanted to reveal. She was insecure, and he didn't want his background to be an issue. It wouldn't be fair to tell her the whole truth. Not now. Not when she was feeling this way. He wouldn't lie, but he would reduce the facts to their most passably general.

"Oh, come on, now," she said, kicking him playfully. "Where are they from? Where do they live? What do they do for a living? What's your relationship like?"

"My mother's name was Elizabeth. A really nice woman who liked to enjoy life. Could do many things. Was a tomboy, actually. Tall woman. I get my height from her. She was about five-eleven, and slender, and loved the arts and political debate yet was also good with her hands. Could fix cars and cut steel and clean and oil her gun. A very confident woman. She was decidedly left-wing in her politics—a democratic socialist—and really funny. Loved life, man. Smoked two packs a day and could knock back a six-pack and drive home on those dark, winding country roads with one hand on the steering wheel and the other one around my shoulders. She liked the excitement of cities but she always lived on a farm. She liked the idea of nurturing things, plants and animals and all that. People too . . . she was always getting a job for this one or writing a letter of recommendation for that one, or running down to the police station to get another one out on bail. Liz was nice, man. She was a real progressive in a place where she could've just gone with the flow and accepted the fact of privilege."

"You say 'was.' Has she passed away?"

He nodded.

"Yes . . . a while ago. When I was fourteen."

He saw restraint in her eyes. It was clear that she wanted

to say something—sorry, perhaps—but didn't want to seem maudlin.

"You said she was privileged. In what way?"

"Well, to be educated in any third world country is to be privileged. To have a piece o' land to call your own makes you more so," he said, thinking of his mother's considerable acreage. "In all honesty, she came from a well-off family. But her father wanted to marry her off at twenty, and she said no and went to the bank and forged his signature and withdrew the money he'd been setting aside to give her at twenty-one, and bought some land out east. I grew up on that property until I was ten and ready for high school. Then I went to Kingston to live with my father. My parents got divorced when I was three."

"What did your mother do besides farm?"

"Worked for Air Jamaica."

"And what's your dad like?"

"Humphrey is a nice guy in an ole-time kinda way. Calls himself a socialist. And he's really progressive in some ways and really conservative in others. Thinks free college tuition is a basic human right, but can't wait for them to bring back hanging."

She cocked her head and spread her arms, grabbing the railing. Leaning forward now, her arms trailing like wings, she stopped her face inches from his and asked: "Okay, where'd you get the name Fire?"

"My father gave me that name when I was eight. I was playing with one of his welding torches and almost burned down the house."

"Is he a welder?"

"No ... he's a teacher," he told her—guiltily, veering toward a lie. "He teaches at the school of art in Kingston."

True, his father had taught there for years. But he'd also been a professor of art history and painting at Cooper Union in New York and the National School of Fine Art in Mexico City, and his work was well placed in the best galleries in Europe. So to call him an art teacher was like saying Colin Powell had done some time in the service. Seeing doubt in her face—as if she were comparing what he'd told her to something that she'd heard—he thought, Fuck, she might know him. She collects art. But maybe not. He added, "And he paints and sculpts as well."

She seemed satisfied.

"And you and Ian have known each other since childhood?" she continued.

"Through an uncle of ours, I-nelik, who's a musician."

A breeze flipped her dress above her knees, flashing her thighs, which were pressed together, forming a shape like the trunk of a cotton tree. He glanced at the strollers and sunbathers. If he were alone with her . . . or if the sky were darker . . . or, he was thinking now, if they were far away from her home, he'd slip his oarsman in her canoe and grunt her name as he paddled.

"I-nelik . . . I-nelik . . ."

One thought was overtaken by another, causing the first to stall then stop. She was standing with her legs slightly open, and the sun was shining through her dress. And it seemed as if—he wasn't sure, for it was just a shadow, wasn't it?—that she wasn't wearing underwear. Because that shadow there, that murkiness below the fabric, was not a wedge of well-cut silk. It was triangular though . . . with wavy edges . . . like a delta seen from a mountaintop.

"You know bout I-nelik?" he said, wondering if she'd seen him looking. "I-nelik is my ole man's youngest brother. I used to find every excuse to spend time with him when I was young. I used to think he was so cool."

"What was so cool about him?"

"He's only fifteen years older than me. So he was in his late twenties, early thirties when I was growing up. So I felt like I could talk to him about anything, especially guy-things I couldn't really talk to my ole man about. Plus he was a romantic kinda guy. I-nelik was a dentist, y'know—did his

D.D.S. at Tufts. He'd always wanted to do music, but the whole family was against it. Not because it was the arts or anything like that—they never fought against my ole man wanting to paint—but because he wanted to play reggae. And in those days—we're talking like the late sixties, early seventies—reggae was street music. You couldn't play it uptown. It was just a ghetto thing.

"The same people who are praising Bob Marley now used to fight it. So about four years after coming back and setting up a practice, and playing one or two sessions at places like Randy's and Dynamic, rasta just buss in him head, and he just knew that he had to play music. That that was his calling. And he sold the practice and became a full-time musician. Of course there were some really hard times. He started growing locks and because o' that people wouldn't rent him a flat in a good neighborhood, so he just went and lived in the ghetto and did volunteer work two times a week at an area clinic. There wasn't much money ... but he was happier than when he was a fat cat named Jonathan Heath. But the thing is that he's all right, now. After linking with Bob and all that, everything worked out. So anyway, I met Ian because he and I-nelik were neighbors. Then when it got back to my father that Ian was a prodigy, it became almost like trading places. Ian would spend most of the summer by me and I would spend mine by him."

"I gather that you didn't spend all your time in Jamaica," she said, intrigued now, seeing in his personality the convergence of two others.

"I came here to go to college."

"Where'd you go to school?"

"Yale."

"Impressive."

"It's a school."

"Well, *be* modest. What did you study?"

"Painting and art history."

"Like your father. Is that what you are? An artist?" Her voice rang out as if she'd made a discovery.

"Not anymore. I gave that up a while ago."

It settled again. "Well, what are you doing now?"

"A little o' this and a little o' that? A little writing, a little farming."

"Writing? What kind of writing?"

"Oh . . . I have an idea for a novel," he said dismissively. This wouldn't draw attention in New York, he thought, where ideas for books were as commonplace as ideas for films in L.A.

"Doesn't everyone," she said, proving his point. "Me too."

"So there you go."

"And this farming thing?" she asked. "What kind of farm is it? Where is it? How big is it?"

"Well, that's a new thing. About a year now. I haven't quite figured out what I'm going to do with it. It will reveal itself. Sarge, the man who grows that coffee I brought you, has some ideas. We'll figure it out when I get back."

"So you didn't plan this whole farming thing?"

"No, it just worked out that way."

"Is that how you run your life?" she said, throwing her hands in the air like a magician demonstrating that the dove has disappeared. "You just let things happen?"

"Pretty much."

"That's so alien to me," she said, shuddering in jest.

"Different strokes," he said, cocking his head and smiling, sure now that she was clothed beneath her dress. The flesh-colored panties were sheer and full-cut.

"So how d'you get by while waiting for this novel to write itself, and the crops to just spring out of the ground?" she asked, sitting on a lower rail. Her face had become serious now. Her tone was not unlike the one a cynic uses on the eve of religious conversion. Respectful but ironic.

"Travel," he said, spreading his arms along the back of the bench. He crossed his legs, trying to make a joke of looking serious, then decided to go along with it when he saw that something in her was demanding to see that. "Read. Listen to music. Talk to people. Maybe take a stab at some writing."

"How long have you been living like this?" she asked. She opened her palms, set to catch an answer.

"Like how?"

"Writing, traveling, painting . . ."

"Pretty much since leaving college."

"Doesn't this make you nervous? Don't you ever start saying to yourself, 'Time's going, I better start living like a quote unquote adult and get a real job and settle down'?"

"No."

"Don't you worry about money?"

"No."

"Why?"

"Because my needs are pretty simple."

"What are they?"

"A place to live. Food to eat. Good friends. Good health. That kinda thing."

"Oh, come on. If I didn't like you so much I'd smack you."

"Why?"

"'Cause you're full of it. Those shoes are a coupla hundred dollars."

"But how many do I own?"

"I don't know. Tell me."

"Shoes total? Four and that includes a pair of sneakers."

He stared at her. She held his gaze, then broke out laughing. He was joking, obviously.

"You're such a liar."

They talked for hours, sitting together on the bench, sometimes getting up to stroll, but talking always, about whatever came to mind—music and art and books and travel and history and politics and cooking—teaching, learning, questioning, and explaining, but always talking, the words splashing down with the authority of abundance.

An observer would not have seen in them the heat of new desire. For this passion that they were feeling now, but hadn't

yet announced, was old, having existed for thousands of
years, in thousands of stories, in thousands of minds as a
thought: If you were going to spend a month on a desert island and you could only take one person, who would it be?

That evening, the sun hit the water in a cataclysm of streaking pebbles. Orange balls with fluttering tails of purple, red,
and gold.

Sitting on the bench, high above the water, Sylvia imagined herself far away. In her mind the Promenade was the terrace of a house on a hill. And the rippling waves, clay-colored
from the sun, were the overlapping roofs of the nearest
town—a hundred miles away.

She'd used their hours of conversation to shade in the
sketch he'd given her. She knew now that he'd lived in several
countries, had met Claire through Ian, and had published two
collections of poetry with a small press in England. But more
important, she now had a sense of his visions and values. He
was an idealist. A romantic. If he weren't so phosphores-
cently intelligent she'd be inclined to say naïve.

How does he function in the modern world? she wondered.
He didn't have a computer, and had no plans of getting one.
He wrote in longhand, then transcribed on a manual typewriter. He didn't even own a date book. He'd never held a job
in his life, had never even tried, and had always done "this
and that" to support himself as he pursued his art.

This and that. She chuckled to herself now, still surprised, as
she considered some items on his résumé—bartender, English
teacher, factory worker, translator, jeweler, cab driver, auto
mechanic, florist, short-order cook, farm laborer, nightclub
bouncer, roadie, encyclopedia salesman, market huckster. And
what did he have to show for all this grunt work? Where was
his payoff after the sacrifice? Where was *his* Wailers gig?

What did he have to show? she asked herself again, as if
the answer were merely waiting on a prompt to reveal itself. A

noncareer as a painter? A coupla poetry books and a piece of land he was *thinking* of farming?

And he clearly hadn't settled down. What had he been doing in London? "Visiting friends," he said, "and doing some writing workshops."

There was something compelling in his madness, though . . . something inspirational . . . something noble in his pursuit. Because he was someone with choices who had chosen to do this, to live simply.

As she thought about this it occurred to her that she was feeling something for him that she'd never felt for any other man in her life. Respect. What she'd thought was respect in the past, she was realizing now, had simply been consideration and courtesy. She'd never been enthralled by their beliefs or opinions, largely because none of those men had equaled or surpassed her in intellect or experience. She had never wanted to be with a man simply for how he made her feel, she admitted to herself now. It had always been for other reasons, none of which, she thought as she looked back now, had been valid.

She looked at him, he was looking back at her . . . and as the air around them was empurpled by the twilight, she sensed the gap between their faces dissolving . . . and his breath searing her nose . . . and his lips steaming the wrinkles out of hers.

"Weren't you scared all those years when you were living hand to mouth?" she asked as they walked along a path to Montague Street, where activity had begun to stir beneath the awnings that shaded the windows of the shops and cafés.

He palmed the back of her head and massaged her scalp, then slid his hand across her shoulder, allowing it to freefall down her back, where it seized the stem of her waist. "No," he said. "I was able to buy all the things I needed. I really don't need many material things to be happy y'know, Sylvia. Not a lot."

"What are some of them?"

The taste of her lips still fresh on his, he steered her down a side street overhung with trees that seemed to drink from the pools of darkness.

"Cut flowers . . . not necessarily fancy ones either," he told her, as his eyes scanned ahead for a recessed entrance where he could lean against her and squeeze the flesh on her hips as he kissed her wetly. "Freshly brewed coffee, two good speakers, enough money to buy a book and a couple of CDs a week. Throw in a nice white shirt and a pair of dress shoes. After that everything is gravy."

"You believe that?" she asked, wondering if that ridge that she'd noticed on his trouser leg as he sat on the bench had all belonged to him, or whether he'd been assisted by a flattering accident of pleating.

"I'm not saying everybody should do this," he replied. "But that is how I feel."

"And you've always felt this way?"

"I've never had any evidence to the contrary. Americans are the richest people in the world—but are they happier than anybody else? Watch the talk shows or the evening news. Look at people's faces on the subway."

She began to think of herself now. A near six-figure salary, an Ivy League diploma, and no dependents. She should feel an incredible sense of possibility, shouldn't she?

A young man on Rollerblades slowed down and gave them a flyer, then sped away into the night.

"Would you like to go to this?" she asked, looking at the flyer. "I know the place. I used to read there quite a bit at one time."

They were standing beneath a hedgerow. They stared at each other, daunted by the challenge of forging a new alphabet to create the new words to describe this new feeling that was causing their skin to gooseflesh. Stymied, they reached out and held hands and began to kiss slowly, braiding their tongues like a poet plaits metaphors.

After walking down a hill through the urban campus of the

Watchtower Society, they came to Old Fulton Street, whose old brick buildings had been turned into restaurants and bars. Holding hands, she led him as they ran across the wide street like kids on a great adventure, first to the median, then through traffic to the other side.

They walked down the gradient toward the river and the old ferry landing, which was marked by a lighthouse and a jetty—a narrow strip of planks where a wedding was taking place on the roof deck of a moored white barge that was strung with balloons and flowers. Beyond the barge, across the river the twinkling skyscrapers seemed to be moving toward them like a hundred tornadoes of light.

Just before they reached the lighthouse she led him round a corner, into a different world, a different time. Behind them was blacktop; here they walked on cobblestones crisscrossed by trolley tracks. Passing under the Brooklyn Bridge, they slithered past the skeletons of old warehouses and rehabbed factories, occupied now by photographers and artists, and filed beneath the Manhattan Bridge, continuing now along silent streets with broken hydrants and pavements overgrown with weeds. They stopped now and then in doorways to kiss and rub against each other, commingling their fluids and scents, till they arrived at a low brick building with arched metal doors, where a crowd of mostly young people were comparing the work of Baraka and Ginsberg. "But neither of them could exist without the jazz poetry of Langston Hughes," a newcomer said. "So y'all better get him up in there."

They paid their five-fifty and climbed a flight of dusty stairs to a third-floor performance space dreamily lit by hundreds of candles fixed in bundles to the chipped and moldy walls. Wading through the tide of dreadheads and baldies they stopped at the bar—two sawhorses and a sheet of ply— and got a lager for her and a stout for him and found a corner in the back, by a window ledge; there she sat with her legs apart and drew him into her private space.

Claiming him completely now she rested against his back,

her chin on his shoulder, knotted her ankles in front of him and chilled. As a kid with yellow glasses freestyled with a three-piece band comprised of turntables, harmonica, and electric guitar, Sylvia wondered if Fire had noticed that she'd answered yes to the question: Do you feel like reading tonight?

Three hours later, at a little after ten, the emcee, a body-builder in carpenter jeans, called her name. As he leaned forward to give her way, Fire asked by puckering his lips, When did all this happen? To which she replied by blowing him a kiss, Wouldn't you like to know.

This is me, she thought, as she made her way to the podium. All around her, hands were fluttering to mark her return. She felt sexy and powerful—a cat among a flock of birds. She felt so natural. Here in this place. With these people. With this man who understood her need to be there. Who could share it with her. Who'd appreciate it. Who could drink a beer with her and sit on a ledge between her legs in a place that smelled of mold, sage, sandalwood, and myrrh.

"Whassup, Brooklyn!" she said, waving her hand in a general salute. "It's so good to be here again, after not taking this stage for . . . what?"—she turned to the emcee—"almost eight months?"—he shook his head—"eight months. But you know how it is. Nine to five and all that.

"This poem is something that I just wrote in my head on my way over here. Maybe some of you won't get it because it's really personal. The title is 'Exile.' "

> *It is wanting to hear the lisp*
> *of the sea, curled on the tongues of passersby.*
> *It is wanting to smell wind, heavy*
> *with rain, wrap itself in the skirts of trees.*
> *It is wanting to see the sun slide*
> *down banana leaves into the thighs of a valley.*
> *It is wanting to taste beads of tamarind*
> *that drop from terraced hillsides.*

It is wanting to feel the pulp of star-apple,
its dark flesh, moist between my hands.
It is, it is wanting you.

The declaration startled them . . . scared them like an accidental discharge from a gun . . . warned them with a sharp report that Russian roulette was not a game for the faint of heart. So when they left, shortly after her performance, they refrained from touching as they retraced their steps past walls and doors still wet with the memory of slow-burning kisses that dribbled like wax. As they passed beneath the bridges, the tremor and hum of traffic was the sound of hot blood rushing through their veins.

"Did you like the music?" she asked, as a police cruiser slowed then continued on its way.

He said yes.

"Is that what you listen to mostly? Hip-hop?"

"I listen to very little of it, actually. But I can dig it."

"Why very little?"

"Hip-hop is the only black music that doesn't have a healthy engagement with women. It's not self-assured when dealing with women. I mean, you can go from funk to blues to afrobeat . . . in black music, even when the lyrics are about heartbreak, the delivery is always from a place of awe, or at most fear, of the feminine—but never hatred. Don't get me wrong, y'know, I still dig it . . . but not to purchase and keep in my personal space. But . . . it's a new music, it will work itself out over time."

"Why d'you think that is? Why're they so angry at women?"

"They're insecure about what it means to be a man. In a culture where manhood is defined by what you own, a youth without money is bound to feel insecure. I mean, men with money have always gotten more than their fair share . . . but the ordinary guy used to be able to pull a girl with sweet talk and nice ways. So to hedge against rejection, ghetto youth get defensive. And it comes out in the music."

She found his perspective wrongheaded, but intriguing nonetheless. Most men she knew did not have opinions. Talking to them was like playing tennis and serving all aces.

"You said this culture defines manhood in terms of what men own—how do *you* define it?"

"Like the bible says, 'As a man thinketh so is he.' Manhood for me is about values, intelligence, courage, and imagination."

"Whadyou mean by values? The term just sounds so . . . I don't know . . . Republican and Jesse Helms and Pat Buchanan."

"Oh yeah . . . alla dat?" He chuckled at her overreaction. "Values for me is a simple thing, treating people like you'd want them to treat your mother."

She patted his waist. He would know the right thing to say, wouldn't he?

They came upon a production crew setting up for a fashion shoot. The models were hankering around the catering table, looking but not eating, their bodies nurtured to emaciation with amphetamines, coke, and cigarettes.

"How much do looks count to you?"

He looked at her. Is she allowing these clothes hangers to make her feel a way?

"As I-nelik once told a woman who was threatening to leave him for a Mr. Body, 'With four months and a personal trainer I could be him. But how long,' he asked her, 'would it take him to be me?' "

Wary of going home, but not willing to admit it, they made a detour at Old Fulton Street and went to sit on the edge of the jetty, their feet dangling over the water that lapped at the pilings and gently tossed the barge, which seemed like an ark now, for all the guests were in twos, paired off against the railing, or dancing to the cover band, a pick-up side of tuxedoed jokers who played everything from Disco-Tex and the Sex-o-Lettes to Basia and the Doors.

"When you get to Oz, Dorothy, will you write to me?" he said of the twinkling skyscrapers on the other bank.

"This does feel strange, doesn't it?" she replied.

"*Good* strange or *bad* strange?"

He was leaning against a mooring post with one leg drawn up toward him, his knee supporting his elbow as he twirled his hair. She was sitting with her legs over the edge and her body turned to the city. Her face, though, which glowed with the sweat of attraction, was turned to him.

"Good strange," she said. "Like wearing Earth shoes for the first time. You just get a whole new idea of what fit means, of what comfort is, and you begin to think of all the shoes in your closet . . . and even the ones you outgrew or threw away . . . and you start to ask questions like, 'How did I wear those for so long? What was I thinking? Can I ever go back to wearing them again?' Do you know what I mean?"

He nodded, hearing in her voice the dirge of a premature decision. It was too early for her to say she wanted this, he thought. Him or his way. She was like Ian in some ways. She needed status and possessions to feel secure. The Earth shoes were a good comparison. Once upon a time they were the rage . . . now they too had been outgrown or thrown away. Time would tell with her. The real test would come when he went away. Would she want him then? Or would she want the life she'd gotten used to? She was lukewarm now, although she thought she was feverish.

She said something that he didn't hear. He looked up, cocking his head interrogatively.

"I said you remind me of Bob Marley," she repeated. "I saw him at the Garden with the Commodores. I'd never seen such charisma in my life. And . . . wow . . . I remember taking a hit off my first joint and thinking, 'Oh shit, I've never wanted to get involved in a concert this way before.' Whenever he would call out, I'd cup my hands over my mouth and scream the loudest. Wo-yoyi. *Wo-yoyi.* Wo-yo-yo-yo-uh. *Wo-yo-yo-yo-uh.* There was a sensuality to him . . . not plain sex appeal . . . but a spiritual magnetism . . . as if he were a shaman . . . as if he had the power to draw people out of themselves into this new space . . . his space, I guess . . . and make them do things they'd always wanted to do or never thought of doing before."

"Bob," Fire said, wondering how this was related to the discussion. She began to hum, and he recognized the bluesy air of "Turn Your Lights Down Low," which the band on the barge was playing now, guiding the ballad with a torch of shimmering guitars.

She turned her body to him and drew her knees in to her chin, wrapping her arms around her shins.

"You look like the picture on *Natty Dread*," she said. Her voice was soft but buzzy like the ripping of damp silk. "The hair is the same . . . not locks . . . but a mantle of Spanish moss. And your nose is similar and your cheekbones . . . they're like fragments of rock. Your eyes are different, though, and your forehead. But especially when you're sleeping, or thinking, the resemblance becomes uncanny."

Her lisp, now that she was getting tired, was becoming more pronounced, investing even the most common words with an erotic sibilance. The mention of sleep aroused in him the memory of her nakedness. And as he thought about watching her through the doorway, he began to undress her with his narrowing eyes, drawing his lids closer so his lashes could coordinate more fluently as his eyes slipped the straps of her dress over her shoulders.

"Did you ever meet him?" she asked.

"Who?"

"Marley. Are you listening to me?"

In his mind she was lying on her back with her legs apart and his tongue was engaging her clitoris. Whispering to it. *How are you? Nice to meet you. Are you shy? Is that why you wear this hood all the time? Here . . . let me help you slip it off. I want to see your face so I can kiss you . . .*

"What are you thinking about?" she asked.

"Yes . . . I'm listening to you."

"What are you smiling about?"

"I'm just having a nice time . . . that's all."

"So . . . did you ever meet Bob Marley?"

He had. Several times. She wanted to know what he was like. Quiet, Fire said. Introspective. Listened more than he talked, and pretended to know less than he did. He didn't like to lose, so he was always good at what he did. Did he have indulgences? None besides women and a beemer . . . not even guitars . . . and the beemer came late. For most of his career he drove a Volkswagen camper or a Bug. Was he a role model? Yeah . . . sure . . . he was roots but cosmopolitan, tough but humble, thrifty but generous, workaholic but laid back. And he didn't take the easy route and go disco; plus he understood love in all its forms—spiritual, fraternal, and romantic. "Forever Loving Jah," "One Love," and "Is This Love?" Oh, by the way, did I-nelik play at the Garden? Yeah, man, he was the guy in the army fatigues on the other side of the drummer from the bass player. The one with the beard all up in his glasses? Same one. Oh, he was the coolest thing that night.

"Could I ask you a favor, Fire?"

"Sure."

"My reggae collection is kinda weak . . . can you suggest a dozen or so CDs to build from?"

"Yeah, man . . . The Wailers, *Catch a Fire*; Bunny Wailer, *Black Heart Man*; Lee Perry, *Super Ape*; Bob Marley and The Wailers, *Babylon by Bus*; Burning Spear, *Marcus Garvey*; Steel Pulse, *True Democracy*; Black Uhuru, *Guess Who's Coming to Dinner*; Third World, *96° in the Shade*; Toots and the Maytals, *Funky Kingston*; Jimmy Cliff, *Wonderful World, Beautiful People*; and the Heptones, *To the Top*. And can you show me your breasts?"

He didn't realize he'd voiced this until she exclaimed in surprise, "Here?"

He looked around—at the people on the barge and the traffic on the street—then looked back at her, the world around him intensified: the lapping water, the driving music, his breathing, Manhattan's glinting lights.

She was biting her lip.

"Come here." His voice was coolly insistent, like a razor.

She'd never been addressed this way before. Or received a request of this nature, much less in a public place.

She slid toward him. She imagined herself leaving behind a silver trail.

His face seductively serene, he reached out and stroked her nose with the magic finger, traced the outline of her lips, dipped it in her mouth like a fountain pen in ink, and made mysterious signs on his face with her saliva. He replaced it in her mouth. She sucked it in with a moan, flaring her lips, collapsing her cheeks around it, playing the role of fellatrix with the emotional truth of a Method actor.

"Come closer," he said. "I want to be near you always."

He opened his legs and she sat between them and placed her thighs outside his and crossed her ankles behind the mooring post. She placed her finger in his mouth and began to feel his tongue transform her tall man into a nub of erectile tissue, wondering, as she felt a shudder in her belly, if her arms would tremble more than her legs if he made her come this way.

Closing her eyes, she imagined her sweat as a film of yellow light, a yellow that was burning into orange now as his tongue investigated then traced the whorls of her fingerprint, the most complicated and privately guarded series of crevices on her body, even more so than the ones around her anus, which, she was thinking, she would surrender to his mouth if he asked.

She grabbed his hair as a wet heat spread from her fingertip. She began to screw his lips now, shoving in deep and backing out slowly, imprinting her knuckles on the walls of his mouth. Then, working slowly, she proceeded to rub her finger around the edge of his lips, teasing him . . . making

him want to grasp it, which he did, pulling her tip to a sweet
spot in the meat of his soft palate; then he moved his jaw in a
slow rub-a-dub, locking into her groove, fusing their sense of
time as the film of light became an iridescent red and the ball
of pressure in her belly, on the verge of rupture now, sought
release through her arteries, causing her arm to stiffen and
tremble, then go numb, then sensate again, then numb again,
as the light around her unwrapped itself from the rest of her
and coiled itself around her arm, compressing itself to her elbow, then her wrist, then over her palm, to the root of her finger where it burst and surged to the tip, showing its electrical
nature by overloading her nervous system and blacking her
out for a second.

He held her tightly, rocking her, whispering her name.
"Sylvia, Sylvia, my darling girl . . . it's okay . . . it's okay."

"Oh fuck," she repeated as he hushed her. "Oh fuck."

When at last she calmed down, she kissed him gingerly
and leaned back on her elbows, not caring who would see, allowing her thighs to fall open. She undid three buttons from
the neck down and peeled away the fabric, exposing first her
cleavage, then her breasts—a pair of droplets with the color
and sheen of virgin olive oil.

"I think it's time to go," she said, directing him to the barge
with her eyes.

He looked up. A couple had their glasses raised in salute.

"Let's go," he said with a smile, "before they ask for an
encore."

She took a bow as they walked away. She had never felt this
sexy in her life.

As they arrived at her house, the pain that had been lying
dormant in her knee began to stir, and she limped slightly as
she moved up the steps. He asked her about it and she told
him that she'd bumped her knee while she was cleaning, not
wanting the story of the fight on the bridge to break apart
their mood.

In the bathroom, which had peach walls and light blue fixtures, she peeled away the floral curtain and sat on the edge of the tub. He knelt between her legs on the mint green tiles and replaced the transparent bandage on her knee, whistling the theme from *M*A*S*H*.

"By the way, Hawkeye, I have more questions."

"Go ahead," he said. "By the way, did you ice it down earlier?"

She hadn't. He went to the kitchen. When he returned she asked him to remind her how he'd met Claire. She'd forgotten, she said. Which was true.

He wasn't sure about her motives though.

"Oh Claire," he began, hoping that she wouldn't delve deeply. Knowing he'd been involved with Claire might color their own affair.

"I met her in Lisbon," he said, studying Sylvia's knee. There was a small cut at the edge of the contusion. "By the way, can I use a piece of your aloe plant?"

She said yes and he returned from the living room with a leaf, which he sliced down the middle, creating two halves that glistened with off-white flesh. He wiped a cotton swab across the meat, dipped it in some hydrogen peroxide, and dabbed the nick.

"I met Claire in Lisbon, remember? I went there to live with Ian after leaving Brazil."

The contact made her wince. He blew on the cut to soothe her, directing soft streams up her thigh.

"And you were painting in Lisbon?"

"No, trying to write a book."

She laughed.

"What's so funny?" he asked, applying the ice now.

The coolness stoked her awareness of the heat between her legs.

"You make writing a book sound like something you just get up . . . and . . . feel like doing . . . and just *do* . . . like mowing the lawn or something."

"Oh, I *never* feel like mowing the lawn," he quipped.

"You know what I mean."

She kneed him in the forehead. He pecked her on the thigh.

"So . . . did you ever finish it? That book?" she asked. She was harboring a smile in the corner of her mouth.

"Yeah."

"Did you ever get it published?"

"No," he told her, reminding himself to pull the manuscript out and revisit it when he got back to Kingston.

He made a monkey face, and she began to laugh and lost her balance, falling in the tub—a bundle of flailing arms and legs. He began to laugh as well.

"Help me up, Fire," she asked, stretching toward him.

"*Mr.* Fire," he replied in an Oxbridge accent.

"Okay . . . *Mr.* Fire, help . . . me . . . up, please."

He was standing now, clasping his hands behind him. "Actually, it's *Sir* Fire."

"Okay . . . *Sir* Fire, help me up, please—why am I even doing this?"

"Because you have no other option. By the way, has anyone ever called you turtle before? Turtle." He placed his index finger across his lips. "Hmmmh, now why did that come to mind."

"I said *Sir*, didn't I?"

He leaned over her with his hands on his knees. "Sorry, I meant *King*. Did I ask you to say *Sir*?"

"Oh . . . I'll show you king," she said, grabbing the edge of the tub to get some leverage. But he was quicker. As she raised herself to come out he turned on the shower and drenched her.

"Bye." He slipped two ice cubes down her dress and chuckled as he left, flipping the light switch and closing the door, leaving her to yell and laugh in the dark.

"Fire . . . Fire . . . you better come back here! Oh you're gonna get it so bad. Revenge is sweetest when cold, y'know. If I were you I'd take mine now. Fire . . . Fire . . . Fire, you *bomboclaat*!"

* * *

They sat in the living room watching television while he dried her hair with a soft white towel, he on the couch and she on the floor between his legs in a light yellow summer dress with a scoop neck and spaghetti straps and buttons down the front to the hem.

She inhaled deeply.

"Do you know what this feels like?" she asked, reaching back to wrap her arms around him.

"Tell me."

"When I was a little girl, I had to spend some time in the hospital because of a breathing problem. And at the hospital I used to make up all these things that I wanted to happen to me, like having a grandmother who would do my hair for me. I had grandparents, obviously, but I never met them. They died before I was born."

She cracked her neck.

"Anyway, when I came home—I was about seven or eight at the time—there was a new family living in the yard. I can't remember where they were from. But now that I think about it, they might have been from Haiti. The grandmother—they were a big clan—was an old woman . . . black like ink, and her back was curled like a question mark. She didn't speak a word of English, didn't speak much at all, and she smoked a pipe nonstop. Gosh—when I think about it now she might have been smoking weed.

"One day my father was struggling with my hair, pulling on my scalp clumsily, trying to loosen my plaits to wash my hair—wow, all this is coming back now—and out of nowhere she just came and took me away from him and led me to the standpipe, pulled the plaits out in no time, and washed my hair for me. Then after that she took me to her back step. She sat first, then she gathered her skirt and put me between her legs and dried my hair for me, and parted it and oiled my scalp with Sulfur 8, and combed my hair with a sparkly comb . . . and brushed it. It was so beautiful. She began to

comb my hair every day. I would just go stand outside her
house and she would call me in with her fingers. And I began
to call her Granny. I would sit with her on her back step every
day without speaking, just sit there motionless while she did
my hair . . ."

"Knowing that if you moved you'd get the back o' the
brush on your leg."

"Oh, but you know it . . . and although she never said it or
showed it in a huggy kinda way I knew she loved me."

"Those old women never tell you they love you."

"Of course not. You just feel it. You know what the feeling
is, Fire? It's the feeling that no matter what you do or turn out
to be in life, good or bad, they will always love you. Their love
is constant. They don't love you for a reason. They love you
because they just love you. They don't know any other way to
feel about you. And if you ask them if they love you they look
at you as if you're an idiot—"

"And if you ask them again they lick you with the brush."

"But you know they love you."

"Do you want me to oil your scalp for you, sweet girl?"

"Hmm-hm."

"Go bring the comb and the oil for Granny. And don't forget the brush. You just might decide to misbehave."

She stayed between his legs when he was through with her
hair, and they sat together watching a rerun of *The Muppet
Show*, which he thought was one of the most brilliant TV
comedies in recent history, along with *Roc*, *Seinfeld*, and *The
Tracey Ullman Show*.

"Hey, Sylvia, you used to watch *Sesame Street*?"

"Yeah."

"I have a question for you."

"Shoot."

"Cookie Monster. What's his story? I mean *Sesame Street*
is educational TV for kids, right? Is he supposed to be like a
special ed monster? Everybody else is articulate. Even Elmo,

and he's only five or so. But grown-ass Cookie has a vocabulary of like nine words and his grammar is all screwed up. 'Me want now cookie eat.' What the hell is that? Really now, what is his story? I mean everyone pretty much knows that Ernie and Bert are a gay couple, but what's up with Cookie?"

"I used to ask the same question," she replied, laughing. "And one day a girl in my class solved the problem. Her name was Shaquina—I'll never forget. Her claim to fame was that her parents used to be Panthers. Now according to her, Cookie was an African monster, that's why he didn't speak English very well. Cause if you checked it out he was the darkest one on the show. But in Africa, she claimed—and she said it all earnest and Cicely Tyson—Cookie was the biggest star on *Sesame Street* . . . bigger than Big Bird, who only went over in America cause he was a blonde."

"Right on!"

"You know what else I used to wonder about?" she asked, enjoying the silliness.

"What?"

"Rastas. Now . . . there's a religious basis for locks, right? So what happens when a dread starts to lose his hair? Does God overlook that, or does it count toward his time in hell?"

"Okay, people who look alike," he said. "Yaphet Kotto and Koko Taylor."

"Morgan Freeman and Jimi Hendrix."

"Snoop Dog and Chuck Berry."

"Denzel Washington and Al Green—"

"No way—"

"Yes, way. Look at the cover of *Let's Stay Together*. Trim up that afro . . ."

He was not convinced.

"Okay, top five rub-up songs of all times."

"What's that?"

"A grind song," he replied, patting her head.

"Of all time?" she asked, turning around and crossing her legs. "No eras or decades or anything? Okay . . . 'Let's Get It

On,' Marvin Gaye; 'Reasons,' Earth, Wind and Fire; 'Me and Mrs. Jones,' Billy Paul; 'For the Love of You', Isley Brothers; and 'Close the Door,' Teddy Pendergrass. Let's hear yours."

" 'Distant Lover,' Marvin Gaye; 'Don't Ask My Neighbor,' the Emotions; 'Sweet Thing,' Chaka Khan . . . and I haffe draw for some reggae now . . . Dennis Brown, 'Your Love's Got a Hold on Me,' and Bob Marley's 'Sun Is Shining.' "

"I didn't know we were including reggae," she said. "Okay, lemme replace 'For the Love of You' with 'Night Nurse' by Gregory Isaacs."

"You should've said this at Club Rio," he replied, narrowing his eyes.

She blew him a kiss. "Everything . . . as you like to say . . . in the fullness of time."

They stayed up after midnight, yapping away like bunk mates at a sleep-away camp, chatting about everything and nothing, erupting without obvious provocation into the raucous laugh of Caribbean peasants and market hucksters—a hand-clapping, leg-flailing, foot-stomping, head-rocking, back-jerking laugh that crouched in their bellies and vaulted through their lips in the form of roars, whines, wails, and rumbles that would have been a true source of embarrassment in different company.

And as the night went on, after they were sure they could really talk about anything without embarrassing either themselves or each other, they ordered a full-house pizza and progressed to higher degrees of outlandishness, rolling on the floor, bouncing off the furniture, banging on the walls, punching the air with their fists, and contorting their faces in visages reminiscent of New Guinean masks.

They switched the brand of humor at will with the intuition that the other would make the transition, like Cuban Americans switching from Spanish to English, or Pippen dishing off blindly to Jordan.

And in the middle of this, as they were both thinking how wonderful it was to be with someone whose interests ranged from Robeson to Robespierre, RuPaul to Romare Bearden, Sylvia looked at Fire, who was down on all fours to illustrate a story about crawling under the school fence to see what he billed as the greatest kung-fu movie ever, *The Snake and Crane Arts of Shaolin,* and fell in love, with a snap, like that.

As soon as it happened, she knew that he knew what she was feeling, that he understood the capacity of the cloud that was seeping out of her mouth and floating over his head, ready to burst and shower him with trust and tenderness and patience and understanding. For he stopped his story and looked up at her, and she could feel him reading her mind, could feel his fingers slipping between the folds of her brain, stretching them apart to view the feelings she had hidden there.

She sat there on the couch and watched him watching her in silence, then reached forward, held him by the chin and pulled him toward her, leaning back, opening her thighs— into whose embrace he fell, his body trembling, like hers, with need and expectation. The lights were on, and the television. They both wanted silence and darkness, but neither was willing to move, to pull away from the other's yielding flesh. They began to chafe against each other, finding crevices and surfaces to move over and under and in between, creating heat like hands being rubbed together over a feast.

Her ears, her nose, her chin, her brows—he studied them, using his tongue as a blind man would a finger, gliding over them slowly . . . pausing . . . retracing . . . then moving forward only when he was sure that he could sketch them in detail from memory. She kissed him as he licked her, dabbing his face as if he'd been in a fight and her lips were a pair of cotton balls soaked in healing oil. She nuzzled his chin, licked his throat, and nibbled his ears before kissing him, consuming his lips hungrily, trailing her fingers through the curls at the back of his head. His tongue searched the walls of her mouth for the soaked-in memories of other men, other kisses, which he tried to cleanse away with hot saliva.

She opened his shirt, peeled it away, and began to lick his shoulders, following trails of salt to his armpits and discovering a musty sharpness like the smell of cloves. Then she took his nipples in her mouth and traced extravagant flourishes on his skin. He stood up and removed his shirt, his eyes twinkling like slices of lime in ginger beer. He had the body of a laborer. Muscular. And hard. His muscles were like crocodile backs in muddy water.

"Tell me," he said, kneeling in front of her and undoing her dress, beginning at the hem, "how do you want me to love you?"

She'd never been asked this before. Had always thought she'd want this. But now she didn't know what to say. Self-pleasure had become such a part of her because of the failings of men.

"Do anything you want," she said. "Explore me . . . teach me about myself."

She let out a gurgle when his hands touched her thighs, gliding steadily toward her hips, shoving before them a thin wave of flesh, which broke over her pelvis. He withdrew his palms to her knees then struck out again, continuing to massage her as he spoke.

"When you touch yourself," he began, "what do you imagine?"

She closed her eyes. "I'm a three-hundred-year-old mahogany table . . . and I'm being polished, and the slightest scratch would ruin my value." She licked her fingers and stroked her belly.

"Okay," he whispered in her navel, "my tongue is a length of silk."

He began with her toes, each one, separately, then worked his way over her instep, around her ankles, over her shins and calves to her knees. He used his hands to wax her breasts as he trailed kisses up her thighs, oiled them with kisses, all the way up to the dampness where they lost a bit of their firmness and became soft, almost chewable—there, in the crevice where the smell of sweat, piss, and feminine lotions combined to make a powerful aphrodisiac. Insinuating his hands beneath her, he took the offer of her upthrust hips and rolled her panties beneath her pelvis. Waiting for him was his supper—what looked like a wet mango with a narrow gash where it had smacked the ground after falling from the tree. Nectar was pooled around the nick. He licked it.

"I like the way you taste," he said as she freed herself into nakedness.

He immersed his face, smearing his cheeks, loving the wetness, inhaling the aroma, peeling away the flesh, exposing the melting pulp to his fervid breath, eating as much for his delight as hers.

As she bucked and trembled, he reached for his condoms, his tongue as fluid as a stream of water.

"Do you want to be inside me?" she asked.

He shook his head, pulled back her legs and tickled the rim of her anus, throwing a vault in her back, causing her limbs to stiffen.

"I want you inside me," she grunted. "But I want to taste you. Will you let me taste you. Fire? Please say you'll let me taste you . . ."

She kissed his torso as it passed her face, then gnawed at the hardness behind his fly, at once excited and afraid of the idea of penetration. She wanted to please him. The excitement came from this—the sweetness of surrender.

She undid his zipper with her teeth as she'd learned from movies, then leaned back a bit to appreciate the size of his wood, a sight as arresting as a *macanudo* clamped in the jaws of a child. She flicked her tongue over the tip as if it were the wheel of a lighter, then rubbed the whole length against her face, over her neck, marveling at its smoothness.

Tightening her lips like a vulva, and maneuvering her jaws to cushion her teeth, she placed a hand on his buttocks and drew him into her mouth, anticipating the fullness of having him all inside her. But he was too big. So she lavished her attention on the head, a scoop of guava sorbet—sucking it, lapping at it, using it to cool the muscles of her tired tongue.

"Let's do it now," she said as she found herself remembering Syd, as she often did while making love. "I'm worried that I might get uptight." He undressed completely and took her to bed. She opened her legs when her skin touched the sea green sheets, and she reached for him, her palms upturned, calling him home.

He cupped her head and stroked her side and began to love her up, his bottom undulating fluidly like a fist directing a pen across a page, the movement subtle, the pressure slight, a grand expression of thought and feeling, like a poem or an essay, or a preliminary sketch for a painting. But still her skin broke out in beads of fear. She began to stiffen beneath him and she asked if he could hold her for a while.

"Are you okay?" he asked.

She explained her anxiety.

"Do you know those stories about heroes slaying dragons?" he asked. She shook her head. "They're metaphors for beating fear. You can't keep running, Sylvia. You have to meet it head on and destroy it. Tonight, sweet girl, if you want, we can fight this one together. Come . . . come here . . . lie on top of me."

She obeyed, hugging him tightly.

"Now," he said, "whenever you're ready, fit yourself around me. There's no hurry, darling girl . . . we have all night."

They lay there for a while, hugging, kissing, fondling, teasing. Then she reached between her buttocks and held him, guiding him to her wetness, feeling the displacement as he steered his way inside her, setting her shores a bit wider.

"See, it's not so bad," he said, kissing her face. "It's not so bad."

She smiled nervously, wincing as she sat upright with her knees on either side of him, her hands pinning his wrists to the bed.

"Now you must ride to meet your dragon," he told her. "Go out there and hunt him down. Close your eyes and listen to me."

She began to bear down on him with more of her weight, her waist stretching and compressing like an accordion, and he began to thrust back, filling her up, cocking his hips and dubbing her up, winding her like a clock. She let his wrists go and grabbed his hair.

"The dragon is near, isn't he?"

"Yes," she said.

"You can see him across the plain. Snorting. You can see his wings and the sun on his scales."

"Yes."

"So ride toward him . . . ride hard."

She dug her heels into the mattress, arched her back, and snapped her hips, pricking him with arrows of sweat. Her moans becoming screams, she drew his hair tighter, holding him on a short rein.

"You can see him now . . . you're up against him now . . . you can't turn back . . ."

"No . . . no . . . but I'm scared."

"Don't worry, I'm with you. If you fall off your horse I will catch you. But you must slay the dragon."

"Oh, fuck, my belly is burning."

"That's the dragon's breath. Come on, Sylvia, you're right on top of him now. I can tell. Take my sword and stab him—plunge it in his heart. Gather all your feelings and deal one deathblow. Stab him. Ram him. Jook the fucker now!"

She eased up and bore down with all her strength and the room turned white and began to spin, and her body was free from weight.

The doorbell chimed, as she floated toward his chest.

"Oh, no," he said, "the pizza man is here."

"Shit, what lousy timing."

"Well, he's not that bad. He could have come a few seconds earlier."

"Forget him. I'm feeling too sweet to get up. Plus I want to hear you call my name when you tremble inside me."

"I know, sweetness, but he's probably some guy from Mexico who supports a whole family from tips. It wouldn't be fair."

"You're right," she said. She sliced her tongue between his thigh and his aching balls, which had not had release in over four months now.

The doorbell chimed again.

"Go," he said. "Hurry. Don't let the man wait like that."

"Okay, Father Teresa," she said with a smile. "I will now go and do God's work."

She threw on a T-shirt and went to get the door. He went to the kitchen for some water.

"Not too much of that," she said, giggling. "Unless you're prepared to work through cramps."

He waved her away. She was still making funny faces when she pressed the buzzer to release the outer door. He headed for the bathroom to urinate, picking up his clothes along the way.

He stood over the toilet and removed the condom, which was fitting him loosely now, flapping about like the wing of a wounded bird. He held it up to the light to check for ruptures, filled it at the sink, checked again, then began to lose the rest of his erection as he considered the larger meaning of this sack—that there used to be a time when making love was about affirming life instead of defying death. He thought about his father. Wondered if he used them. They didn't discuss that sort of thing. Private lives.

He dropped the condom in the toilet. Fuck, he thought, I don't have another one. He hadn't thought that sex would happen this soon. Now he'd have to go to the store. He could ask her—but no, he could not. Whatever she had was for her and the man—that is, if they used them. They'd better. This is fucked up.

And will she tell him about this? he wondered, as he pulled

on his trousers. The urine had not come. And if so, what will it mean for them? What has it meant for her? What does it mean to me, all that has happened in these last few hours? Oh fuck! Phil! I forgot to take him his dinner. I didn't even call. Fuck! Fuck! Fuck!

Would she understand, he wondered, noting the second toothbrush in the holder, if he told her that he was no longer in the mood? Would she take it personally, as some sort of affront to her womanhood, if he said that things had happened too quickly, and that he needed some time to think about what this means, and what, ideally, he would like it to mean?

This is a dangerous space for me, he said to himself. Again he was in love with a woman who was involved with another man.

He looked at his face in the mirrored door of the medicine cabinet. Are you in love? You, with that whitish glaze on your cheeks. Are you in love?

I am.

How do you know this?

The smell of molasses. It's everywhere.

There has to be more than that.

Lemme put it to you this way, I know that I'm in love with her because I know deep down in my heart that if she asked me to be her man right now I'd tell her yes.

Why?

Because I believe we've connected for a reason . . . I can give her a lot of what she needs . . .

Her voice pulled him out of his thoughts.

"Who is it?" she asked, inquiring by rote. Who else could it be but the pizza man?

"Lewis."

Fire sat down on the toilet and held his head in his hands, prepared to lie for her if the man came inside and found him. But what could he say? How would he explain being shirtless in her apartment at—what time was it? He'd taken his watch off. He always did while making love as a rebellion against the idea that sex had objective dimensions.

"Oh . . . what are you doing here?" he heard her say. Her voice was poised between guilt and anger. "Why didn't you call?"

"I was in the neighborhood . . . sort of . . . having some drinks . . . I think I might have had one too many. So I was wondering if I could stay the night."

His voice was timid but taut, as if the meekness was taking effort.

Fire finished dressing quickly, but without panic. The man didn't scare him. But if the man needed a bed, it wouldn't be right to cause the man to be denied. A drunk driver is a danger to himself and others. And in any event . . . he just needed to go . . . to get away from this mix-up and bangarang.

"Who were you having drinks with?" She sounded genuinely curious.

"Why can't you just open the door?" Lewis snapped.

"I didn't know we were still speaking to each other. I still haven't gotten over yesterday, y'know."

"So we have a petty falling out and it's come to this, Sylvia? Jesus Christ!"

"Who were you having drinks with? Don't lie to me."

"Margaret."

"I thought so. Oh, you know I hate that bitch. Are you sleeping with her again?"

"Listen, it's nothing like that. She called me. She's having some problems. And why can't you let me in? Do you have company?"

"Don't be ridiculous . . . listen . . . I was only up to get some water. I'm going back to sleep."

"This is so . . . Listen, I have some stuff for you . . ."

"What is it? Can it fit beneath the door?"

"I guess . . ."

There was a shuffling sound.

"Oh . . . wow . . . thank you." She was deeply touched by whatever it was. But what could it be?

"I heard there was a problem . . . I found them at the house."

"Okay. But I've got to . . . go back to bed."

"Okay . . . and listen . . . I'm really sorry about yesterday. You were right. I should have stood up for you. I love you, Sylvia."

There was silence. Then her voice. Weaker than before.

"Okay . . . but now's not a good time for this."

So this is what it's all about, Fire thought, as her footsteps drew nearer. She and the man had been fighting.

She knocked at the door. He told her to come in. He was slouched on the edge of the tub, his face as rumpled as his clothes. Redolent of sex and sweat, she leaned against the clothes hamper, clutching the envelope with the receipts. She was wearing a sarong now. Nakedness seemed inappropriate.

"I'm very sorry," she said. Her voice was defensive but pleading. "I had no idea that he would come by . . . and . . . I didn't want you to hear all that. I mean, it wasn't fair to you. But the only other choice I had was to let him in. Which I think would've been worse. And why are you dressed? Don't go."

"What can I say," he began, entangling his fingers in his hair. "I shouldn't have even been here." He was speaking more to himself than to her. He was blaming himself for the mess, and edging toward the conclusion that things could only get messier. "You're involved and I should have just left you alone. I shouldn't have forced things so much."

She shifted her weight from leg to leg, her arms folded across her chest.

"I'm a grown woman," she replied. "I can't be forced. I must have wanted it just as much as you or else it wouldn't have happened."

"What is *it*?" he asked without raising his head.

"I . . . don't know."

"What is it you don't know?"

She began to think now. She couldn't sleep with two men—well, not habitually—and in retrospect she shouldn't have allowed this affair to happen. But what to do now? Choose, obviously. But she wasn't prepared for that. If she didn't have a history with either of them, the choice would've been simple. But this was not the case. She wanted one man in her life. That's what she wanted.

"Could you please look at me, Fire? I hate when people speak to me without looking me in the eye."

He looked at her. "What is it that you don't know?" he reiterated.

She looked away. He sucked his teeth.

This is just completely wrong, he thought. It was best for him to go now and pick up the discussion the next day, when both of them had had some time and distance. But still, he was angry—less with her than with himself. And further, he felt clammy. Unlike her, he hadn't showered since that morning.

"I need to bathe," he said. "I feel sticky and miserable. May I have a towel, please?"

She returned from the linen closet with an orange one with white stripes. Her face was rolled tight like a cabbage.

Did showering mean that he was staying? She hoped so. But she was scared to ask. Scared of rejection. And embarrassed. He'd heard her lying. What did he think of that? That she lied all the time? She hoped not. Would he doubt everything she'd told him now . . . about herself and her life?

"Do you have the number for a car service?" he asked. "Or could you tell me how to get home by subway?"

"I'm not chasing you out, y'know."

"I understand that."

She was feeling abandoned now. Which made her angry.

"Is that your usual style?" she asked. Her lips were drawn tightly against her teeth. "To fuck women and leave them?"

"What're you saying?" His voice was still soft and warm.

That irked her. Made her feel as if none of this had mattered.
So she provoked him.

"I'm saying that you feel as if sauntering out of here after
fucking me makes you some kind of hero. You're just like the
rest, aren't you?" Her voice was raised now. "You're a sham,
Fire. How could I have been so dumb—to get involved with a
man I'd met on the street? I knew I shouldn't let you fuck me.
Now you feel you have some kind of power over me. Well
lemme just tell you"—she jammed a finger in his face—"you
don't. Go ahead . . . I'm not about to beg you to stay. You got
what you came for. You only wanted one thing."

He allowed himself to be snide now. "Are you trying to get
a rise out of me? Your ability to do that has diminished exponentially. I think you should desist."

She began to reply, but held back when she felt tears starting. No. She would not cry in front of him. She had her pride.

"I can't believe what I'm hearing," he said. "*I* wanted one
thing? I won't even address that, because we both know that's
ridiculous . . . but let's say for argument's sake that is true.
How many things did *you* want?"

"Let's just drop it, okay? I'll be in the living room if you
need anything."

She left him sitting on the edge of the tub, his face hard.

Fire felt a wave of resentment rise up in him. Sylvia
seemed self-righteous and accusatory. Lumping this in with
the fuzziness of her involvement with Lewis and her feelings
for him made the prospect of getting closer to her less and
less feasible—or desirable. He had planned to ask her about
her relationship with Lewis. After they'd sprayed each other
with their love. Not that he was calculating, but there are
some things that one never risks while dangling on the brink
of a great romance. As a man of experience Fire knew that
nothing prevented a good fall better than firm and reasoned
reflection.

As the water jets buzzed his head, he thought about how

they'd met by chance, how they'd met again by greater coincidence, how he'd pursued her, how she'd resisted, how he'd charmed her, how she'd relented, how he wasn't sure if she knew what she felt for him, how he wasn't sure if she knew what she felt for the man, how *he* knew what he felt for her, and how vulnerable that had left him.

Something had to give.

She was sitting on the couch when he came out of the bathroom. He went to the kitchen for some water. Would she like some? he asked, dropping a wedge of lime in his glass. No, she wouldn't, she said, without looking at him.

He sat next to her on the couch.

"I'm going to take a shower," she said, staring ahead at the TV.

"Okay," he replied.

She didn't move though. She was waiting for someone to say the right thing. Preferably him.

They were inches apart, but their attitudes projected leagues of distance, like black and white riders in a subway car.

"Are you hungry?" she asked, trying to make conversation.

"Not really." He slurped the water.

"Do you want me to call to find out what happened to the pizza man?" She turned halfway toward him.

"I'm not hungry," he said, without looking at her.

This flustered her. This lack of attention. "Well, you were so concerned about him and his family a few minutes ago, I thought you'd want to know."

"Yes, that was a wonderful pie, wasn't it? Pie in the face."

"Do you still want that cab number? I can't find it." She was lying. She was only saying this to give him a path to come to her.

"I'll just take the subway."

She was angry now because he didn't take the opportunity she'd offered. "So you're leaving then?"

"I think it's the best thing."

"Go ahead. Do what you want."

"At least I know what that is."

"And what is it?" she asked quickly.

"I should correct myself. I know what I used to want."

She stomped away to the bathroom and slammed the door. Fire finished his water, washed the glass, and left, as the sound of the shower filled his head like a round of applause.

chapter six

On Monday morning, blades of light slipped through the blinds and slashed her face. Torpid from melancholy, she barely stirred. Fire was gone.

She'd made three calls to his hotel, leaving messages the first two times and discovering with the third that he'd checked out, which saddened her because there was so much that she wanted to tell him. She would not have answered the doorbell if she'd known it was Lewis; she'd wanted Fire to spend the night with her; she was feeling something for him that she had never felt before. But she also needed time to make up her mind because Lewis, after all, had been in her life for a while. They had a history and that had to count for something.

But there was something else that she was feeling, that she would not have said: that it scared her that he could be satisfied with just the basics in life. She aspired to more than that, and had achieved many of her aspirations, and she didn't want to slip, didn't want to be with anyone who she thought might bring her down.

That Lewis was ambitious was not insignificant, she told herself as she dressed for work. What was so wrong, she asked herself, for wanting to be in a relationship with someone who was driven in the same way that she was?

And further, was it pragmatic for her, as a black woman over thirty, a member of the demographic group that was least likely to be married—irrespective of looks, talent, or education—to enter a relationship primarily for love?

She left for work in a pensive mood. Her first stop was accounting, where she dropped off the receipts. Then she dragged herself to an editorial meeting, announcing her arrival with little more than a polite nod to her colleagues assembled around the conference table in Virgil's office.

"Hey, Sylvia, what's the matter?" asked the art director, a fey man in a pink shirt; he had a birdlike face to match his movements.

"Nothing," she replied blankly.

"You need an aspirin?"

"Girlfriend needs some dick," said the travel editor, whose three chins were dusted with four different kinds of doughnut sprinkles.

Virgil entered the room. Smarting from the DeVeaux issue and his on-again crush on Lewis, he opened the meeting by picking on Sylvia.

"What do you think about this idea?" he asked. "A four-page story on ecotourism in the Caribbean? Y'know, the Blue Mountains in Jamaica, the Caroni Swamp in Trinidad, the El Yunque rain forest in Puerto Rico—"

"I think it's great," she said, pretending to be excited. She knew better than to disagree.

"I think it's crap, actually," he replied, lighting a cigar. "Black people don't like nature. It reminds them of cotton fields. Let's feature the all-inclusives. They buy lots of ads."

I need to get out of here, Sylvia said to herself as her colleagues championed Virgil's idea, a story they'd done every January for the last three years.

She began to recede into herself as the meeting dragged on, wondering how she'd come to this. She'd had a sense of mission when she began. She'd actually believed that she could make a difference. Bring in better writers. Develop a global vision. Energize the copy. Galvanize the art direction. Shit, she'd even thought she could be honest about the shortcomings of public figures who happened to be black, or more accurately, light brown.

Searching the faces around her for passion, she found none. Like her, the others were all there for a paycheck. Some of them, she remembered, used to come to meetings with ideas. But that lasted for the first year at most, by which time they learned the rules. If an idea didn't start with Virgil, it was bad. After he'd claimed it, it was good. If an editor cared to debate this, she was bad. After a closed-door session, she was good—or fired.

But for all its drawbacks, the job had perks. A good salary, comp tickets to exclusive events, and a direct connection to the black power movement—leading figures in the arts, entertainment, sports, and business.

And in any event, it would be hard to leave. She'd gotten lax since she'd been there. Why pursue excellence if it wasn't required? So her book of clips was less impressive than when she arrived from *The New York Times Magazine* four years ago. Further, Virgil banned the staff from freelancing, so she hadn't been able to publish work of the highest quality elsewhere. Ideally, she wanted to work for a *Time* or a *Vanity Fair* or a *New Yorker*—a publication where she could stretch out and show true brilliance. Maybe then she'd be motivated to work on her novel.

But then there was something else to consider. If she left black publishing, she would lose stature, not in the larger world of professionals, but in the smaller world defined by race, where her status was inflated because so many talented black people lacked the access needed to gain the qualifications and experience she had. She was like a third-world student with an American engineering degree who can choose between an entry-level job at Bell Atlantic, where she can grow in value and experience, and going home to become Junior Undersecretary for Telecommunications with a villa and a chauffeur and direct responsibility for maintaining the four rotary-dial telephones in a far-flung province.

Which to choose? Satisfaction or status? She was thinking about this when the meeting came to a close.

She called Claire when she got in that evening, suspecting that Fire was there, hoping that he would answer, unsure of what she would say. She paced her room as she dialed, changing from her cream-colored pantsuit to a light brown shift.

She would apologize immediately, she said to herself as the phone rang. Yes, she would do that first . . . then . . . she didn't know . . . she would just—

Claire clicked over from the other line. "Hallo."

"Oh, hi Claire, how are y—"

"Fine, but I can't talk now. I have to rush a friend to the airport. Can I call you back?"

"Oh, which friend is this?" she asked, taking pains to sound disinterested.

"Fire . . . I'm sure you remember Fire. You were flirting with him shamelessly on your doorstep."

"Oh him? Oh, stop, we were just joking around. Tell him I said hi."

She wished for the courage to ask to speak with him. But so many things were rushing through her head. He might accidentally say something to give Claire the idea that they were having, or had had—she wasn't sure—an affair. What would she do then? Their world was so small. Claire knew Ian, Margaret, and Lewis. Margaret and Ian had recently broken up, and according to Fire, she and Phil were together now. That tramp. And of course Margaret and Lewis used to be involved.

"Do you want to tell him yourself?" Claire asked.

"No. It's all right," she replied. "Just tell him Sylvia says hi. Who knows? He's probably forgotten who I am."

She heard him in the background, urging Claire to get off the phone, and began to wonder if he knew with whom Claire was speaking.

"Listen, Sylvia, I'll talk to you later," Claire said. "We have to go, okay?"

He must know for sure now, she thought. In fact he must have raised his voice to make me hear it—to torture me. I opened up to him in ways I've never opened up to Lewis. He knows more than Lewis about my past, my insecurities, my passions, my sexuality. Jesus, how can he not know that I'm sorry?

"Listen . . . Claire . . . could you ask him . . ."

"I really can't talk," Claire said. "We have to go. He's already missed one flight. Bye-bye."

"Okay, but could you tell him that—"

Click.

She sat in silence with the phone against her ear, listening to the dial tone. She was in the kitchen now, sitting on the countertop with her feet on a stool. What if he'd answered the phone, what would she have said?

Would I have told him that I love him and miss him? she thought. She began to hope that she would have. She didn't know. Suddenly she was feeling abandoned, and the hands of the clock on her wall were whittling time like a pocketknife, and there was nothing she could do with the pieces.

book three

chapter seven

Dear My Son,

I hope this leter cachis you in the best of helth. I hold my head and cry when Fire come back an tell me that he see you becus I thout I would go in my grave and not here from my ondly son. I get the money that you sen for me with Fire thank you but Im an old lady I dont have any use for so much. I dont really want for anyting. Fire have me retyred. I have a nice room for myself and he use to kuorrel if I pick up even a pin, but I tell him that I am boring when I dont have nothing to do so I cook and take care of my littl garden. I am trobling with my heart nowaday. Im going on haiti years old now. I can dead anyday so come and look for me. Son rich or poor you are my son no mater what hapen I am glad to see you. My birtday is coming at mont end and Fire ask what I want I tell him my son to come and he say right and ask you. I tell him if you cant get to come then to go to Jerusalem and see were Jesus walk woud be my other wish. As I say I dont have much use for mony so here take back a tosand pounds and by a plane ticket if this can by it and come for my birtday next month in october. If you cant come keep the mony and come another time. I am so glad to fine out your adres to right you. I learn to right a littl bit well now so you will here from me again. And dont tell Fire I send the money for you or he will kuorrel with me. Dont let me die before I see you my son. I will pray for you

that you will fine a nice yung lady to care for you. Fire to.
He need the same. Boat of you are good childran.

—Your mother Gita Bhagwandhat

It was Labor Day. The summer was gone.

Sitting on the edge of the low iron bed, in his illegal conversion in the Brooklyn Navy Yard, shirtless and shoeless,
dressed in a pair of pea green boxers, Ian looked up from his
mother's spidery script into the sheet of silver sky that filled
the windows like wrinkled foil. He withstood the bite of the
glare, vowing not to cry even as the tension in his head began
to buckle his face, deforming it like a hand squeezing water
from a sponge.

On the kitchen counter at the far end of the loft, beyond the
barber chairs and low glass table that marked the den, and the
scuffed floorboards beneath the basketball hoop, the West Indian Day parade—a lava flow of rum-loosened revelers in
fringes, sequins, and feathers—hissed across the TV screen
like the beckoning smile of a femme fatale.

My life has turned to shit, he thought as he placed the letter
on the dresser and looked out the window for Margaret. He
had never in his life felt so vulnerable. For he'd always depended on the strength of others. Since the argument at the
gallery three months ago, he'd withdrawn from Sylvia, and
she hadn't tried to reconnect; Margaret now belonged to Phil;
and he hadn't heard from Fire since the argument about the
watch. Every time he spoke to Claire he felt like confessing
his arrangement with Lewis. So he'd begun to avoid her
as well.

But even with all these people out of his life, he thought,
looking down the street toward the entrance of the sprawling
brick-and-concrete complex, he still didn't want to see his
mother, whom he resented for reasons he'd long recognized
without really understanding. He loathed Miss Gita because
she was East Indian. A coolie. A despised and stereotyped

minority in an overwhelmingly black country. *Coolie.* The word seemed to knock the wind out of him. He leaned against the window ledge, which was wide and trimmed in mauve. The walls were a powder blue and hung with the work of friends, including, over the bed, a Jean-Michel Basquiat portrait of him as a king, in acrylic on hardboard.

In his head he heard the taunts. *Coolie baboo shit pon hot callaloo. Coolie gyal ave white liver. Coolie can tief milk outta coffee. Sixteen coolie weigh one pound. Coolie cyaah dance. Coolie batty flat. Coolie drink dem own piss when dem thirsty.*

Coolie. It was worse than *nigger.* Because even a nigger could call an Indian "coolie" and get away with it. But the black people don't see it that way. They expect you to forget who you are. It's okay to celebrate Diwali because they like to come and eat the food, the curry this and the curry that, and they like to watch you jig to the tabla drum because *coolie cyaah dance* and *coolie gyal wi gi weh pussy once dem get excited.*

Coolie gyal have white liver. Coolie gyal cyaah satisfy nuh matter how hard yuh fuck dem. Coolie gyal mighta likkle but dem big underneat. His own friends used to say these things. Like the nigger in America, the coolie in Jamaica is invisible.

So knowing this, Mama, he thought, as his shadow stained the wall, why you had six children for six different men? Why you never married even one o' dem? Everyone—you included—likes to emphasize that I'm your only son, as if it's the same thing as being your only child. What about your daughters? My sisters? Wha'appen to dem? Dem cyaah help you?

Now that you old everyone sorry for you. But I remember you when you was young and the cyaar man-dem used to draw up a de gate and everybody used to look and point behind your back when you walk past the standpipe in your tight-up dress—which you still used to wear when your ass and your belly start exchanging places.

And being the youngest—remember, you had me at forty-five—I grew up hearing that my sisters, most of whom had left the house by then, was just like you: some white-liver, fucky-fucky coolie gyal. Which is why I used to spend so much time with Fire's old man although him was a faggot. But a faggot better than a whore. Faggots fuck a lot but at least they doan breed.

Mama, you doan know how it feel to walk past a bar and hear a man bawl out, "*Bwai,* call me 'Mister' cause ah coulda be yuh faada."

Now you talking about Jesus and Jerusalem. It easy to turn Christian, eeh? Now that you old and nobody doan want you. Why now, Mama, and not then?

He heard Margaret's key in the front door. He checked his TAG. It was four-fifteen. She'd called a half hour before to say she was leaving. In his mind he followed her from her house to his.

She lived about six blocks away, on South Elliot Avenue, but the six blocks could have easily been sixty miles. Fort Greene Park, a rolling green with tennis courts and a jogging trail, sits between DeKalb and Myrtle Avenues, not so much as a barrier but as a sieve, leaching the rehabbed brownstones and shade trees from the streets that enter it from the south. From DeKalb south to Atlantic, Fort Greene is a historic district of boutiques and cafés. It's the manger of African America's future—the home of acclaimed and emerging figures in music, fine art, and literature. Filmmakers. Architects. Choreographers. And fast-moving corporate executives. Beyond the park, though, is Myrtle Avenue, and the Fort Greene projects, acres of low-rise boxes like a jumbo pack of roach motels; and incorporated storefront Pentecostal churches; and bulletproof Chinese take-out joints; and liquor stores that cash welfare checks; and teenage boys who will enter manhood with the burden of children; and young girls pushing strollers when they should be pushing for a promotion. The Navy Yard, where Ian was waiting, was north of Myrtle, north of the elevated BQE, north of the Brooklyn Correctional Facility, on the northern edge of Fort Greene, on the southern bank of the East River.

The Navy Yard, which was now an asbestos-ridden commercial park, did not allow tenants to live there. But Ian had converted some space into a residence. He needed somewhere to live. And the rent was cheap.

He showed Margaret the letter when she arrived. She sat on the bed. Her hair was pulled away from her face and tied in a knot above her head, a style that drew attention to her eyes. They were dark with thick lashes whose shadows gave the effect of kohl. She was wearing a velvet shirt that he'd given to Phil. She hadn't wanted it when it was his, Ian noted. Brown didn't suit her, she'd said.

The fuck is wrong with her? Wha she a-try say? This thing with Phil is serious? He laughed inside. She'd even tried to cut him off—had said she'd never sleep with him again. But here she was, only weeks beyond her declaration, ready to let off, because Phil didn't know how to slap her despite being taught by the master.

He went to the fridge for a Guinness, asked Margaret what she wanted. She said, without looking up, red wine.

Despite all the mix-up, Ian liked having Phil around. He was jovial and domestic. He cooked and cleaned and washed. Went shopping and ran errands. Without any sort of prompting. He had a nice spirit. And hearing him practice on his trumpet from dawn till noon was indulging in aural sex.

He also liked having Phil around because he gave him access to Margaret. Because of Phil's presence, Margaret visited often, and had even spent a few nights.

Ian pretended to be unaffected by her visits, and he kept out of her way under the guise of giving her some privacy with Phil, although she didn't seem to cherish it. As a matter of fact she tried to outrage him by being openly sexual with Phil.

So Ian was faced with a choice between two hurts—the hurt of seeing Margaret with Phil, and the hurt of losing touch with her altogether. Through Phil, he learned about the goings-on in her life—what she ate, where she went, how she was feeling. And gleaning this information was easy because Phil spoke about Margaret constantly. He adored her.

About a month ago, Phil had made an announcement. He said it very simply: "I'm thinking about living with Margaret." He and Ian were sitting next to each other on the staircase having dinner.

"Why? What appen?" Ian said. "You tink I runnin y'out? Stay as long as you want, man."

"It's not that you're making me uncomfortable or anything," Phil replied. "It's just that I'm thinking of staying in America for a while and I guess I'd need my own place."

Ian heaved a sigh and swallowed. "I mean if you get the Philharmonic gig then you'll be over here for a while, but you can stay here for as long as you need, man," he said, worried about the prospect of losing touch with Margaret.

"I've kinda soured on the Philharmonic, Ian," Phil replied laconically.

"What you mean?"

"I'm not sure if my future is in classical music. Margaret's been suggesting that I start thinking about jazz. She could do things for me, she says . . . open doors . . . She knows a lot of people, being at the station and all."

"Me never know you like jazz all dat much, Phil."

"I do. I've been playing more in the last couple of years . . . but come on, America's where it's at. Not England. New York. Not London."

Ian sucked his teeth.

"Listen," Phil continued. "It's not just about music . . . I *love* Margaret, and I want to stay near her."

"But does she love you?" Ian asked, trying to sow seeds of doubt.

As he thought back to a conversation they'd had that morning, Ian admitted to himself that Phil buttressed his sagging ego. Make me a stud, Phil had asked when he came out of St. Vincent's. And in daily chats and quizzes Ian had been trying to teach him what most men had learned in a lifetime—not really expecting him to learn. He taught him out of arrogance. Even with his help, he thought, Phil could never be as good as him.

After a slow start, Phil learned a lot about sex, got the hang of it—at least in theory—as evidenced by his good scores on Ian's pop quizzes, which came without warning or regard for place. On the train. In the tub. At breakfast. During trumpet practice.

"If you don't want to come too fast, what you must do?" Ian asked one day as he and Phil waited on a supermarket checkout line.

"Is that before or during?" Phil replied.

"Don't answer me back a question wid a question. Before."

"Easy. Jerk off at least twice, at most an hour before you go. It'll take you longer to come the third time."

"Good. What about during?"

"When you feel it coming, look away, don't engage in explicitly sexual talk, and think of yourself pushing your dick in the blades of a fan."

"What if de *poompoom* big?"

"Deep or wide?"

"Don't answer me back a question wid a question. Deep."

"Well . . . if you've got her in missionary, put her legs over your shoulders, grip her by the ass, and raise yourself to a kneeling position. This combination shortens her vagina and allows an extra inch and a half of your dick to get in compared to the basic missionary."

"What if dat don't work?"

"Take her from the back."

"Just from de back? You know how much ways you can fuck a woman from de back, *bwai*? Specify."

"Oh. Let her kneel with her head down flat, like a Muslim at prayer . . . then kneel behind her on one knee with the other foot flat and that knee bent . . . y'know, basically crouching on one knee. Hold her by the waist and work it. It shortens her vagina more than leg-over-shoulder, plus you still get the extra inch and a half."

"What if it's wide?"

"Legs crossed to constrict vagina. Good positions are standing face-to-face, lying face-to-face woman on top."

"Now, quickly. Five rules to live by de first time you fuckin a woman?"

"Always have an extra pack of condoms. Always with the lights on so you can see what you're getting into. Always before dinner, never after—cause it's never worth it on a full stomach. Always do it her way today to improve your chances of getting to do it your way tomorrow. Always do it twice in case tomorrow never comes."

Margaret's voice pulled him out of the reverie. "I think you should go and see your mother."

She turned up the ends of her mouth to seal her opinion, hoping the conversation wouldn't go any further because they'd argued several times about his distance from Miss Gita. She'd said to him quite often that he resented all women because he resented his mother. To which he'd often replied that she was defending her because she was a whore as well.

He was thinking of this now as she began to undress.

Fuck, they would have to be quick, he thought. Phil would be returning from the parade soon. And he didn't want to hurt his feelings. The poor boy was naïve enough to believe that Margaret would be faithful.

"Do you want me to strip for you?" she asked, taking a sip of merlot. She smacked her lips, which were painted a coppery brown.

"We don't have time," he said, feeling bad for Phil momentarily. He was too nice. He didn't deserve this.

He was feeling the heat of her lips from a distance. Those lips, he thought. Those lips.

A few days after she'd said she would never screw him again, she came to see Phil and did everything to get in his way, to rub it in. Walking around half clothed and shit.

As he lay in bed resting, he heard them in the sleeping bay above the kitchen, then on the stairs, then on the bed beside him while he pretended to sleep. He heard her moan. Heard her sigh. Heard her tell Phil to come in her mouth. Heard her slurp and swallow through these same lips.

But he didn't respond. He held it in.

He would break her, he knew. And he had. She'd apologized afterward. By phone and in a letter. But that wasn't the proof he needed. This was it. She was peeling the shirt down to her waist, revealing a white teddy into which her body was poured like a cup of coffee. Her breasts spilled over the top like cream on mugs of cappuccino.

You're such a nasty bitch, he thought. He felt the urge to smack her. Which drove—or was it driven by?—his need for her to hold him and rock him and tell him that she loved him best and not Phil and that he didn't have to worry about Miss Gita, because she would mummy him whenever he needed. As he watched her slide out of the rest of her clothes he found himself comparing the woman he'd first met with the one in front of him, the one with the fleshy hips who was lying top-less on the bed in a transparent G-string, the one whose fatness pulled the spit into his mouth like the breast of a roasted chicken.

It was 1985, Ian remembered. Fire had just moved to London, and he'd begun to make a name for himself. It wasn't a spectacular meeting. He saw her in a Paris metro station, followed her onto the train, and slipped her a drawing that he'd made of her while she stood on the platform—an opening flush that had served him well in the past. Five stops later she

agreed to meet him for dinner. And the next evening he arrived at the restaurant with flowers and high expectations and
met her boyfriend, whom she'd invited. She was from St.
Louis, he discovered over dinner, and her boyfriend from Tal-
lahassee. They were music students at Berklee—she in jazz
piano and he in trumpet—and they were both traveling outside America for the first time. There was an endearing green-
ness to them, a provincialism that he liked because it defined
him as cosmopolitan. So he adopted them for the rest of their
stay, which was three months, and they willingly surrendered
authority. He picked up the tab at meals, took them to galleries and museums, and drove them out to the country in his
Alfa. Then he moved them into his apartment for the last
three weeks because they ran out of money. That's when he
began to spend time with her, because her boyfriend continued to move with a crowd of posey Americans that he'd met at
their hotel.

I've never met a man like you, she used to say all the time.
You know so much, you've done so much and seen so much.
Gosh, Ian, I wanna be like you . . . y'know . . . make money
from my art. She wasn't sure she'd be able to do that, she
would say. She felt she had the talent. But she was afraid of
the cycle of feast and famine. Her father, a pianist who'd
recorded with Gerry Mulligan, had died in obscurity, so she
knew the danger of life on the edge.

I've never met a man like you. Whenever she said this, he
would put his hand on her shoulder, and feel her innocence
drawing the anger from his soul. She created beauty so easily,
he would remark to himself. Even when she played the piano.
Her touch was so light it seemed she barely touched the
keys, as if the keyboard were connected to her fingertips by
invisible lengths of string and creating the lushest melodies
was a simple matter of flexing her knuckles.

Two weeks before she left, he told her over a bottle of wine
in his studio that he thought he was falling in love with her.
What would it take, he asked, for her to love him in return?

Nothing, she said. She was in love with him too, had fallen in love at first sight. It was his eyes, she said. She'd fallen in love with the pain there.

They kissed. It was awkward. Her tongue flapped like a child's excited hello. No, he said, holding her face. Not like so. Like so. And taught her.

Under his guidance they kissed, they touched, undressed, and . . . went no further because, she said, trembling as he mounted her, she was saving herself for marriage. Promise me, she said as she dressed herself quickly, that we will never do this again. And don't mention it ever, she added. Not even to me.

And everything was normal again—until two weeks later, when she was leaving for the States.

They got high together at the going-away party and tried again in the wine cellar. And again, as he tried to penetrate, she began to cry. She was guilty, she said. He tried to reason with her, which made her cry even more, and he became frustrated and stormed away.

Returning to the studio to brood, he caught her boyfriend cotched on a pedestal with a nodding crew cut between his legs, and he went back to find Margaret. The only way to get her for himself, he thought, was to break her heart. He led her to the room feigning innocence and made her open the door. And she ran away screaming.

It took him a while to find her. He drove around looking for her, ashamed of himself and completely in love, wanting to comfort her and beg her to stay with him. He'd never loved like that in his life. Had never loved a woman at all.

He eventually found her in the studio—at two o'clock in the morning, drunk and coked-up, lying on a workbench with her skirt up, giggling then moaning in chemically dulled pain as three of his German acquaintances had their way.

Ian still loved her then.

He loved her until, instead of stopping it as he knew he

should have, he took one look at her luscious thighs and pliant lips and lay on top of her like the others and smothered his love to death. He would always hold her dear. Always have a special affection for her. Always like being close to her. But he could never love her, he told himself, because she was a whore. Since then a part of him always hated Margaret, for he blamed her for his inability to love.

"Come here," she whispered, sliding her panties over her hips.

He glanced up at the TV as he lay down in her softness. How would he explain this to Phil? She locked her ankles round his neck. How would he explain that he and Margaret have a connection that no one else would ever understand?

"Who do you love?" he asked. He wanted to beat her. But mental pain was deeper and more lasting than physical pain, he knew. So he loved her up sweetly, told himself he was an anxious finger slipping into a wedding ring.

Who did she love? Margaret wasn't sure anymore. She'd been with Phil for a couple of months now, and she was falling in love. Not so much with him, but with his innocence, his naïveté, his faith in human goodness—but most of all his acceptance of her as a person. She was thinking now of the first time they'd slept together after the ménage with Ian.

"How is it that you make love so beautifully?" he'd asked as they showered.

"Because I've fucked a lot of men," she replied. She wanted him to understand that it was just a fling. There was a part of her that didn't think she deserved more than that.

"Good," he replied, "because I haven't slept with many women, so maybe you could teach me. I'm quite inexperienced for my age."

After he'd come out of the hospital, she'd told him to come and stay with her until his new audition date. He couldn't afford to fly back to England and return, she knew; she also knew it would be difficult for their relationship to prosper in

Ian's shadow. After a few days, however, her neighbors began to complain about his practicing. So he went back to Ian, without knowing the depth of their history together—he thought that she and Ian were just fuck buddies.

Ian.

The man she lived to please. The man who knew her body like a musician knows his chosen instrument. The man whose touch was so unerring that when she was flat—like now—he could slide his fingers down her spine and bend her back in tune.

"Who do you love?" he asked again.

His eyes were half closed, the skin on his face rumpled like the damp sheets beneath her.

"You," she said, smiling. In her mind her cervix was the head of a talking drum, and he was playing a love song to the gods.

"If you love me, then prove it," he whispered. "Surrender everything. Turn over." He reached for the lubricant. "I want complete surrender."

He was sweet and attentive afterward, wiping her down with a cool, wet towel as she lay on her back hugging herself, her shoulders drawn up to her ears, as if she were afraid that her fluttering legs would propel her body through the open window. He brought her water, and held the back of her head as she cotched herself on her elbows to quench her only remaining thirst, and he kissed her brows as he wiped her lips. Addressing her as "baby," he went to draw her a bath, his brows flexed haughtily after breaking her down with his cock, which was badly chafed but throbbing with excitement after escaping the noose of her anus.

"Is it wrong for me to be doing this?" she asked when he returned. She was sitting up with her legs crossed. There was a sweet burn beneath her.

His arms were splayed on the window ledge. He was pulling

deeply on a Craven "A," jetting blue smoke in the face of the reddening sky.

"What you mean?" he replied without looking around.

"Sleeping with you behind Phil's back. Fucking you again after telling you I didn't want that anymore."

He turned around, his face ablaze with triumph. She gathered the sheets around her to shield herself. Fuck! She'd taken the light in his eyes for compassion. Recognizing her mistake made her angry. Gave her strength. She lay down again, feeling the urge to spit on him.

He sucked his teeth, looked at her and sucked his teeth again, thought she was cowering. Of course you can't look me in the eye, he thought. I've just reminded you of how much you need me, of how you can never be faithful to any man as long as I'm alive. I've got the handle, baby. You've got the blade.

"There's nothing wrong," he said, stonily. "You're a whore. Y'have a whore mentality. You cyaah get away from yourself." He crossed his ankles and flicked some ashes in his palm, trying to appear controlled; then, forming his lips in a kiss to taunt her, he took a sip of smoke to calm his nerves.

"What makes me a whore?" She threw off the sheets and stood in front of him. Naked and afraid, but determined to protect on Phil's behalf the seed of pride within her.

"Because you open your legs for any man," he snapped.

"Call me what you want, Ian, but opening my legs is easier for me than opening my heart. You of all people should understand why."

He crumpled beneath her words—a cornstalk in a shower of hail. "Why *Phil*?" he heard himself say. "What about *me*, Margaret?" His thoughts imploded, sucking in his cheeks and eyes.

"Ian," she replied, "have you ever opened your heart to me?" She jabbed a finger in his face. "Phil has."

"So why are you *here*?" he said, his voice breaking. His hands were at his sides with the palms turned toward her—

ready to catch mercy if it were thrown his way. "Why are you here if he means so much to you?"

"Because I keep hoping that one day you can make me feel like it wouldn't be a risk to open my heart to you," she replied, taking his hands and wrapping them around her waist, holding him now and speaking into his chest, which was bare and smelled of tar and sweat. "But how can I when you call me a whore?" She pulled away and stepped back two paces as she felt herself becoming weak again. "Ian, until you can look me in the eye and tell me you'll respect me . . . and that you'll leave the past alone and judge me by the goodness I always try to show you, I'll remain with Phil. Can you look me in the eye and do that?"

He looked away quickly, scared by what he saw reflected in her pupils—himself, or a version thereof, trying to look at her through different lenses. To humanize her would make it too easy to forgive her. And forgiveness was the first step to redemption. He was afraid of that. It would make him vulnerable. Bitterness had served him well as a strong defense.

"Let this be the last time," he said, walking away from her. There was a gun beneath the bed. In a suitcase. A Ruger nine millimeter. Black handle with chrome barrel. Loaded. Two clips. With fifteen rounds each. "Leave now . . . I'm beginning to fucking hate you."

"This is goodbye," she said. "I hope you know that."

She began to button her shirt. He lit another cigarette and leaned out the window. At the water's edge, giant cranes rusted on thirty-foot legs, hooks dangling from their arms like hands with broken wrists. Was it true? Is this really the last time? As the smoke filled his chest he felt his heart shudder, then spark, then spin. Then it fell through his body in a whining spiral, a helicopter gunship downed by fire.

I made her this way, he said to himself. It's not her fault. He was thinking now of her first return to Paris—of how much she'd changed just a year later. She was worldly and confident. Sexually experienced. They fucked the first night. He wanted to make love but she didn't want to do more than fuck. She told him that. Placed her hand over his mouth and said that, when he told her that he loved her. Love, she said, meant entanglement. Which was why she was single—and would always be. You're a man, she said, when he tried to discuss it . . . you should understand . . . we know how we feel about each other . . . fucking other people shouldn't change that . . . sex is just release . . . so let's be open . . . lies are too hard to live with.

And he accepted this. He had to. He had made her that way.

You don't know how this feels, he thought now as he watched her jam her foot in her shoe.

The best work of his best years had been secretly dedicated to her. He was thinking especially of Seoul now. The Olympics. The commission to create the ornamental friezes for the stadium. Each of the female figures—six hundred and seventy-two of them—had parts that were modeled on hers. Eyelids. Kneecaps. Shoulder blades. Toes. Guilt was a brilliant muse. Fire thought he'd come to America to run down fame. What did he know? But then what had he told him? Nothing. Why add more to his plate, which was already filled up with Blanche. He'd even asked her to marry him—this fucking bitch who was leaving now—and she'd said no. Said some fuckery like, Only if we're allowed to see other people.

And he'd beaten her. Kick way her leg-dem. Siddown pon her chest and pin down her hand-dem. Take out him stiff-up cocky and baton her face. Buss up her lip. Blood up her mout. Swell up her wandering eye.

Then tried to kill himself . . . sucked on a pistol for a half a day, but the bullet wouldn't come.

"Goodbye, Ian."

He looked up from the floorboards. She was on the landing now. Her hands gripped the railing as if she were thinking of vaulting downstairs to get out of his life a bit sooner.

"What should I say to Phil?" he asked.

"That he should pack his things and leave." There was a gun under the bed. Maybe he should pull it out and shoot her.

Ian went out for a walk at about eight o'clock that evening, dressed in black. The Puerto Ricans were out on the sidewalk in their lawn chairs listening to salsa and watching the Mets on their portable TVs. Ian stopped for a little bit with a group outside a bodega and sat on a beer crate and watched part of the game, shaking hands with all the neighborhood folks who came to pay their respects to El Jamaiqueño, whom they hadn't seen in a little while.

He moved on, and walked up Kent Avenue—the foreshore road that runs from Fort Greene up to Long Island City in Queens—through Williamsburg, where the Hasidim scurried out of his way; to Greenpoint, Little Poland, where he stopped in at a bar and shot a round of pool; then on to Astoria, Little Athens, where he had dinner at Uncle George's.

He walked a lot that night, moving in a hunched-over shuffle like a laborer carrying a sack of cement. And he stopped in at many places. Illegal gambling dens. Warehouse raves. Strip clubs. Churches. Crack houses. Poetry readings in performance spaces. Artists' studios. Cafés. Liquor stores. Record shops.

He walked around until he could find nowhere else to go, then walked back home.

It was two A.M. The street was deserted. The lights in the tortilla factory across the street were on, and a few cars were parked along the curb. But there was no sound—at least none that he could hear, because his hearing, like the rest of his senses, had turned inward.

Sitting down heavily on his doorstep, Ian began to think about himself and Margaret, picking up their history at the point when she left Paris.

Margaret had been the reason that he'd moved to the States. He'd kept in touch with her and continued to see her whenever he could, which was about three times a year. Because of what she'd experienced on her last night, Margaret left Paris a changed woman and in very short order had jettisoned Mr. Boyfriend along with all the trust and stability associated with a committed relationship. She neither requested nor expected a commitment from anyone, including Ian. Out of this came the ground rule that permitted—and to a great extent encouraged—openness about their myriad involvements.

At the time, Ian thought he was being cool. But as he sat on his doorstep, thinking about his past with Margaret, he realized that they'd done this to avoid dealing with the wedge that had been driven between them when he'd participated in her violation.

He would fuck her friends. She would fuck his. He would talk about his kinky experiences, she would talk about hers. And over time they succeeded in burying each other beneath the dirt that they shared, creating a thick coat of crusted muck that made it difficult for them to really touch.

Margaret's departure sparked a creative explosion within Ian that set off a chain reaction of commissions, media hype, and skyrocketing prices throughout Europe. Striding confidently between the classical, postmodern, and primitive, Ian was on his way to stardom. What was not known, however, was that all his work—his grand statues in expansive plazas and detailed architectural friezes on public buildings and exquisite accessories in expensive homes—was an attempt to win the love of Margaret Weir. All his work, in his heart, was dedicated to her.

It didn't matter to him that she had never made it as a musician, or that she had made only a minor success of herself in broadcasting. He knew what it felt like to love her, and he wanted to love her again. And he wanted her to love him—at least initially. But once he began to believe that winning her love was futile, he tried not to love her. He decided that it would be a bad thing. Whenever he found himself coming too close to loving her, he intentionally screwed things up. But still, he needed her.

His decision to move to New York came one night when he

attended a party at the Factory—the kind of party where a rum and coke was an unchased drink and some powder, and a girlfriend was more likely to be a friend than a girl, even in those days of shallow relations.

Contrary to his reputation, he was quiet that night. He was just interested in smoking as much herb as he could, and wasn't talking much. Freddie Mercury came over and tried to make conversation, and as they talked, Keith Haring joined them with Sylvester and Diego Peña in tow.

"André Six come yet?" Ian muttered into Diego's ear.

"Why? You wanna see if he should be renamed André Neuf?" Diego replied jokingly.

"I want see who him coming wid," Ian replied flatly.

"You know these models, Ian, they always come with some tired bitch."

As Ian anticipated, André came a few hours later with Margaret. He was doing a lot of work for Calvin Klein then, and Willi Smith. He was tall and big-boned.

Margaret had told him a lot about André—too much, in fact, for too long. For once it seemed as if she was becoming involved above the waist, at least as high as the liver. And he found that threatening.

He had invited her to the party and she had turned him down, saying that André had already invited her.

"Well, I'm asking you now," he insisted.

"But I already told him yes," she replied casually.

"Well, cancel," he commanded.

"I can't," she replied nonchalantly.

"Why?"

"He wouldn't like that."

"So?"

"So he wouldn't like that, and I don't want to hurt his feelings."

"When did feelings begin to count?"

"They count sometimes."

"When do *mine* count?"

"You don't have any."

"But *he* does, right?"

"Yes."

"And I don't?"

"C'mon, Ian, I was joking. Don't tell me you're serious. We've never been like this. It's always been come and go as you please."

"I'm tired of that," he said, stonily.

"Well it suits me fine," she snapped, put off by his insistence.

"Fuck you!"

She laughed to annoy him and walked away.

He watched her and André as they elbowed their way through the crowd. He watched them dance and he watched them kiss, unaware that he was crying until Diego told him discreetly.

And he felt something taking over his body. He called it mischief then, this thing that took him over to a bubble gum machine in a corner . . . this thing that made him insert coin after coin until he got a ring . . . this thing that made him walk up to Margaret and whisper in her ear to meet him in the stairwell . . . this thing that made him stand his ground when she said no.

André was standing next to her, looking on intently as he held her hand and slipped the ten-cent ring on her finger and told her to read his eyes.

"What do you see?" Ian asked.

"Immaturity," Margaret whispered.

"Yes, but that's not it," he whispered back.

"You've got some nerve," she whispered. "You—"

"You're mine, Margaret," he interjected. "And we're leaving. Let's stop pretending. We're special to each other. Let's . . . stop . . . pretending."

He squeezed her hand and pierced her soul with the pins of his eyes, determined to bully her, beg her, bamboozle her—anything to make her leave with him.

He felt it when she relented. It was nothing that she did. He just knew. They were connected that way.

Emboldened by her collapse of will, he turned and walked to the door without so much as a backward glance, then stopped and waited with his arm outstretched behind him . . . waiting . . . a little nervous . . . but waiting . . . willing her to come to heel . . . a little unsure . . . but waiting . . . until he felt her hand in his. And he decided on the spot that he was not going back to Paris.

He had called it mischief then, this thing that made him make that bold move. But as he sat on his stoop thinking about all these moments he began to wonder if this thing was more than that. And the longer he thought about it, the more he was convinced that it was in fact more. And although he had screwed things up back then, it had taught him something. Maybe he needed to make another dramatic move—if it turned out that he really wanted to risk hurting her and himself again.

Ian tried to clear his head, then went inside.

He paused downstairs in the studio. The unsold pieces from the show that Fire had seen were packed up in boxes. Only two of them had sold. What did Fire think? He hadn't said. Which meant something. He started up the stairs. And Miss Gita? Would he go and see her for her birthday? And . . .

Phil was on the phone speaking to Margaret. He was packing. Fuck. How would he be in touch with her now?

Ian stood still in the dark, straining to hear every word. Yes, Phil was leaving. A cab was on its way. He picked up a hammer from a workbench. Tapped it against his palm.

Phil told Margaret to hold on. "Is someone there?" he called out.

Ian didn't answer. He was tapping harder. But he couldn't feel it.

Phil called out again and he grunted a reply.

"Could've lost your life," Phil said when Ian reached the landing. "I've got your gun here."

"Oh yeah?" Ian mumbled. "You have a gun. I have a hammer. But you have something to live for. I don't. I think you luckier than me."

Ian feel asleep with murder on his mind. He heard the voice in his head for the first time. *Kill Margaret. Kill Phil. Kill me.*

chapter eight

Halloween fell on a Monday that year.

Two months after the flight of Fire, Sylvia, committed to writing a page a day, had written a hundred and two pages of a new novel, a love story, set in Jamaica, about a writer who meets a blues singer on vacation and comes to believe they're reincarnated lovers from the days of slavery. The novel on which she'd been working for the past several years was out of her life. Gone. The manuscript bound up with old newspapers and left on the curb with the trash. For trash it was, she'd come to realize. The best novels, she learned, after taking the time to reread the work of Toni Morrison, were not just about skill. They were also about honesty.

The new shape of her consciousness, she knew, was largely the result of her collision with the mind of the man on whom her main character was based. And there were times when she would allow herself to consider that this novel, which came to her slowly but easily, like the dawn with which she rose to write, was not just a piece of fiction but a clever way to engage him without incurring any risks. Being a character in her story, he couldn't walk away from her, he couldn't slip off her screen as easily as he'd slipped out of her life. For she controlled him.

From a distance, by being forced to explore him in order to render him as a character, she began to understand him, began to sympathize with his decision. For she was wrong to have accused him so, to beat him about the head with her own guilt and insecurity. He didn't deserve that. Not after all he'd done. But he should've written, or called. For the first month, she would cry whenever she thought of him. But the process of shaping her emotions into art had helped to heal her. She still thought of him as a person distinct from the character she'd drawn—a left-wing rasta who lived in Brooklyn—but less and less so as she became involved with molding her story.

This didn't happen naturally, this mature objectivity. She was feverish and weak for three days after he left. She went to her doctor, worried that she might have caught an infection, and after several tests and referral to a specialist was told that her symptoms were psychosomatic. She was lovesick.

She couldn't allow this, she told herself, and began to look for reasons to dislike him. She sat up in bed and made a list: He didn't respect her time—he was always late. He didn't respect her privacy—he asked a lot of personal questions and had gone through her things while she slept. He was presumptuous—had come to her house and to New York without calling, just assuming it was a good time for her. And there were so many things that didn't seem to add up or weren't clear. How did he make his living? And what was he *really* doing in England? And there was no proof that he'd actually done those drawings in the book he'd sent her. He could've easily bought it somewhere.

She threw out anything that reminded her of him. His flowers, the vase in which she'd placed them, the book of drawings, even the plates from which he'd eaten and the glasses from which he'd drunk. Even the towel he'd used to dry his body.

Drawn into a Zenlike calm by the meditative ritual of writing at first light, Sylvia began to find a lot of things more bearable—work, for instance. She had begun to accept it as an imperfect situation in an imperfect world. Writing fiction was her calling. She was clear now. She understood this because she was crafting a novel from truth. *Umbra,* she could say now, without wavering or rancor, was just a gig to pay her bills.

Her relationship with Lewis had improved as well. They didn't argue as much, largely, she believed, because she wasn't as tense about work; also, she admitted, she had become more forgiving since the affair with Fire. What had he done, she would ask herself, that could compare with her infraction? Being arrogant? Condescending? Philistine? And even that thing that Ian had told her about in a rambling letter the other day. What drug was Ian on at the time? That thing about their under-the-table deal. It wasn't exactly illegal.

Should she tell Lewis?

Admittedly, she had come to feel more for Lewis in the last month than she had ever felt for him. He had been very kind to her, and attentive, and seemed warmer.

Swaddled in denial, she never asked herself if she was feeling this way about Lewis because she felt abandoned by Fire. She had convinced herself that Fire had been an insignificant dalliance that had almost cost her a valuable relationship. And she shooed away thoughts of him as though they were germ-infested flies.

Lewis would be coming over soon. To pass the time as she waited, she watched the Jets play Cleveland. When a string of commercials interrupted the game she switched channels randomly until CNN grabbed her attention. It was another story on the high proportion of black males in jail or on parole. As she leaned back to absorb the statistics, a follow-up story covered the plight of professional black women in search of partners of equal status. She listened intently as sister after sister produced the same I-got-everything-a-brother-would-want-but-no-brother-to-give-it-to sound bite in different words, accents, and degrees of demonstrated desperation.

When that was over she switched again and got a CNN promo: "Educated. Professional. Good-looking . . . and *very* lonely. Single black females in America."

As she sat quietly considering all this there was a knock at the door.

She knew it was Lewis. He never rang the bell. He'd become adept at slipping inside the front door without being buzzed up.

She opened the door to find him holding flowers and a picnic basket and was overwhelmed by emotion. She took them from him with a smile and hugged him, then pulled him toward her and kissed him on the lips, blessing their first intimate communion in months.

"I guess you're glad to see me," Lewis said as he stepped inside.

"Very," she replied.

She placed the roses in some fresh water in a vase in her bedroom. Then they made a little picnic in the living room and watched the game, wolfing down smoked salmon and chardonnay like hot dogs and beer, while moaning for New York.

At the end of the game, they sat together on the couch. She had a leg thrown over his and he had an arm draped around her shoulders.

"I came to talk seriously," Lewis began. "You know that."

"Yes," she said.

"Sylvia, I love you."

"I know, Lewis," she replied, kissing him on the cheek. He took her face in his hands.

"Sylvia, you mean so much to me," he said. "I want you back in my life. I want us to be together again. I'm not perfect. I know that. And I don't know if you've noticed, but I've been trying my best to win you back. And if I've failed I'll just keep trying harder, because I refuse to let you go. If I have to cry and plead for your sympathy I don't mind, cause you mean so much to me . . ." He couldn't hold a straight face as he recited the lyrics of "Ain't Too Proud to Beg." Sylvia laughed too.

"Lewis," she said, "you're making me laugh too easily nowadays, and that's dangerous."

Lewis chuckled.

"Bottom line though, Sylvia, is, Do you want me back or not?"

"There's something I have to do first before I answer that," she said, thinking about the CNN feature. She got up and went to her bedroom.

Lewis sat nervously until she returned. But he smiled when Sylvia reappeared with the candleholders in her hand.

"Remember these?" she asked.

Lewis nodded wryly.

"They don't mean that much to me," she said, then went outside and threw them in the garbage. Lewis stood at the door watching her. As she ascended the steps he realized that she was crying.

"I'm sorry, Lewis," she said, as he held her close at the doorway. "I hurt you so much. I'm so selfish."

"It's okay, Sylvia. It's okay," he murmured, leading her inside.

As she pressed against him she felt a hard lump against her pelvis.

"Been a while, hasn't it?"

"Like an eternity," he replied sheepishly.

"Come inside the bedroom then. I'll make it up to you."

Lewis kissed her deeply and massaged the mound between her legs as she undid his buckle. Leaning against the wall, she slipped out of her shoes and came to his assistance as he tried to ease her jeans over her hips. She trembled as he touched the waist of her underwear. But before she could savor the sensation his hand was up inside her, his tongue was on her lips, and his penis was on the tips of her fingers.

"Take me to bed, Lewis," she said as she felt herself being lifted off the ground.

Aware that he was in charge of the moment, Lewis laid her down on the bed and took his time as he undressed. Standing in the center of the room, he removed his shirt, undoing just the neck, then hauling the shirt over his head to reveal his muscled torso. She stroked herself beneath the sheets as she watched him. She liked his upper body, the way it rose out of his narrow hips and bloomed into his shoulders . . . the way his chest was bisected by a deep, hard furrow that proceeded down his middle, where it became overgrown by wispy hair.

He turned around and removed his pants. He had a nice ass. The kind that women like to pat and men like to penetrate. Hard. And clamped shut. When he turned back and came to bed, his face was flushed with a look of mischief.

She opened her legs and parted her lips for a kiss, a heat racing through her body as she felt him fumbling around between her thighs, searching for the gateway to her softness.

Then he kissed her and she felt something in her mouth. She was curious. Then startled. It was hard and it had edges and it . . . oh God!

She pulled it out—a three-carat diamond in an antique setting.

"Oh, Lewis," she said. "Lewis, oh, Lewis."

"Will you marry me, Sylvia?"

Delirious from the heat of the moment, she said yes.

He placed the ring on her finger.

"Make love to me," she said, "and wash away the past."

As Lewis poured himself into her, Sylvia felt fire in her heart and between her legs.

Standing backstage at the Blue Note on the cusp of his first New York engagement, Phil fidgeted nervously with his trumpet valves as tenor saxophonist Marshall Davis ran down the number they were about to perform. The gig had come about after some serious arm-twisting on Margaret's part, and Marshall was getting edgy, because Phil seemed unprepared.

"Pabadabbadabbadabbadoobidido, pipideebideebideebideebididee, spaa-rooo-sipsideeeee, deee-deeeeeee," Marshall scatted, his acned face contorted as he reiterated the intro to his signature tune, "Kamikaze," a hard-bop number that was aptly named. "Get it? That's in unison. You and me together.

Then we repeat that phrase, then it's alternating improv for twelve bars each. You and me. I go first, then you. And we just work it like that back and forth till we run outta shit to play. You with me now? Cause you're looking kinda spooked."

"No, I'm fine actually. I'm just thinking of what I'm going to play," Phil replied.

"Don't do that cause you're gonna forget it all when you go up there, and you'll freeze and fuck up and make us look bad. Too much thinking makes your improvisation sound scripted. We're going for that spontaneous feel. We wanna go out on the edge here—throw caution to the wind. Think of a Jap nose-diving in a Zero."

"It appears problematic for you," Phil replied, "and I'm sorry, but I need to think things out in my head first. Sketch them out a bit."

"I can see this shit ain't gonna work," Marshall said, flashing his green-tinted dreadlocks out of his face.

"Well, it's too late for that now, isn't it," Phil said with muted aggression.

Marshall turned to Margaret. "Where'd you get this fucked-up boy from? Coming in here acting like he know everything?"

"Relax, Marshall, everything will be fine," she replied ingratiatingly.

"Fuck relax! We go on in five minutes and this nigger making me nervous."

"I'm clearly not a nigger," Phil retorted.

"So who's a nigger, me?" Marshall replied. "You calling me a nigger, you cracker son of a bitch?"

Margaret jumped in front of Phil as Marshall lunged at him. Phil went to a corner away from the other band members and quietly tamped a cigarette against a chair.

"Marshall, look," Margaret said, primping the lapels of the lanky sax man's double-breasted jacket, "relax, okay? It's only one number. You rehearsed with Phil and you didn't have any problems. You were doing great out there. The crowd's loving you. Now you're on your break and you're gonna go back, and they're gonna love you even more. Now Phil's only coming on for the finale. Can he really spoil all that for you? Marshall Davis? *The* Marshall Davis? I don't think so." She lowered her voice to a whisper. "Look, you're doing me a favor, right, cause I've done some for you. I've had you on the station how many times this year? About four. I put your records in regular rotation. I can stop doing favors."

Marshall took a look over Margaret's shoulder at Phil. "He's smiling like nothing even happened."

"See, Marshall, he's a nice guy. Give him a break already. And listen, I invited those A&R people here to see you. A little thank-you for doing this favor for me."

Marshall's pockmarked face broke into a grin. Margaret stepped out of the way, and Marshall shook Phil's hand and apologized, saying he was a little bit nervous because some A&R people had walked in just before the break. Phil said it was okay and they worked out the number one more time before Marshall returned to the stage.

Margaret walked Marshall downstairs. On her way back to the dressing room, she thought about how important this evening could be for Phil. The A&R people who were giving Marshall the jitters were actually there to see his guest trumpeter. She didn't tell Phil this, because she wanted him to remain calm.

She had been selling Phil diligently and had prepared his look carefully and didn't want his sound to spoil things. In fact she hadn't mentioned his playing much to the record scouts. Not that Phil couldn't play. But she knew from experience that from a record company's point of view Phil had more important attributes in his favor than talent: he was white, from Britain, had a classical background, and lacked a mind of his own. She had worked very hard to set things up. Phone calls here, faxes there, long lunches, phony greetings. Finally, the time was ripe.

On her way back she paused at the top of the stairs and

straightened her dress, a black crêpe mini with a plunging neckline and a single button holding it together in front. She opened the door and entered the smoky room, each step revealing a vista of high thigh. Phil was standing with his back to her, head bowed, shoulders hunched over, sketching his solos vaguely with the trumpet's mute in place. Margaret quietly closed the door behind her, and watched him as he stood oblivious to her in the diffuse light, dressed in a three-button black suit like a mystery man in a fog . . . or a dream . . . or a fantasy . . . or, perhaps, in a smoky elevator at the Factory. As she watched him, she felt a quiver below her belly button as if a pouch had been punctured. She willed the man in the black suit to turn around . . . and close the distance between them . . . and ease away the curtain of her dress . . . and take a peek at her thighs . . . and ease them apart . . . and slip inside her with a thrust that would reach her heart.

Phil turned around and found her staring. He smiled at her, his newly grown mustache framing his mouth.

"Come here," she said, "and touch my legs. Quickly, before they come to get you."

When Marshall summoned him to the stage, Phil bowed politely. Holding his horn primly across his chest, he waited for the applause to drain out of the room, nodded at Marshall and the sidemen, then spoke softly into the microphone.

"Thank you very much, ladies and gentlemen. Margaret Weir, I love you."

The rhythm section cranked up to a blistering pace, the drums slashing a jagged path along which the bass walked in earnest. The piano played a catch-up game, hanging lazily behind, then leapfrogging across great spaces, only to straggle to the back again.

Pabadabbadabbadabbadoobididoo, pipidideebideebidee-bideebididee, spaa-roooo-sipsideeeee, deee-deeeeeee. Unison. Repeat the phrase again.

Marshall launched into a gymnastic solo, sending notes

tumbling and somersaulting and vaulting from his alto sax around the room. At the end of his twelve bars he nodded to Phil.

Phil stepped up to the mike, and as he was about to fill in the middle and edges of his solo sketch he found himself with a blank sheet. So he did what any intelligent musician would have done in such a crisis: he paraphrased Marshall's solo and tried to pass it off as commentary.

He thought fast during Marshall's next turn, but before he was finished he was up again. He stepped up to the mike again, directionless, getting himself in and out of jams guilelessly like a desperate thief on the run in a strange neighborhood, as the pianist lobbed chord changes at his chest, and the drummer stepped up the tempo.

Marshall stepped back to the mike again, announcing his return with a loud honk above the roar of the crowd. Reveling in the fast tempo, he took off on long runs that melted notes into each other, and took sudden dives into deep blues cries, sweat glistening on his wrinkled forehead. He played fast, hard, and reckless, making adventurous shifts like a confident driver with a Porsche on an Alpine road. He careened over chord changes, redlined the tempo, and skidded around turns in the melody. He cocked his sax flamboyantly and rocked his body wildly, bucking and railing like a Pentecostal minister caught up in the spirit.

Phil watched all this in amazement while he tried to sketch something out. But he couldn't concentrate beneath Marshall's barrage.

Taking a glance offstage, Phil saw Margaret's disappointment and blew her a kiss, which she returned feebly. It touched Phil's heart to know that he had let her down, and right then and there he decided that he had to do something to redeem himself. Before he had time to chart what it was, though, he was up again.

Having no idea what he was going to play, Phil took Marshall's advice and played without thinking. And out of his soul oozed Welsh ditties, barroom songs, fugues and arias, bits and pieces of symphonies, themes from BBC programs and Tom Jones hits, and Gregorian chants. He turned them inside out ... upside down ... crushed them and mixed them ... compressed them and extended them ... swallowed some notes, suggested others, warped some this way and others that, and formed them in a bolus that he regurgitated and rammed them down Marshall's throat bar after bar until Marshall called it a night ten minutes later.

"You had me scared a little at first," Marshall said as they made their way upstairs, "but you're all right, Phil. Come sit in with me again sometime."

Margaret took Marshall aside, thanked him for giving Phil a break and revved him up about his performance. After that she got Phil, and they went downstairs.

"You did great," she said.

"Thanks. I almost chucked the whole lot in the beginning though," he replied.

"But you really turned it on in the end, Phil. And it really moved me when you said you loved me in front of everyone."

"But I do."

They stopped at the foot of the stairs and kissed.

"Don't mess up my new suit," Phil said, "it was hard enough straightening it out after you raped me before I went on."

"Wrong. Rape is a crime of violence. That was love."

They went outside to catch a cab. It was freezing and windy. They huddled together in their coats.

Outside, they ran into Sylvia and Lewis, who saw Margaret too late to turn away. She came up to him and said hello, kissing his cheek as a casual greeting.

"This is Phil," Margaret said to Lewis.

"Nice to meet you, Phil," Lewis replied. "And this is Sylvia."

Phil shook her hand firmly.

"Oh, I'm sorry, Sylvia," Margaret said. "I'm forgetting my manners. I forgot to introduce you . . . but I didn't recognize you at first. You look different. Have you gained weight?"

"My hair has grown."

She ran her fingers through it, admitting to herself that this was all quite petty, this need to make it clear it wasn't a weave. The lights of the traffic glinted off the ring.

"Congratulations to the both of you," Margaret said, drawing Phil closer. "When's the big day?"

"We're working on it," Lewis replied. "Next spring. No firm date yet."

As Lewis and Margaret talked about weddings and marriage Phil and Sylvia stood silently.

I'm not jealous, Sylvia thought as she listened to Lewis and Margaret. I'm just doing what any normal person would do. They used to fuck! They know that I know this. So why is she standing so close to him? And why did she have to kiss him? Whatever happened to shaking hands? And this moron she is with, why is he looking at me like that? As if he is afraid of saying something.

"If you don't mind my asking," Phil said, "what's your last name?"

Sylvia told him.

He lowered his voice. "I know the connection."

So did she now. The accent. The pitch.

"Nice to meet you, finally," she said quietly, masking her distress.

"Nice to meet you too," he replied.

They flashed each other embarrassed grins.

Panicked, Sylvia excused herself from Phil, turned to Lewis, and told him she was cold.

Sylvia felt as though a giant fist were gripping her chest. She could hardly breathe. Fucking Phil recognized her. She had done a good job of appearing blasé, she thought. But then she hadn't seen her face.

She didn't speak much on the way home, claiming that she

had a headache. Lewis put on some soft music and told her to recline the seat.

Sylvia's first concern was damage control. She gathered her forces and considered her options. Just do nothing and if it ever comes up with Lewis, deny it, she thought. Naw, because most likely it won't come directly from Phil to Lewis, it's gonna pass through Margaret, and who knows who else *she's* gonna tell, and I don't want people in my business.

Talk to Phil and ask him to keep a secret? Naw, because then that's like admitting to things that Fire might have told him that weren't true. I mean what *does* Phil know? That Fire was interested in me and sent me a package or something? But what if he knows the rest? That might be worse than any lies Fire might've told him. Co-opt Phil? Tell him everything, then . . . naw, he's gonna know too much and he might tell Margaret and . . . naw.

Confess to Lewis? He might understand, if I edit it correctly. Then if he hears anything else I'll deny it. And if he dares to interrogate me I'll deny it down to the ground and threaten to leave him. But then all that might put pressure on the relationship and it might not be worth much after that. Confess to Lewis . . . but only after I get *him* to confess. Maybe I could bring it up in a joking kind of way about his fooling around while we were apart . . . somehow use what I know about him and Margaret to get into it . . . then after he fesses up just say, Well, baby, I understand because I came close too, kinda, but I know it's you I want, and then . . . naw. No matter what, never confess.

Sylvia gradually receded from tactical considerations, partly due to fatigue and partly due to competition for her mental energy from her memories of Fire. Until this evening, she had been comfortable in her belief that she had gotten over him. But now she began to feel unsure, as thoughts of him replaced the tightness in her chest with a tightness of a different kind—instead of suffocation there was the feeling of a zealous embrace.

She saw Fire at her doorstep with the flowers, crouching to console her. At the train station. Dancing at the bar at the Club Rio. Sitting on the bench with her on the Promenade. Kneeling in front of her to mend her knee. Leaning against the phone booth the first time they met. Parting her hair, combing it and brushing it, oiling her scalp like Granny used to do. Touching her body like no man had ever done before, and as no man had done since.

She didn't realize that she was smiling until Lewis asked her what she was smiling about.

"It was nice to have met you," she said softly.

"It was nice to have met you too, Sylvia."

Sylvia began to sing "You Go to My Head," thinking of her wait on the Brooklyn Bridge.

Lewis hummed along, out of tune.

"No," Margaret said, as she leaned against Phil in the cab.

"Yes," Phil insisted.

"No way."

"Yes. Why would I make up something so stupid?"

"I believe you but I can't believe it. Sylvia and Fire?"

"You're not going to tell anyone, now are you?"

"Who's there to tell?"

"C'mon, Margaret, promise."

"Why should I have to, Phil? You can trust me."

"You don't sound sincere."

"I am."

"If I ever found out that you told someone I'd be very upset."

"Lewis would flip if he should ever hear this."

"Look, drop it right now."

"Okay it's dropped."

chapter nine

About two weeks after seeing Margaret and Phil at the Blue Note, Sylvia received a message from a Jane Smith—a familiar name that she couldn't immediately place.

"Did she say what it was about, Boogie?"

"Only that it was important."

Something told Sylvia she should call.

"*Q&A* magazine."

She knew the publication. An oversize, black-and-white arts and culture monthly with lots of one-on-one interviews. It was hugely successful in Britain. The U.S. edition was three years old. They used good writers. Martin Amis. Henry Louis Gates. Wole Soyinka.

"Oh, hi, Sylvia," Jane said when she came on the line. "I'm a little frazzled here, bear with me, darling. Diego Peña referred me to you, by the way."

"Oh, yes, I know Diego very well."

"Well here's the story, darling," Jane continued. "I'd like to talk to you about doing an interview for an upcoming issue. The assigned writer called me last night from rehab, telling me he had to check himself in. God, I didn't even know he was doing heroin. He'd always seemed more cocaine to me. But anyway, I just happened to be speaking with Diego when I got the call. He's gonna be our March cover. And he said I should call you. Said you're absolutely brilliant. What're you doing for lunch today? Do you wanna meet at around say . . . two? I know it's really short notice, but we're running crazy here—there is just so much drama—and I *must* go now. But I *must* talk to you some more."

"Aah . . . lemme check my schedule."

She put the phone down and leaned back in her chair. *Q&A* was the kind of magazine she wanted to write for. But if she took the assignment she'd have to use a pseudonym. "Two sounds good. Where do you want to meet?"

"How about Café Beulah?"

"Café Beulah at two then."

Jane's purple Blahniks swept her into the southern bistro a half hour later than they should have. A fiftyish peroxide blond with short, spiky hair, she had a pale, bony face whose angles weren't softened by horn-rimmed glasses. Wearing a camel-colored smock over black suede leggings, she toted a big leather pouch that contained, among other cargo, bottles of organic vitamins and minerals, and something labeled "Spirit Water," which she explained to be H_2O filtered through the ashes of a long-departed Navajo medicine man.

"It gives you this dramatic flow of energy," she said, taking a swig. "I'd let you try it, darling, but each person's spiritual profile is different and special incantations are said over each bottle before it's shipped—it's special-order, you know—to match your spirit profile. Otherwise, it doesn't work."

Sylvia shook her head and smiled. Even if this didn't work out, she thought, at least she'd have some fun.

Over she-crab soup and vegetarian gumbo, they had a free-ranging conversation about the arts and politics. Jane was quite bright, Sylvia realized. She was a big blues fan. In between flirting with the ephebic waiters she would pat her chest and swoon. "Listen to that. That's Freddie King. He sounds like he's playing your spine." And she didn't place much emphasis on time. Whenever Sylvia tried to loop the conversation to business, Jane would ignore her and ramble on. When Sylvia checked her watch for the seventh time, she dug into her bag for her Nokia.

"Callem and tellem you're lunching. You're an editor. You *must* have long lunches. How else do you show your power?"

Then finally, when the table was cleared, Jane got around to business.

"Okay, here's the drama," Jane began. "You've heard of A. J. Heath, the novelist, haven't you, darling? *The Rudies*? *Miriam*? *Dangling on the Brink of the Edge*?"

She hadn't. But she knew better than to say that.

"Well, he's who we want you to interview. He's really neat and bright. He turned down a Rhodes Scholarship because he said Cecil Rhodes was a racist. He was short-listed for the Booker Prize this year but he didn't win. He should've won though. But I think there's been a backlash against non-British writers. After Rushdie and Okri people started complaining. From talking to you I think the both of you would make a very good interview. It would be five thousand words, at a dollar per word plus expenses. There are basic guidelines for our interviews but our interviewers basically make up their own. We like their personalities to come out as well. And you've got loads. Does it sound like something you'd like?"

"Well . . ." She was hoping Jane wouldn't ask any deeper questions about the work. She knew nothing of British literature.

"I don't mean to rush you," Jane said. "But I do need to know by tomorrow morning."

Sylvia had been a journalist long enough to know she could do this piece—any piece, really—with a good press kit and some research. But as she walked down Park Avenue to Union Square, thinking about her luck, five thousand easy dollars, she cautioned herself about getting excited. If she took the assignment and was discovered, she would lose her job. But this was the kind of assignment that her résumé needed. She was still thinking of moving on—after finishing the new novel, which she estimated would take a year.

I need to call Diego, she thought as she crossed Fourteenth

Street and picked up Broadway. And I need to get copies of those books.

She went to the Strand, a musty used-book store with scuffed wooden floors and shelves and crates packed with books. She found used editions of *Miriam* and *Dangling* in rough condition—hardcover without slipcovers.

She asked a clerk for *The Rudies*.

"Can't keep it in hardcover," he said. His nose was pierced in five places. "We don't get many and when we do they don't last. Try paperback."

She squeezed past the crowd milling around the art books table and went to the paperbacks.

"*Rudies*? We had one today but I think it might be gone. See that trough of books over there? Dig somewhere in there."

She found the book after a difficult search. It was a thick volume, with a porkpie hat and a .38 Special on the cover. She began to read it on the train platform. The gangland epic engrossed her so much that she was almost home before she realized that she was headed in the wrong direction. There was simply no point in returning to her office.

She called in sick and continued reading and taking notes until three A.M., by which time she was sure she wanted to do it. There was an honesty to the writing and an eye for detail that she found compelling. She began to find the author fascinating. What did he look like? All she knew of him was his blurb. So he was Jamaican and had won a Somerset Maugham and a David Higham, two outstanding awards.

Fuck, she would have to lie to get the time off.

She called Diego.

"Hello?"

She didn't answer.

"Hello? . . . Hello? Hello?"

She tried to say something.

"Who the fuck is it? Okay I'm jacking off too, *maricón*.

I'm wearing lace lingerie and I have an ass that's big like Brooklyn—"

"Hi, Diego, how are you? It's me." She sighed heavily.

"Heavy breathing. I knew it had to be some pervert calling me this early in the morning. Lemme go on . . . I got an ass that's big like Brooklyn but I wish it was as big as Sylvia Lucas's ego, because it took her so fucking long, after all the shit we been through, to call me, not to say sorry, but just to say, 'Motherfucker, how you doing?' "

"I'm sorry, Diego," she whispered. She didn't want her voice to crack.

"I love you, *mi hija*."

"I love you too, Diego. I miss you. I'm sorry about everything."

"It's okay. We're all allowed three stupid things in life. That was one. Getting engaged to Lou-Lou was the second—don't ask how I know. And if you're calling to tell me you're not gonna take the assignment, that'll be the third. I worked hard to hook you up. I even licked Jane Smith's lily and I'm allergic to flowers. Come on, fuck it. What're you worried about? *Umbra?* Fuckem. What've they done for you lately, Janet Jackson? Tell them a relative died in Jamaica. They'll give you the time. Whose gonna question a death in the family?"

She began to laugh as he outlined the scenario, using different voices.

"You're right," she said. "I should go. Even if it's just to see what it's like to work at another level again. I owe it to myself."

"Good. Give Jane a call and tell her you're down and give me a call back, okay?"

They stayed on the phone for over an hour when she called him back.

"What're you doing later, by the way?" he asked before hanging up.

"Stay home and read. It's Saturday. Jane's sending over a press kit, so I'll be in."

"Good. I'll bring you breakfast."

He arrived an hour later with juice and croissants. The messenger arrived as soon as he sat down.

"Oh shit . . ."

Diego looked up. Sylvia was shaking.

"What?"

She was sifting through the package on her way back from the door. "Oh shit." Her voice was trembling.

"What's the matter?" he asked.

"I can't take this assignment, Diego. I can't."

"Why?"

"I can't do this."

"Come on, you're a professional."

"You don't understand."

"Well tell me."

She gave him Fire's photograph. "I had an affair with this guy over the summer."

November 10, 19—

Dear Fire,

I need a break from this fucking place. Feel like I losing my mind. I hope you get these lines in time. I'm coming to Jamaica on the twenty-fourth at 3:30. I don't have the flight number. Fuck, how much flight coming from New York at that time? See you then, soon. Mama have a good birthday?

—Ian

chapter ten

Ian paused at the top of the ramp and loosened the neck of his shirt. The sky was a steaming iron, and the hills that backdropped the terminal buildings were wrinkles in a piece of cloth. Kingston hot nuh rass.

As he walked across the tarmac to the gate, and shuffled through the long airless corridor past wilting palms, he reminded himself that this was his country, the place where he was born. But, God, he felt so alien here. How long had it been? Ten years maybe? Fifteen? Did it matter?

He tied his shirt around his head. Sweat ran down his withering frame, stained the waist of his khaki shorts as he tried to adjust to the heat. There was the sense of an air force barracks about the place. As if they designed the place for people who didn't associate flying with comfort. Fuck, if they asked he would volunteer to beautify the place. At least some healthy plants, man. Wasn't this supposed to be paradise? A yucca plant was dying in a planter, slowly turning to ash like a piece of coal. This is what this place can do to you, he thought. Sap your strength and dry you out. That's why the best of us had to run away. Even Bob. They don't appreciate artists here. A voice from behind said, "Move." Without looking, he told it to fuck off.

If I returned, he said to himself, it would be to die. But then, the very act of living here would kill me. He thought about this even more after he went to the bathroom and there was no paper. He had to wipe his ass with his boxers. And when he tried to flush it, the toilet began to grunt and spit and bubble up toward him. Why would a government have people living with such indignity? he thought. Why?

But the indignities weren't over. The immigration officer wouldn't let him in until he spoke some French to prove his passport was valid. He'd never seen a coolie with a French passport, he said. This must be some kinda racket. Look what I have to go through—in my own country, Ian thought. This would never happen in Paris.

Neither would this. He'd walked into baggage claim, which looked like a huge hangar with a carousel. Three flights had come in, and the frustrated passengers were shoving and shouting as if they were ringed around fighting cocks, as if two bloodied birds were spurring each other for the kingship of that mountain of vinyl grips and cardboard boxes.

He circled the crowd cautiously, poised on his toes, ready to pounce at the first opportunity. He saw a crack but before he could move the crowd spat out an old man in a three-piece suit who backpedaled with a carry-on bag in his hand. Ian shook his head and opened a pack of cigarettes. Fuck, he needed a hit. Crack. Heroin. Speed. Something.

Outside, he sat on the curb of the shaded walkway and waited for Fire, assailed by heat and sweat and noise. Taxi? No. Taxi? No, star. Taxi? There was a feel about the place of a bus stop at a market or the waiting room at a country clinic. He looked around. The waiting area for arrivals was over his shoulder—a few plastic chairs in front of a TV set that was hung from the ceiling and encased in iron bars. There weren't enough seats for everyone, but no one complained. Maybe standing gave them the feeling of hanging out.

Fuck, where was Fire? He must've been waiting over an hour now. He wasn't sure. He'd sold his watch. Maybe he should give in to one of the cab drivers. And go where though? He needed a place to stay. Somewhere safe. He had money in his bag for his mother. What did she look like now? He closed his eyes and tried to form her face.

Through the rumble of voices and the grunts of cars he heard his name. He opened his eyes and Fire was standing in front of him, in sandals and cut-off jeans. His gauzy yellow shirt was rolled up over his forearms and open at the neck. And his hair, which was in dreads now, was knotted on top with a leather thong.

"Pussy, where you was?"

The ruffneck greeting made Fire smile. And in the sureness with which he took his hand and pulled him to his feet, Ian knew him again as a brother.

With Fire at the wheel, they set off for home, leaving the flowered parking lot to join the speeding convoy that raced along the single-lane highway down the center of the beach-trimmed peninsula, an overgrown sand spit really, that stuck out from the rest of Kingston like a thumb.

Ian had forgotten about the beauty of the drive. And as the salt spray tickled the hair on his arms, and the sea breeze licked his sun-warmed skin, he was overwhelmed by the sense of space and freedom, and felt the urge to cry. On his left was Kingston harbor, gray water brushed into waves by doting breezes. On his right, undulating sand dunes shimmered against each other like sea-wet nudes arranged for the lens of a dirty magazine.

At Harbour View they shunted left at the roundabout and picked up the Rockfort Road, which slithered between the bay and the scrub-covered hills, a two-lane highway with a grassy median littered with gay pink flowers.

"You know what I like about this drive?" Ian said. "Although Kingston is so near ... well, technically we are in Kingston ... you don't *feel* Kingston. I can't explain it."

They had just passed the cement factory and the flour mills.

"I know what you mean," Fire replied. "I felt the same way when I returned. And after thinking about it I realized I wasn't feeling Kingston, because it's no longer a seaside town. It has evolved, y'know, like fish into amphibians, then reptiles, then mammals. Over the years it's grown away from the docks to the hinterland, to the plains up into the hills."

Ian didn't quite understand what Fire meant. But as they discussed the city's history, Fire pointed the wheels through the deep curve after the oil refinery, and it all became clear. The sea dived away from the land and the hills ran away from the road and the road collapsed its width, and suddenly the expansive Rockfort Road was the rowdy, crowded Windward Road, where goats loitered between overcrowded minibuses, and unemployed youths sat on broken fences, and old women sat on stools in shop piazzas hawking bad fruit and loose cigarettes, and men pushed homemade carts with stuff nobody wanted to buy, and reggae thundered from the speaker boxes set up outside record shops, and people crossed the street against the traffic lights, and the pungent smell of jerk chicken wafted from smoky pans set up in front of the kind of bars where the only mixed drink was rum and water, and the beautiful homes with their shingled roofs and hardwood floors had become ugly tenements, and the memory of the heady days of the sixties when a zoot-suited guy named Bob Marley used to croon at La Parisienne and the Bournemouth Baths, and Desmond Dekker and the Skatalites used to rule up de town had faded along with the hope for better days.

They pulled up to the curb and bought some chicken and a round of stout, then headed north, ascending in a steady incline toward prosperity past the stadium, a small bowl overlooked by grand villas on Beverly Hills, along Old Hope Road, past the old mansions converted to administrative use, up, up past the Sovereign Center, a Miami-style shopping mall where local kids ogle Benetton gear while fine-tuning the mores of the Jamdown mall rat, through the commercial bustle of Liguanea, where it seemed all vehicles were Mitsubishi Monteros or Honda Accords, past the botanical gardens and the two universities, up into the fern-draped foothills of the tall Blue Mountains, along a narrow road that wound along a river valley before forking off through hamlets and switching back across steep, green hillsides dotted with brightly painted houses that from a distance looked like plastic thumbtacks.

At an altitude where the air was crisp like seltzer, and cows outnumbered cars and people, they entered a dirt road and continued uphill through a stand of eucalyptus trees that led them to the house, which was modest in size but well restored.

"Where's Miss Gita?" Ian asked, as he thought about his own living situation.

"Somewhere in the Mediterranean. She and Sarge gone on a cruise for her birthday. She said she wanted to see Jerusalem."

"Sarge is her boyfriend?"

"No, man. Sarge is the foreman. He runs the farm . . . a nice bredda from the area . . . has his own little coffee farm and all that. Nothing going on between them or nothing like that. I just sent him to keep her company and look after her."

"Oh . . . okay . . . when they coming back?"

"About two weeks."

They stepped off the verandah into the empty living room, which felt like a gallery. There was art on the walls but no furniture.

"Is so the whole house stay?" Ian asked.

"No, man. Upstairs set up awright. Everything in the fullness of time, nuh. This place was really a mess when I got it, y'know. Me and Sarge rebuilt a whole lot of it by weself."

Ian looked outside, down the hill.

"You supposed to get a good amounta pussy with a base like this. If these walls could talk, eh?"

"Pussy," Fire replied. "I don't know if I coulda recognize one right now. I'm not really in the head space for that right now, anyway."

"What, you thinking of getting married or something?"

They sat next to each other with their backs against the wall.

"Not now," Fire told him, "or soon. But I'm at the stage now where I could do that. Have a couple of children and all that. Yeah, man."

"How old are we now, Fire?"

"Thirty-three and thirty-seven."

"And we have neither chick nor child."

"Believe it or not."

"I'da love get married, y'know, Fire. I want children and all that ... but ... I guess y'haffe meet the person first, right?"

"But . . . in the fullness of time, nuh."

"Y'ever feel like kill somebody yet?"

"What?"

"Okay, lemme put it to you this way. What it woulda take for you to kill somebody?"

"For me to kill somebody right now? Means, motive, and opportunity. I wouldn't need more than that."

"You take everything for joke, eeh man."

Fire punched him playfully. "Y'hungry? Y'want some food? I steamed some snapper."

"I need to sleep first."

Fire led him to one of the guest rooms, where he was lulled to sleep by the sound of the voice he'd begun to hear in New York. *Kill Margaret. Kill Phil. Kill me.*

They had dinner on the upstairs terrace that evening. Kingston's lights were gems on satin.

"So how you know about this place?" Ian asked.

"I just buck it up one day while I was hiking, and it just stuck in my mind. What it was, I think, was seeing eucalyptus in Jamaica. There's a guy named Butch who owns some cottages over the hill deh"—he pointed with his fork—"and I was staying in one o'dem. When I told him I'd run into the place he told me it was for sale. Later, when I decided to move back, I found out it never sold yet, and I took it. I bought the farm separately. Y'ever think bout coming home, Ian?"

"To live?" Ian buttoned his shirt against the cold . . . tucked his legs beneath him.

"Yeah," Fire said. "To live."

"No way, sah."

"Why not?"

He began to shift around. "*Bwai,* Jamaica just too . . . I don't know"—he didn't want to bring up the Indian thing; he wasn't sure he'd be understood—"inefficient, everything just so . . . nothing works . . . too much crime . . . everything expensive . . . food, clothes. And the price of a car is fucking ridiculous. And the people, man, don't respect artists. As a culture, we don't respect our own."

"I hear you," Fire began slowly. "But if you want to see inefficiency just go to any government office in the States . . . not even that . . . go to a bank. Crime? Come on, Ian, you live in New York. I hear what you saying about food, but if you eat local and earn money in U.S. dollars it's cheap. The pint of freshly squeezed orange juice you pay three dollars for in New York is fifty cents here. Talk about expensive, if you married right now in New York, could you pay a live-in helper to help with the child at home? You can do that here. I can hear you on the car thing. But I don't have a new car. I have the same old one. And when I want a new one I know who to bribe so that I don't pay more than a quarter of the duty. And in any case the duty-dem not high like one time. One time it was a hundred percent of the price of the vehicle. So you had to buy the car twice.

"But I won't lie to you. It took some adjustment. It was hard to leave a place where things work for one where they don't work. I had to put in a water tank because up here water get lock off at least once a day. Then I had to get a generator because y'know how electricity go down here. Then I had to get a cellular phone because it took longer to get a regular phone. Then I had to get a satellite dish because local TV is trash. Even news. You can't believe the news. But the thing that bothered me most, though, was getting a gun. But I'd be stupid not to have one in an isolated area.

"And doing business is another story. For example, y'know why I reach so late for you today? I was waiting for a meeting that didn't happen. There is this bredda named Donovan Mackenzie who works for one of the airlines, and him do some little *bandooloo* on the side. Basically, him use the airline plane-dem to import goods from Miami for resale. I paid him for a washer and dryer about nine months ago and I still don't have them yet. Why? Every day is another excuse. But that is just life on this rock.

"I can't tell you what to do, Ian, but for me Jamaica is the place. I mean I miss London y'know, but when I was there I missed Jamaica. And when the urge take me now, I jump on a plane and go where I feel like go. But this is my base, Ian. This is where I'm rooted. I'm a Jamaican, Ian. Yardie to de *bloodclaat* core. I love stout more than wine. I love cricket more than baseball. I love rice more than pasta. And I love Bob Marley more than Beethoven or Count Basie. I call women I don't know 'darling.' When a fight start I look to throw a stone quicker than a punch. And I think that the fat on a woman batty and hips is a sexy thing that they shouldn't try to lose at the gym."

"Drink to dat one," Ian said, clinking stout bottles with Fire.

Ian and Fire laughed. They sat on the verandah and listened to music, chatting and drinking until sunrise.

Fire set aside a few hours each day to listen to Ian, who had pulled together his doubts about living in Jamaica into a somewhat incoherent political theory, which he labeled Gore-Tech, the central idea of which was that he, Ian Gore, should be benevolent dictator of the island, ably assisted by a cadre of Caribbean technocrats recruited from overseas. To Fire, the point of engaging him was not to indulge his political vision, but rather to steer him into discussions of his youth, their youth, in the hope of locating the exact time and place when he'd begun to resent Miss Gita. He'd given Fire the money that first night, had simply placed the envelope on his lap while they talked. There were no thank-yous or you're-welcomes, yet there was an understanding, as subtle as salt on a strip of beach, that one was sorry and the other forgiving.

By the end of the third day, Fire could get him to talk about adolescence, and for the first time he began to really understand the weight of Ian's class baggage, for none of his reminiscences about the pranks they used to pull, and the girls they used to like, and the parties they used to crash were centered in his own environment. Downtown. The ghetto. Which was strange, because they'd spent a lot of time there, playing soccer on dustbowl fields, and learning to flash ratchet knives, and going to dances at the primary school to dub against the chain-link fence to the heavyweight sounds of Jammy's and Arrow's and Ray Symbolic.

And the stories themselves, of concerts at the Police Officers Club and disco nights at Toppsi, in their lack of detail, sounded like adaptations from the secondhand account of someone else's life, someone distant, a stranger, about whom he didn't care. They didn't have the vividness of adolescent memory. Which was like a stage play. Alive. Expressive. And emotionally engaging.

Had he chosen to forget? Fire would ask himself. Or is he talking about things he thinks I'd remember—the things he thinks I'd value? And what does that say of his impression of me? That I'm a bourgeois? And what does all this say about his impression of himself?

Most of their time was spent apart though. Fire would rise with the light and go running, then make breakfast when he returned; he would eat alone. Ian would come down usually after noon and sketch in the shade of a magnolia tree at the side of the house, while Fire read or listened to music or worked on refining some ideas for a novel. His mind was always active. It had to be. His emotions were safer in a crowd.

One morning, as he was about to do some laundry by hand, Fire went up to Ian's room to look for dirty clothes. He heard him singing in the back and leaned out the window and asked if he had any washing. He said no. On the way down, Fire noticed a sketch pad on the bed. Ian was a master draftsman, so out of a sense of admiration Fire picked up the pad to glance through it, expecting to see landscapes, still lifes, and a few figure studies. The first page took him by surprise. He studied it for a couple of seconds and flipped to the next. To his disquiet it was worse. The entire pad, he discovered, was a meditation on the same idea. He flipped through from end to end again.

Ian was coming. He replaced the pad quickly.

They left the house that afternoon to meet with Donovan at his office in New Kingston, the commercial and cultural hub of the city. A cluster of low-rise buildings in the international style.

Like a lot of local professionals, Fire confided in a whisper as they waited in the reception area, Donovan was not just a professional. He was also an ICI, an informal commercial trader—in short, a higgler. He traded in home appliances. Some traded in car parts. Some stationery. Some clothes. Some jewelry. But something. They would fly to Miami on weekend buying trips with written orders, do business, bribe their way through customs, and get their wares to the buyer at a markup plus a service charge. And after all this the dealers' prices were lower than the prices in the stores. He liked working with Donovan because he had an excellent hookup through the airline. His goods were cleared easily, the turnaround time was short, and he could travel at short notice. Donovan was a prick though, Fire added. Sometimes he tried to fuck you around.

Short and tubby, with a pea-shaped head, Donovan was cruising porn sites when they went in.

"So," he began slowly, after a bit of small talk, "the washer and dryer. There's a slight problem."

Fire tightened his jaw and began to hum. It had been the better part of a year now, and Donovan had already been paid.

"I see the look on your face," Donovan said, toying with his pinkie ring. "I can understand if you're upset. But just sit tight. Everything soon work out."

"What's the problem, exactly?" Fire asked. "Why you fucking me around?"

"Look, there's no need to be out of order. Don't act like you don't know how things are here, man. A million and one things can happen."

He began to lament. If he could get just one tenth of the Jamaicans in the States to return home, he sighed, he could make the country into Singapore or South Korea. All this he said while gesturing grandly. His graduation ring from Miami-Dade Community College glinted.

"Okay, fine, Donovan," Fire said. "A million things can happen, but what *did* happen? I've heard so many different stories from you: It's at the warehouse. It's still in Miami. It's at the warehouse in Miami. You have it here now, but customs is giving you a hard time. Something broke in transit and you have to send it back. C'mon, Donovan, tell me the truth. I'll work it out with you. Just level with me."

Donovan leaned forward in his chair and placed his hands on his desk in his best imitation of earnestness. Fire and Ian leaned forward as well, expecting to hear an apology.

"You're calling me a liar?" Donovan asked, wagging his head slowly. "I can't believe my ears. I go to the Ark of God Pentecostal Church with my wife and three kids every Sunday. When was the last time either of you set foot in a sanctuary?" They didn't answer. "And you have the temerity—in fact the corruptness—to call me a liar? Gentlemen, I am very disappointed, not to mention hurt."

He leaned back in his chair, stared up at the ceiling, and made the sign of the cross while whispering in tongues— "shala-pala-shala-mala"—then leaned forward again.

Fire and Ian looked at each other in disbelief.

Fire threw up his hands in frustration, but Ian continued to argue, jousted with Donovan, wore him down until he confessed.

"Okay, okay, okay," he said. "Somebody else bought them, so I have to bring down another set when I go up again."

"Who?" Fire asked.

"Can't tell you that. Confidential. Just like how I don't discuss your business with other people, I can't discuss other people's business with you."

"Don't give me no confidential fuckery, Donovan. I want to know who has my fucking washer and dryer!"

"Listen, man, get a hold of yourself. Don't raise your voice at me. And is not *your* washer and dryer, is *theirs*. They paid for it!"

"But I gave you the fucking money," Fire shot back.

"But they gave me more." He covered his mouth quickly. He'd said more than he'd meant to.

"Look," he said, "it's fucked up and I'm sorry. Listen, Fire . . . don't let that come between us though y'know, man. Two more weeks and you get it."

Fire narrowed his eyes. Ian got up to go to the bathroom.

"We have to call this meeting over," Donovan said as Ian left. "I have a function to attend at the Pegasus, and I have to leave here now. Call me tomorrow morning and we'll straighten things out. Come on, let's deal with this intelligently. Call me Monday. And Fire, tell you friend to cool it. The man is acting like I'm a tief—like anybody tief like coolie."

Coolie. Fire wanted to break his jaw for that . . . crack his teeth . . . bust his lip . . . spill his blood. The Glock was heavy on his waist. Shoulda gunbutt de fucker fe dat, he thought. Fe diss de man like dat. You cyaah call a man a coolie. No man. Dat nuh right.

Ian returned. "Tell you what," he said. "Just give us back de money then and call it quits."

"What you talking about?" Donovan replied. "A deal is a deal."

"Gi wi back de money now." Ian hammered the desk.

Donovan sucked his teeth.

"Okay, then," Ian said. "We'll come for it next week."

"Can't do that either," Donovan said nervously.

"Why?"

"It's kinda tied up."

"In what?"

"Well . . . I had to give some money to this chick I have."

"So wha appen to de money you get from whoever buy de washer and dryer from you?"

"I gave her that as well."

"Suppose I just kick you in you face right now, Donovan?" Ian asked. His voice was calm but purposeful, as if he were asking the time.

"Are you threatening me?"

"No. I'm just asking a question. Suppose I just kick *you* as an individual in *your* particular face right now? Would you cry? Would you run? Would you try to fight me and get kicked some more? Or would you just go into a drawer somewhere and get the money and hand it over? Tell me, because I don't want to waste a good kick. I mean, instead of kicking you I could kick my nicotine habit." He paused to light up a Craven "A." "So tell me, what will it be? Money or kick-up? Kick-up or money? How many kicks you think de money worth? I think about seventy-nine. What do you think, Fire?"

"Just cool, Ian," Fire said. He was thinking of the sketch pad now.

"You think ah fraid for him?" Donovan said to Fire. "Let him try nuh. I have my connections."

"Donovan, shut you ass before de man mash you down."

Donovan began to mutter to himself while shuffling some papers to show that he wasn't concerned with whatever was on their minds. "Dis likkle coolie bwai feel say . . . cho—"

"Weh you say?" Ian asked. "Is me you calling coolie?"

Donovan sucked his teeth.

And Ian sprang on top of the desk and kicked Donovan in the face.

"Gimme de fucking money, Donovan," Ian whispered as cocked his boot again.

"I don't have it," Donovan said, clutching his broken nose.

"So who have the fucking washer and dryer?" Ian asked, pulling the smoke in deeply.

"Dr. Lewis at the children's hospital," Donovan replied. Blood was splattered on his light blue shirt.

"Good. Make him fix you up."

Fuck, Fire was thinking now. How did it get to this?

At the same time that Ian and Fire were hustling out of Donovan's office, Humphrey Heath was finishing his figure drawing class at the Edna Manley School of Visual Arts. Puffing on his Hoyo de Monterrey Double Corona, he spared some time for the students' questions, then went to have his lunch.

Although he was approaching his seventy-fifth birthday, Mr. Heath was still a handsome man—tall and willowy. His salt-and-pepper hair was swept away from his face in an exuberance of curls, and his white beard clung to his face like ivy on a parish church.

He walked slowly—but lazily rather than feebly—with rounded shoulders and the slight limp that he'd been carrying since the Libyan campaign of 1942. He liked to tell students that he'd been hit by a Mauser slug at El Alamein, but in truth his patella was damaged during a pickup game of cricket in a rearguard supply station.

He sat in the outdoor amphitheater at the drama school and broke off bits of bread with his gnarled hands. A class was rehearsing a play onstage, and when they had a break, the students came to sit with him on the limestone tier. He had been teaching at the school for some twenty-five years and was immensely popular. Budget cuts and arthritis had forced him to reduce his hours, but he could always be found at the school, usually in the center of a group of young artists.

Mr. Heath left the amphitheater after about a half hour, and walked across the campus to the gate, stopping every few yards to talk with the groups of students who called out to him.

He crossed the street and walked on the shady side of Arthur Wint Drive down to Tom Redcam Avenue and sat on a bench in front of the library and smoked another cigar, relaxing in the shade of a poinciana tree as traffic crawled by. He resumed his walk over to the military headquarters at Up Park Camp where he was due for his afternoon scotch with Major Daley. The corporals on duty gave him a mock salute and admitted him without question. He returned their salute jokingly and hitched a ride in a jeep to the major's house, a cream-colored clapboard bungalow with sky blue trim that had been built by the British army in the 1940s.

Damian, the major's six-year-old grandnephew, leaped off the verandah and ran to meet Mr. Heath, who couldn't help smiling on seeing his vigor.

The major admonished Mr. Heath for being late. But being casual about time, like his son, Mr. Heath shrugged his shoulders and asked for his tonic. Soon the maid brought out a decanter of Johnny Walker Black and left the two men to chat and bicker and watch the boy play.

"I saw your Fire the other day," the major remarked. "I was going up to Newcastle and I glimpsed him flying off Mammee River Road. I blew him but I don't think he knew it was me."

"When I look at Damian," Mr. Heath said, "I see Fire. He was such a strong boy. Full of life."

"He's so much like you," the major said. "Loves to talk to people and always late."

Mr. Heath sucked his teeth.

"But it's true. Both of you have no concept of time."

Mr. Heath sucked his teeth again and poured another drink. "You know Ian is here too?" he said ominously.

"No," the major replied.

"I haven't seen him yet, but I spoke to him on the telephone. Maybe he's too embarrassed to come and see me, since he ruined his life in America. I don't know why that boy doesn't come home. What is holding him in America?"

"I don't know," Major Daley replied. "But who cares? Why do you even bother with him? You took in that boy like your son and tried to point him in the right direction. But he's just born to be bad. Listen, some people just come from bad seed."

Mr. Heath shook his head. "Sometimes I'm inclined to believe that bad seed thing," he began. "If Ian is from bad seed, though, is from the mother, not the father. The father was a good man. I don't know . . ."

"Don't even bother," the major said. "You're old now, and Fire and Ian are grown up. Rest."

Mr. Heath took a sip and shook his head.

chapter eleven

Although Sylvia had assured Diego that she wasn't going to change her mind, she called Lewis as soon as she was alone. Without Diego's counsel she began to feel unsure, and she wanted to be able to blame her change of heart on someone else.

She could have called anyone for the second opinion. But Sylvia wanted to discuss things with Lewis because she wanted *him* to give her a reason to stay. After all, he was the one who stood to lose the most if she should see Fire again. Because she knew that even if nothing happened between her and Fire . . . even if all they did was talk . . . even if she never got close enough to his neck to inhale the subtle aroma that clung to his skin . . . she knew she would return to Lewis with less of her belonging to him than when she left.

Since reading through the press kit, she'd begun to feel more intensely for Fire than she ever had. It wasn't that she realized he was *somebody* and not a loafer. The package filled in some of the blanks in his biography, and the knowledge eased her apprehension. From the sheaf of clippings enclosed, she learned a lot about him.

She was very impressed with his work and academic credentials, but what impressed her most of all was that he hadn't used them to attract her; he didn't wear them on his chest like medals, as most men would have. He just approached her like an ordinary guy, just a bredda who liked her off and wanted her to like him off too. And he didn't solicit advertisement from her either. He didn't ask her about her position at *Umbra* or where she went to school; neither did he engage her in name-dropping, although he could have littered a field with names like John Barnes, Derek Walcott, Euzhan Palcy, and Garth Fagan. He just liked *her*. Basic her. Stripped down. Base model without the options. Plain *bullah* cake without even a piece of pear.

Fuck, she was still in love.

Diego had made some good points during their conversation. "How would you feel," he'd asked, "if the shoe was on the other foot and you didn't know how he was feeling about you? And he was involved with somebody else? How would you feel if you were really feeling a connection with a man and then he came and crapped some reality on your little romantic fantasy—you know, like his woman turned up. And then while you were feeling hurt because you realized that the other person was more important than you, he accused you of some stupid shit? How would you react?

"The man was right," he added. "Look whose rock you're wearing." Then he said something that made her feel very small.

"*Mi hija,* your relationship with Lou-Lou is like your relationship with *Umbra*. You are not there because you wanna be. You are there because of status. In both cases you really want to do something else that you're scared of doing because stupid appearances mean too much to you. Ask yourself this question about your man and your job. Do you love them? If you say no, ask yourself why you remain. And if the answer is too embarrassing, you do not have to answer aloud."

They didn't talk about it anymore. Diego left hours later.

Just as she was about to call Lewis, he called her and invited her over for dinner.

As she'd requested, the driver woke her up when the bus reached her stop. A low murmur vibrated through her bones as she alighted on the sidewalk, and she looped her scarf around her head against the cold. She seemed frail as she walked, frail and unsure, her usually confident stride replaced by ginger steps.

Lewis got out of the Range Rover and walked toward her. Greeting her warmly with a hug and kiss, he led her by the hand to the vehicle.

"Are you okay?" he asked, noticing her quietness.

"Yeah . . . kinda," she replied with a forced smile. "I think I'm probably just hungry."

"Well, I cooked," he said. "Poached salmon."

He served dinner in the kitchen of his rambling house, and they sat on stools at a small high table next to a picture window that framed the sundeck and the covered pool. The backyard was professionally landscaped—islands of shrubs in lakes of grass. There were no leaves on the ground.

"How is it?" Lewis asked, pointing at her plate with his fork.

"Good," she replied.

"And the wine?"

"Good."

"It's a cabernet sauvignon from an Argentinean cellar, believe it or not," he said, trying to make conversation.

"Oh."

"You know who turned me on to it? Marlon Gaines. He sorta discovered it when Citibank sent him to Buenos Aires last year." She held her face down as he spoke. "When I tasted it I couldn't believe it was from Argentina . . . actually I didn't know what to expect from Argentina . . . I always choose a French cabernet."

"Yeah. I have noticed that."

"A few California wineries have produced some decent bottles . . . but generally the California wineries are inconsistent."

She wished he would shut up, but he went on and on about the frigging wine. She felt an urge to smack him. Or jab him in the Adam's apple with her fork.

"I think Washington State is going to begin outdoing them soon," he went on. "Look at what Beringer is doing. The first time that I had one of their wines was at this restaurant in Toronto called Jump, greatest place you could ever imagine, right on Bay Street, I think, and the waiter presented us with the wine list, *we* meaning me and Joe Strong, I don't think you know Joe—do you know Joe?—well, whatever, and before I could make a decision, Joe says, 'Bring a bottle of whatever you think goes best with this,' and the waiter brought out this 1989 Beringer cabernet, and I couldn't believe it. So . . . Washington State . . . look out for them."

She didn't answer and they finished dinner in silence. They went to the den and she took a seat in a leather club chair, and he went poking around his Sony ES system.

"Wanna hear some Luther?" he asked as he flipped through his CDs.

"Not really," she replied, tucking her legs beneath her.

They went on like that for a little while, he asking if she wanted to hear something and she saying no.

"Wanna hear the radio, then?"

"Sure."

He pressed the scan button and told her to tell him when she wanted him to stop. She listened disinterestedly for a while as the KEF speakers aired New York's Babylon of beats, accents, and points of view. Then she heard some calypso.

"Yeah, there," she said. It was a low-power college station on the Island. The host was a Bajan kid who talked a lot—too much, in fact—in the rhyming patter that has become the signature of Caribbean radio because of the influence of 1950s American rock 'n' roll deejays.

Sylvia chuckled to herself as she listened, because to her the kid was a recognizable type. Lewis, though, found the kid irritating. The music as well. And after about fifteen minutes he hinted that he wanted a change.

She didn't protest, but it rubbed her the wrong way. So she

decided not to talk about her trip until she was in a better mood, because she didn't want them to have an argument if they happened to disagree.

Sylvia woke up early the next morning after an uneven sleep and lay quietly for a few minutes with her eyes closed, in the position in which she had fallen asleep: prostrate on top of Lewis. As she listened to his heart she wondered how it would sound if she ever told him about Fire. Would it beat faster and faster, then end in a crescendo? Or would it beat slower and slower until it faded into a sizzle like an old 45?

Peeling herself away from Lewis stealthily, she slung a robe around her shoulders and stood in front of a mirror and examined herself: her face, which needed a good ironing . . . the archipelago of hickeys across her breasts and shoulders . . . the crusted semen in her belly button. She looked a mess. As she considered her reflection—the Fezza silk robe, the diamond ring she couldn't have afforded, the background of bedroom as large as her childhood home—and listened to the satiated breathing of a man she didn't love, tears began to spill over the rims of her eyelids and run down her cheek. She went downstairs to the kitchen and made a pot of coffee, gathered the Sunday *Times*, and went to the den. She reclined on a divan to read the paper, but try as she might she couldn't get comfortable. After shifting and stirring in vain, she went to lie on the thick Berber rug in the middle of the room and switched on the television.

She soon abandoned the rug for the sectional. When the TV began to bore her she switched on the stereo. She put on a gospel station and went back to the couch and tried to relax, rearranging herself diligently, trying to feel comfortable in her own skin.

chapter twelve

Donovan filed a criminal charge, and the following morning, two detectives came to the house in a battered white Corolla. They parked beneath a tamarind tree, and as Fire watched from an upstairs window, the driver, a meager man in a Lakers vest, slung an M16 across his chest, slipped on a pair of wraparound sunshades, and paused to light a cigarette. Soon the car began to pitch and roll, and his partner, a grossly fat man in a red shell suit, gripped the roof and pulled himself to his feet. He reached into the car for an Uzi and then led the way to the door.

Fire felt the wad of bills in his pocket as he went downstairs to meet his guests. The pendulous moral weight of the bribe—a thousand U.S. dollars—made him feel unbalanced. Of all the adjustments he'd been forced to make since moving back to Jamaica, bribery was the one that bothered him most. It was a form of theft. More important, it outraged his sense of social justice, for bribery, in his opinion, was a tax against the poor.

This is shit, he thought, as he opened the door. What does this say about me . . . the socialist . . . the one who all his life has railed against class privilege . . . the one who refused a Rhodes because it was named for an imperialist . . . the one who spent three glorious years in Cuba? Ian committed a violent crime, and he's a violent man . . . has always been that way. And although I will defend myself—I'm a man of peace. Poor people in Jamaica routinely go to jail for things

like this. Why should Ian be any different? Because I am his
friend? Because I have money? I was raised to defend the innocent. Not the guilty.

This is shit, he told himself as he offered the men some
drinks.

They sat on varnished wicker chairs around the breakfast
table, an inlaid door from a Cuban church, and talked
over Chivas Regal—scotch, they said, was their drink of
choice . . . they drank only the best. The request for the
money would not come directly, Fire knew, so he was neither
relieved nor misled when the slim one began to bemoan the
officer's life—the low pay, the poor conditions, the rotten
public image.

They were misunderstood, the man said. It was not that
they were cruel; it was just that Jamaican people cooperated
only out of fear.

"You really think so?" Fire asked, trying to get a sense
of him.

"Yeah, man. Jamaican people have a warrior heart. They
born to hate authority. And American journalists don't understand this, so they come down here and write a whole heapa
things bout how Jamaican police wicked. But what about
the people? I deal with them on the road every day. Them
wickeder than we." Then, as his partner followed him in lay-
ing his rifle on the table—a warning disguised as goodwill—
he asked, "If New York send fifty of their police out here and
we send fifty of our police up there, what you think would
happen?" Before Fire could answer he said, "Our gunmen
would kill their fifty out here because they wouldn't fraida
dem. And our fifty would go to jail up there because they
woulda beat and manhandle the people dem and kill anyone
they catch with a illegal gun."

Understanding this for what it was—a threat in thin
disguise—Fire responded with a threat of his own. Pretending to lean forward to refill his glass, he snatched his Glock

from the small of his back and laid it between the police-men's guns.

"Just want you to know I'm armed," he said. "A lot of tragedies arise from confusion." He leaned back and watched as they placed their weapons across their laps, their eyes blinking busily like lamps flashing an urgent message: Help, this will not be easy. He's more streetwise than he seems.

"I know y'have a license," the slim one said. "You really wouldn't diss we da way deh. You smarter dan dat."

"You're the boss," Fire replied. "If you say I have a license, then I have a license. If you say I don't have one, then I don't have one." Steering the conversation to Ian's charges, he went on, "What you say carries a lot of weight, which is why it's important that we"—he turned to the fat one to include him—"agree on what you are going to say when you get back to the station. The stakes are very high . . . as, I assume, will be the cost."

"You realize this is a serious thing," the fat one said. "Your friend could go to jail for a very long time. The court-dem back up bad as you know. It could take a long time before him case get call . . . months. And ah know him as a farriner not used to the conditions we have down here. I hear up in America where him come from dem have toilet in jail for prisoner. Down here we have shit bucket, and we doan have TV, and prisoners have no rights. Anything could happen to him in there." He took a sip of the whisky, closed his eyes, and swallowed. "That would be a tragic thing. But"—he glanced at the slim one—"we like how you flex, so we'll try and work out a ting. And as you know, if you don't help the police then the police cyaah help you." He rubbed his hands together. "So where im is, by the way?"

"I don't know," Fire said. Ian was upstairs. "I haven't heard from him since yesterday. So what should I tell him . . . in case I hear from him . . . that the police came and didn't see him and will continue their search elsewhere?"

The answer piqued the fat one's love of games. He reached

into his pocket for a copy of the *Gleaner* and unrolled it on the table. Beneath the headline AIRING DIRTY LAUNDRY were pictures of Fire and Ian. For Fire there was a publicity shot, for Ian the picture from the cover of *Time*.

Less patient than his partner, the slim one cleared his throat and placed his hands behind his head. "Tell him to turn in himself," he bluffed. His teeth were chipped like old dominoes. "If we decide fe look fe him, him mightn't reach the station."

"Anything," the fat one added, "can happen on the road." His overeagerness suggested desperation.

Fire placed his elbows on the table and cotched his chin on his knuckles. The arrogant casualness of the threat had sparked his indignation, and in a moment of anger he allowed himself to rationalize Ian's behavior. Fuck the police, he thought. There is only one side, the side of my friend. Fire decided to exercise the power of his family name as he'd never done before. He would call the commissioner's office and have the charges dropped. These fuckers sitting before him would not get a dime.

"What d'you mean that anything can happen?" he challenged. He heard in his voice the return of an accent he'd worked so hard to unlearn, the near-British cadence of old Jamaica, the vowels forming high in the back of the mouth, the lips barely moving. This was the voice of the legendary barristers and parliamentarians—of more than money. It was the voice of breeding, of people with family names like Manley, Hart, Matalon, Desnoes, Ashenheim, Issa, and Blackwell.

And for a moment the men couldn't reply . . . didn't feel they had the right. Then the fat one spoke, in a timid voice. "He didn't mean it no way, boss."

Fire turned his stare on the slim one, demanding without words a prompt explanation.

"I said what I have to say," he muttered, trying to sound defiant.

"And what is that supposed to mean?"

"That the road is dangerous . . . that's all. Nutten more than that."

"Let me tell you something," Fire said, rising. "You don't want the kind of trouble I can bring to your insignificant life. Considering who my family is, you don't want that at all." He held his fist in front of his chest and cracked his knuckles one at a time. "This is what you will do. You will go back to your station and say you searched as best as you could but you didn't find that man. You'll say you will keep on looking, but you won't. And you will never mention this conversation to anyone. Also, and I really can't stress this enough, you will never return to this house again; neither will you call me." He paused as he heard Ian coming down the stairs. To Ian he said: "Come and have a drink." As Ian swigged from the bottle, Fire said to the policemen: "Go now."

As they looked at each other, not knowing what to say, Fire was bubbling with anger. There was no pleasure in bringing this charade to its rightful conclusion.

"Time to go," the fat one said.

"Thanks for the drinks, boss," the slim one said.

Fire walked them past Ian to the door. As he watched them drive away, he felt the wad of money in his pocket grow heavier.

When he returned to the kitchen, he washed up the glasses and sat at the table. There, with his legs crossed, a glass of water in his hand, he called the commissioner's office. He was assured that everything would be fine. How? he asked, and there was silence. He puzzled a moment and then he remembered where he was—in Jamaica, people of privilege do not consider details. Details are for minions and fools.

Fire felt strange when he hung up the phone—oddly weak when he should be feeling potent. Taking a sip of water, he leaned back in the chair and closed his eyes to clear his head, opening them to see the chessboard pattern of the coffered ceiling, a pattern mirrored on a smaller scale in the terra-cotta floor. With his poet's eye, he saw in this a metaphor: life is a game of luck. Some people are pawns and some are kings.

Who decides which we will become? The answer came quickly—fate.

He took off his shoes and placed his feet up on a chair and reflected on his life. Although his family had some money and he'd been left a small inheritance by his grandfather, he'd made it on his own. He'd worked hard, first as a painter, then later as a writer, and, with the recent sale of the house in London, he was now independently wealthy by Jamaican standards. With few indulgences beyond travel, books, and music he wouldn't have to work for the rest of his life. So in a material sense, he'd made it on his own. But had he done so in more important ways?

How much of my love of adventure is the result of my class privilege? he began to wonder. Or the ease with which I endured hard living while I pursued my art? How would I be different if I had had Ian's parents? How much like Ian would I be? In his head he heard a term he'd used at university— lucky sperm. These were kids who were accepted because their parents were alumni. He'd won an academic scholarship. But in many ways, he was admitting now, he was a lucky sperm. His father was a well-regarded painter. His mother's family owned a large estate. Michael Manley was his godfather. And through I-nelik he'd become friends with Marley.

Fire began to consider now how hard he would have had to work to be a failure. He had always assumed success because he'd been given the tools to succeed, so he'd never worried. Never felt intimidated by life. At Yale he'd been aware of the whiteness of the place, but his blackness and his sense of worth had been so deeply ingrained at home that he felt no sort of pressure to fit in, to stand out, or to prove any points. He realized now that this ability to be himself and love himself was something he'd taken for granted.

As he reexamined himself he thought of Ian, and then

Sylvia. And he began to feel, more than comprehend intellectually, her insecurities and fears. Sylvia was not the one who was out of step. It was him, for he was a privileged romantic in a competitive world barely open to black artists. He wanted to see her now, to apologize for his arrogance, for disappearing without saying goodbye. To hold her face and say, Sweet girl, I am sorry.

Should I call her? he began to think. Or should I write? As he considered his options, the phone rang. It was his father.

"Hello, Dada. How are you?"

"Have you seen the *Gleaner*?"

"Yes."

"Well, how do you expect me to feel? You and Ian are on the front page looking like two criminals."

"I don't want to argue right now, Dada," Fire said. At times like these, he thought, I wish that I could just hang up or tell him to leave me alone. But for all his flaws the man was an elder, and elders must be respected.

"I have to go," he said as his father paused to take a breath.

"I'm not finished."

"I don't know what else to say."

"Well, we can finish tomorrow. The Major and I are going up to Newcastle, so we'll come for tea in the afternoon. And tell Ian I have some words for him—acting like a damn ruffian like that."

"It shocked me when he struck him too," Fire said in a low voice, looking over his shoulder for Ian and feeling like a traitor.

"Not me," Mr. Heath said. "He's always been like that. I thought he would grow out of it eventually. But breeding is something that you just can't buy, Fire. Look how I try with that boy. I took time away from you so I could help to raise him and look what happened. Left on his own he fell almost right back where he came from. And on top of everything he hasn't called or come to see me since he's been here. Take it from me, ingratitude is worse than witchcraft, and that boy is ungrateful. He'll take, take, take, but he will never give. Anyway, tell him not to worry. The Major says he'll call the commissioner and get the charges dropped."

"I see," Fire said distantly.

"So we'll see you tomorrow, then."

"Yow, pack," Fire shouted to Ian as soon as he hung up. "We're going to the Lighthouse first thing in the morning."

Later that evening, as the sun withdrew so the moon could shine, Fire sat at the kitchen table and wrote a letter to Sylvia.

There are two ways to get to Port Antonio from Kingston. There is the Junction Road, a looping ribbon of asphalt that gift wraps rugged hills, and then there is the East Road, the longer route, which shadows the coast through the parish of St. Thomas like a ruffled hem on a dress. The Junction Road is shorter and more scenic, but also more dangerous. It flirts with the lips of hungry gorges and dashes toward blind curves.

Fire and Ian took the East Road, descending through the city as the sun began to rise. The roads were empty at first, but became busier as they left the newer suburbs and their tile-roofed gentility and picked up Mountain View Avenue, which took them past the national stadium, whose parking lot was cracked and filled with weeds. Soon they fell into a convoy of beachgoers in Monteros and Accords, and looped and swayed and dipped and rose with the narrow, rutted road. Fire, shirtless in denim overalls, kept thinking about the letter in his knapsack as they drove through east Kingston, where his father had lived as a boy, a swath of verandahed bungalows with shingled roofs and wide bay windows. Bourgeois forty years ago, it was a ghetto now. A ghetto with blue-collar dreams. From time to time, Fire and Ian would pull themselves away from their thoughts to talk above the sound of the engine and the onrushing wind.

Fire had spent the night in a chair on the terrace, afraid of falling asleep, knowing that he would dream of Sylvia if he slept, aware that this could send him tumbling into the pool of emotion in which he'd nearly drowned when things had ended badly in New York.

Ian had lain awake in bed, worried about their friendship, afraid that he had damaged it beyond repair. Late in the evening he went downstairs to apologize to Fire for the trouble he had caused him and found him writing at the table. Believing it was a poem, he asked if he could see it and Fire told him no—said it sharply without looking up, as if he were a pest. This had pitched Ian down a briared slope of old hurts and jealousies . . . prickly anxieties about class, and race, and natural gifts and talents.

They followed the convoy along the edge of the harbor past the silos of the cement factory and the flour mill to the flowered roundabout at Harbour View; there the beachgoers tooted and took the peninsula road that leads to the airport and Port Royal, where hired fishing boats would take them to the cays.

Moving into the countryside with greater speed now, Fire and Ian saw fewer cars but more people, especially in the larger towns like Morant Bay and Yallahs, where small groups waited for buses to take them to church, the women in hats and stockings and the boys and girls in suits and frilly dresses. Beyond Yallahs the land became more mountainous, the vegetation wetter, and the towns—with names like Priestman's River and Poor Man's Corner—quainter, smaller, and more widely spaced. Over the hood of the dusty truck, the country rushed toward them in rippling waves of pastureland and banana groves and hamlets by the sea.

Fifteen miles outside Port Antonio, about two hours after leaving home, they came upon a fork where the main road cut inland for the next five miles to bypass a ragged line of sheltered coves.

"Thirsty?" Fire said. "Want a Guinness?"

Ian wiped his face on his white T-shirt.

"Yeah, man."

"We have to get some from Buju then, because a dance keep last night and I know Mr. Bartley sell out."

Fire turned off on the country lane that led to the town of Battery, passing beneath an arbor of tamarind and mango and crossing a Bailey bridge that spanned a little stream; there, naked children splashed in the easy current and women washed their clothes.

"They normally do the washing after church," Fire explained. "But Mr. Bartley, who owns the bar, is also the pastor of the church. So whenever he has a hangover everybody knows that church gweh late."

After passing the path to Snapper Bay, the road was straight for a hundred yards, then veered to the left, crawling along a sheer rock face before swishing around a triple bend and fluttering into the town.

Battery was built on an English fort on the lip of a low-rise cliff. It had one street, Battery Square, a narrow brick road around a rectangular park that used to be the parade ground. Around the park was a tall, stone fence.

The church and the school were on one side of the park. On the other side were ice-cream-colored clapboard houses, each with a garden and an overgrown hedge. Behind the houses was the common.

In front of a light blue house with yellow trim Fire pulled up and honked the horn. Soon Buju came down the walkway, a gangly man in a red mesh vest and a blue Knicks cap. He had a wide face with a flat chin and a nose like a lump of clay.

"You remember Ian," Fire said to him.

"Yeah, man. How you mean?" Buju replied, booming Ian's fist. "Yeah, man, him use to come by you modda when oonoo did likkle." To Ian he said, "Respek, *rude bwai*. Long time, long time. Years without fears."

"Y'have any stout?" Fire asked.

"Yeah, man. How much you want?"

"You drinking too, right?"

Buju nodded.

"Bring bout a dozen, then," Fire said.

"Before I forget," Buju said as he went inside, "Stereotone a-play down yah tonight, y'know. Oonoo must come, cause me hear a talk seh some big deejay suppose to come from Kingston. Plus me a-go run my usual chicken ting."

"Buju make the wickedest jerk sauce," Fire said to Ian as Buju disappeared inside. "We selling it to some hotels now. But we really trying to get it into supermarkets."

"Who is we?"

"Me and him. Well, him, really. I'm just helping him out with a couple of things . . . some seed money and thing. Is a trying yute. When you see a yute like that, y'haffe help him out. Plus I'm his son's godfather, so I haffe look out for him."

"Oh," Ian said, feeling jealous now. "That's nice."

Buju returned with a six-pack and they sat on the curb and talked about sports and politics. When the six-pack was done another one appeared and they began to joke about the absurdity of life in Jamaica. In a sense, Buju said, Ian was a hero, for he'd stood up for his rights. A man shouldn't tek certain disrespek. Fire laughed with them, but he didn't agree.

"So hummuch dat?" Fire asked as he got up to leave.

In his mind Buju counted the bottles at their feet. There were four stouts remaining.

"Just pay for the four," he said, hoping for a chance to pay back Fire for all his help. Fire had helped him in so many ways, from listening to his ideas to encouraging him to create an education trust for his son.

"Just cool, Buju man," Fire replied, punching him playfully. "We haffe pay for what drink off, man."

Buju jabbed him in the chest and they began to shadowbox.

"*You* cool," Buju said as Fire slipped a cross and touched a hooking pat on his cheek. "You cyaah siddown wid a man and reason wid him in fronta you house then charge him for de juice. Wha kinda Yankee ting you comin wid? Just cool, man."

"But this is your business," Fire replied. "Everybody know you have a little shop in your house. If we did go out to a bar that's a different thing."

As he said this Buju feinted with an overhand and palmed his face.

"Okay," Fire said as he flopped on the sidewalk. "That was the knockout punch."

As they laughed he reached into his pocket and thumbed through the money he'd taken out of the bank for the bribe, and as Buju jerked him to his feet he palmed him a couple of bills.

"This is not for the stout," he said under his breath. "This is for my godson's trust fund."

Buju shook his head and accepted the money, then watched them drive away.

Back on the main road, sweetened by the bitter stout, Fire sent the Land Rover charging up the hill. On the left, from a thousand feet, the jungle fell toward them in a stream of palms and shrubs and trees hung with furry vines. Breaking across the road, the greenery resumed its cascade on their right, roiling and frothing down the steep incline and splashing into the sea, where forest green and ocean blue became a minty teal.

At a dip in the road by a jackfruit tree, Fire turned off on a rutted track and the Land Rover bucked and grunted as it burrowed into the heart of the forest; there, the trees grew tall and light drained through the canopy in amber streams like drafts of beer. As they came out of a fording, the track became a wide dirt road that curled around the mountain, switching back through bamboo groves and stands of wild bananas.

Picking up a grassy trail, they rode on the edge of a deep ravine to the top of a high plateau; there at the end of a gravel road was the Lighthouse, the writing retreat that Fire had bought and renovated two years before his return—a nineteenth-century windmill that had lost its blades to vandals and the weather. From a ring of white hibiscus it rose up forty feet, a column of stone with six-foot yellow shutters that opened from the top like wings.

Zachy, the caretaker, was playing cards with his cronies beneath a poui tree aflame with scarlet flowers. The wind blew the fallen blooms across the crabgrass . . . sifted them across the slatted table where the old men sat with mugs of rum and milk. Zachy waved and flashed a toothless grin when Fire and Ian arrived and returned to his game. His dentures, which he only wore to church, were stuffed in a pocket of his blue Sunday suit.

As he passed inside through a tall, arched door, Ian began to compare himself with Fire. On one level he felt superior, because Fire had not achieved as much as he—had not earned as much money or enjoyed as much fame. On another level he was embarrassed because he had so little now and Fire seemed to have everything. As Fire went outside to cut some roses and birds-of-paradise for his vases, Ian stood in the doorway and looked around. A wooden staircase with scrolled iron banisters curled along the book-lined walls to the bed-room, a cantilevered loft that extended three-quarters of the way to the door. In front of him on a raised platform were a sofa upholstered in saffron chenille and a pair of honey-colored club chairs in braided rattan with arms like the fend-ers of a forties sedan. The chairs were arranged around a bowlegged table, which sat low on a caramel-colored rug that Fire had purchased years ago while cycling through Mo-rocco. Ian had never owned a space like this, one that was a part of him, an extension of himself. When he could afford it, he had always paid the best designers to beautify his homes. But Fire had worked with Sarge to renovate his home, had built the loft, had helped to lay the floorboards.

"I need to bathe," Ian said, as his jealousy revealed itself in the form of an itch.

"The bathroom is outside," Fire told him as he slipped some stems in a stoneware urn, "between the kitchen and Zachy's cabin. Anything you want is in the cabinet."

Upstairs, Fire put his knapsack on his writing desk, a draft-
ing table from the twenties, and removed the linen from the
tall trunk bed. Glancing at the hamper, he saw that Zachy, old
and forgetful now, had not remembered to have the washing
done. Luckily, he'd brought a few things from Kingston.

From the mirrored armoire he dressed the bed in tangerine
sheets, then leaned out the window and gazed at the sky,
preparing to discuss the sketch pad with Ian. Am I reading too
much into things? Fire wondered. Still, his instincts told him
that the sketch pad and the Donovan incident were related. It
would be good to talk with I-nelik now, but he was on the road
with Ziggy.

He stood there thinking till Ian returned.

"What you have to eat?" Ian asked as he came up the
stairs.

"What you feel like?"

"Like I woulda eat some fish."

"Look in the armoire you see a walkie-talkie," Fire said as
he dug through his knapsack for underwear. "Call Teego
down by Snapper Bay and find out what him catch."

When Fire left the room, Ian went to his desk, sat in his
chair, and swiveled in front of his typewriter, continuing the
quiet sobbing he'd begun in the shower. He imagined himself
having Fire's life—being confident, and kind, and forgiving,
to naturally love himself and others. Ian felt the room begin to
spin. He hadn't slept all night and he'd had six stouts on an
empty stomach. As he closed his eyes to regain his balance,
he began to feel that he was shrinking, that his skin was tightening on his bones. He stumbled toward the bed. Lying there
on his back in the hard stone tower, naked except for off-
white boxers, feeling small and useless, Ian began to imagine
himself as a denatured sperm, a dot being carried in another
man's stream. Fire was taking care of his mother. Fire had
taken care of the police. Fire. Fire. Fire. What the fuck would
he do without him? Apparently nothing. He'd depended on
him for something or other all his life, it seemed.

If it hadn't been for Fire's father he would've never been an artist. But Humphrey Heath saw in him the talent he had hoped to see in his son and nurtured it . . . took him away from his mother and moved him from the ghetto to a Jack's Hill villa with a tennis court and a pool, and pulled strings to get him transferred from a trade school to Wolmers Boys, the most prestigious school on the island. There he worked twice as hard to prove himself worthy; there he lied, saying that Humphrey was his father to gain respect and acceptance; there he battered a curious boy who began to whisper that he wasn't Humphrey's son, and that Humphrey had left his wife because he was a beeps. Ian knew this was true but forced himself to disbelieve it, for he didn't want fear and pride to make him lose his focus. He could never go back to where he came from.

The voice in his head, the same one that kept urging him to murder Phil and Margaret and kill himself, grew more demanding. *What kind of man needs so many people to prop him up?* it challenged. *A man who isn't a man,* said his demon.

Across the room, on a scullery table, was an electric kettle, and utensils for making coffee and tea. From the fridge he got a piece of ginger, peeled it, mashed it with the back of a spoon, and steeped it in hot water to make some tea. Retracing his steps on shaky legs, the voice aglow in his head, he tripped over Fire's knapsack, which, the voice explained, had been placed there for that purpose. Sucking his teeth, he threw a T-shirt on the spreading spill and as he replaced the things that had fallen out of the bag he saw a folded sheet of lilac paper—which he recognized from the night before.

His first response was to put it away, but the voice in his head was insistent. *Don't be a fool,* it said. *Didn't you hear him whispering to his father last night? Who do you think they were talking about? What do you think he was saying? Read the letter and you'll know. They're hatching a plot against you, man. Don't know why or for what but Fire was*

*acting too strange last night . . . too secretive. How does he
really feel about you? You'll know if you read this. He's
always been jealous of you . . . of your talent . . . because his
father spent more time with you.*

He'll never know if I read it, Ian thought as he glanced outside. Guilty but vengeful, he squatted next to the desk, aware
that this was more than Fire's room. This was his most private
place, his refuge, his sanctuary. His desk was the altar where
he summoned his muse by drumming on the keys of his Un-
derwood manual, a 1930 No. 5 that had once belonged to
Claude McKay. Eyes darting furtively, Ian unfolded the letter
and began to read.

December—, 19—

Dearest Sylvia,

You are writing this letter. Every word is yours. For as I
sit here miles away from you, you occupy my soul. The
spirit that used to live in me is a wanderer now, a thin dull
shadow that haunts the places where we met and loved
and laughed like careless children. Do you remember our
kisses, our tongues full and strong like Spanish wine? The
warmth that would invade our bones? The weakness in our
legs? Then, I did not think a letter to you would be this
way—a plea for forgiveness. Writing should be a sweet indulgence, the letters arriving damp with musk and long-
ing. This is not right, Sylvia. This letter should be amusing,
a reminder of how often we forget the things we say . . . because we talk so much. Perhaps you don't remember, but
we met and fell in love by chance. When did you first love
me, Sylvia? And do you love me still? If you do then you
should be here, writing poems in the shade and drinking
tea with condensed milk. Come and spend some time with
me, bathe with me in a secret river, and *wine* me in the
shallows where the mullets lay their eggs, the current moving slowly, the deep mud sucking us down. Come feed me
your sweet fig nipples, wet my lips with red wine kisses,

dip my head in the healing stream that flows between your legs. This is the end of this letter, my love, this letter that you have written. But I won't say goodbye, because I'm afraid of what that means, so I will say I'm sorry. I am sorry, Sylvia Lucas, for walking away from you, causing you pain. Now, I'm going to think of you, your crooked smile, your slender waist, and touch myself, dreaming you will be here when I wake.

After reading the letter, Ian began to feel another self rise within him, an old self really, one that was deaf to reason and blindly male, that drew its power and sense of worth from the weakness of others. Fire's vulnerability produced a perverted sense of safety in him—the kind of cunning self-pity that breeds unchecked in prisons and hospitals, infecting healthy brains and causing people to say to themselves, "I'm all right because he's worse off than me." Ian read the letter again, warmed for the moment by the knowledge that he was not the only one confounded by love and its often contrary demands. As he sifted the words for clues—the whens, the wheres, the whys, and the hows—he felt a chill. He'd been left out of this love affair, which he was sure now must have begun in June.

Through the window he heard Fire singing as he came along the walkway. So you doan have nutten over me, Ian thought as he replaced the letter quickly. Fuck wha'ever you make of yourself. When it come down to it, you worse than me because you get fraid and apologize, and me still a-stand firm.

When Fire returned from the shower he found a new mood in the room, as if old grudges has been scrubbed away—loofahed off like dead skin. Ian was extraordinarily talkative and the light had returned to his eyes, which for days had been in shadow.

Looking around the loft, which was lined with books to the

twenty-foot ceiling, Ian said, "How many books you have up here?"

Fire was sitting on the edge of the bed, massaging his skin with almond oil. Ian was leaning against the record changer, an old Grundig which resembled a casket on legs with its wooden cabinet and lidded top.

"About one thousand," Fire replied, pausing to consider if by books Ian meant just novels.

"And downstairs?"

"Another thousand."

"And you read off alla dem?"

"Most. As Oscar Wilde said, 'There is no such thing as a bad book . . . only bad writers.' "

Shaking his head and laughing, Ian tapped the Grundig and asked if it worked.

"Yeah, man," Fire replied. "Them old tube ting-deh doan break down. I swap a guy in Port Antonio for a boom box. When I throw it in the back and bring it up here I couldn't believe it, man. Only the speaker did need a little work and ah get that fix for little and nutten."

"Good. So let's lick some music, then."

On the front of the Grundig, on the left-hand side, was a corrugated sliding door. Ian opened it and found a trove of old LPs. As he stacked the record changer with his favorite Charlie Parkers, Fire made some lemonade. Soon it began to rain, and for the next three hours they leaned against a windowsill drinking out of jelly jars, talking about music and history and writing and art, voices swooping and swerving like kites.

When the sun came out they went to get the fish from Teego. The trails were wet and slippery, and in some places covered with mud. As they talked and laughed in this landscape of fragrant earth and lustrous leaves and burbling streams, each began to feel the presence of the woman he loved. The knot on a branch was her navel, a bunch of bananas her toes. Papayas and cacao pods were her breasts, and an overripe mango, split from falling, brought to mind the sweetness of the fruit between her legs. And their conversation, which had been about cricket, turned suddenly to reflection on their lives and loves.

"You know what the big difference is between me and you?" Ian asked as they stopped to descend into the fording. "I am a pussy man and you are a woman man. See . . . a pussy man wi fuck any kinda pussy . . . ugly pussy, pretty pussy, lean pussy, straight pussy . . . cause him jus love pussy. Him nuh business bout nutten else. Him doan care how the woman look. Or her personality. Or wha she want outta life. Cause is about pussy and pussy doan laugh, pussy doan cry, pussy barely even crack a smile. And pussy doan have no great ambition. Pussy just waah get fuck. So my life simpler. A woman man like you now have too much distraction. Yeah, you love pussy to an extent, but you really into women first. You waah understand them and get to like them and get emotional with them. Y'see like how you can stop fuck a woman and be her friend—me cyaah do that. But I see you do it with Claire, and I see you do it with Nan. Me couldn't do that. I doan have the time fe be a woman friend after we done fuck."

It was true, Fire thought, as he laughed with Ian. He had lost his virginity at fourteen, while Ian had slept with thirteen girls at the age of twelve—and by sixteen, thirty-four. In high school Ian developed a brooding disposition that girls used to think was cool, but which was in fact a form of shyness: he didn't like the way he spoke. In high school, Fire wasn't cool. No one wanted to sleep with him. They thought he was funny, and nice to talk to, and wicked with words—which they didn't find sexy till their college years, when these same traits were recognized as the base ingredients of charm.

"I was such a loser," Fire said jokingly, as they reached the jackfruit tree that marked the entrance to the main road. The muddy tires slipped before they gripped the blacktop. "When I look back now, there were so many girls I coulda clap."

As Fire went down the list of failures, Ian laughed along while mocking him inside. You was always one big pussy, he thought. Always Mr. Nice . . . telling gyal you sorry and all that kinda fart. Before I bow to a gyal again ah mash up her *bloodclaat* first.

From the country lane to Battery they turned off on the narrow path that led to Snapper Bay. From the top of the hill, the beach was a wedge of white between lush green points that stretched into the sea, spreading then hooking like crab claws. Away from the shore, at the foot of a hill, was a cluster of huts within a rusty fence whose flapping sheets resembled strips of mudcloth.

"Yow sah!" Fire shouted as he parked at the edge of the sand.

As Teego looked up from his soccer game, a gaggle of laughing children scrambled over the beached canoes.

"Is Ian dat?" Teego asked, champing on his spliff. He was thin but muscled and his locks had been bleached by the sun and the sea. "Rope een man. Long time nuh see. Come lick a chalice wid me."

They took off their shoes, boomed fists with the bredren, and took their place in the circle, talking and laughing as they juggled the ball like seals, diving and twisting and jumping to keep it from touching the ground. As he caught the ball in the nape of his neck, Teego asked Ian about the fight: "So you really do dat or is lie?"

"All now ah doan read it," Ian replied. "Wha dem say? Dat ah fuck up a pussyhole who disrespek me? If is dat dem say then is true."

"Is wha dem do you?" another man asked.

"De bwai start diss up Fire bout a washing machine dat him done pay for long time," Ian said. "And you know how Fire stay—is a man wi make people step pon him—so me haffe jump in and defen it." To Fire he said: "Me and you is like blood, y'understand, so me couldn't stan up and watch a man pussy you up." To the others he said: "So me a-try work out this thing fe Fire now and the man come call me 'coolie,' star, and me just haffe gi it two small kick and mash it down."

"*Bwai,* you cold nuh *bloodclaat*," Teego replied through a chuckle. "You really beat up de man fe dat? Dat is just words, man. Me glad say a *bwai* like dat get a beaten, still, cause dem man-deh support the Babylon system dat hold I down . . . but if you shoulda beat every man inna Jamaica dat use de word 'coolie' then, you would tired out yuh hand and foot. Is just a word, man."

"If is so you feel then done the conversation," Ian answered, glancing at Fire's reaction. He had never heard him use the word, but he'd never heard him denounce it. Fire looked away and sucked his teeth.

When the game was over, Fire got the fish from Teego's hut and walked down the beach to sit in the shade of a gnarled and ancient sea grape tree. Sweeping his feet across the cool, wet sand, he cleared a space in the mess of sour grapes and set down his basin. He unwrapped the fish, which were packed in dry ice and burlap, and began to clean the snappers, ripping their gills and guts with his fingers and scaling them with a wire brush.

At first he did not know that he was angry. He could feel a tightness in his face, drawn lips and narrowed eyes—but he thought that this was due to concentration. But as he worked in the spray of blood and scales, there began to appear on the edge of his mind a column of swirling thoughts. Slowly, like the advance of a horse across dry ground, the cloud produced a form, and Fire saw the outline of an old resentment: Ian had always thought that he was soft because he didn't like to fight. There was a pettiness in the idea that annoyed him, a certain small-mindedness. When they were boys it was understandable, even tolerable, but they were in their thirties now. He'd tried to explain to Ian years ago that fighting didn't solve many problems, and that as a means of causing pain it wasn't very effective, for a black eye would heal in a week, and a broken arm in four, but the right words, sharpened with the right inflection, could damage someone for life.

What irked him most was that he was allowing himself to

be bothered. So what if Ian portrayed him as some damsel in distress? He knew he wasn't soft. From I-nelik he'd learned some martial arts, and from Zachy, who used to be a ranger on his mother's farm, he'd learned to use a gun. And while researching *The Rudies* he'd met and befriended many gunmen and posse leaders.

Why was he so bothered? The answer came quickly—disappointment.

He'd begun to hope they'd regained the place of comfort they had lost. But as he thought some more he changed his mind. They had never really found that place. They had simply grown to love each other while they continued their search.

It was clear now as he gazed into the eyes of the gutted fish, that their search for a comfort zone in their friendship had been abandoned many years ago. Exactly when, he didn't know . . . but certainly by the time he lived in Cuba. As he pondered this he asked himself, Do I love Ian less? No, I don't, the answer came. I just love him differently . . . like a parent loves a young child . . . with few expectations. Children always break your heart.

He found himself tracing patterns in the sand with his toes, and began to think of the sketch pad again. He had to talk to Ian.

Returning home to the Lighthouse, burdened by the weight of love and disappointment, the two men went their separate ways without explanation—Ian upstairs to read and look at old photo albums, and Fire to the kitchen to season the fish, which he left to soak in a marinade of onions, garlic, scallions, and thyme.

Later, in the living room, Fire took off his shoes and lay on the couch and thought about his letter to Sylvia. Had he said too much? Had he said too little? Had he said the right thing in the right kind of way? Should he mail it?

There was a part of him that thought the letter was self-indulgent, less a way to speak to her than a means of addressing his deepest self. As he lay there considering this, a breeze blew some blossoms from the poui tree through an open window. A few fell on his chest and he imagined that the light red pedals were kisses from her . . . his darling girl, his lover and his love, whose absence he was feeling as a presence in his belly, an incandescent burning. Tired from not sleeping the night before, he didn't resist the entreaties of the soft chenille beneath him.

He awoke an hour later to the sound of Ian's snoring and went to the kitchen, where he fried the fish in coconut oil, then stewed them with tomatoes and allspice while boiling rice and making a salad of avocados, cucumbers, carrots, and watercress. He placed the food on the table beneath the poui tree.

They ate quietly with the polite but restrained conversation of strangers on a plane. Ian, chewing slowly as he continued to go through albums, would look up from time to time and smile a bit and nod his head. It was strange, Fire reflected as he guessed at Ian's thoughts, how fragile our moods are, how quickly they change or die.

It was in this mood that they finished the meal and went to sleep, Ian upstairs and Fire outside in a hammock that was strung between two almond trees; so it was with great surprise that Fire woke up at sundown to see Ian standing over him, his head held low, his shoulders hunched, his hands concealed in his pockets.

"Y'awright?" Fire asked, searching his eyes.

"Yes," he said, scuffing his feet in the grass. "I just need to talk to you."

The sketch pad, Fire concluded. "Where do you want to talk?" he asked, extending his arms to communicate his expansive desire to make the conversation easy. "Inside? Out here? In the kitchen?"

Ian bit his lip, then spat as if he'd drawn blood by accident.

"Somewhere where we can sit ... but not inside though..."

"So whappen?" Fire asked as they returned to the poui tree. In the distance the sea was turning orange as it slowly ate the sun.

Ian drummed his fingers on the table. "There's something I need to tell you but I don't know where to begin."

Fire began to wonder if he was ready. How should I act when he tells me? he asked himself. Should I let him know that I have seen it? Maybe I should act surprised. To Ian he said, "Take your time and get it out. Do you want me to get you some water?"

Ian shook his head and continued to drum his fingers. "You don't understand what I am going through," he mumbled. "You don't know how bad I'm hurting inside."

He's speaking standard English, Fire noted. He only speaks that way at the gravest moments.

"This isn't easy," Ian said. "It won't be easy at all. But I have to unload. This thing is just eating me inside."

Each word contained a bent blue note of melancholy that reverberated in Fire's head. "Give it a try, Ian," he said. The words felt like a guitar pick on his vocal cords. "Just take a deep breath and take your time."

"Okay, then. As I was going through those old albums today it really dawned on me how much you and I have been through ... You are my brother, Fire. And your father is the only father I know."

As Ian began to sniffle Fire looked away. Being perceived as hard was important to Ian; Fire knew better than to try and comfort him. He just sat there waiting, hoping he'd have something to say when Ian opened up.

"Your opinion matters a lot to me," Ian continued. "And I hope that what I say won't change that—but I know it will."

Feeling especially close to him now, Fire said, "Nothing can break us apart, Ian. We've been through too much already. If it didn't happen before it won't happen now."

"You mean that?" Ian said, wiping his eyes.

"Yeah, man."

"Okay then," he said, lowering his eyes to the table. "Don't stop me until I'm through."

"I won't."

"There is so much that I owe to you and your family, man. Cause you've done so much for me. I've been feeling like shit since the Donovan business, man, cause I brought a lotta trouble on your head. And on top of being embarrassed, I was so damn fraida going to jail. And without my even asking you came to my rescue, like always. So last night, I came downstairs to talk to you, to just say to you, for what it's worth, 'Man, I don't know how to thank you for helping me out . . . this time and all the other times before.' But you wouldn't even gimme a chance to say it. As soon as I opened my mouth you just snapped at me. You just shut me out, man . . . just lock yourself off. And that really fucked me up because I'm sitting there thinking, Is it all over now after all these years? Have I crossed that line?

"We're driving down here this morning and you're not speaking to me, really. You're all quiet . . . quiet that is, until we see Buju. Then suddenly you become yourself again. And I am sitting there dying, saying to you with my eyes, 'Fire, you really don't check for me the way you used to,' and I began to feel so low . . . so angry . . . like everything we had was nothing. So I was feeling all this now, when you went to bathe today. And while I was in your room something happened—I accidentally knocked over your knapsack, some things fell out, and I saw the paper you were writing on last night . . . the one you didn't want me to see. And it was like I started hearing this voice in my head. This voice telling me all kinda fuckery, and I started to get really paranoid . . . started to think you were writing things about me that you wanted to hide. Fire, I was carrying so much feelings that I couldn't help myself, and before I knew it, I read it. And now I know about you and Sylvia. That was a fucked-up thing to do . . . I know. And I thought that I could live with it. But I can't. Not after looking through those albums and seeing us as boys. I had to tell you, star. As I said, me and you are like blood. Fire, I know how you feel."

"No you don't," Fire said, closing his eyes. "You don't know how I feel." There was no one word to describe what he was feeling—anger, sadness, shame, confusion.

"You must be really angry, now," Ian said quietly.

What right do I have to anger? Fire thought. Haven't I committed the same crime? I'm just as guilty as you.

"I know how you feel," Ian said, reaching out to pat his hand.

Fire believed he didn't deserve this, so he pulled his hand away. "No, you don't."

"I do," Ian said, as he closed his eyes to fix Margaret's face in his mind. "Believe me, dread. I do."

Fire wanted to walk away and was asking his legs to try, but his thoughts were blocked by his swollen heart.

"Cry if you want," Ian said to him. "Go ahead and cry."

"It's okay," Fire said, unable to overcome for the moment the perception that he was soft. He sat with his head in his hands till his mind began to clear, then he walked away across the grass. And as he flashed his arms and legs to energize himself he found himself doing a silly dance. The sequence of events, he began to see, had turned comic. The cosmic joke was on him. Why did he think that he could look in Ian's sketch pad without the same thing happening to him? What gave him the right?

From behind, he heard Ian crossing the distance between them.

"So we're still friends then?"

"I guess we are," Fire said. As he turned around he saw in Ian the boy who became his closest friend.

"Fuck it," Ian said, as they hugged. "Who is this Sylvia to ruin what we have between us? Let's light a fire and roast some corn and talk. Then later on we can go down to Battery and listen to Stereotone tonight."

"It's nice to know I can depend on you," Fire said.

"It's good to feel so useful," Ian said, squeezing him tight.

Tented by a starry sky, Fire opened himself and told Ian about the love affair, from the meeting on Spring Street to the falling out in Brooklyn Heights, sparing only the details of sex, which he thought should still be private.

Ian was surprised to learn that Fire and Sylvia were like that. Now he understood the whole story . . . about how they met, about Fire's visiting from London, about how the two of them became lovers, about how she made Fire feel small when Lewis unexpectedly appeared, about how Fire hurt for months after he left . . .

The flames pitched shadows on their faces. In the forest around them, the coos and shrieks of the lizards and bugs were locked in an ancient groove, a groove so old as to be modern, like Hendrix meeting Fela Kuti.

"So why you love her so?" Ian asked, his thinness and black T-shirt making him almost one with the darkness around them. "I am trying to understand that love thing. As a pussy man is not easy."

Fire looked up at the stars to buy some time to order his thoughts, then answered. "It's a weird thing," he said. "I don't really know why I love her . . . in the sense that people very often don't know why it is they love someone."

"Not a good answer." Ian turned some cobs with a stick.

"It's not the most eloquent thing I've ever said," Fire defended. "But off the top of my head it's the best I can do."

"Well, think about it."

"Ask me a more precise question."

"Okay, do you love her . . . are you in love with her?" Ian asked.

"Yes on both counts."

"How do you know that it's love and not just infatuation?"

"Love *is* infatuation."

"What you mean?" Ian asked as a challenge, thinking that Fire was trying to blow him off.

Fire asked Ian for a cigarette, his first in almost a decade. "I am infatuated," he said as the smoke filled him up. "She inspires me to do fatuous things. I used to feel this way a lot when I was younger. The difference is she still makes me giddy when I'm old enough to know better. I like the dizziness that comes with it. It's a very nice high." He paused to smile with Ian, who was looking at him, beaming. He liked to hear Fire philosophize.

"I think infatuation has gotten a bad rap," Fire continued. "That's why a lot of relationships break down. Love without infatuation is not enough. Cause it's infatuation that brings playfulness, indulgence, romance. Love, on the other hand, is about patience and loyalty and, very importantly, nurturing— that impulse to take care of someone and see to their needs. So when you hear people saying, 'I love you but I'm not in love with you,' what they're really saying is that the infatuation is gone. So yeah, they'd die for you; but they wouldn't go with you at two in the morning to find a pint of Häagen-Dazs anymore."

"So you're infatuated?" Ian asked, thinking about his feelings for Margaret. The word "infatuation" seemed too sweet. His feelings required a more clinical name, one that would include the image that was in his mind now. Margaret was lying down, smiling, in a coffin.

"So what about people who are infatuated and then fall out?" Ian asked, trying to gauge the odds of Margaret and Phil breaking up.

"Sometimes it wasn't infatuation in the first place," Fire said, "but another kind of attraction . . . money . . . sex . . . a whole heapa things."

"And how you tell the difference?"

Fire shifted around on his haunches as he felt the urge to gloat. Ian seemed so denatured now. So who was the pussy after all?

Blowing the smoke through the side of his mouth, Fire leaned toward him, watching his eyebrows rising with anticipation, and said, with a raspiness brought on by the cigarette, "You feel infatuation all the time, while you feel other kinds of attraction only in certain contexts. If your attraction to someone is sexual, you don't feel connected unless you're fucking. If it's money, you don't feel connected unless you're buying. But infatuation doesn't need a context. Because when you're infatuated you feel connected to that person in countless ways. And that's why society is terrified of it. Infatuation doesn't respect the rules. So why not take the day off and lay up in bed with your woman? So why not max out a credit card to go watch the sunset in Negril with a two-hour advance purchase?"

"Or why not get involved with a woman who already has a man?" This was said with a flourish, Ian's voice beginning low then rising to a sarcastic climax.

"That's why it's dangerous," Fire said, the rawness of his nerves suddenly revealed. "It can make you do some crazy things."

"So what you going to do with the letter, then?"

Fire puffed his cheeks. "I don't know. The situation is kinda no-win, isn't it? I mean, what would it say about her if she left him for me?" He paused, more to gather himself than to think. "Plus I know from experience that that kinda mix-up is usually not worth it. If she really wants to leave him she'll leave him . . . on her own . . . and if we happen to meet again when she's single, then . . . who knows? Fate makes all these choices, man. What is for me can't be un-for me."

"But you knew she had a man when you met her though?"

"Yeah . . . but it started as a kind of joke, y'know. After Blanche I didn't think that that kinda thing coulda happened to me again. So when I met her on Spring Street then met her again at Claire's and she kissed me, I was taking it as one of those humorous things that I could just maybe write about.

But we flirted with each other that night and I lost my balance and fell over the edge."

Ian crossed his arms and turned one of Fire's favorite questions back at him: "So what are you going to do about all this?"

"Nothing," Fire replied, slightly chafed by the irony.

"Just nothing?"

"That's right. Sylvia doesn't want to be hot or cold, man. She wants to be lukewarm. And I can't deal with that. Trust me, I won't be waiting in vain. But if she becomes single again and she makes the move . . . well . . . you never know."

"And what if she should just turn up right now."

Fire's eyes came alive and he began to laugh, booming fists with Ian over the top of the flame. "She would go back to America with a pregnant belly—then she woulda really haffe leave de *bwai*."

They began to debate now. What should Fire do? Ian, who had seemed enlightened earlier, was insisting that Fire get his closure by taking some revenge. Send the letter, he implored, and win her heart again, then fuck her good at least once before letting her go. It wasn't good for a man to go around with a big what-if, he argued. Things like that can make you crazy. Laughing with Ian, who presented his ideas with a comedian's sense of timing, Fire disagreed, hiding his true feelings, while countering that sleeping with her would be giving her the victory, because she would believe that she could have him and eat him too, like cake. The real reason, however, was that he was afraid that his infatuation might take control of him and make him believe that he could conquer fate—which he believed was the true force that directed the universe.

When the corn was done, they peeled away the blackened husks and entered into the ritual of eating, a bonding marked by burnt tongues and scorched fingers, into which little boys were initiated by older men. You have to know how to blow the corn or else you'll singe your lip.

"So what you have there?" Fire asked, referring to the CDs

that Ian had brought outside along with the kitchen stereo, a
Bose Acoustic Wave Music System.

"Foreign Exchange, Cassandra Wilson, Salif Keita,
Oumou Sangare, Al Green, ZZ Top, Nusrat Ali Khan, Johnny
Winters, Shabba Ranks . . ."

"Gimme some Shabba. I feeling like a bad *bwai* tonight.
The thought of getting her pregnant just gimme a vibes."

They began to talk about Sylvia again, as Shabba horse-
galloped on a rugged ragga beat: "Love punanny bad / Love
punanny bad . . ."

"You think you guys would make a good couple?" Ian
asked. "Let's say Lewis wasn't in the picture."

"Yeah," Fire replied, as he cooled down the corn with a few
bursts of his breath.

"Why?"

"Because we seem so compatible. It's been a while, Ian,
since I met a woman that I can talk with about so many
things . . . and I'm not talking about open-mindedness—
which is important—but a shared set of references, man. One
afternoon we strolled the Brooklyn Promenade and talked
and talked and we covered so many things, just moving together, man, like athletes out on a Sunday run. There was this
immediate understanding that nobody was trying to outrun
anybody and the pace picked up and slowed down with the
clear sense that nobody's brain would be tired or that no one
was being held back. That's it, man, she's got a great brain.
And that's really hard to find. And I personally need that.
Everybody doesn't—but I do. *I* need someone that I can talk
with about Nabokov and Leon Forrest but also Stephen King.
Someone who can leave a museum and go see a karate film. I
want partnership, man—someone that's wired for me outta
the box, someone with the same intellectual and spiritual vocabulary. I check for Sylvia, man. She's not big-headed about
being smart . . . and with all that she is, at her core she's really
a cool West Indian girl."

"Being West Indian matters?" Ian asked.

"Not anymore. But I must admit that it used to.

"In some ways it makes things easier though. It adds another set of shared assumptions. Y'know . . . you don't have to explain certain jokes and you might have similar expectations of how you should act and how you should raise children and that kinda thing. But no . . . being West Indian isn't so critical to me anymore. Today everybody has to step outside themselves and learn about other people, other ways of thinking."

"I can't believe you used to be so stupid," Ian said. "To limit yourself to one kinda pussy like that."

"I never said I used to limit myself," Fire said, bitingly. "And it's not a pussy thing. And I've already said it was a foolish thing to say."

"You didn't say that."

"Well I meant to."

"So why you getting so hype?"

"I'm not."

"Yes you are. I can hear it in your voice."

Fire was annoyed now, but he didn't show it as he gave his explanation.

"I used to feel that way, because to me West Indian women were my mother, my aunts, my cousins, my teachers, the first girls I fell in love with. And so I was drawn to them in a special kinda way, even after living abroad and traveling the world." Then he felt something unraveling inside him. "But why do I have to explain this? Isn't this how most men feel about the women that raised them?"

Ian shrugged.

"So when you stopped thinking this way?"

"I can't remember exactly. Some time in my twenties, I guess. At college."

Ian chuckled.

"When you start to fuck whitey?"

"That has never been my style. You know that. There are boundaries that still remain."

They became quiet for a while as they attacked the corn and listened to Shabba. There must have been about ten cobs on the fire, and they were all gone in less than thirty minutes.

Out of the blue, Ian began to laugh. Fire looked up from his cob and asked him what was up.

"Boy," Ian said, "just listening to Shabba right now I just got a mental picture of him face when him come."

Fire burst out laughing and sprayed Ian with spit and corn mash.

"Is awright, man," Ian said, wiping his face with his shirt-tail. "Is awright. But seriously," he continued, "if your woman have a fling with Shabba it wouldn't make sense take her back. Shabba woulda blow her engine and twist her chassis. Oil woulda start seep inna her crankcase."

Fire was cracking up. Ian was on a roll.

"*Bwai,* Fire, me woulda love borrow Shabba wood and just walk down de street wid it out and terrorize women. Just frighten dem."

"Ian, and you say me talk plenty fuckery?" Fire said.

"You think is joke, Fire? Me woulda love borrow Shabba wood. Cause me sure say Shabba wood is about twelve inches long."

"Ian, nobody no have no twelve-inch wood! In any case what de fuck would a man do wid a twelve-inch wood?"

"How you mean, Fire? *Fuck!*"

"Fuck who? Zachy donkey?"

Ian rolled his eyes as if Fire had just questioned the earth's roundness. "Fire," he began, "me meet women already dat woulda love twelve inches."

"A twelve-inch tongue maybe," Fire quipped.

"No! Twelve-inch wood."

"Ian, which woman you know coulda take a twelve-inch wood?"

"Plenty."

"Ian, trust me, size matters to men more than to women.

I've talked to enough women to know that size is over-rated . . . is how you work with what you have."

"Hey, Fire, watch it, y'know . . . is only a small-wood man say things like 'size don't matter,' y'know. Well, let's just say I prefer to err on de side of excess."

"You know who look like she coulda take on Shabba . . . come to think of it?" Fire replied as he thought of a way to introduce the topic of the sketch pad. "What she name again? From New York?"

"Who?" Ian responded jauntily.

"Pretty girl, man," Fire replied, pretending to forget Margaret's name. "Yeah, man, you know. Big breasts, look kinda soft and milk-fed, healthy body—"

"Who de fuck is dat?" Ian said, hoping that Fire would drop the subject.

"Phil say you introduce him to her . . . aah . . . aah . . . Phil girl, man . . . Margaret! Right, Margaret! When she told me that Phil was her boyfriend I almost flipped. She look like too much for Phil to handle. That's one sexy woman, Ian. She coulda take on The Ranks. Speaking of Phil, I haven't heard from him. Having a girlfriend has really changed him. Did he make it with the New York Philharmonic?"

"No," Ian replied quietly.

"He's still in New York?" Fire asked quickly.

"Yeah."

"What's he doing?"

"Fucking Margaret, probably. That's all they do."

It took a great deal of strength for Ian to answer Fire's questions without betraying his true emotions. His head was a sphere of warring jealousies. Competing for his attention was his anger about Margaret and Phil and his envy of Sylvia, for she had come out of nowhere, it seemed, to claim Fire's heart. Fire came to New York in June to see me, Ian thought, met Sylvia and avoided me. Then he came back to see Sylvia again in August and did not call. What did this mean? What did it mean that Phil was a part of Fire's love affair and he himself was not? How could he talk to Fire about his troubles with Margaret now, when Phil, it seemed, had displaced him.

"Y'awright?" Fire asked. "You cool?"

"Of course I'm awright," Ian answered, running his fingers through his thinning hair. "It's just that this whole thing, y'know"—he gestured with his hands and head to the world at large—"is just a nice thing, y'know . . . to siddown and talk with you. I feel like ah know you better."

Fire knew Ian long enough to know that he was lying. It was the sketch pad, he said to himself. It had to be the pad. "What's really going on?" he said, trying to draw him out. "I think this is a good time to put some things out on the table." The flames were dying now. Fire couldn't see his face very well. The voice will tell it all, he thought. The voice will tell it all.

"I just feel a little left out, that's all," Ian said. "You came to New York to see me, and you ended up spending all your time with Sylvia. Is kinda childish anyway, to think like that. You're a grown man. You can do whatever you want."

"Oh, don't say that," Fire replied. "Is not simple like that."

"You said we should put things out on the table, right? So I'm putting things out."

"Okay," Fire said. "Oh, fuck!"

The corn that he was eating had slipped out of his hands. And in that moment Ian saw him spilling the beer on Sylvia at the gallery, and remembered that they hadn't spoken about his exhibit.

"Can I ask you something?"

"Go ahead," Fire said, fanning the embers with his hands to revive the flames. The movement kicked up ash and sparks.

"What did you think of my show? And I want you to be honest."

His voice was small but razor sharp, like a baby's fingernails.

Fire wasn't sure how to answer. "I don't know," he said, realizing as he heard the hesitation in his voice the depth of his disappointment. "It wasn't the Ian Gore that I'm accustomed to. Let's put it that way."

"Don't tell me that kinda bullshit, man. You said we should lay things on the fucking table."

"Well, maybe I shouldn't have said that. What makes me qualified to judge?"

Ian sucked his teeth.

"Come on, Ian, man. Be cooler than that."

"Ah Fire, you'll never change."

"What you mean by that?"

"You always try and pussy your way outta things."

"You can say anything," Fire replied, angered by the word. "You can talk all you *bloodclaat* want."

"But is true . . . that's how you are."

"What the fuck you talking about, Ian?"

Ian began to chuckle as he felt himself burrowing under Fire's skin. "Everybody knows that," he said. "Your father knows that. Look at this. A grown man like you had to run away from Kingston because his father was going to scold him. That's what I'm talking about. And you allowed Sylvia to dangle you. And Blanche did the same. You're not *nice*, Fire, you're a pussy."

"Ian," Fire said, narrowing his eyes, "if you call me that again, you won't like it."

Ian dusted off his jeans as he stood up, jabbing his finger in Fire's face and saying, "My show was shit and you know it."

"You're right," Fire said, rising to his feet. "I hated the fucking show. What next—painted wooden fish to sell to tourists in Negril?"

As Fire stared at him, prepared for a shouting match, Ian began to laugh. "See, that's the Fire I like to see." He began to imitate Fire's bowlegged stance. "See, I always knew you had some Shabba in you."

"You're a sick man," Fire replied as Ian's hyena laugh blew most of his anger away. "Come here, you fucking moron, gimme a hug and promise to be good or I won't let you out tonight."

As they slapped each other's backs in the dark, Fire said to himself, What can I do with this madman but love him?

They left the house for Battery at eleven-thirty, jerking along the main, stopping and starting in the traffic jam that clogged the road like arterial plaque. Fire was wearing black tonight, a linen shirt and baggy jeans. Ian, who'd shaved, and washed and brushed his hair, had dressed himself in white—a ribbed tank top and slim-fit jeans and a pair of vintage tennis shoes. There was a hopeful anxiety between them. Stretched almost to the point of breaking, their love had shown its strength and elasticity, but had given birth to envy, anger, and mistrust. Fire was still resentful that Ian had called him a pussy and meant it. And Ian still burned from the remark about painted fish.

Along the lane that led to town, higglers edged between the cars, hawking gum and cigarettes, which they carried in homemade wooden trays strapped across their shoulders. The night was humid and the thick air trapped engine fumes and the scent of roasted nuts and sweet colognes and sweat. Crashing in waves of echo from the hills and cliffs around them, the music claimed their bodies with its tidal ebb and flow. They began to float along in their own ruminations, so it was with great alarm that Fire saw a young peanut vendor jump in front of his wheels. Slamming on his brakes, he stopped in time, and the youth quickly pointed to the culprit, a racing bike that had almost run him down.

"Pussyhole!" Ian shouted into the night.

"Don't do that shit!" Fire snapped. "You don't know who is who!"

"I'm not like you, y'know," Ian replied. "I can't be a hypocrite. I have to say what I feel."

To Fire the reference was clear. "So we're fishing again," he countered.

Ian sucked his teeth.

Fire shrugged, noting to himself that this was not the mood in which to discuss the sketch pad.

In town, they parked with the rest of the cars on the common, which had been turned into a temporary parking lot. Picking their way through the thick crowd outside the bar, Fire and Ian pressed knuckles with Mikey Magnum and Trigger Finger, who immediately gave them some big-ups over the microphone. Then they went to help Buju at the stall set up in front of his house, stirring sauce and slicing bread and turning meat in the smoker, an oil drum sliced in two and set on legs. The dance was being held in the yard of the primary school beside Mr. Bartley's bar, but there was rival entertainment in the theater of the street—people skanking on the sidewalks and telling jokes in the street and whistling at the girls who sauntered by in colored wigs and *poompoom* shorts. Sometimes a girl would stop, and the town would pause to see how long a man could hold her attention; they would shrug with him if all he got to say was hello, and raise their fists and Guinness bottles if she came out with her number. Later on, a woman caught her man by the park with a sweetheart and beat him with her platform shoes, chased him round the bend by the seawall and came back walking hop-and-drop to cheers of "Nuff respek."

At nearly three in the morning, as a crowd converged on the stall to buy food for the road, Fire heard a stranger say his name. He looked up, searching pairs of eyes for recognition, which he found in those of a tall woman in a red T-shirt with a hood.

"Can I see you for a minute?" she said.

Ian leaned into his ear. "Is long time she a-watch you, y'know. She walk by couple time and look, then turn back . . . You might get lucky tonight."

The hood, in which her face was shadowed, created an aura of mystery.

"Can it wait?" Fire asked. "My boss, Mr. Buju, only be-lieves in work. He doesn't believe in pleasure."

"I have time," she said. "Meet me by the seawall." To Buju she said: "Don't work him too hard . . . I think he'll need his strength."

Then she left, walking away on long, thick legs, and the crowd said, "Woiieee!" and people began to boom Fire's fist and slap his back.

"*Bomboclaat,*" Ian said. "You see the way she walk. Jesus Christ, is like she have a egg between her leg and she doan want it break."

And in all the commotion, Fire kept watching her, as the sway of her hips, wide and languid, fanned hot coals in his belly. It was not the walk so much that was pulling him in. Ja-maican women tend to walk that way. It was the boldness of her approach, a confident directness that said that she could fuck without commitment, which he was prepared to try now . . . now that he'd decided that he wouldn't wait for Sylvia, but would go on with his life. Sylvia was his love but not his destiny.

But could he do that again? Just screw and be friends? He needed to know, and this woman represented possibility. He took off his apron, used Buju's bathroom to straighten himself and freshen up, then sauntered down the street to meet her.

She pushed back the hood when he reached the sidewalk. Like him, she had dreads, but hers were short and tinted maple red. She had nut-brown skin and a broad, flat nose and cheekbones that defined her face.

"So . . . you wanted to talk," he said, stopping directly in front of her.

"Yes," she said, looking up at him. Her eyes were dim and moody like candles. "But first you must do me a favor." Her voice was low and softly modulated, the voice of someone equally equipped as masseuse and dominatrix. He looked at her appraisingly, trying to see which side of her was easier to engage, using his longest dreads to tie a ponytail, his fingers working deftly, like a gypsy playing a Spanish guitar.

"What would you like me to do?" he asked, raising his brows indulgently.

She planted her hand on his belly and said, "Take your cock outta my face." Oh to have it there in the first place, he thought.

"My name is Dr. Yvonne Lewis," she said, as he allowed her to ease him away so she could stand. "I heard that you and your friend had a licking to give me over a washer and dryer. Don't worry, I didn't come looking for you. I just happened to be doing some work in the area, and I came down here by chance. But when I heard the deejay bigging you up all night, I decided to come and find you. We women need a straightening out from time to time. I just thought I might get mine tonight."

The words came in a flurry like a series of punches, sending him in retreat.

"Look," he said, speaking slowly through a daze, "I'm really not in the mood for this. Have a good night."

He began to walk back to Buju's stall and she followed him, cursing and spearing him with taunts.

"Is wha de *bloodclaat* this?" Ian said as Fire came up the street with her.

"She has problems," Fire said. "That's all I can say."

She began to draw a crowd now, and rumors began to spread. "Is him babymodda." "She ketch im wid a gyal." "Ah hear seh him give her gonorrhea."

"You cyaah talk to the big man so!" Ian said from across the table, speaking not to a person but to a symbolic emasculator. Dr. Lewis, whom he addressed in his mind as Hectoring Bitch, was every woman with power over his life: Margaret, his mother, Claire, and now Sylvia—who, it seemed, had pushed him toward the edge of Fire's life.

Defend the cause, he thought as he glared at Fire, who was standing there looking bored. Just box her down for me.

Don't be pussy now. Act like a man. Grab the *gyal* and shake her at least.

"Is awright, Ian," Fire said to him. "Let her run off her mouth. If you talk to her, all she gweh do is get more hype."

Ian leaned into his ear. "You cyaah make she disrespek you in fronta people like this, Fire. People know you, y'know."

"Leave it alone," Fire said. "She not fazing me at all."

"Well, fuck, she disturbing me. So I gweh deal wid her," Ian said. "Ay, *gyal*," he said to her. "Shut your *bloodclaat* mouth!"

The crowd fell silent—from excitement, not fear. They wanted to hear the exchange.

"Baldhead *bwai*," she said, jabbing a hand in his face. "Shut your ass when big people talking. Because you come inna newspaper you think you're a big shot. I will never let any man threaten me publicly or privately and get away with it. Too many men feel they can bully women in this country."

Some women in the crowd began to nod.

Before Ian could reply, Fire grabbed him. "Done it, man," he said. "Cut out this fucking back-and-forth."

"I'm not a boy, Fire," Ian said defensively. "You cyaah deal wid me this kinda way."

"If you're a man then act like a man, then," Fire told him. "Men don't argue with women. That's for little sissy boys."

"Who tell you that," Ian replied, feeling let down and betrayed, "you battyman father? Why y'haffe gwaan like a pussy all the while!"

The crowd began to whisper and Dr. Lewis laughed.

"Ian," Fire said through his teeth, "you better say you're sorry. And you better say it fast."

"Man, fuck you," Ian said, as he pushed him aside and stormed away. "You always a-make woman rule you. Sometimes I feel y'is a battyman too."

Fire turned to Buju; his eyes were pilot lights of rage. "Did you hear that?" he said quietly as he felt his temperature rise. "Now, if ah fuck him up people gweh say ah wicked."

"Him shouldn't did say that," Buju said. "How you fadda coulda be a battyman and bring you? Idiot argument that."

Fire sucked his teeth and turned away. Buju didn't know. Didn't really understand.

As he considered this, there was a jostling in the crowd, and he looked up to see Ian lunge toward Dr. Lewis with a stick. He knocked her to the ground with a chopping blow and her head struck the cobblestones. Then he leaped on her and began to punch her, his fists coming left and right like the horns of a bull that has downed a matador.

"Stop it!" Fire yelled, pulling him away "You outta you fucking mind?"

Dr. Lewis, blood on her face and on her clothes, was doubled over. As two women picked her up Buju ran inside to get some rags to wipe her face.

"Stop it!" Fire said, as Ian kicked and writhed. "Control you fucking self."

"Awright," Ian said. "Awright. Just let me go."

"Let you go and what?"

"And everything will be over."

"Better be," Fire said, shoving him to the ground. "Better fucking be."

He stood there, trembling, hands at the ready, legs wide apart, resisting the urge to stomp him because he was Miss Gita's son and he wanted her to see him, and she would be coming back soon.

"Is one reason why I doan beat up you *bloodclaat*, y'know, Ian. Jah know."

Ian got up slowly, a smirk on his face. "Because you're a pussy."

Fire kicked him in the chest, sending him crashing into the crowd, which threw him back to fight.

"So you can fight, pussy," Ian said, through the pain. "I use to think all you had was words." Then he stood still and addressed the crowd: "You see this man here, he's what you call a pussy. Him went to farrin in June and meet a girl, and the girl have a man, and him try deal with the girl and it never work out. The *gyal* treat him like shit and disrespek him because she tink seh him never have no money. And you know what him do? Insteada deal wid her the right way as a man, you know wha him do? Him write her love letter and tell her how him love her and miss her and how him want her to come to Jamaica so him can eat her pussy and how him gweh go to him bed and masturbate. Now, people, isn't that the behavior of pussy?"

The laughter in the crowd set off an explosion in Fire and he rushed toward Ian and threw a punch that began as a contraction in his calves and traveled through his thighs along his spine, gathering force before shooting through his shoulders into Ian's gut. As Ian went down, Fire kneed him in the temple, grabbed him by the collar, and slapped his face back and forth, for all the people whom Ian had used and betrayed and brought so much pain.

"I'll fucking kill you," Ian screamed defiantly. "Stop or I'll fucking kill you!"

"Kill me?" Fire replied. "Kill me? Ian, all you think about is killing yourself. You have a sketch pad filled from cover to cover with drawings of yourself committing suicide—hanging from trees, slashing your wrist, falling in front of trains, drinking poison, shooting yourself in the head. You think I'm an ass, Ian? In every single drawing Margaret is watching you and crying. Don't flatter yourself, Ian. If you should die no one would care . . . not Margaret, not me, not Claire, not your mother. Do you hear? Nobody. In fact we'll be happier when you go, because all you do is bring us grief!"

chapter thirteen

Sylvia dispatched Monday's task before noon. As rehearsed with Diego, she was away from her office when the call came and pretended to be alarmed when Boogie Boo paged her and gave her the news that her mother was ill. Exclaiming soft "Oh Gods," she closed her door, implying that she was returning the call. Then she emerged with a solemn face.

By the early afternoon, events were developing as engineered. Boogie had spread the news in the break room and at the water fountain, and by the afternoon editorial meeting Sylvia was the object of oblique support—an extra hello here and how-you-doing there.

Virgil asked to speak to her after the meeting, and, following a little small talk, inquired about her state of mind. She said there was nothing wrong, displaying just enough contrary body language to suggest that she couldn't talk without breaking down.

Virgil began to pry with less subtlety and Sylvia stood her ground, evading his interrogative charges with the arrogance of a matador—courting danger, then eluding it with grace.

She had to be careful though. It was important to not tell an outright lie. A fuzzy lie was more difficult to uncover than a clear one and it was usually considered a lesser infraction. It was also important to seem resilient. She knew that Virgil admired feminine strength and that her time off might actually come as a reward for valor, so she deceived him, radiating grief that made him soften his approach.

"Are you sure you will be okay, sister?" Virgil asked, getting up from behind his desk and sitting on the arm of Sylvia's chair.

"Yes," Sylvia said with a sigh. "I'll be fine."

Virgil put his arm around her paternally and drew her near. "If there's anything we can do for you, Sylvia, just tell us. Don't hesitate . . . we are family here."

We, she thought. I didn't know you considered yourself part of any family except the Holy Trinity.

It was slow in coming, but finally it came. The rest of the week off. Three for vacation. Two to be counted as comp time.

"Listen, girl," Virgil said just as she was getting up to leave, "I know how you feel. Sometimes I don't like sharing my problems with others either . . . but listen, if you ever need to talk, you've got a friend here . . . Virgil Pucci. It hasn't always been easy between us, Sylvia, and I know you feel that I pick on you at times. But of all the sisters at *Umbra*, I think you're the most capable. That's why I work you so hard. If you ever want to talk, Sylvia, call me, come see me, my door is always open. Here . . . take my home number. And don't discuss your time off with anyone. I don't want them to think I'm playing favorites. Okay?"

"Okay," Sylvia replied. "Thanks, Virgil. What you said really means a lot to me."

"It's all right, sister. I have a mother too."

Virgil held Sylvia and hugged her tightly. They both dabbed their eyes with tissues when they loosened their embrace.

As soon as she left the meeting with Virgil, Sylvia called Diego to let him know that everything was fine. But although she shared a quiet laugh with him she ended up feeling guilty for the rest of the afternoon. She hadn't been prepared for Virgil's show of tenderness.

She had never thought of Virgil as a man with feelings. After all, he never showed them. But after the conversation she knew better. Virgil was not just a living, breathing, thinking person, but a *feeling* one as well. So, she couldn't help but feel remorse. *I have a mother too.*

Mother. Hopefully she would find out more about hers when she went to Kingston.

But just as everything seemed to be going smoothly—right as she was packing to leave the office—she got a frantic call from Lewis. And before she had a chance to say anything, even hello, Lewis shot her a question. "What is this about your mother being dead? Is there something I don't understand?"

Sylvia sat back in her chair and held the phone away from her face for a minute. Already struggling with her conscience for deceiving Virgil, she felt overburdened by this new development. How did Lewis even know there was gossip about her mother's health floating around the office? she thought. And dead? How many cycles of gossip did it take to get to death? Shit!

Pissed with herself and the world at large, she answered tersely, "My mother is dead, Lewis. But you're right, she didn't die today."

"Why are you angry with me?" he asked. "I'm only telling you what I heard."

Her scalp began to itch. She didn't know what to say. She cursed herself silently. After all, it was her screw-up that was causing this awkwardness now. She should've dealt with Lewis over the weekend, she thought. But the right time had just never come. And she had been too annoyed with him to guarantee a civil discussion. And she didn't want to fight.

"Who . . . who told you this . . . this . . . ridiculous thing, Lewis?" she asked, trying to buy some time.

"Does it matter?" he asked sarcastically.

"Yes, it does," she replied.

"Why?" he demanded before her answer had fully passed her lips.

Feeling desperate as she found herself getting cornered, Sylvia held the phone silently, trying to make sure that what she was about to say would make sense. She struggled to find a suitable answer, but all she could raise was: "Because I just want to know."

"Is there something the matter with your mother, Sylvia?"

"I can't talk now," she replied indignantly.

"Why?"

"I just can't! Okay?"

"When *can* you talk about it, Sylvia?"

"Can we meet somewhere this evening, Lewis?"

"I'll see you at yours at eight."

Lewis arrived at Sylvia's apartment with a prosecutorial demeanor. After a cursory greeting he sat on the couch and demanded the facts. Embarrassed, she did not tell him the entire truth.

"First of all," he began, "I think what you've done is misguided, immature, treacherous, and . . . just plain dumb. If they find out, you're outta there. And then what? After you're fired, will it all have been worth it? Think about it."

"You don't understand."

"I don't understand a few things, Sylvia. Like how you could risk your job at *Umbra* for an assignment on some guy nobody"—meaning him—"has ever heard of for *Q&A*." He pronounced the magazine's name as if it were *Shit & Piss*.

Sylvia weighed the idea of telling him that A. J. Heath was Fire. Maybe that would somehow help her to make sense to him. But she decided against it, although she didn't think that he would have made the romantic connection. It just seemed too sleazy to masquerade so close to danger, cavalier, as if the interview were being done for a thrill.

"A. J. Heath, Lewis, is an award-winning writer," she began. "A lot of people have heard of him. Also, with *Q&A* I can do the kinds of things I can't do at *Umbra*. That's what it's all about."

Lewis listened quietly as Sylvia outlined her frustration with *Umbra*. He was thoroughly disappointed. Didn't she realize that white people didn't play fair and that she was better off sticking with her own? Look at what happened to him. Chosen for an executive training program. Worked his heart out. Late nights. Early mornings. Lunch? Business only. Weekends without prompting. AVP came on time. VP right on target . . . But then no more. Others went ahead, but not him. And there were no overt signs of discrimination. No patronizing quips. Nothing he could put his finger on without turning it to dust like some relic that had existed since the beginning of time. And it wasn't as if the ones who got ahead were slouches. They put in just as much as he did . . . but they got more out. He knew why. But he couldn't prove it. He couldn't produce any sort of evidence. Couldn't patch together any idea that didn't have a hole. And all it took was one hole for the idea to be invalidated. But he knew why. It took a while to know. But he knew . . . the way a woman knows when her man is sleeping with somebody else instead of working late. That's why he abandoned corporate America for the safety of his own people.

"Sylvia," he said, interrupting her so that he wouldn't have to hear any more, "why didn't you talk this over with me? I could've talked you out of this."

She flung her hands in the air. "Don't trivialize me, Lewis! See . . . I'm trying to show you how I feel about something that's important to me . . . and . . . and you don't even wanna hear it—"

"You listen, Sylvia—"

"Lewis, don't talk to me like that."

"Like how?"

"In that *tone*."

"*What* tone?"

"That *man* tone."

"That's what I am," he replied smugly, "a man. I can't help it."

"Sometimes I wonder if you really are."

"You can be such a fucking hard-headed bitch sometimes, Sylvia," he spat. "Do you know that? Such a motherfucking bitch."

If a string had been attached to that outburst he would've sucked it back into his mouth. And as soon as he said it he began to apologize. But Sylvia cut him off.

"How dare you call me a fucking bitch? And in my own house, Lewis?" she said, her voice descending to a fierce whisper. "Go and never come back. Just go."

"Look . . . Syl . . ." he said as she got up and walked halfway to the door.

She turned around to see if he was following. He was still seated.

"Lewis . . . go," she said, her eyes narrowing to cruel slits.

"I'm sorry. I'm sorry. I'm sorry," he said, as he slumped on the couch.

She frowned and turned away.

He walked up behind her and spoke to the back of her head. "I'm only trying to help, Sylvia. I'm sorry for what I said. But you really frustrate me sometimes, I mean, *think,* Sylvia. What if you lose your job? Would it all be worth it?"

"Who told you about my mother?"

"Does it really matter?" he replied. Gathering a bit of sarcasm, he continued, "And by the way, don't refer to it as fact. You made it up, remember?"

"Can we stop playing games, Lewis?" she asked, ignoring his jab.

He paused for a second to see if he should tell her or not. After weighing the decision carefully, he did, believing that it would change her mind.

"The same person who told me about the receipts," he replied.

"Who?" she asked, with an interrogative tilt of her chin. It dawned on her that she hadn't solved that mystery either.

Lewis paused again. This time for effect.

"Virgil Pucci."

Sylvia felt her heart explode. What treachery! What deceit! How could he? She couldn't believe that Lewis had had the low-down, corrupted nature to discuss her business with her boss.

"Get out! Get out!" she screamed.

He tried to calm her down with words, but words were not enough.

"Get out! Get out!"

"What's the matter with you, Sylvia?" he implored.

She stared at him in amazement, then spun around and threw herself on the couch. She couldn't believe his nerve . . . asking her what was the matter with her after he'd just told her that he'd been discussing her with her boss . . . She looked up at him, her mouth filled with the hurt that she'd regurgitated like bile. How could he? That motherfucker . . . that *bomboclaat*!

"I hate you, Lewis," she hissed. She said it over and over again. Harsher. Louder. Faster.

Speechless, Lewis stood watching her, understanding her rage but thinking she was overreacting, wondering if there was anything he could do to not hear her, hoping that her eruption was some kind of spontaneous scream therapy that would leave her purged afterward so they could go back to the original issue. He swallowed his pride and put on his meekest voice and tried to get her to hear him. But it was like responding to a blitzkrieg with bows and arrows. The more he tried, the more frustrated he became, and each time that he swallowed his pride it came up again with a bitter coat of bile that made it harder to keep down.

"I hate you too," he said limply. But she didn't seem to hear him. It was as if she had chanted herself into a trance, like one

of those Pentecostal women in the storefront church beside
his father's liquor store in Baltimore.

"IhateyouIhateyouIhateyouIhateyouIhateyouIhate
youIhateyouIhateyouIhateyouIhateyouIhateyouIhateyou . . ."

Finally, he couldn't take it anymore and he snapped.

"Fuck you," he said. He had grown tired of taking the high
road. "Fuck you, Sylvia!"

It felt good. He turned to walk away.

His hubris, though, had caught her attention. "Where are
you going?" she demanded.

"Fuck you, Sylvia," he repeated.

He stood with his back to her and she could see his shoulders heaving with rage. He sounded resolved, which upset
her, because it meant that she hadn't stung him hard enough,
that he hadn't paid the full price. Desperate to make him
writhe, she concocted a mix of venom.

"Where're you going?" she screamed. "To fuck Margaret
Weir? That fucking whore you were chatting to when you had
me waiting in the cold outside the Blue Note?"

Lewis turned around.

"Maybe you don't have to pay her," she continued. "Maybe
you lent her money like you lent Ian. And what is she paying
you in? Blow jobs?"

"Shut your fucking mouth!" he yelled.

She went on, retching up undigested feelings about him.

Stunned by the deluge, by its suddenness, by its volume, by
its violence, Lewis stood still, although he wanted to run.
Words like *pompous*, *insensitive*, *selfish*, *snob*, *shallow*, *op-
portunistic*, *venal*, and *materialistic* rained down on his head,
until their bitterness shocked him into action.

"Me?" he shot back. *"Me?* Sylvia, you say all this shit
about me. What about you? If I'm all this and we're together,
what does it say about *you*? You can't say anything about me
without saying it about yourself, Sylvia. 'Show me your company and I'll tell you who you are.' Ever heard that?"

He paused and wiped saliva from the corners of his mouth.

"You're a sorry bitch, Sylvia," he said with a mocking laugh. "You are one sorry bitch. Talking about me like that as if—shit, you said it outta your own mouth, Sylvia: if I wasn't who I am you wouldn't be with me . . . said it with your own mouth at Claire's . . ."

She began to reply but, emboldened by the obvious shift in power, he bulldozed her.

"You call *Margaret* a whore, Sylvia? Then what are you? A . . . a . . . a call girl? A . . . a . . . an escort? Or should I be a little literary and say *strumpet* . . . or *courtesan* . . . or . . . *slattern*? At least Margaret is honest. She sleeps with whoever attracts her, whether it be preacher or pimp. Doctor or deli clerk. *You,* on the other hand, choose men by rank, by position . . . profession, stature . . . status. Of course you wouldn't be with me if I was a cop or a fireman or a . . . an accounting clerk. I know that. And I wouldn't be with you if you were a word processor or a lab technician. *You,* though, are trying to make me feel bad for feeling this way. And I refuse. Who knows, Sylvia, maybe you want me to feel bad because you feel bad about your whorish interest in me. I don't feel bad, Sylvia. I'm a whore and I accept that about myself. You're a whore and you don't. In fact you can't."

Sylvia got up and walked to the window, her shoulders rounded and her head slung low.

She seemed so frail to him, and he began to feel sorry for her, but his anger overrode his affection. His face bore a faint smile, but his victory felt hollow, like that of a boxer who has killed his opponent in the ring. He had to face the possibility that he had perhaps gone too far, that there were limits in even the most savage battles. So he walked over to her and stood behind her, wondering what to do next. Speak to her? Touch her? His hand reached out and touched her shoulder.

"Take it off," she said stonily.

He kept it there, wanting to maintain some kind of connection between them.

"Take it off," she repeated. "I'm a whore, remember. Why would you want to touch a whore?"

Earnestly wanting to defuse the tension, but wary of losing his edge, he decided to be philosophical. Maybe it was the right philosophy but just spoken in the wrong voice to the wrong person. Or maybe the air was so flammable that any admixture of right and wrong ingredients would have had the same result.

"Cause we're both whores," he replied.

She whipped around to confront him and her hand accidentally smacked him in the mouth, splitting his lip. And before he could stop himself he had slapped her in the face.

Whap! Bap! She took the lick and hit him back.

Then they froze. Eye to eye they stared. Neither one evincing fear, pain, or remorse, anger or love. Just resolution. Without shifting her stare, Sylvia slid the ring off her finger and pressed it into Lewis's palm. He closed his fingers around it.

"So that's it, huh?"

"I guess," she answered.

They stood there for a minute. Then began to cry.

Bundled in a hooded parka, Sylvia walked him to his car, where they stood quietly as it began to sleet.

After he left she went back to her apartment and made some tea, then sat on the couch with her legs beneath her and watched TV. How long would it have taken her to leave Lewis if they hadn't fought? she wondered. Another month? After two years of marriage? Around their seventh anniversary? Then a more immediate question arose. How would she handle the news of her breakup with Lewis? Tell people before they asked? Or could she trust them to be delicate and not inquire?

She continued to watch TV but it wasn't distracting her enough, so she called Diego. He was out, so she called Claire.

"Can I call you back?" Claire asked as soon as Sylvia said hello. "I'm on the phone long distance with Ian."

"Okay," Sylvia replied. "Call me."

When Claire mentioned Ian, Sylvia remembered that he'd sworn her to secrecy about Lewis and Margaret and the loan. Fuck, she'd broken her promise too, which was a screwed-up thing to do—understandable, but screwed-up nonetheless. She decided how to handle that situation in an instant, though: shut the hell up until something came out of it. Ian was too unpredictable.

Claire called back an hour later.

"Hello," Claire said with a sigh, "How are you?"

Sylvia heard distress in her voice. "Okayish," she replied, "but you don't sound so good."

"Sylvia, what the fuck am I gonna do with Ian? I got a call from him. He and Fire had a big fight and he ... I don't know."

"You don't know what?" Sylvia asked, piqued by the mention of Fire's name.

"Sylvia, I need to talk to you. My bike is in the shop and Ian may call back. Can you come over?"

Fire. The name sent Sylvia's mind tumbling. Had she not met him, she wondered, would all of this have happened with Lewis? As the cab skimmed over the Brooklyn Bridge, the windshield wipers resembling desperate hands trying to wipe away tears, she reflected on their meeting and couldn't help but smile. She began to think of what it was going to be like when they saw each other again. She didn't know if he knew she was coming, and she hadn't asked Jane, because she'd been procrastinating about facing the possibility of ... well ... she wasn't sure ... a number of things ... danger? disappointment?

She closed her eyes to get away from the world. When she opened them, the world was still there, appearing more eldritch than before, the reflection of nearby emergency lights oozing through the frosty, rain-streaked glass like something from the imagination of Stephen King.

Claire lived in a big apartment in a half-shabby building on a partially gentrified block in the East Village. The lights were off and the room was lit with shimmering candles.

"I'm gonna roll a J," Claire said as Sylvia sat on an Ashanti footstool. "Want some?"

Sylvia thought for a second, then accepted. She hadn't smoked a spliff in years.

"Take off your coat and gloves," Claire said.

"I'm still cold."

"Suit yourself."

Claire sat cross-legged on a Turkish cushion and rolled the herb in tobacco leaves, talking as she worked.

"Ian and Fire got in this big fight in Jamaica . . . I mean a fistfight, not just words . . . and now they're not talking. I asked Ian what they fought about, and he said ask you. According to him you know. So I'm asking you. He couldn't tell me anything intelligent. I guess he was high."

"I don't know what Ian is talking about," Sylvia replied.

Claire shrugged her shoulders and gave her the spliff. She took a long drag and blew the smoke through the corner of her mouth and handed it back to Claire, who savored it with a murmur.

"You want some music?" Claire asked.

"Sure."

Claire put on some Black Uhuru and came back to her seat.

"My life is in shit," Claire said emptily, staring through Sylvia and beyond. "I feel so betrayed. Do you know that Ian has sold pieces to Lewis behind my back?"

"No," Sylvia replied quietly.

"Ian told me he had to get it off his chest . . . he couldn't hold it anymore. I had to drop him, Sylvia. I had to drop Ian. I've suffered too much with him for him to do this to me. Pardon me, but nothing Lewis does surprises me."

"I left him," Sylvia heard herself saying.

"Gooood," Claire replied. "I'm gonna sue them . . . Ian and Lewis."

"Gooood," Sylvia heard herself saying.

"Did you give Lewis back his ring?" Claire asked.

"Yesssss," Sylvia replied.

"Baaaad," Claire said. "Never give back a ring. You never know when you're gonna be broke."

"Truuuuue."

"You miss Lewis, Sylvia?"

"Noooo."

"Whyyyyy?"

"Don't . . . know."

"Still love im?"

"Nooooo."

"Gooooood . . . because . . . I'm gonna fuck im up . . . baaaaad."

"Gooooood."

"You hear that drum? That's Sly Dunbar. Drum roll sounds like thunder. That's the sound you hear on Judgment Day . . . a big drumroll . . . and you have to account for all the fucked-up things you do."

"Sad . . . but true."

Sylvia got back to her apartment around eleven. She felt better on the ride home than she had on the way out. She and Claire had been good for each other. They shared their feelings in a woman kind of way . . . tender without being sappy . . . open without being self-conscious . . . frank without being arrogant. Afraid of what might meet her eyes, she hadn't examined her tingling face. Claire hadn't mentioned anything, so it couldn't be bad, she thought, as she switched on the bathroom light. There was a slight ridge about an inch long on her cheek, and a little nick where one of his finger-nails must have scratched her. The subtlety of the damage was no consolation though. The man had hit her. Before this . . . this incident . . . she knew what she would've done to any man who laid a hand on her. She'd often recited the list in her mind. Cut off his balls. Burn him with oil. Stab him in his sleep.

As she stood there looking in the mirror now, she realized that she did not have in her the dark avenger. Nor had she known that she would feel this way—embarrassed more than angry. She reached toward the bruise. Stopped short. Held her hand an inch away and felt her skin reacting to the cooling shadow. Her lips parted like the skin of an orange, showing the white of her smile underneath, as she felt again the sting of his flesh on her palm. She'd gone toe to toe with him. That was good. For what it meant to him more than for what it meant to her. To her it meant she didn't take shit. To him it meant the same. But she had always known this. Apparently he didn't.

She began to undress, smiling still. Then she saw the pools of blood beneath her skin where his lips had recently trampled her shoulders. She was a part of this, wasn't she? How could he have walked across her if she hadn't lain down beneath him? Whyyyy?! she screamed inside. Tell me! Whyyyy? Why did you let this happen to you? Why didn't you leave if you knew you didn't love him? And you call Margaret a whore? What are you then? Whyyyy? She ripped open the medicine cabinet and grabbed a pair of scissors, scattering bottles and tubes, smashing jars, dispersing pills like pollen; then hacked the clothes from her body, raking her skin without flinching. Whyyyyy? She was naked now. Gathered around her like wet leaves were her clothes, soaked in Listerine and rubbing alcohol. I hate you, she thought. I really fucking do. From the scraps of cloth she fished a roach she'd brought from Claire's . . . lit it with the lighter that she used for disinfecting pins and tweezers. I hate you. I hate you. I really do. She began to hear a new voice in her head. It sounded like hers but with a new inflection.

So wha you sayin . . . you jus bruk up wid a yute you was engage to, dat you know seh you never really love? So wha you engage fo den? Wha kine a life you did expect fe live wid him? Happy? No? So why you deh wid him fo? Me no believe dat. Come on . . . you is a attractive, intelligent, talented woman. You no need no man fe status. Wha bout love? Oh . . . ah see . . . you learn fe love status. But him mus did make you feel good some o' de time though? Well, at least you being fair. But most o' de time him make you feel nutten at all is wha you sayin? And a whole heapa time him make you feel bad. So why you never leave? Security? Wha kinda security? You have a degree and a nice apartment, a likkle lump in de bank, a profession. But you did waah fe make sure you nevah lose these things . . . you did waah keep up . . . you did fraid fe slip. I see. You cyaah really explain it, nuh true? Cause you no really understan it. You cyaah even understand why me a-make dis in a big ting. Me know wah you a-tink, y'know— dat everybody dweet so is a normal thing . . . fe go fe status insteada love. Me can see you point, y'know. Me know how it go. It tough out deh fe de woman-dem. Man hard fe fine. And after you love plenty bad one when you young it easy fe say love no so important again when you feel age a-run you down. But tink pon it now. It did wort it? You cyaah answer? Don't worry. Me and you know dat you know.

Her head was a cup. Her thoughts were clattering dice. Smoke pimp-rolled across her tongue in a blue-gray velvet suit.

And Fire, she thought. What will it be like to see him? What will he say when he hears my voice? How will I explain myself, my fears, my failings, without breaking down? She was standing where he'd stood that time . . . that time . . .

The alcohol fumes were stinging her nose. Questions. Questions. Tumbling like a diviner's bones. Oh, shit. She grabbed her head. The splifftail slipped from between her fingers.

Flames flew toward her, beaks sharp and orange, like fluttering birds-of-paradise.

* * *

Fire, meanwhile, was slouched in the Land Rover outside Mr. Bartley's bar, alone in the empty square. The headlights stared toward the horizon, a faint line between black water and black sky. It was the time of night when the sea shed its bluster and hugged the feet of the embankment and confessed with a lisp to the presence of pain, the constant prick of the broken bones of the sons and daughters of Africa. The Caribbean sea, frivolous by day, does not rest well at night. It murmurs. It whimpers. It wheezes under the weight of guilt.

A dog barked. Up on the main road a truck honked its horn. A rock-steady riff, dry and ashy like waifish feet, hop-scotched through the open door.

The sounds of the world were calling, but Fire didn't answer.

Where was Ian? Teego and Buju were siding with him. They hadn't said anything, but he knew. He hadn't heard from either of them since the fight. Well, if is so, is so. You shouldn't mash down de man so, Buju had said. Teego had just looked away and shook his head. They were simple men, he was thinking now. They didn't understand the power of words.

He didn't realize he'd closed his eyes until he opened them. A blade of lightning chased its sound above his head. There was a crack, which had startled him; then the sky split apart like smoldering wood. It would rain soon.

Where was Ian? he wondered, as he raised the tarpaulin. Miss Gita would be home soon. He had to find her boy. That's what he was, a boy. Maybe Buju and Teego were right. As a man, he should've known better. But look at what the boy had done. He'd unfettered dangerous thoughts and feelings. The letter was a pen full of perilous words, words that had roamed his mind in packs and cornered his wounded self-esteem, yelping as they sank their teeth in and pulled it down.

He was thinking of writing to her again now. *Dear Sylvia, On the flight back to London I locked myself in the bathroom and cried so hard . . .*

Dear Sylvia, If your clit was a spliff I'd smoke it . . .

*Dear Sylvia, The only woman I've ever loved as much was
my mother* . . .

According to I-nelik, the two women resembled each
other. That's your mother, the dread had said, peering at
Sylvia in carnival dress. They had been viewing the stolen
image on the edge of a hilly grove in the back of the family
land, taking shade beneath a nasberry bush beside the radio-
active spring they called the Jah-cuzzi. They'd been going
there since his teenage years to soak and talk and burn a stick
of weed, which they treated like a sacrament for communing
with nature, the living, breathing temple of God.

At the time he'd been back from London about two months,
he was thinking now as he secured the canvas, and was carrying an extra thirty pounds from trying to eat away the depression that was eroding his soul. He'd been having ice cream
daily, at least a quart, and had backslid to red meat, mainly
pork, which he'd fry in coconut oil and smother in butter
sauce and eat with buttered mashed potatoes and mounds of
buttered rice. Depressed, he'd begun to lock himself away in
his room. He stopped answering the phone, and stopped going out, and told Miss Gita to tell everyone he was still away
in England. When he wasn't eating he lay awake in bed, fighting sleep and memory. Sleep was more dangerous. Memory
he could challenge while awake. In sleep he was defenseless.
She would float on his dreams like spilled crude oil and make
him cry like a drowning gull.

Finished now with raising the canvas, he slid the picture
from his pocket. That's Betty, his uncle had said at the spring.
Check the smile. See the lean-mouth flex. And prip the
cheeks.

Fire looked at her face now as it began to drizzle. He
leaned inside the cab. It was dark there, but this picture must
not get wet. I-nelik had a point . . . sort of. Yeah . . . the cheekbones in a way. They were pointy like arms akimbo . . . or the
handles of an urn . . . a terra-cotta urn . . . a terra-cotta urn

with flowers . . . tulips, maybe . . . or sunflowers. Baby, I love you and miss you so much.

But where was Ian? Fuck. He had to find him. He put away the picture, strode into the bar, and ordered a hot Guinness. The barmaid reached beneath the counter for a bamboo coaster and gave him the drink in the bottle.

"Is awright," she said. He felt eyes on his back. Circles of heat like spotlights. "Make Teego and Buju gweh. Ian nevah have a right. Those are not things that supposed to talk."

He looked around the room as if he were a stranger—the scuffed wooden floor, the sheet metal tables, the plastic mats, the strings of 45s hanging from the rafters—then took a sip. What were these men thinking now? He knew. Pussy Sucker. Masturbator. Baggy Follower. Mother Wanter. Big Crier. All the things they were themselves but were all afraid to admit. Man a wall, they liked to say. Man fe stand firm. He poured, raised the glass, and pressed his lips into the foam, whose warmth and yield and soft brown color recalled the fat on her inner thigh. Baby, he thought, what are you doing? Do you miss me? Are you hurting too? But man a wall. Man fe stand firm. He downed the glass and ordered another stout. He was ready to look them in the eye.

Shaking hands as he passed each table, trading "wha'appens" firmly, he discreetly searched the room for Ian. At the jukebox, which was by the door, he punched some Desmond Dekker, twirling a trail of ska in his wake as he walked back to his drink. He sat with his back to the counter and faced the room, silencing the whispers.

"Where Mr. Bartley?" he asked over his shoulder.

"Ah don't know, y'know. Im gone from eight o'clock. Ah ope im come back soon cau is soon eleven an me haffe lock up."

Mr. Bartley was the only one he'd directly ask for Ian. As a pastor he understood these things.

"You know what time him coming back?"

"Hol on make ah try fine out." She jangled through the beaded curtain. "Ah hear him went to carry Ian go Kingston."

"Oh," Fire said. His gullet collapsed. He couldn't swallow. He dammed the stout behind his teeth.

He told her goodbye, nodded to the others, and went outside.

As he opened the door and entered the cab, the night soaked up the mist of rain. But soon the rain was hard again, egged on by a vicious breeze that made the streaking raindrops hiss like sputtering, sparking power lines. At the main road, he thought of what to do. Wait at the Lighthouse or go to town tonight? Shit, man, he should've asked where Mr. Bartley had taken Ian.

Lightning crashed again. Struck a tree he couldn't see but whose burning bark he smelled. Something dread was about to happen. He could feel it. There was a mystical power in all this flashing of lightning and trembling of trees. As he thought of this, a ton and a half of English steel was brushed aside beneath him as if the wind had found within itself the power of a hurricane. This wasn't natural. The road to Kingston was treacherous. Especially around the double bend that folks called See Me No More.

He began to think of another night as his foot came off the clutch. *So what you going to do?* The question was I-nelik's. They were driving along this very road—they'd just left the Jah-cuzzi—a few miles to the west, near Hope Bay, a little town on the edge of the sea with a train stop and post office. The sharp front end of the E-type Jaguar was chiseling through the darkness. The night had dropped from the setting sun like golden grains of sugar and hardened into caramel on contact with the soil, which was red like molten rock and held the heat of many days. The top was down. I-nelik was gangster-leaned against the door, stiff-arming the pearl white car along the narrow road, which dipped and curled as it shadowed the edges of bays and narrow inlets.

"So what you going to do?" his uncle asked.

He dipped into the bag at his feet. Peeled an orange with his fingers. Offered a piece. "I don't know, dread. I really don't know. I believe in destiny, and it's clear that that woman is not for me. I shoulda did know better. I mean the whole thing wasn't right from the start. Checking a woman who has a man is really not my style. But this one, man . . . this one . . . was just so . . . I just felt like I'd found the one, y'know. I didn't know her very well, but there was a sweetness, man . . ."

"So what you going to do?" the dread interjected. He took off his tam and let the salt breeze take his hair.

"I don't know . . ."

"You dealing with anybody?"

"No . . . not really. I mean, there is Blanche. We not to-gether anymore. We started to work things out, reason things out while I was in England, but . . ."

"But what?"

"But she's not the one I really want. I love Blanche, I-nelik . . . I'd be a liar if I didn't say that. She and I have too much history. There were some fucked-up times, but I can't deny the sweetness. But she's not as dangerous as Sylvia. Well, she is, which is why she isn't. I fear Blanche. I know what she can do. She's charming and manipulative. So know-ing this I keep my distance. I haven't seen her since I left for London. We began to speak on the phone, but I haven't seen her since I came back. Haven't even spoken to her. She called, but I think Miss Gita cuss her off. I haven't heard from her in a while. The easiest thing to do right now is to run back into her arms, I-nelik. I know that. If I should see her right now that's exactly what would happen. Nobody likes to be lonely."

"You know why that is, Fire? Blanche has always intimi-dated you. When you met her you were half-formed and she was more or less complete. It was a rookie gainst a seasoned vet. You've never really recovered from that spanking she gave you. That's why you took her back all those times. It was more than love, man. It was awe. Cause there you were, this bright and talented guy who could charm the drawers off any woman, and then came this person who was that much quicker, that much more experienced, and able to control you. Make you want to come back for more. But you have to be careful with this Sylvia chick. I know what's running through your head, y'know. Deep down you think that you're smarter than her, more experienced. And you believe, then, that with enough time you can bend her your way. But before you say another word, I want you consider this. Considering how things end fuck up, you'da really waah deal with a woman like that? She have two major strikes against her as far as me concerned. She materialistic and she self-righteous. That's two big flaw right deh so. And to make it even more complicated, she don't know herself. She don't know if she coming or she going. Y'haffe know yourself in this world, y'know, Fire. If you don't know yourself you get caught up inna Babylon system. Y'see, when we was on the road with Bob in the early days—a-play de likkle small club dem—nuff people used to say we shoulda cross over cause this reggae thing couldn't work. Cause nobody don't know it, y'know. Like we shoulda play funky or rock or dem ting deh. But I-n-I never even consider that. I-n-I listen those music and like them, still y'know, and even borrow from them, blues especially for the guitars, but I-n-I wasn't going get caught up inna Babylon system and sell I-n-I soul. Cause I-n-I know who I-n-I was. And I-n-I was reggae. And I-n-I come from Jamaica. And within six years to rass I-n-I was the biggest touring band in the world. Bigger than the Stones. The Commodores. Don't run down what is not for you, Fire. Leave da girl-deh alone. She don't know herself. And that is something that you cyaah do fe her. She haffe come to a certain understanding in the fullness of time."

"I think you're being harsh on her, man. As I told you, she's been through a lot. I mean . . . how can we sit here and judge her and we've never had to live her life . . . never had to make her choices?"

"I bet you any money that if she knew you was a big writer and have coupla dollars she woulda lef de *bwai* and come and deal with you."

"How you know that?"

"Experience will teach you these things in the fullness of time."

"I'm not convinced of that."

"Because you in love."

"Come on, I-nelik, man . . . think about the kinda life she had as a child. Scarcity will turn you into a hoarder, man. Look at people who came of age in the Great Depression."

"Fire, I'm not saying that some rough shit never reach her, y'know. But who says these things actually cause her to be this way? I know nuff people who grow up poor and never turned out so. So wha dat tell you?"

"That we still can't judge her so soon."

"You're making excuses for her, man."

"These are not excuses, I-nelik. They are facts we must consider."

"Sylvia has been away from Jamaica too long, Fire. She doesn't understand how to share anymore. America is a self-ish fucking place."

"Isn't that self-righteous?"

"No."

"What is it, then?"

"Facts."

"I see."

"Listen to me, Fire. Have I ever steered you wrong before? Forget both Blanche and Sylvia and start afresh with some-one new."

"Come on, I-nelik, it's not that simple. Is like she inside me. She's like a part of the muscle fibers now. I can't separate myself from her that easily. Trust me, if ah coulda do it ah woulda do it."

"You can do it, Fire. You mind weak right now. You need to purge it then feed it again. Your body too. You should go on a retreat. Spend some time in the bush, man, and fast and cogitate and take long walks and come back to yourself."

"You think so?"

"That's the only way, really. Otherwise, you'll go mad."

"So a retreat then . . ."

"Yeah, man. Is not me say so y'know. Is Jah the Father. The one that sitteth on the holy throne of Mount Zion. I am just a messenger."

He began to laugh . . . and sing: "Jah send me come / Jah send me come, come." And suddenly lightning burst from the sky, raining down in white-hot sheets that burned away the darkness. Then there was thunder. And battling winds crisscrossed the rain like broken bicycle spokes.

"Jah!" the dread exclaimed. "Rastafari! King of Kings and Lord of Lords, the Conquering Lion of the Tribe of Judah, the Elect of God, Ever Living God, Earth's Rightful Ruler, Negust Negast. Jah! Rastafari!"

The next morning Fire hitchhiked to St. Elizabeth, a gindry parish in the south. He shouldn't drive, I-nelik had said. And he shouldn't take more than a knapsack and whatever he needed for hygiene. For he was going back to nature. To himself. So he needed to leave the world behind and trust in the wisdom and goodness of God. Go to Black River, I-nelik had said, and no matter what time you get there, walk to Treasure Beach. When you reach, ask for Shiloh. He will know that you are coming.

How?

Cause there's a natural mystic blowing through the air.

He arrived in Black River in the late afternoon, riding in the back of a flatbed truck, his fourth ride of the journey, whose long gaps between stages had given him lots of time to think. In work boots, T-shirt, and cut-off jeans, he walked in

the middle of the asphalt road. Fifteen or twenty minutes
would pass before he heard the sound of traffic, and sound
traveled far and quickly in this place, which was flat like the
Serengeti. The trees were low. The grass had been burned to a
golden brown like wheat. The dirt was red, and brittle. Even
the cry of a bird would stir the dust, coating everything: the
gingerbread houses, the cows so lean they looked like horses.
Even the people, it seemed. Their skin was coppery, like dust
had clogged their pores, preventing sweat from washing away
the base from which they were made, the form to which they
would return.

He saw the beach after a three-hour walk and collapsed at
the root of an old sea grape, sheltering beneath its skirt of
leaves. He took off his boots and shirt and went for a wade in
the water, which was deep and rough. Boys were kicking a
football on the shore. Some older men were steaming fish and
fixing their nets beneath a shed. He asked them for Shiloh after he finished his soak. One man pointed to the hills in the
distance—he lived up so. The yellowtail snappers were simmering in a butter sauce fragrant with garlic and tomatoes.
How much for the fish? he asked. If you going to see Shiloh,
one of the men replied, you not suppose to eat . . . everybody
know dat. Hurry up, the man added. When night come nobody cyaah see you and car might lick you down. How long
will it take to get there? he asked. The man said about four
hours. Most of it was uphill. Y'have any water? The man
pointed to the sea. Fuck, I-nelik had told him not to bring any
money.

There was a small hotel down the beach. He could go there
and call someone collect. He thanked the men, who gave him
directions, then gathered his things. His stomach grumbled.
His tongue was a strip of leather. It not far, one of the men
said from behind him. You know how far man did haffe walk
inna de days of slavery? True dat. He went into the hotel
lobby and walked out again. What was his load compared to
the burdens of his forefathers? Those men who would have

seen in this place the savannas where they'd been trapped like antelopes. *Do you remember the days of slavery?* He began to hear Burning Spear in his head. Heard the bass and the horns, the marshaling of the troops, and he began to march from the beach to the road, which he followed all the way to the top of the hill. There, in a clearing among some acacia trees, was a wattle-and-daub hut. Below him, night was coloring the plain like ink dispersed in a glass of water. He ambled forward on burning feet and called out hello. No one answered. The place seemed deserted. He walked around the hut and peered through a window. There was no one there. What would he do now? It was eighteen miles to Black River. And he was tired and hungry. And broke. And dizzy. He slumped down against the side of the hut and opened his bag, hoping to see something he hadn't packed there. He could eat a little toothpaste, but that would only increase his thirst. No, not the soap. Not the soap. *Do you remember the days of slavery?* He began to sing in his mind again. *Do you? Do you? Do you?* Black River was a clump of lights to the left. The others he was sure were fireflies in the nearground. In his mind he saw tall ships in the estuary, unloading men in chains. Men like Marcus Garvey and Bob Marley and Michael Manley and Harry Belafonte and Colin Powell and Claude McKay and Peter Tosh. *Do you remember the days of slavery?* This was hard, he thought. But he would overcome. For he was descended from kings.

There was a flash on the edge of his vision, and he looked up to see the lights of a jetliner smearing a path through the maze of stars. From the outline of the landing lights he could tell it was a 737, and from its bearing he could tell that it was headed for the Caymans. His mother flew that route for years.

What would she think of all this? he wondered. One of the things that had always perplexed him, and which he'd begun to consider more seriously as he entered his thirties, was the ways in which his relationship with his mother had affected his relationship with women.

Of all the women he'd been involved with, he wondered, how many of them had been like her? As he thought about that he began to remember the women he'd slept with. In his mind his lovers were gemstones strung together like a necklace. He counted them now for the first time, touching the tip of one finger after another to his lips as he called each name in his head and saw a face that triggered the memory of a time and place that seemed so distant now, so unconnected to this person that he'd become. He stopped counting, surprised, when he'd run out of fingers. One should be able to count on one's fingers and toes, he said to himself. And I don't believe I can.

He'd had sex for the first time at the age of fourteen—with Nan. She had come to Jamaica to spend the summer at his mother's farm as he'd spent the previous summer with her family in London. She was awkward-looking then, pimply faced and knock-kneed, and her new-grown breasts did not have the effect she had anticipated. Instead of drawing attention to themselves, they drew attention to the tabletop flatness of her ass. It was bad sex, he was thinking now. He did not want to do it. He'd only done it because she'd said she'd heard a rumor that his father was gay, and asked him quite frankly, as they built a kite beneath a tamarind tree, if he was too.

"No," he said.

"Are you sure?" she asked.

"I don't think so."

"You don't seem sure," she said. "My friend said only gay boys like to paint. If you're not, then let's fool around and prove it. You don't have to use a rubber—Mum put me on the pill because she's scared I'll get pregnant."

So they did it, right there, she bracing herself against the tree, he glancing around to see if anyone would catch them as he pulled her panties to the side and took her from behind. It saddened him that he was glad she couldn't see his face . . . the pain there . . . the anxiety . . . the disappointment that she was not someone he cared about in a romantic way.

He would feel this way several times in college. He would sleep with women he did not love, but who, he knew, loved him. Why was this? he wondered now.

In the clarity of the night it came to him that he'd been involved in these relationships to save himself from disappointment. Deep down, in his core, he was realizing that that was why he'd grown so attached to Blanche. In a sense I-nelik was right. Blanche had been his mum in many ways.

The next morning, when I-nelik came to pick him up, he was cured.

"Nice to meet you," the rastaman said as he gave him his hand. "My name is Shiloh."

They hugged each other and blessed this victory with the shedding of tears.

"I want to mark this stage in my life somehow," he said to the dread as he sipped some water and lime juice from a bottle.

"Never cut your hair again," I-nelik said. "And live as if your body is a temple. Fly your dreads, my son. Flash it in the face of Babylon. You are now the lion king."

Fire was thinking about all these things as he pulled up to the Lighthouse. As the headlights swiveled around the final bend he saw a figure huddled in the doorway. Then he saw the car. The white Corolla. It was Blanche.

"What are you doing here?" he asked as he stepped out into the downpour.

"I heard about your troubles and thought that you might need me. It's late to go back to Kingston. Can I spend the night?"

"Blanche . . ."

"I can understand if you say no," she said, shivering. Her cream cotton dress was drenched. Her makeup was running down her face. "I just wanted to know that you were okay."

Inside, surrounded by his books, he felt new confidence in

her presence. They were not the same people who'd splashed in each other's wetness on a rainy night ten years ago in a country ninety miles away. Those two people, the teacher and the student, had died, sprouting, as a dead log shoots up orchids, new lives with new beginnings . . . new purposes and meanings.

"I'll get you a towel and some clothes," he said as she followed him up the wooden steps, splashing in the puddles he left behind.

On the landing she slipped and held him, her hand brushing his back from shoulder to waist. As he helped her to her feet she saw a newness in his eyes. Like coal, they used to smolder when he looked at her. Now they glinted, hard and self-assured like diamonds. She reflected on her new expectations. From the letters they'd written to each other while he was in away in London it was clear they would never be partners. He did not want her; this she accepted. But she wanted him to fuck her every now and then. She deserved that, she thought, for all that she had done for him. And hearing about his troubles, and guessing that he might be weak, she'd rented a nearby villa and pretended to have driven from Kingston in the rain, knowing he wouldn't turn her away, but prepared nonetheless. Just in case.

To create distance, he took a towel and some clothes and went downstairs to change, telling her as he left that she could wear whatever she wanted. When he returned, in gray sweatpants and a black T-shirt, she was standing by the scullery table, making coffee in an off-white slip and a black brassiere, her hair coiled up in a light blue towel.

"Want some?" she asked, looking over the top of her reading glasses. She'd placed some books on the nightstand. Her skin, he saw, was damp in places.

He nodded.

"Sit down. I'll bring it to you."

And as he watched her assemble the coffee press, slipping the carafe into the aluminum frame, screwing the long, hard

plunger stem into the round mesh filter, he began to regret his
decision to spend a rainy night alone in the company of this
great seductress, who had stacked the record changer with
bossa nova, to which she was swaying almost imperceptibly
now, forcing him to look, pulling him in to wait in anticipation for each shimmer of her fleshy hips, each insidious dip of
her waist, which was narrow, but had grown a lip of fat, in
which it seemed she stored the oil that kept it supple.

"Oh it smells so good," she said as she filled two mugs.
Pouring from a punctured can, she sweetened them with condensed milk, stopping the flow with her fingertip, which she
dipped into her mouth, seducing him from inside himself,
pulling from his brain into his belly recollections of her
tongue—its hunger, its heat, its artful pliancy.

She brought his coffee and paused in front of him, sipping
hers, so he could see for himself that the heftiness between
her legs was not a chicken breast, but something just as
smooth—for it was shaven—and just as good to eat.

She sat on the swivel chair across from him and crossed
her legs, the lower one pinching the underside of the one that
lay on top of it.

"Mind if I smoke while we talk?"

He was afraid his voice would betray his weakness so he
nodded. She lit a Rothmans.

"You know you shouldn't be doing that," he said.

"What am I doing that's so dangerous?" she asked, shifting her weight and recrossing her legs the other way, luxuriating in her own wetness.

"Smoking," he said. "After all you've been through."

Uncrossing her legs, allowing her thighs to fall apart, she
leaned in his direction, elbows on her knees, the cigarette
limp in her rose-colored lips—a pistil between two petals.

"I'm not afraid of death," she said, lingering over each
word as if it massaged her tongue. "I have beaten death.
Death should be afraid of me." She reached behind her and
unsnapped her bra, slipping the strap over her sun-baked

shoulders, down over her arms and over her wrists and fingers. Cupping her breasts she said, "These are my medals. I wear them with pride." She ran her hand down her stomach. "Here, I carried my children. Four of them. And in here"—she slid her hand into the waist of the undergarment—"is where I pushed them out, gave them life . . . breed them, as they say down here. Death, my boy, doesn't scare me."

"What does?" he asked. As he felt her power encircle him, his cock, like a general to a diplomat, was offering hawkish advice.

She was coming toward him now, unwrapping the towel and allowing her hair to fall in wanton ringlets.

"This doesn't make any sense—y'know that," he said as she sank to her knees and slid his pants down his thighs, which trembled from the force of the hot blood rushing through them on their way to his groin. Her palm was warm against his cock, her tongue was wet against his tender balls, which she lapped, masturbating him slowly, urging his veins to show themselves beneath the skin.

"You don't love me and I don't love you," she said as she bundled her slip around her waist so he could see her parted ass. "Sex is all we have. Let's enjoy it to the fullest. We tried for more before and hurt ourselves. This is simpler now." She began to lash him with her tongue again.

"You're right," he said, removing his shirt, thrusting deep inside her mouth. "I don't love you. All that you can do for me is fuck me."

She pushed him into the sheets and peeled his pants away, and stood over him, admiring his body—the wide chest, the narrow waist, the furrows which defined the muscles, forming rivers of sweat—and his cock, brown and rippled.

As she leaned over him to kiss him, she said, "If you tell me you love me I'll believe you till it's over. Make it sweet. Lie to me."

"If you lie to me too," he said, as he took her in his arms.

And they began to kiss, excited by the enigma of history, of how soon the old becomes deliciously exotic.

Fragile, desperate, clinging to the last of his self-control, Blanche's body coming toward him in waves of flesh, Fire thought, Can this humping, this fucking, this struggle toward release, ever bring the kind of peace I need . . . the peace that I can't bring myself whenever I'm alone?

As she rolled onto her back so he could dig until the source of life revealed itself, he heard himself say, "No." And he ran downstairs through the door out into the rain and sacrificed his seed to earth, howling, then smiling as he collapsed in the mud because he had come close to losing but had won.

"You cannot stay," he told her when he returned to the bedroom. "You must go."

"You are a fool," she said as she dressed herself.

"No, Blanche," he replied. "I just don't love you."

chapter fourteen

The next day, when the telephone stirred Sylvia from her sleep, the apartment still smelled of smoke. It was two in the afternoon. Shit, how the heck did she sleep so late? She'd gone to bed as soon as she'd doused the fire, which was around one. It was the weed, she realized. Weed always knocked her out. That was one of the reasons she didn't like to smoke.

"Hello."

It was Jane. Sylvia sat on the edge of the bed with her elbow on her knee, her forehead in the palm of her hand.

"Oh, hi," she said. "How are you?"

"Well, not so good."

"I sense some less-than-good news."

"Where've you been? I've been calling you all morning. I've left lotsa messages on your machine."

"I've been out."

"Well," Jane began, "there's a slight problem."

"Just go on with it. I can deal with anything right now." She didn't really believe this.

"I spoke to Adrian Heath this morning, just firming everything up. And as soon as I mentioned your name he said he was no longer available."

"What?"

"Yeah . . . it was quite weird, actually. I'm not saying it has anything to do with you. He never said that. He just said something about scheduling problems and apologized. He was very apologetic. Very sweet. Said he'd been meaning to call us."

"Oh." Sylvia lay on her side and curled into herself.

"But don't worry," Jane said. "You'll get a kill fee. And I want to do some more work with you down the line. But I have to go now. Call me in a coupla weeks. Let's go lunching."

"Okay."

She flopped over on her back, feeling simultaneously heavy and light—heavy in the head but light in the body. She would have never thought this would feel this way. He probably hated her. That's what. It was a shame that things should be this way, she thought, as she began to experience a kind of reverse crying—tears being pulled from their ducts back into her head, drenching her thoughts, shorting out her ability to think, causing her senses to shut down; and she began to feel that she was running on emergency power. Soon she could barely think. She could just take things in. She couldn't react.

Jane had said she'd left many messages. Sylvia felt for the play button and stared at the ceiling, absorbing the messages as if through her skin, rather than hearing them.

"Hi, Sylvia, this is Jane . . . there may be some bad news about Mr. Heath. Call me ASAP."

"Sylvia, Jane here. Need to talk to you."

"Hi, this is Jane. It's official. The piece on A. J. Heath got canned. Sorry about this. Call me as soon as you can."

"Shaquita . . . I'm not even sure if this is your number . . . cause I lost the piece o' paper that I wrote it on . . . Anyway, this is Shamar that you met at the Sound Factory . . . gimme a call, okay? Peace out."

"Sylvia, you fucking little bitch, this is Lewis. I've been talking to Margaret . . . remember her? The little whore? I've been talking to her and I told her your opinion of her, and you know what? She had a coupla things to say about you. But not just you, though . . . you and Fire, or maybe I should say 'A. J. Heath.' You played yourself, Sylvia. I shoulda slapped the

black offa you when I had the chance. Lemme tell you, Virgil
will be very happy to know how you lied to him. Bitch, you're
history. Fuck you! Was it fucking worth it, Sylvia? Was all
that fucking worth it? If I were you I would just move outta
New York, cause you're fucked here. As long as I live here
you're fucked. After all I've done for you . . . Do you know
how many people you wouldn't have known if it wasn't for
me . . . how many circles you wouldn't have cracked . . . how
many contacts you wouldn't have made? And this is how you
turn around and fuck me! Fuck you, Sylvia! Fuck you!"

"*Mi hija,* how are you doing? This is Diego. Are you there?
Pick up the phone. Are you taking a shit or something? Okay,
wipe quickly and come to the phone . . . I'm not gonna hang
up . . . I'm gonna wait . . . Okay, I guess you're not there.
Somehow I know that as soon as I hang up the phone you're
gonna get to it . . . Okay, call me. Love you, baby."

"Hello, Sylvia, this is Virgil. Please come to the reception
desk to retrieve your personal items. They will be in a box
with your name on it. And don't worry about returning your
keys. The locks are being changed . . ."

She didn't hear the rest of it as she drifted off to sleep.

She was disoriented when she opened her eyes a few hours
later. She felt weightless and numb, and ordinary objects
seemed unfamiliar, as if she had been reincarnated into a
world that shared only some features with the one she knew.

Fuck, she thought, I've been fired. She lay looking at the
ceiling and thought about this, and asked herself what she
was going to do, but withdrew the question when she realized
that it would only lead to others, and she didn't have the energy to focus. So she directed her strength to simpler considerations, namely looking on the bright side. Maybe losing her
job was a good thing. If it hadn't happened, when would she
have gotten outta that frigging place? Jobs were hard to
get . . . but she was qualified . . . more qualified than many
people. She chuckled when she thought about her breakup
with Lewis—laughter would've required more confidence.

What a waste of time. What a relief it was done. It had ended badly, but it was over. That was more important. It'd lasted too long, and it shouldn't have begun in the first place. He was a pathetic, petty man. And a coward, that was all, and she knew he was feeling worse than she was. For how could anyone have done what he did, smack her around and spitefully get her fired, without feeling bad about himself? How? And that Margaret . . . that trifling little bitch, what did she have to gain?

And then there was Fire. Sweet man, she thought, do you know how close I almost came to you? If only you knew, my loved one. If only you knew.

The phone rang again. It was Diego. She'd left him a message about Lewis.

"How you feel?" he asked.

"Weird, I guess." She couldn't find a better way to express her emotions. She was happy yet anxious. "I don't know where I belong, Diego. I feel like I'm a round hole and life is a square peg—"

"I know what you need," he said, trying to make her laugh. "A round peg. See, Lou-Lou was fucking you with a square peg, that's why you didn't like him."

"I set myself up for that one," she replied. "But seriously, Diego, I just feel adrift, man. I don't have a job . . . I don't have a relationship. I'm accustomed to stability. I feel unstable, like my whole life is going to be in vertigo from now on."

"What do you mean, you lost your job?"

She told him about Virgil's call, surprised herself at how matter-of-fact she was managing to sound, as though it had all happened to someone else.

He arrived in about an hour with breakfast and a thousand suggestions for her next move. By this time she'd taken a bath and changed into a black turtleneck and leggings. She'd eased out of her funk a bit. It was the bath. As she pampered herself with scented soap, she realized that she hadn't had time for herself in a while, certainly not in midweek. Her schedule was so packed. Her entire life was rushed. All she took were showers. After her bath, she searched for some cocoa balls she'd bought in Tobago some time ago but had never found the time to use. She grated one into a pot of boiling water, added a half stick of cinnamon, and let it simmer. There'd be no microwaved Nestlé today.

"What the fuck are you doing looking so happy?" Diego said as he kissed her hello. "You're supposed to be in a bathtub full of bloody water by now."

"Do you know why I'm not depressed anymore?" she asked, as she buttered some muffins at the coffee table. "I have time. It felt so strange this morning to have time. It's something I haven't had in a while. It feels so good."

"So what're you gonna do with it?"

"I don't care. I really don't care what I do. As a matter of fact I don't want to do anything except finish my new novel."

"There's a new one?"

"Yeah. A love story."

"What happened to the old one?"

"I trashed it, man. You were right. It was shit."

"I wouldn't say all that. It was a fart. Fart. Yeah, that's what it was."

"You're so fucking crazy."

"Now that you've got all this time, why don't you work with me? Come work on some screenplays."

"I don't know. I'm really into this novel—"

Then she remembered. "Oh, shit, I have to get my stuff from *Umbra*. Lemme call the front desk to see if it's packed."

Her confidence stalled as she picked up the phone. She was embarrassed about the firing. Not losing her job so much as the reason behind it. She'd betrayed a whole lot of trust. Everyone at the office had been so nice to her when they'd believed her lie. Now they all had something over her. She was a liar.

"Hi. This is Sylvia. Are my things packed and ready?" She sounded assured enough, she thought.

"Yes, as a matter of fact." The reply was normal. As if nothing had happened.

"How many boxes are there?"

"Could you hold a minute?" There was silence for a bit. "Six."

This surprised her. "Are you sure that's all mine?"

"I wouldn't lie, now would I?"

Then came the laughter of other people on the line.

Sylvia thought she recognized some of the voices; but she didn't know what to say. She wouldn't sound tongue-tied though, and give them satisfaction. Fuck them. She'd call Boogie Boo at home and apologize personally.

"Thank you," Sylvia said. "Thank you very much. I'll come by this afternoon."

Diego went with her in a rented van. She should let him get the boxes, he pleaded all the way, and she should wait outside. She protested vehemently, but he eventually won her over. He could carry more stuff, he said. And someone had to be with the van or else it would be towed.

The receptionist looked him up and down from behind the U-shaped desk, told him to wait, then whispered into the intercom. He paced the floor. There were two people in interview suits sitting on the couch.

"Sir," the receptionist said, "would you like to have a seat?"

"No. I'd like the boxes," he replied sharply.

This is the bitch, he thought, who'd fucked with Sylvia.

"I can't give them to you," she snapped. "Sylvia has to get them herself, because she has to sign."

"Sign what?"

"A form saying it's all hers and that nothing's damaged."

"That doesn't make sense."

"It does to the company."

Don't get upset, Diego. Set an example for Sylvia. He bit his lip and went to the elevator.

Sylvia sat up when she saw him without the boxes. "What's the matter?"

He tried to sound relaxed. "You need to sign something to say that it's yours and there's no damage."

"Okay, I'm ready," she said as she jumped out onto the sidewalk.

Diego didn't like the look in her eye, and he told her that.

"I'm cool," she said, reassuringly. "I just want my stuff. I don't care about their bullshit."

No one else who'd been fired had gone through this, she thought. Former employees were usually allowed the courtesy of collecting their things in the company of someone senior.

She started off quickly and he jogged next to her.

"Who's going to stay with the van if you go with me?" she snapped. "One of us has to stay put."

"Don't start any shit, Sylvia," he said, putting his arm around her shoulders. "I'm trusting you. They're a bunch of dunces. You're a genius. Think about it: in the grand scheme, do they really count? Letting them get to you is like an elephant being bothered by a mosquito. They are little black insects, Sylvia, that's all they are. One smack and they're done. Fuckem."

She said she'd be calm. He leaned against the van and let her go.

She was caught off guard by the hiccups in her heartbeat as the elevator opened.

"Let me have the form," she said when she got to the front desk.

She signed it quickly and handed it back. Fuck, she'd left the hand truck. The oversight pissed her off.

"How'd it go?" Diego asked when she arrived outside.

"I need the hand truck for the boxes."

He patted her on the back.

"Now that everything is signed," he said, "stay here and let me get them."

She let him go.

Just as he was about to lift the first box, however, the receptionist said, "Keys first."

"What keys?"

"Office keys. Sylvia still has office keys."

"Why didn't you tell me this before?"

"*She* shoulda told you."

"So I can't get the boxes now is what you're saying."

"Exactly."

He couldn't hold it anymore. "You're such a stupid fucking bitch," he muttered.

She heard him. "Sir, do not call me outta my name. I'm not having it."

He took a deep breath and began to walk away. Fuck, man, he thought, why'd you have to do that? He was about to turn around and apologize when he was startled by three words: "Fucking Puerto Rican."

"Listen you fucking nigger bitch," he said as he charged toward her, "I'll break your fucking face."

She screamed for help over the intercom as he slammed his palms against her desk and scattered her papers on the floor. She hit him in the head with a pencil sharpener as he stormed toward the elevator. Out of nowhere, it seemed, anxious employees were filling the reception area.

"They want the fucking keys. They want the fucking keys." This was all he could manage to say when he got back to the van.

"What keys?" Sylvia asked.

"The office keys."

She threw up her hands in disbelief. "Virgil said I didn't have to worry about keys because they were going to change the locks. They're getting on my fucking nerves now!" She kicked the side of the van.

"And that big fat pig of a receptionist called me a 'fucking

Puerto Rican'! Does she know who I fucking am? But you know what? She doesn't need to respect me, because I'm Hispanic. Niggers talk all this unity shit and then they fuck you over!"

"I apologize," Sylvia said as she marched toward the building. "But I've had enough of their shit for one day."

They stepped out of the elevator together, anger raking their brows, to find the reception area jammed with employees. They loaded the hand truck methodically, trying to keep their anger under control by focusing on their task. They could feel the eyes on them. But they didn't look. They just wanted to get out of there. There'd been a clamor of voices when they entered. Now there was a hush. The silence of an office. The silence of ringing phones and cooling systems and humming computer printers. Then there was a new quality to the silence. At first they couldn't place it. Then they realized they were at the center of one of those collective hushes that descend on black people whenever the police appear.

"What's the problem? We have a report of an assault and trespassing and disturbing the peace."

There were two them. One was undoing his holster clip. You couldn't take a chance with so many niggers.

Sylvia explained the situation as calmly as she could while the colored people faded through the walls, it seemed, to the safety of their cubicles.

"Who was assaulted?" the other officer asked. The receptionist said she was—by Diego, who began to cry. This wasn't right. How could Staten Island trash make him feel this way? Him, an award-winning filmmaker. This wasn't right, man. It wasn't right at all. And with her hero broken, Sylvia began to cry as well.

"Do you work here?" the officer asked her.

"Not anymore."

"Are you authorized to be here?"

"I'm just here to pick up my stuff," she said, looking around her for support. There was none.

"Lock them up," the receptionist yelled. "She's trespassing. And he tried to choke me."

The cops moved toward them. Then Boogie Boo came out.

"Y'all have gots to fire me," she said to the others before addressing the police. "It's all been blown out of proportion," she said to the policemen. "If they just take the boxes and go everything will be okay. It's all a misunderstanding. And there's no need to have your hands on your guns. This is a place of business, not the streets. Sylvia, I apologize to you from the bottom of my heart for all these punk-ass negroes who work here."

Sylvia hugged her.

"It's okay, girl," Boogie Boo said. "After this I might as well just come with you."

The police escorted Sylvia and Diego out of the building with the boxes. The van, however, was gone. A homeless man said the same cops had given it a ticket and called to have it towed.

It was Diego who began to laugh at first. Sylvia held back—but she broke down completely when it began to rain. The situation was so absurd.

"You cried like a little girl," she said, punching Diego's arm. "You almost shit in your pants, didn't you?"

"And you actually did," he said.

"Can you imagine . . . after all that . . . the damn truck got towed?"

"And now it's raining!" he added.

"What next?" she asked, gasping for air in the downpour. "We're gonna get hit by lightning?"

"Don't push it."

They leaned against the boxes and laughed until they were tired, amusing the skittering passersby, who stole glances from beneath their umbrellas and shook their heads at the two maniacs getting soaked to the skin and loving it.

"Is there anything here that you really need?" Diego asked her.

She thought for a second. "No," she said.

"Good. Let's get coffee."

They left the boxes in the hand truck and went downtown to an Irish dive near Times Square and settled into a musty booth and ordered two scotch and waters from a waitress whose eyes told them she'd seen patrons at their worst. The scotch warmed Sylvia's belly, and the dim light put her in a sober mood.

"I was just thinking of how many things have happened to me in the last couple of days," she said, checking off events in her head.

"Hmmm-hm." She wanted to talk, he realized. And he wanted to listen.

"I feel like such an idiot, Diego. Blind . . . phony. I should've left *Umbra* a long time ago, because I wasn't happy. But I guess a lot of times when people aren't genuinely happy, they try to destroy their beliefs. It's hard to face your soul every day and not like what you see. It's easier to face something so destroyed that you can say it is not really you . . . it makes it easier to remain in denial. Do you understand what I'm saying, Diego? You go from standing for something to standing for nothing in particular; you make everything relative, when you damn well know in your heart what is wrong and what is right."

She leaned back in her chair.

"D'you know what you should do," he said with a wave of his hand. "Take a vacation. Go somewhere quiet and spend a couple of weeks. Relax. Think. And come back."

"I would love to," she said, "but I've got to be careful with money . . . I've got to think about the future."

He placed his hand on hers.

"The future, *mi hija,* is gonna happen whether you think about it or not. It doesn't need your thoughts. *You* need thinking about. Go to vacation and think about *yourself* and see how you gonna prepare you to meet the future."

She tossed back the balance of the scotch and found herself agreeing with him.

"Are you gonna come with me?"

"No, *mi hija*. You need to walk this path alone so that when the time comes you can lead someone."

They spent the rest of the afternoon planning her trip. They would see about the van later.

Using one of Fire's credit cards, Ian took a room in a small hotel on the cliffs of Negril. He barely ate any of the food that he ordered, and the maid complained to the manager about shit stains in the sheets. Two weeks after checking in, the six quarts of rum and pound of weed he'd brought with him were nearly done. He was hungry but he didn't eat. No one cared about him. But care they would, he thought, when they saw his emaciation. He'd lost fifteen pounds and was down to a hundred and five. His skin was dry and it sagged around his joints. And he smelled. He hadn't changed his underwear, taken a bath, or brushed his teeth in all that time.

Margaret. She shadowed his mind as it wandered to the edge of delusion. Sometimes she was with him in bed, mopping his brow and crying. Other times she was calling him on the phone from New York to tell him she was leaving Phil, and was on her way to save him.

Why, he was asking himself this morning, couldn't he just ask her to leave Phil? He knew why. She'd remind him of her ultimatum, and he wouldn't be able to meet it, because . . . he just couldn't accept her past. The fact that she could accept his was irrelevant. They called this a double standard, but so what? Fuck them. Whoever they were. That was how he felt and he was too old to change. This was the crux of his problem, this knowledge that he was being unfair. A less intelligent or a more evolved man would not have been as troubled. A less intelligent man would not have recognized the incongruity in his argument; a more evolved man would have simply gotten over it or not have made it into an issue in the first place. But Ian was in the middle. And he just couldn't cope. If he didn't love her, then he wouldn't have had a problem. But he did.

This morning, though, he was seized by an overwhelming feeling that he would die soon—from a gunshot. Phil had taken out a contract on him. He lit his second spliff of the day. Fuck, he thought, those seagulls were really eavesdroppers. He closed the sliding door, pulled the blinds. Margaret was the only one who could save him, he thought as he pissed on the carpet. Phil would listen to her if she begged him. He couldn't die right now. He had to live to see his mother so he could spit in her face.

He sat on the bed and dialed Margaret's number.

The telephone entered Margaret's consciousness slowly. She was lying on the carpet in her living room with a throw pillow under her hips and Phil had his wood inside her moving at the right speed, at the right angle, with the right amount of force.

It was uncanny, she was thinking to herself, how much he'd begun to feel like Ian. She tightened her glam to savor the sweetness.

"Get it," Phil said gruffly. She'd let him play dominator at times.

"Why?" she asked meekly.

"Because I say so," he growled. He smacked her lightly on the hip.

"No, I won't," she said, inviting him to smack her a little harder. He did. She told him no again. He bit her shoulder and pinned her wrists behind her head.

"Get the phone," he said again, ramming her deep for punctuation.

She felt a crackling in her bones now. She wanted to roll onto her belly so she could feel him deeper. But he held her down.

"Get the fucking phone or I'll stop," he said.

Desperation shook her. "No. Don't stop fucking me. Pleeease! I'll do anything. I'll do anything,"

"So get it then."

He raised his weight and she lowered her legs and slithered to the phone, using the opportunity to turn over and cock up on her knees with the pillow beneath her belly.

A heat sliced through her body when he entered her again. He gripped her by the waist.

"Tell whoever it is that you're getting fucked."

She picked up the receiver. "Hello," she said, out of breath now. "I'm getting fucked. And I'm loving it and I don't want it to stop and—"

"No one ever fucked you like this," Phil dictated.

"No one ever fucked me like this," she said.

"Ever has, does, or will."

"Ever has, does, or will. Oh fuck, Phil . . . I'm coming! I'm coming! I'm comiiiinng!"

She collapsed on the floor.

Phil replaced the receiver and lay down beside her. She licked the sweat off his forehead. She was glad she had him, she thought. He was wonderful.

The phone rang again and they both began to laugh.

"Will you please get that, luv?" Phil asked, falling out of character now.

"I'm too embarrassed," she said. "It might be the same person calling back."

"If they ask, tell them they must've called a wrong number."

Giggling, she picked up the receiver. "Hello," she said, trying to sound nonchalant.

It was Ian. She felt her heart leaning against her ribs. He was disoriented. Slurring his words. She had to be strong, though, she thought. She couldn't let him mash up her peace. She made up her mind to be very sharp if she had to.

"Margaret, I going dead. Phil . . . Phil . . . him is there with you? You was making love to him when I called, Margaret? Tell me no. Tell me that white pale dog wasn't fucking me woman. Margaret, Phil hire a man fe kill me. Call de police. Send them quick. Margaret, you sleeping with a murderer."

"Why are you calling me?"

"Because I want to love you, Margaret. Lawd. Do. Don't make him kill me."

"Where are you?" she heard herself asking. Fuck, she thought, why can't I be cold? Why can't I just hang up? "Where are you?" she asked again.

"Hell."

The word bounced hard in her head like a marble. She fought her instinct to help him. But before she knew it she was asking him how she could help.

"Leave Phil," he replied. "Kill him before him kill me!"

"Don't talk like that," she said.

"You won't kill him?" he asked.

"No," she snapped, exasperated not just by this mad request but the whole fucking situation.

"Then I will kill him when I come," he said. His voice had gathered the conviction of a pledge. "And when I kill him, I coming for you, you fucking whore. Is you send de white boy fe kill me. I going cut off you titty-dem and stuff dem up you big pussy hole."

She slammed down the receiver and screamed. Phil held her and tried to console her. But her pain ran too deep for him to truly understand.

Ian swallowed a mouthful of rum and passed out. He came to about three hours later, then lapsed in and out of consciousness until he fell off the bed and hit his head, which woke him up.

He didn't know how much time had passed since speaking to Margaret, and could only remember the gist of the phone call. He knew he'd upset her though. What about, he wasn't sure. He needed her. That was the most important thing. He felt sick. He leaned over and retched and retched but nothing came up but stinking air.

He called her a few hours later, sober but hungover. As the phone rang, he thought of what he would say, but she picked up before his thoughts had cohered.

"Hello," he said, searching for a suitable entrée, "aah . . . aaah . . ."

"Is this Ian?"

"Yes . . . aah . . ."

"Haven't you hurt me enough? Why don't you just leave me alone? I hate you, you fucking bastard. I hate you for the way you try to manipulate me. I can't have you in my life anymore. You've gone too far this time. Don't ever speak to me again. Do you hear me? Ever!"

He tried to remember what he'd said before, but he couldn't. He needed to know to apologize. Having no alternative, he asked her.

Stunned, she didn't answer.

"Answer me," he asked quietly. "Please. I'm having a rough time."

She didn't respond.

"Margaret, please talk to me. I want to love you, Margaret," he said, exhaling the words like they were his last breath.

She still didn't answer and he became very afraid.

"Please . . . Margaret . . . talk to me. I need you. I'm so down . . . don't hurt me when I'm down. I don't want to lose you, Margaret . . . I want you in my life . . ."

He paused for a moment, thinking he had heard her begin to speak. As he listened keenly, desperation gripped his body. "I going kill myself."

When he heard the dial tone, he began to consider it seriously. He was adrift with no one to look after him. Fire was gone and Margaret too. And he didn't feel the strength to go it alone. He wanted to lose the ability to feel because his senses seemed tuned only to pain. He lay in a wreck on the floor with the phone to his ear and whimpered like a mangy dog.

chapter fifteen

"Four!"

The crowd under the bamboo pavilion applauded Fire's cover drive. The next ball, though, was a bouncer, and he scuttled to the pitch.

"Don't hurt me, nephew, y'know," I-nelik yelled jokingly as the bowler returned to his mark. "Cricket is supposed to be a gentleman's game—I don't know what a cruff like you doing here."

The crowd tittered, then settled down. Fire brushed off his white flannels and tapped his bat slowly, watching and waiting. The bowler dropped the next one short as well and he shuffled down the pitch to meet the ball and lost his offstump in the process.

He took a seat in the pavilion after his beautiful eight and watched the innings collapse. Buju, the only batsman to reach double figures, was soon caught in the slips. After that the Battery Eleven flowed in a steady stream to and from the crease, and they lost the match by six wickets.

Everyone went to Mr. Bartley's bar after the match to drink and eat a just-killed-and-curried goat and sip hot mannish water.

Fire and I-nelik sat on the hood of the Land Rover and ate and talked. Buju kept his distance. He and Fire still were not completely cool since the fight with Ian. They'd talked things over, though, and agreed to let things slide.

Fire was taking lots of ribbing for his elegant eight. He was a good batsman, but impatient, and had been slipping steadily in the batting order. He used to be an opener, but was now batting five.

"Dat eight is a prophecy, y'know," Zacky said, interrupting the conversation. "Last match you did make five. And you bat five today. Make twelve next time nuh, so me can get a game. I was a boss opener in me time y'know. Ask you father. I wasn't pretty like you though . . . but I used to score more runs."

The three of them had a good laugh.

"Everybody say is the prettiest eight dem see in years, man," Zachy continued. "Only Lawrence Rowe coulda make eight runs look so good."

Zachy went to shark down a domino game inside.

"That Zachy is something else," I-nelik remarked. Darkness was rolling in off the sea.

"Someone told me he used to be a class bats one time," Fire said.

"I'm sure it was *him*," the dread quipped. "Him brag about it, but is true. Zachy was a class bats when him was young. But unfortunately for him, he was an opening bats when Allen Rae and Jeffrey Stollmeyer were opening for the West Indies. That was a team . . . Worrell . . . Weekes . . . and Walcott . . . Ramadhin and Valentine as spin bowlers. Remember when Ian was young we used to call him Ramadhin?"

"He was a good spinner," Fire said blankly.

"He went back to the States, right?" I-nelik asked. "Y'ever heard from him?"

"Well the last I heard from him was when he was out here," Fire replied. "I presume he's back in the States."

"I want to talk to him, y'know," I-nelik said.

Fire was staring out to sea.

"Something is wrong," I-nelik went on. "The way Ian beat up that Mackenzie bredda . . . was not a normal kind of anger. *I* know that anger. *You* know that anger. We're all artists. That is frustration . . . and a special kind. Artists tend to be very controlling—you can't create without control. You can only imagine, but you can't create. And they carry this need for control into everyday life. Ian is losing control over something, Fire. And it's making him lose his mind."

Fire steeled himself against feeling sorry. He wasn't guilty anymore. As time had passed and he'd thought about things, he'd realized how paternalistic he'd been toward Ian, and how little all his efforts had done to make him change. And he had his own damn troubles. He'd almost slept with Blanche that night. He would've if there'd been a condom. She was seeing someone now. No one he knew. And to his surprise this didn't bother him. This was good. It meant he was over her. Being able to just fuck her, he realized, was its own twisted kind of triumph.

"Honestly, I-nelik," he said, still looking out to sea, "I can't be Ian's conscience forever. When you get to a certain age, it's your duty to search out the meaning of right and wrong."

"So what really go down with the two of *oonoo*?" I-nelik asked. "I-man hear a whole heapa things."

Fire told him about the fight without revealing the letter's exact contents. I-nelik listened quietly.

"Ian was reaching for help," he said. "Ian didn't want to kill himself. He wanted you to think that and ask him about it, then he would talk to you. When people want to kill themselves, Fire, they don't want people to stop them, so they don't tell anybody. When they're getting close to the point where they *think* they might kill themselves, though, then they cry out for help . . . maybe they botch the attempt or have people 'discover' their plan and talk them out of it. But in any event, a person is far gone when they get to that point. It means they considering it seriously."

"How you know so much about suicide, I-nelik?"

I-nelik pulled him closer and whispered, "Every artist thinks about suicide at some point in his life."

"So what we should do, dread?" Fire asked.

"Let's go up to the Lighthouse and call him."

Fire was consumed with anxiety as they drove up the hill. He imagined Ian dying . . . hanging himself . . . and he heard his own words urging him to do it during the fight. All self-interest left his body when he reached the door, and in his mind he began to see Ian with a noose around his neck, preparing to take the step.

Fire dialed Ian's number in New York. The phone rang without an answer.

"If he's not at home, call Claire and find out," I-nelik said.

Fire dialed again. "Claire, it's Fire," he began urgently. "Have you seen or heard from Ian?"

"Let me tell you about your fucking friend," she said. "Ian has stabbed me in the fucking back and his ass is mine. Ian and Lewis have defrauded me of hundreds of thousands of dollars, okay? Ian has sold pieces to Lewis behind my back . . . cutting me out . . . after all I've done for him . . . after how close we used to be. Well, I'm suing them both!"

He pretended he didn't know. She would be angry with him as well.

"And you know what pissed me off even more?" she continued. "He was calling me to comfort him because Margaret told him she doesn't want him anymore. Me! Me who he's fucked over . . . he was calling me!"

She'd spoken to him, Fire thought. Which was good. He was alive.

"Where'd he call from?" Fire asked.

"So what about me?" Claire snapped. "Don't you care about how I feel, Fire?"

"Yes, Claire . . . but . . ."

"But he's more important?"

"Does it really matter?"

She hung up.

He threw the phone on the bed, but it bounced off and hit the floor. He put it to his ear. It was dead. He tried to dial anyway.

I-nelik was annoyed now. How could the boy lose his cool

at a moment like this? The dread reached out and grabbed the phone. Fire grabbed it back.

"Listen, I-nelik, I'm a big man, okay?"

The dread waved him away and began to use a penknife to pull the phone apart. Fire stormed through the door, jumped into the Land Rover, and drove to Mr. Bartley's to call and apologize to Claire, his best bet for finding out where Ian was. He thought of what he'd say to her as he gunned the engine.

"Claire," he said, as soon as she picked up. "I was wrong and I apologize. I shouldn't have said what I said. You know I love you best . . . I'm just under a lot of pressure, that's all."

He spoke to her softly, counting every minute on the Air Jamaica clock over the door. She eventually warmed up, but he was forced to listen as she poured out her emotions. This took fifteen minutes, during which time Mr. Bartley kept hinting to him to get off the line. This was a business, he kept saying. And his daughter was supposed to be calling from Canada. Finally, after about twenty minutes, Fire felt safe to ask about Ian.

"I want to give him a piece o' my mind about what he's done to you," he said. "Where'd the fucker call from?"

"It's okay, Fire," she replied. "Don't get involved."

He thought quickly. "If it concerns you then it concerns me, Claire. I need to know where he is. He wasn't at his house when I called him."

"Of course not," she replied. "He's in Jamaica . . . at a hotel in Negril."

"Which one?"

"Sea something. I can't remember—"

"Sea Cliffs, maybe?" he asked. Fuck, so many of them began with "Sea."

"Aaah . . . that could be it."

"How did he sound?"

"Weak . . . and hoarse."

"This might sound strange . . . but . . . did he mention suicide?"

"Not at all. He just sounded very depressed . . . and rightfully so . . . he should be ashamed of what he did. Can you blame me for how I feel, Fire?"

He didn't answer. He was too busy thinking about I-nelik's words: *When people want to kill themselves, Fire, they don't want people to stop them . . .*

He apologized to Mr. Bartley and dialed the hotel. There was no Ian Gore there, the woman said. He described him. No, they hadn't seen anyone fitting that description. Maybe it wasn't the Sea-something, he began to think. Maybe Claire was mistaken. And again, Ian could've registered under an alias. Fuck, he had to find him. Miss Gita was back and didn't know her son had been there.

"Call the police," Mr. Bartley said, when Fire told him what had happened. "Have them check all de hotels. Dat *bwai* wasn't looking good at all when I did take him go town. Call all the hotels and see if him is elsewhere. We can't let him kill himself. If you kill yourself you go to hell because you don't have any time to ask forgiveness."

"Ian needs no introduction to hell, Mr. Bartley. He lives there."

He took Mr. Bartley's suggestion, picked up I-nelik, and headed for Negril, which was more than five hours away.

Kill Phil. Kill Margaret. Kill me. The first time that Ian had heard this, it was clearly the voice of someone else. It had an accent he couldn't place . . . the kind of British accent you'd hear in a Peter Cushing film. The voice he began to hear after Claire hung up on him was also from a film—his film. He was the star of this film, as well as the scriptwriter, producer, and director. The voice in this film was his own.

In his film, he was good and Margaret and Phil were evil, so he had to kill them. Then, to show how powerful he was, he would kill himself . . . then . . . then . . . he hadn't finished the script yet . . . but . . . he knew that he would come back to life . . . or . . . maybe he wouldn't kill himself . . . aaahh . . . he would have a fake bullet for himself and wouldn't die at all . . . he would survive . . . somehow . . . because star cyaah dead.

As fate would have it, Ian was scheduled to leave Jamaica on the night he spoke to Margaret and Claire. The voice told him what to do: *Leave but don't check out. Be strong. Go to New York. Don't tell anyone about your plans. Kill Phil. Kill Margaret. Kill me.*

He slept during most of the flight. About a half hour outside JFK, though, turbulence shook the plane and he awoke. His first impulse was to machine-gun the passengers with his cock, but the scene wouldn't have worked with his script. So he thought of opening an emergency door and flying the rest of the way on his own power. That could fit the script, he thought, but with a bit of a rewrite. But by the time he'd figured out how to open the door he fell asleep again.

He worked on his storyboard as he rode home in the cab. He would go home and get his gun from beneath the bed, wait for Phil to come. He would force him at gunpoint to invite Margaret over, then kill him while she was on the way. When Margaret came, he would force her to suck Phil's dead cock while he fucked her with his gun. Then he would fuck her to death with the real thing. When she was dead, he would put the gun in his mouth and pull the trigger and the bullet would ricochet off his hard palate.

About an hour after Ian had reached New York, Margaret and Phil were having an argument.

"Phil," she pleaded, "why can't you see what I'm saying?"

"Because you're overreacting, luv," Phil replied, reaching across the bed to stroke her hair. "Ian was just high. He's not going to kill us."

"He threatened us and that's enough. All I want you to do is go over there and get the rest of your stuff before he gets back."

Phil put his arm around her and pulled her to his side. He kissed her on the forehead and wiped a tear from her face.

"Babe," he said reassuringly, "in any case he's in Jamaica. It's not like he can fly over here in a flash."

"Please, Phil . . . please . . . for my sake . . . pleeease."

"Okay, don't answer the phone," he told her as he got up to leave. "Let the machine pick up, in case he decides to call again."

Phil pondered his future as he rode in the back of the gypsy cab. He'd been gigging around a lot, and Margaret had been saying that the A&R people were interested. But these things took time, he knew; in the meantime his money was running out. He didn't want to depend on her. And fuck, man, he'd had no idea until now that Ian had been feeling this way all this time. Then he began to think about something that had been simmering in his mind.

There was no life in the Navy Yard that night. Even the wind was still. As he stepped onto the curb, a streetlight coughed and fizzled.

"You will wait, right?" he asked the driver as he fumbled in his pockets for his keys. Something about the blown bulb made him afraid of going inside.

"Pay first," the driver said.

Phil gave him the fare plus extra. "Funny how the light just popped . . . weird, wasn't it?"

"I was saying the same thing. It had me kinda spooked there for a sec . . . but being in New York and all, you got other things to be scared of, like ignant motherfuckers with guns."

The driver cracked a smile. Phil felt okay to crack one too.

"Where you from?" the man asked, sliding over to the passenger seat. "You sound kinda different."

Phil squatted so that their faces were aligned.

"The U.K.," he replied.

"Where's that? Canada?"

"No. Britain."

"And where's that?"

"Like England."

"Okay, I gotcha now. So the U.K. and England are like Queens and Jersey then."

Phil didn't understand the comparison, but he said yes. "Where are you from?" he asked.

"Me? Originally? Georgia . . . Columbus. Little Richard's from there."

"Are Georgia and Columbus like Queens and Jersey too?"

"Well . . . not exactly . . . but kinda. You vacationing over here? . . . aah . . . scuse me but I didn't catch your name."

"Phil."

"Doug."

"I came to try out for an orchestra . . . I'm a trumpeter . . . but I ended up meeting a girl and we fell in love . . . but"—Phil paused a bit and searched the driver's eye for sympathy and experience. He didn't find them to the degree he wanted, but he needed to clear his mind—"she's black. I'm not . . . being a racialist or anything," he continued, "but it scares me. See, her boyfriend before me was black . . . and he's going crazy because he wants her back. And it's affecting her so deeply. She's in tears, hysterical. She says it's over his threats . . . but I don't believe her completely. I think a lot of her tears are for him . . . for the sadness that he's feeling. And that's making me feel insecure, and I can't help feeling that it's a color thing. I mean he treats her like shit . . . always has . . . and I treat her like a queen . . . and he still can touch her in this way that I don't feel I can. I can't help feeling that it's a color thing, Doug. Maybe I can't connect with her in the same way a black man can . . . I don't know . . . maybe a white man has to be twice as good."

He told Doug about the threats and explained why he had come to this address in his cab.

"Get on back to the U.S. of K., man, and leave this shit

behind. You said this nigger got a gun *and* he threatening her
on the phone *and* he saying he think you out to kill him? I
know people like that . . . I done been shot by one jealous nigger. No woman's worth a bullet, Phil. Leave her ass and go
back home. And if I was you I'd quit all this talking and get
my shit together. Cause you never know when he'll appear."

Doug made sense but Phil was still confused. It took him a
while to open the lock—his fingers were trembling and he
couldn't get the key to fit.

The lights were off inside, which made him even edgier,
claustrophobic, as if he were trapped in a coal mine. He felt
for the switch as his heart swelled to fill his chest. The feel of
the stubby plastic relieved him. Smiling to himself, he flicked
it. But nothing happened and he panicked. Shit. He flicked it
again. Nothing. And again. Blackness. More fear. And silence. At the base of his skull, a hammer began to bang a tat-
too that almost drowned the sound of his heavy breathing. He
reached out again. And then he felt it—this cold sensation
that he was not alone. He listened keenly. But he didn't hear
anything. Fuck, he thought he saw something move. "Who's
there?" he called out timidly. Sweat soaked his shirt. He
didn't see any movement or hear any sound, which rather
than reassuring him led him to question his senses, and this
made him feel even more vulnerable. As his vision adjusted
to the dimness and he still wasn't able to see anything un-
usual, he began to relax and suddenly, out of nowhere, the
reason for the darkness hit him. He'd forgotten to pay the
electric bill.

Laughing at himself a bit, though still uneasy, he felt his way
to the kitchen and got a candle. As he walked under the basketball net, he mapped out the most efficient route for gathering
his things and devised an emergency plan—grab spare horn
and scores first, everything else after. Then he saw what looked
like a figure in the bed. He stopped. Then crept closer. Then
stopped again when his breath blew out the light. Crouching
slowly, he placed the candleholder on the floor. Could it be Ian?

He didn't want to go any closer if it was. Maybe he's asleep. But don't be daft, Phil, he's in Jamaica. Now you're overreacting. Just get your things. He felt his way to the dresser, felt for his scores, then stooped to pick up the trumpet. He felt the handle of the case and grabbed it. But it was empty. The trumpet must be in the room. All he would need to find it was light. As he scoured his memory he focused in on the form in the bed. If it was Ian he would have answered, he thought. It may be just a bundle of pillows and sheets, for heaven's sake. Why am I getting so hyper? "Ian?" He jumped at the sound of his own voice. But he calmed down when there was no reply. Feeling bolder now, he called out again, a little louder. "Ian? . . . It's me, Phil . . . Are you sleeping? Ian . . . Ian . . . Oh fuck, there's no one there!"

Convinced he was alone, Phil went to the kitchen for another match. He came back and lit the candle, but he wasn't completely settled. He saw his trumpet and he quickly put it away, but he was curious about the bundle in the bed. He went there and pulled back the sheets and stood there . . . and stood there . . . and stood there . . .

The gun was still in Ian's mouth, and his hand still held it in place, as though it wanted to be ready in case his brain, which was splattered against the bed frame and the wall, decided to reconstitute itself. Taped to his chest was a piece of paper. Phil peeled it off carefully, recoiling when his hand brushed the warm skin. He began to wonder now: How long had Ian been dead? The gun had a silencer, he noticed. Fuck, it could've happened while he was outside with Doug. The note said:

Bury me in Jamaica. Play lots of music. Tell lots of lies about me. Say I was a good man.

book four

chapter sixteen

On the day of Ian's funeral Fire woke up from a hard-earned sleep with death trapped in his pores. Yawning and stretching, he wiped the sleep from his eyes, and tied a noose with a lock of hair and dangled it over his thumb. He lay there on his back awhile, in a lime green poplin shirt, breathing nonchalantly as if survival were not instinctive but a curious afterthought. Digging in with his elbows, he raised himself to the edge of the bed and gazed through the open door. A bright, red dawn was bleeding through the mist. The mist was gray . . . not white this morning. Gray, he thought, like the sea must have been on the trip that brought the Africans here. Red, he thought, like it must have been when the bravest chose the mouths of sharks. Death before dishonor.

He leaned toward the nightstand and spilled a cup of water as he tried to tune the radio. White noise surged and popped and snapped. Down toward the hundreds he tripped over a rising sound and held the knob with trembling fingers. He couldn't afford to lose it now. A horn was sailing through the blues, surging on an ancient tide. The Bird was playing "Now's the Time."

He drew the purple sheets against himself, sat up hugging his knees, then lay down again. It had rained last night and the air was damp, adding a bite to the mountain breeze. He hadn't eaten since Claire had called to share the news—nine days now—and he'd lost a bit of weight. How much, he didn't know. But these khakis in which he'd slept last night—

he gathered the waistband now—would slip over his hips if he didn't wear a belt.

At first he'd told himself that he was fasting. After that he said that he was busy. Which he was. He'd been taking care of everything: writing the obit, shipping the corpse, arranging for cremation, planning the funeral, and covering the costs—because Ian had died penniless, and Miss Gita couldn't afford to bury him. Even in death he felt a need to care for him.

But there was another reason, one which he only discussed with himself, and even so, always in a whisper, and never directly: deep in his heart he believed that he had failed Ian, that he had allowed his infatuation with Sylvia to distract him. Why, he would ask, had they spent their last hours together discussing only *his* hurt? And wasn't he the one who had told Ian that no one would care if he killed himself?

The least he could do was to give him the kind of funeral he would've wanted . . . or at least the kind he deserved.

Convinced there was a need to reunite him with his family, Fire had tried to persuade Ian's sisters to go to the funeral in Battery. The first two, sensing that his urgency was greater than theirs, said they couldn't go because they didn't have clothes that were suitable for church. Stripping some bills from the wad he'd withdrawn to bribe the detectives, he told them to go and get some. And wha bout de pickney-dem? they asked. It wouldn't right fe bring dem inna tear-up-batty pants . . .

Conversations with the rest of them were simpler: Fuck Birdie . . . when him was alive him nevah know we.

Downstairs in the kitchen Miss Gita was sniffling. Poor woman, Fire thought. She'd returned from seeing where Christ was born to hear her son was dead. No, woman . . . nuh cry . . .

Dead, he thought. Dead. The fan was an axe suspended above him. Ian is fucking dead? He lifted his shirt and pinched his skin . . . placed his palm above his heart.

He breathed in deeply and his belly caved in, touching his

spine, it seemed. And he promised to eat at the nine-night, when family and guests would nyam up fish and clap dominoes and dance ole choons and lick white rum and sup black coffee, making noise till way past midnight, speeding the spirit home.

How would he die? he wondered. He really didn't want to know—tried to fight it—but the thought swelled up like dough.

When he was ten he wanted to die in war . . . as a pilot . . . in a dogfight . . . trailing a scarf and a plume of smoke behind his twirling plane. At twenty he wanted to die in bed, wallowing under a stranger.

Now he wanted to die in his sleep, to go to bed and live within his dreams.

He felt his eyelids drooping, and sat up quickly. Not now, he thought. Not now. He must not fall asleep right now.

He hitched up his pants and went to splash his face with water, then went to the terrace and slouched in a blue Adirondack chair.

The mist was melted away by now and all was green before him—green and wet with dew and life. The low sunlight was dripping off the coffee plants. And the orchard blazed with pulsing color—yellow papayas, orange mangoes, fat magenta plums.

And Charlie Parker was riffing still.

He asked himself what time it was. Around five by the sun, he thought. A crowing rooster confirmed this as an army chopper shot across the sky . . . thukkering . . . thukkering . . . whipping a breeze, bending plants and shaking trees and stirring dust and grit.

He closed his eyes. Fuckers, he thought, dissing the dead like that. His face was wet when he looked again. It must be the wind, he thought. These could not be tears because my heart's too dry to make them.

I have no blood left. No sweat. I haven't pissed or shit in days. Maybe I too have died. Maybe I'm dreaming. Maybe this is how it feels when the plane goes down or when you come in a flutter of flailing limbs into arms that do not know you.

He reached for his pocketknife and looped a finger through the ring. If I cut myself I would not hurt, he thought. I know this. As he laid the blade against his wrist a flock of birds curled into view, circling the house then flying away, chirping toward the horizon and the comfort of the sea. Can I come with you? he thought. Can you take me where you're going? He bit his lip and clicked his teeth.

And Charlie Parker was riffing still.

Placing his feet on the banister, he took his time to count the wedge of birds ... started from the left-hand side ... worked his way across the crook. There were thirty-three of them. Thirty-three garlings.

Birds, he screamed inside his head, go around the world and sing my lament. Sing that I did not want this boy to die ... that I wanted us to age and join the elders of our tribe. Birds, go around the world and sing my lament. Sing that I do not want him to take that trip alone. For who will instruct him in the ways of the life that he has chosen not to know? Who will beg and plead for him with the guards outside the village? Someone has to tell them that he is not a stranger, that he is still our brother even though his hair and nose are different. I do not want them to press their spears against his spleen and order him to go. For where would he find his resting place? In India he's untouchable.

Miss Gita began to wail downstairs.

Ian, he thought, as he threw the knife on a stack of books, look what you do to your mother ... you dutty, wutless coolie ...

He began to moan. And Charlie Parker was riffing still.

chapter seventeen

The funeral procession began at a quarter to five on the Bailey bridge on the narrow road that wriggled down to Battery. The river, which was brown with silt, fizzed like a stream of spurted Coke, splashing over bright green ferns and leaping off protruding rocks to lick the fruit that dangled forth from overhanging trees, nobbly sweetsops and wedgy carambolas and round passion fruit. It had rained that morning, and the air was cool. The clouds in the washed-out sky were hard and gray like steel wool.

"I shoulda had something before I came," Fire said to I-nelik. "Or brought a sandwich. I had no idea we'd run so late. Everybody's in town already."

They were seated in the cab of the Land Rover.

"Well . . . we couldn't leave before Miss Gita calmed down," said I-nelik. "And maybe it's better that they went ahead. So many people on this little road could cause a lotta problems."

"How many you think down there?" Fire asked, feeling within himself a preemptive disappointment. There was no figure, he knew, that would make him happy.

"Bout a half grand," I-nelik said, hearing in Fire's melancholy a keynote that confirmed his suspicion that he was staging the funeral for selfish reasons. "I didn't know so many people liked him. But then they always love you when you're dead."

Dead. Fire reclined in the vinyl seat, creasing his purple robe.

"If you hungry then drive, then," I-nelik said, glancing in the rearview mirror at the milling crowd behind them.

"Couldn't do that," Fire replied. "Miss Gita asked me to lead the band."

"But suppose you faint?"

"Is a mind-over-matter thing," Fire said through a stomach cramp. He laid the keys on the dashboard. "Your mind must be strong in times like these."

He climbed into the back of the Land Rover and raised his hands, and the clashing sounds were slowly drawn into the surrounding forest, sucked away by silence, the silence of ants digging soil, and roots drawing water, and leaves making life out of sunshine. And Fire forgot his hunger and smiled. Arranged in rows before him was a Pentecostal mass choir, three hundred and twenty-six women from neighboring towns dressed in black robes and purple sashes, fussing with tambourines and hymnals. Behind the women were two hundred and twenty-four rastamen with long beards and white robes to match their headwraps, warming up their instruments—kete and funde drums, cowbells, chimes, and calabash gourds. And behind them, sitting crossways on a mule led by Sarge, who was wearing a too-tight suit, was Miss Gita in a bright red sari trimmed in gold, clutching the urn with her son's remains.

"I am not a Christian," Fire said, cupping his hands to project his voice. "And I'm not a rastaman. But that shouldn't matter, because we are here today in the name of love. And love is bigger than religion. For religion was made by man . . . and love was made by God. So let us walk together and make a joyful noise and sing that song that binds every one of us who came across the Atlantic in the belly of the whale— 'Amazing Grace.' "

He blinked the mist from his eyes and I-nelik gunned the

motor and the funde drummers began to beat a call on the drums strapped across their chests.

Boom-boom. Boom-boom.

Then the calabash gourds replied.

Boom-boom. Boom-boom. Boom-boom-sheke-sheke-boom-boom.

Then the kete drums.

Boom-boom. Boom-boom. Boom-boom-sheke-sheke-boom-boom-tock. Tock-boom-boom. Boom-boom. Boom-boom-sheke-sheke-boom-boom-tock.

As I-nelik eased the vehicle forward the cowbells and chimes began to titter and the women's voices railed up high and the choir began to dance across the bridge with their hands above their heads, tambourines shimmering, shaking out a sound like rice being poured into a skillet. Sweating, jostling, dipping sometimes then falling back, the procession made its way along the narrow, rutted road, curling around the jungled mountainside, rising and falling as it descended along the edge of the valley, which followed the natural lay of the land designed by the whim of the swerving river. Nine times in the five-mile journey women were picked up and thrown down by the power to froth and wriggle on the coarse asphalt, to rise, lurching and sweating, speaking tongues of remembrance without a scratch on their skin or a speck of dirt on their shining robes.

The church was too small to hold the service, so Buju and Teego had built a three-foot stage out of bamboo and palm fronds outside the door. I-nelik steered the Land Rover to where the cars were parked on the common and the rest of the procession nudged and squeezed its way to the stage, then split in two to form an aisle, up which Sarge led the mule with Miss Gita. She handed the urn to Reverend Bartley, who'd dressed himself this evening in a black-and-gray-checked three-piece suit and a Panama hat with a purple band. Sarge lifted Miss Gita down from the mule onto the stage; there she sat in an aluminum chair beside a plastic table decorated with pink and purple doilies and a portrait of her son.

Clutching a tattered bible, Mr. Bartley approached the microphone and asked to be joined in prayer. The crowd sardined between the gated park and the gingerbread houses bowed its head, and the ochre light from the setting sun washed over heaving shoulders.

"Dear Lord and Heavenly Father, we are gathered here before you now as sinners begging forgiveness. We are not worthy of Thy sight, O Lord. We do not deserve Thy love. But still You sent Your only son to die for our sins, so great is Thy forgiveness. The poet Dylan Thomas said that death shall have no dominion. But we don't need no book to tell us that. For in You we have eternal life. You alone have loosed the bonds of death. So we ask that You grant each and every one of us the wisdom to look into our hearts and admit that we are sinners, to confess our imperfections so that we may be humble in our actions before You and each other, in Jesus' name we pray. Amen."

"I still can't believe so many came," Fire said to I-nelik as they walked to the square from the common. "We have about five to six hundred people and about two hundred vehicles with a lotta minivans." He'd taken off his robe and was dressed now in a black-and-navy windowpane suit with flaps on the three patch pockets. As he surveyed the crowd, he pulled his hair into a ponytail and loosened the neck of his lavender shirt. People were clinging to branches and perched on shingled rooftops.

I-nelik stopped and looked at him, smothering his anger by stroking his beard. He began to whistle as he felt an urge to shake his nephew. Instead, he tapped him on the shoulder and addressed him frankly in the voice of the dentist he used to be. "You're sounding like a concert promoter. Okay, Fire, you've managed to attract a horde of people through a focused marketing plan. But so what? What does that mean? It means a lot to you, obviously. But fundamentally, Fire, what does it mean? None of this will bring him back. Accept that."

Fire stuck his hands in his pockets; he did not want to hear this now.

"You are using your brother, Fire. His funeral has become your personal sacrifice for what you believe are your sins. Look into your heart, Fire, and ask yourself if this is about Ian or about you—realizing, though, that if this is about you it will be refused like Cain's offering to God. Who knows, most of these people probably came for the food."

None of the people who were close to Ian came, Fire reflected. Claire had said she wasn't over the treachery. Margaret was still recovering from a breakdown, and Phil had decided to stay with her.

"And there is something else you should consider in all this," I-nelik said. "From what you have told me and from what I know about Ian, he did not deserve that woman. And deep down I know you know that. Fire, you can't go around blaming yourself for Ian's behavior. You've been doing that for twenty-odd years. Everybody has free will. Everybody has to make choices—choices they must live with, sometimes die with. Ian made his and you've made yours. He's died with his. Now what are you going to do?"

I-nelik stood there stroking his beard, watching his nephew clenching his jaw, grinding the words that came to mind like a calf chewing its cud. "Lately I've been getting this sense from you, Fire," he continued, "and it's very disturbing: you believe that all Ian's problems are related to class and that you'd be just like him if you'd been born in his situation. That's the kind of thinking that gives us of the left a really bad name—that kind of simplistic economic determinism. There are many struggles in life, Fire, and class struggle is only one of them. Everything in life is a struggle, and the greatest one of all is holding that commitment to keep struggling no matter what. Cause when you lose that one, you can easily lose it all."

"You are right," Fire said to end the discussion. "You are

right. But everything has begun. There is nothing I can do about it now."

The sun was halfway into the wrinkled sea.

"As I said," I-nelik replied, "we have to live with our choices. And," he began, moving to another point, "are you still insisting on taking his ashes out to sea today? We're running late. It might be dark coming in. Why we don't do it tomorrow? It will be safer then."

Afraid of what he might say and how he might say it, Fire looked past his uncle into the sun's red eye and began to debate going out alone. On the stage, a mento band was leading the crowd in "Rock of Ages." The service would be over soon. Short and sweet, he'd told the Reverend. Ian had wanted a party.

As they began to walk again he felt the need to be alone. I-nelik was right, he thought. How many of these people had really loved the boy? How much of the turnout was due to his effort? He began to do the math in his head. Fifty percent? No, closer to seventy. Then as the figure pushed past eighty-five he felt another cramp in his belly. A man was pacing behind the crowd, chattering into a mobile phone. What the fuck, Fire thought, could be so important?

Ahead of them, advancing from the edge of the crowd, whose members were singing and holding hands, Fire saw Mr. Heath and Major Daley.

"Well, look who's here," said I-nelik in a sarcastic voice. "The First Couple. I'll check you later. They might start holding hands too."

"This is not the time for that," Fire said, grabbing his arm. "We're family, man. Blood."

Searching Fire's eyes I-nelik said, "Stop pretending. You've never liked having a battyman father. Don't get sentimental now."

"That has never been my issue with him—and you know that."

"Well it should be."

The dread sucked his teeth, pushed his way between the men, and burrowed into the crowd. Fire began to feel queasy, as if he'd eaten sour bananas. There was a part of him that often wondered if his relationship with his father would've been different if the man were straight. Or if it would've been any easier if they didn't live in Jamaica—a stubbornly homophobic country. He thought about this awhile and reassured himself that this had nothing to do with it. They'd been distant from the beginning.

"Come," Mr. Heath said from a few paces. The neck of his black shirt-jacket was open, revealing a red silk ascot. "Come and hug your father."

Fire tried to feel the closeness, told himself it would feel natural if he tried. They'd hugged like this maybe three times, he thought. He couldn't remember the first time. The last time had been at his mother's bedside.

"We are family," Mr. Heath whispered. "No matter what, son, we are family."

"Yes, Dada."

"You are my only child, Fire. We can't keep living like this. Jesus Christ, man. I know that I'm not a perfect man and that I might have done things to alienate you . . . but come on, man . . . gimme a chance. Life is too short, man. Look at Ian and Miss Gita. Let that be an example to us. Things aren't right, so let's try and fix it. You are my only child, Fire. My only son."

"I understand that," Fire replied. "I understand that."

"Are you sure you understand?"

"Yes . . . I'm sure I understand . . . so we can let go now."

Fire stepped back and turned to the sun. The light would be gone soon. Did Buju and Teego remember to line the gravel road with flambeaus? The procession needed light to go down to the beach for the nine-night. Shit, did he order enough Portosans and tables?

"How much did all this cost you?" Mr. Heath asked, puffing on his cigar. Major Daley was standing to the side.

"Money is not the object, Dada," Fire replied, as he thought of what I-nelik had told him.

Mr. Heath wagged his head.

"You let that boy use you to the grave, eeh man?"

"Let it rest," Fire said.

"I keep forgetting that I can't tell you anything."

"That's not true."

"Of course it's true."

"You know it's not true."

"Name one piece of advice you've ever taken from me . . ."

"I'm not in the mood for challenges now."

Mr. Heath dabbed eyes.

"That hurt, you know . . ."

"I understand that."

"No you don't. You won't know what I'm talking about until you have children."

"Fire, Fire."

Over his father's shoulder Fire saw two of Ian's sisters approaching.

"Dada," he said, taking their hands, "remember Pearl and Junie? You know them—"

"Oh . . . yes," Mr. Heath replied, finding quick use for his hands—stroking his beard and holding his cigar. "How are you girls really doing?"

"So weh the children?" Fire asked brightly. He wanted to see them in their new Sunday outfits.

Junie, the older one, a fat-bottomed girl with droopy eyes, rubbed her hands down her green minidress and squirmed in her go-go boots, which were yellow like her back-length wig. Her sister, in a vinyl midriff to match her black battyrider, scratched her bouffant weave and giggled. She had a face like a truck—like a truck had hit it.

"So where are the little ones?" Mr. Heath asked.

"At home," Junie said.

Fuck, Fire thought. So these are your church clothes.

"How many you have?" Mr. Heath asked.

"Junie has six and Pearl has four," Fire said, speaking on their behalf. "They are really nice children and —"

"So why they didn't bring them?" Mr. Heath insisted.

"We goin to a dance down Oracabessa later and we doan know when we a-go reach home," Junie said.

Pearl slipped a hand around Fire's waist and snuggled up against his chest. "Y'ave any money? We want fe take a taxi."

"No!" Mr. Heath said, slapping Fire's hand.

"Dada!" Fire said as Junie picked up the billfold.

"You're just like your mother," Mr. Heath exclaimed. The veins in his neck were thick like high-voltage wires. "You just give, give, give, give, give . . ."

"I can't help you," Fire said as the women walked away. "I really can't help you right now."

The music ended and the crowd began to separate slowly. Fire felt his limbs trembling. So what if the old man is right? he thought. He doesn't have the right to treat me this way. And look at them . . . their brother is dead and they don't even care.

"See what I mean," Mr. Heath said, as he pulled on his cigar. "Coolie-dem just disgusting. I tried with Ian but—"

"What is wrong with you?" Fire shouted. "Who do you think you are?"

"Adrian!" Mr. Heath snapped.

"What?" Fire asked, shoving his fists in his pockets.

"Don't forget yourself."

"I didn't mean to do that," Fire said while looking at his pebble grain shoes. He wasn't bowing to his father, he told himself. The shoes were really interesting.

"You don't think sometimes," Mr. Heath said, clasping his hands behind him, afraid that he might reach out and be denied. "That's always been your problem."

"Just leave me alone," Fire said.

He plunged into the crowd, twisting and pushing against the mass. The rastamen had started to play again, and the crosscurrents of their polyglot rhythms echoed off the build-ings and smashed against each other, creating a kind of sonic dust that hung over the murmuring conversations of the slow-moving crowd. Darkness was falling like a mist of rain, blow-ing like a purple haze.

Fire shook hands without looking and blindly returned hellos as he fought his way around the edge of the park, pressed against the stout stone fence, reaching for handholds and pulling himself along like a climber on a horizontal cliff. A woman fainted and he was crushed against the fence in the rush to pick her up, and an elbow gored his side. This is mad-ness, he thought as the taste of bile rose to the back of his throat. He had to eat, he told himself as he watched the woman being passed overhead like a log. He had to eat . . . and reach the stage . . . and get the urn . . . take it down to the beach and out to sea.

According to his plan, as soon as the service was over, the choir and the rastamen should have set off up the hill to the gravel road with Miss Gita and the guests in tow for the nine-night and the spreading of the ashes. Because he'd been argu-ing with his father, he'd not been at his post when the ceremony was over, and, left to themselves, the choir mem-bers had drifted off to socialize with friends, and the rasta-men had formed a groundation circle and begun to smoke weed and chant down Babylon.

Now he was trapped across the street from Buju's house. To get to the stage he needed to work his way along the fence in the direction of the seawall, then slip around the short end of the rectangular park. Accepting the fact that the recession would never occur, he cotched against a ledge in the fence and waited for the crowd to pass. A breeze brought the smell of fried fish from Snapper Bay on the other side of the hill . . . the garlic . . . the pimento . . . the Scotch bonnet pepper . . . the heavy perfume of coconut oil. He trawled the conversa-tions as the crowd swam by. No one was talking about Ian.

They were talking about the fish, though—how good it smelled—and describing how they'd like to have theirs. Some wanted hard dough bread, some wanted festival, one or two were hoping for rice or steamed vegetables. Could I-nelik be right? Could they *all* have come for the food? He began to wonder now. It didn't make sense, but he still gave it thought, to keep himself from thinking about the quarrel with his father . . . and the argument with his uncle . . . and the way the service had ended in disarray. Maybe the old man was right.

He plucked a program from the sidewalk; but he lost his idea by the time he'd reached for his pen; and he sat there for a while with the Uniball suspended over the paper, waiting for a thought.

"Fire, ah just want to tell you that you shouldn't feel bad about what happen," a voice interrupted.

"Is awright, Zachy," Fire said without looking up. "But we can talk bout this later."

The crusty voice became a whisper. A bony hand fell on his shoulder. He imagined the toothless mouth. "I am really de one to be blame fe dis what happen here, because I get de dream and never tell nobody. Cause de day Ian dead me did dream mushroom . . . and anytime me dream mushroom dat mean death. Ah doan know what to do with meself now, Fire. Ah doan know where to go."

"Never mind," Fire said, as he tried to turn his mind in on itself like a Roman villa. He lowered his lids and listened to his breathing, and judged the saltiness of his mouth by running his tongue over his palate. Soon Zachy's voice was beaten into the droning world outside his head—from which another voice was calling.

"Hello," the voice said in a tone both timid and insistent. "Hello, can you hear me?"

And he opened his eyes to see Sylvia standing there in a black cotton dress with a flouncy hem, holding a pocketbook against her breasts like a schoolgirl clasping a three-ring binder. For a moment he wasn't sure if he knew her. Her hair was longer now, tumbling to her shoulders in waves and curls from a part in the middle of her head. Unsure of how he felt, he made a simple declaration. "I didn't know you were here."

chapter eighteen

She didn't answer immediately. She just stood there, leaning back on one leg, using her body weight to keep it from shaking. The melancholy in his voice was making her want to hold him, but he seemed to her so different now. Mischief no longer danced across his brows.

"How are you?" she asked.

He raised his palms and shrugged. Through the neck of his open shirt his collarbone dipped and rose, and she noticed that he was thinner. His skin was tighter around his mouth and his cheekbones seemed higher, making his face appear impregnable. Tears, she thought, could never breach those high embankments.

"It's so sad about Ian, isn't it?"

He nodded.

She had been standing at the edge of the crowd when he arrived, and had watched him from a distance as he talked first with I-nelik and then his father, both of whom she knew by instinct. Twice when he stood on the edge of the common it seemed as if he'd looked at her, but fearful that she wouldn't know what to say, she'd merged into the shifting crowd. She had arrived on the island the day before, using a provision in her airline ticket to stop over en route to St. Lucia, where Diego had arranged for her to stay in a villa with a view of Les Pitons, the twin volcanic plugs that overlook the languid village of Soufrière. There she planned to rest and regroup and write for a month. She'd landed in Montego Bay and

taken a commuter plane a hundred and twenty miles across
the island's hilly spine, landing at an airfield that was obviously a pasture till the pilot told her different. As they came in
low across the turquoise water she half-expected the plane to
sprout pontoons and skim to a halt on the rippling waves,
through which she made out schools of fish. Panicking as the
nose went down, she closed her eyes and squeezed her knees,
and in a moment of suspended weight and expectations she
found herself imagining that she wasn't going to a funeral,
but rather to spend a month with her lover, who'd be waiting
for her in that shed with the funky turret—the terminal, she
soon realized—with one arm outstretched to take her bags,
the other to pull her close, and his warm lips wet and slightly
ajar to taste her tongue with decorum, delaying the release
until they were alone. So when she didn't see him, she cried,
and she kept on crying during the forty-minute drive along
the coast to her hotel. In her room she thought of him as she
lay beneath the netting in the four-poster bed, wondering as
she gazed at the redwood rafters if he, her lover, loved her
still—believing no, but hoping yes, regretting now the choices
that she'd made.

But she was refusing to live with those choices, because
this man in front of her now, looking at her with downcast
eyes, was too special to lose. He was not just the one she
wanted to sleep with every night. He was the one she wanted
to wake up with every morning.

"How are you, Fire?" she asked.

He shrugged again.

"Is it going to be like this?" she ventured, looking at his
locks and wondering if he'd changed inside as well. "Me talking and you not saying anything in return? I hope not . . . because I think there's a lot for us to talk about . . . I know that
you and Ian were very close. Maybe this isn't a good time."

Fire rubbed his palms together and looked away from
Sylvia toward the sea. She followed his gaze through the thinning crowd, past the street lamp and the rubbish bin at the

corner where the street curved around the park, over the top
of the low seawall, through the gaps in the line of silhouettes.
In his disengagement she saw a bit of herself at their first
meeting, when he wore her down, charming her into his trust.
Turning his strategy against him, she pointed to the program
that was idling on his lap and paraphrased something he'd
said to her in the kitchen at Claire's gallery: "Okay, before I
go, I'd like to leave you an address and phone number so you
can get in touch with me . . . so we can be in touch only at
your convenience. Can I use that paper there?"

He handed her the program and she asked for his pen. In
the exchange, their fingers touched, and, ignoring for a second the restraint of the arms to which they belonged, curled
around each other in a brief embrace. Fire, who had been
feeling disconnected from Sylvia until this moment, felt her
life force race through him—the hydraulic pressure of her
blood, the electric pulse of her thoughts, the heat from the
chemical reactions that fueled her emotions. And as he felt
her filling him up, he found the room within his heart to tem-
porarily displace his guilt over how their affair had con-
tributed to Ian's demise. It was in this new mood that he
received her note, which she creased like a greeting card and
placed on his shoulder like an epaulet, holding his gaze as he
removed it.

Fire had been too deep in his own thoughts to see the moment when Sylvia wiped the paper against her neck to infuse
it with the scent she had dabbed there. She had bought the almond oil from Winston's Roots Apothecary when she stopped
to get a remedy for the headache that had worsened as the time
drew nearer to meet him.

Reining in the smile that played across his lips, Fire unfolded the paper and found there a drawing of a cookie and
an aroma that evoked in him the memory of the night in
New York when he'd sought refuge in her house and arms
after spending thirteen hours at the hospital with Phil, and
she indulged him with almond cookies. As he sat there

flashing through the memories—their lunch under the cherry tree, their walk along the Promenade, the reading at the warehouse—he felt something leap in his throat, a roar shaking his ribs, claws raking his stomach. It was hunger, he knew—the kind that could not be quelled by food. Shrugging to loosen the tension in his bones, he stood up, and stretched his neck, and rolled his head in languid circles. He settled his gaze on her, demanding through his posture that she show him a sign. Anxious that he might not see it, he looked toward the sea again, his face serene with contemplation. She saw something new in him now, a maturity accented by his meditative gaze. And there was power in the muscle that pulsed at his temple that reminded her that his was a mind unafraid to embrace serious issues. No, he wasn't just Fire. He was A. J. Heath.

He inhaled deeply and rested his palms against his temples, trying to fight the thoughts that were attacking him. It would be dark soon and he had to take Ian's ashes out to sea. But spending time with Sylvia was important—even if all he achieved was closure. In his head he heard his uncle's voice: *Everybody has free will. Everybody has to make choices— choices they must live with, sometimes die with. Ian made his and you've made yours. He's died with his. Now what are you going to do?*

What was he going to do? He allowed his hands to free-fall to his thighs, felt the sting through the light wool fabric.

In the process a button on his shirt became undone, and Sylvia remembered the night when he held her in the back of the cab on the way from the concert . . . his nipples small and raisin sweet.

"I wanted to call you so badly," she said, as her skin began to gooseflesh. "So many times . . . but I was afraid of you. In some ways I still am. You're too easy to love. You changed my life, Fire. I see myself differently because of you. You helped me find the me that I wasn't sure existed . . . I know now that my writing is more than just an advanced hobby. Writing

is my destiny, and I'm ready to struggle and fight for it—
because of you. There was a time when I couldn't relate to Jamaica. I didn't even want to relate to love. Now I do—again
because of you. And with you at my side I slew a dragon that
had me terrorized for most of my life. How can I not love
you? Oh, Fire, I was so scared, so, so scared of you. Because I
hardly knew you, and I was ready to run away with you if you
asked me. And that kind of passion is frightening. I love you,
sweet boy. That's all I can say. And I hope you love me too."

She felt the first tear when it bounced against her cheek.
She'd been studying his face for signs that he understood and
believed her.

She pressed herself against him and cried, while the drumming of the rastamen faded as they made their way out of
town, and up the hill. Their departure signaled to Fire that it
was time for him to leave. But how could he, when his darling
girl was crying? Holding her, he felt her sadness passing into
him. But what should he do? What did she want? What did he
want? As he considered this, Sarge appeared with the urn in
his hand, stopping at a respectful distance to ask with hand
signals if he should wait. Fire shook his head and, using signals himself, urged him to go on, indicating that he'd meet
him at the beach and wouldn't be much longer.

"This is not America," he told her, feeling the stares directed toward them. They were near to the spot where he and
Ian had fought. Everyone would know this was the woman
now. "Out here people are not accustomed to seeing this
kinda thing in public." Then he thought of how she'd cared for
him when he'd gone to her house after the hellish time in the
hospital with Phil.

"But fuck them," he added, "let's find somewhere to sit
and talk."

Wiping her face quickly, Sylvia ignored the stares and held
her pocketbook against her side as she followed him to a corner where the seawall joined the concrete fence of a peach-
colored house; there in the overhang of a mango tree they sat

side by side and spoke quietly, as the sea continued to hammer rocks below them.

Unaware that she was leaving that evening, Fire asked her to tell him about her novel and sat with his arm around her as she told him about the love story she was writing, blushing when she described the male protagonist, a novelist from Jamaica, a richly embroidered version of himself. They really wanted to talk to each other about the implications of their unexpected reunion, about the significance of this second chance. But what if I want it more than her? Fire thought. Sylvia was thinking the same about him. Nervous and afraid, but concealing it well, they talked about the things they knew were safe, drawn like magnets to what had first attracted them as they had sat on the Promenade in Brooklyn when he had come to see her from London—books and music. Glancing at her watch, she realized that time was running out, so she dared to be bold.

She placed her hand on his lips and said, "Do you realize that we've never danced?"

"We can dance tomorrow, if you want," he said. "Where are you staying? I'll pick you up."

Stroking the back of his neck she said, "But I'm leaving today . . . in a few minutes."

"What?" Fire lost his balance and almost fell over the wall into the sea. He wanted to ask her to stay, but he didn't feel he had the right. To his knowledge she was still involved. "Where are you going?"

She told him.

"And what does that mean?" he asked. He wanted to add "for us" or "for me" but he didn't feel he had the right.

She stood up, pulling him to his feet. He sat down again, trying to stall her. She remained standing, holding his hands, willing him to ask her to stay.

"I don't know," she said. "I guess it's up to us to define."

"But we can't have any more crying now."

"Don't worry," she said. "I won't embarrass you."

"I'm not worried about you," he laughed. "I'm worried about me."

She gave him her address in St. Lucia and told him to write or call.

"Tell Walcott to write you a love poem on my behalf," he said, feigning levity, running his hands along her sides now, feeling the dip of her waist and the flesh on her hips, which felt damp beneath the fabric. "I couldn't write you the poem you deserve. My brilliance is lament. And I'm happy now. Happy that we're parting like this."

"By the way, I have a bone to pick with you, Mr. Heath. Why didn't you tell me you were a famous novelist?" Some twenty yards away, in the direction of the church, some boys were pointing toward the star-filled sky, discussing UFOs. She looked back at Fire again and was seized by desire. What if she unzipped him and pulled her come-slick panties aside and sat in his lap? Did she have enough control to do that—to have him inside her and not gyrate or cock her waist and throw it back?

"I didn't tell you I was a writer," he said, "because I was naïve enough to think it didn't and shouldn't matter . . . but ultimately it did, didn't it?"

"Yes," she said, with a sigh. "My head was in a crazy place."

"And I guess mine was as well," he replied, "to believe the world was simpler than it is."

Sylvia found herself in a dilemma now. She wanted to make it clear to him that she wanted him now not just because she knew he was A. J. Heath, but because she had discovered her own values and had finally discarded everyone else's. There was no way to tell him this without telling him how much she wanted him. What if he didn't want her?

"How are you getting to the airport?" he asked.

"I paid a cab to wait for me."

He felt the tears well up from his belly and burst into his chest and he said, "I have to go take care of some things down at the beach. Ian's ashes must be taken out to sea. I won't be able to walk you to your car."

"It's okay," she said, sniffling. "Be good."

He closed his eyes to hide his tears and felt her lean away. When he opened them she was walking across the street toward the park, her toes pointed outward and her neck held loose.

"Call me when you get to St. Lucia," he said.

She stopped at the corner, next to the rubbish bin, and slowly retraced her steps. "I will," she said, placing her hands on his shoulders.

"I know you will," he told her. "You will, won't you?" As the hunger railed inside him again, he held her gaze and ran his hands along her legs, then looped his arms around her slender waist.

"Of course I will," she said. A breeze began to rustle the tree, spotting their faces with shadow.

They looked at each other with watery eyes.

"I have to go," she said as she used her knees to spread his thighs so she could hold him closer. In her mind her nipples were flickering candles. Extinguish them, she wanted to say to him, use your breath to blow them out. "Your hair is nice," she said. "Can I touch it?"

"Yes," he said, caressing her throat with the tip of his nose. "You can touch it. You can touch my hair."

She reached behind his neck and pulled the knot. The locks fell over his shoulders. "Would it be mad," she said, "if I asked you for a piece of it to keep with me forever?"

"That wouldn't be mad," he said. "That would not be mad at all."

"But what would I do with it?"

"Keep it as a reminder of what if . . . y'know . . . what if, what if . . ."

"I have to go," she said as she kissed his forehead. "And so do you. It's night now. Will you be going out to sea alone?"

He sighed deeply. "Yes."

"Don't go alone," she said, stepping away. "Take someone with you."

"Like who?"

She stopped and looked at her shoes. She tried to hint him: "Someone who you could talk to for days and days without getting bored if a wild wind blows you off course to a desert island."

"Those kind of people are so hard to come by," he said, leaning forward to pull her toward him by the flouncy hem of her dress. "This is why these things are so difficult."

She kissed him on the lips, suddenly, before he had a chance to stop and think about his neighbors. Desperate now, they searched and found in this mundane inconvenience the wisdom of prophecy, and he said to her, "I'll go with you to the cab."

They walked arm in arm to the common without speaking, zigzagging to draw out the time, their feet falling lightly, their bodies limp, as committed to their journey as sheets of wind-blown newspaper. The air was wet with the scent of roses, tangy with the smell of the sea, and heavy with whispered words. "Is de girl dat?" "She look nice though." "Is she make de man-dem fight?" "Me nevah think she woulda mawga so." "Is a farriner?" "Them look like bredda and sister."

At the edge of the common she stopped and pointed to a tan Corolla with rust around the wheel wells. By lamplight a group of men were playing Ludo on a homemade board on the hood.

"Okay," Fire said, waving to the driver. "That's Pan Head. I know him. He's a good driver."

She pressed her ear against his chest. His heart was pumping fiercely and his breathing was very shallow—like a drowning man. And once again, as she had when her plane was coming in to land on the island, she began to think, what if this was her last chance? "You were wearing those shoes when you came to see me from London," she said, hoping they could draw from the power of memory the energy to struggle for this love that belonged to them by right, but which they seemed so close to losing. "You brought me flowers," she continued. "That was so nice of you."

"Your cab is waiting," he replied.

"Is there anything you want to tell me?" Sylvia asked.

"Like what?" he asked, clenching his jaw as he looked at her, trying to fight the hunger.

"Do you love me?"

"I don't want to tell you that."

"Do you?" she insisted.

"I have to go."

"So go then," she said weakly. "Go."

He kissed her palm and stroked her face and walked away.

"Fire!"

She was twenty yards away from him, standing on the edge of the grass, with her arms at her sides, her palms facing forward. She watched him turn back, and saw that he was smiling.

"Was that your smile or the reflection of mine?" she said, pulling him in with the very first question he'd ever asked her. She could see in his face the recollection of that night on Spring Street, when he turned around in his muddy boots and dungarees and saw that she was admiring him.

"Neither," he replied. "It's the reflection of hope."

"It was nice to have met you, Fire," she said, repeating the words they'd said to each other before meeting again at the gallery.

"It was nice to have met you too, Sylvia."

"We can't just end like this," she said as he held her and rocked her and called her sweet names. "We can't just end like this, Fire. We must not end this way. Is there somewhere we could go," she asked, "and have a last dance?"

As he led her across the common, beyond the driver's feeble torch into the womb of darkness, they held each other closer, snuggled into each other's crevices like twins unborn.

Breaching the last of the vehicles on the field, leaving the sounds of the town behind, the blood rushing to the surface of their skin, they began to feel a heightened sense of each other and their surroundings, as the spirit of their passion, dead before, rose again and struck them down to lie in the middle of the open field, on a bed of grass, their sheets the sky.

As Fire's kisses fell against her face like melting candle wax Sylvia pulled up her dress to her neck and undid her bra so he could kiss her belly. She felt her body crest and fall like a wave, his fingers hook her panty-crotch, and the wind coming low and cool across the moss-laden stone that hid the spring that trickled out, enriched with natural salts, from the secret cave within her. With the stretch of his entry she gasped, and felt the greater heat of his mouth on hers. He'd kept his pants on but opened his shirt so she could feel the sweat-slicked ridges on his belly slide and tighten as he led her in a dance to a rhythm so primal as to be nameless, the rhythm of tides, of seasons, of phases of the moon. She felt herself becoming one with the earth beneath her and she looked up at him, as her soul left her body and returned, in that brief moment of death in which she screamed and called him "Dada" as she trembled.

They lay together, panting, dazed, bonded like survivors of an earthquake.

"I will love you forever," she said, running her thumb down the dip in his back.

"Just love me today," he said. "You know I'm afraid of promises. Promises frighten me. As I told you when we left the concert in New York, I don't deal with disappointment very well."

"I won't disappoint you, Fire. I won't."

"Promise me you won't," he said, hearing his voice thinning out to the one he possessed as a boy.

"Will you write me in St. Lucia?"

He didn't answer. He thought of the letter he'd written to

her, the one that Ian had found, the one over which they argued, the one that led indirectly to this moment. Feeling overcome by the burden of free will, he began to retreat to the
comfort of his belief in fate.

"Is there anything you want to tell me, Fire?"

In his heart he said, "I love you." To her face he said, "If
we're meant to be, Sylvia, then nothing can stop it."

Sylvia grew quiet and did not speak until they arrived at
the door of the cab, their clothes wrinkled and flecked with
grass.

"It was nice to have met you," she said.

"It was nice to have met you too," he replied.

Fire turned and walked away as Sylvia stood with one hand
on the car door, smiling, willing him to turn around. Everything else, it seemed—charm, reason, sex—had failed. Turn
around, she said to him telepathically. Maybe that will be our
sign that we are meant to be. She closed her eyes. Turn
around, she continued to say. Turn around. Just turn around
and smile at me.

When she opened her eyes he was gone.

chapter nineteen

With the urn tucked between some ropes at his feet, Fire put out to sea in a yellow canoe, the throttle eased back, the motor putt-putting, the prow riding low. Behind him, on the beach, the congregation had put away their dominoes and cups of rum and were holding hands at the water's edge, their bodies thrown into silhouette by the shimmering flambeaus perched on bamboo poles behind them.

After clearing the headlands and the reef, he gunned the engine and the outboard diesel sank the stern and raised the bow, and the boat sped toward the horizon pointing to the sky like an accuser's finger.

What will happen to us now? he thought as panic rose within him. When will I see her? Where will it be? And what will I say when I call? According to his beliefs, pursuing her was unwise, because fate, which decided all things, punished those who tried to work against it. Look at what had happened to them before. She was obviously not his destiny, because she was involved; but he'd gone ahead and forced it, bringing pain to himself and everyone around him. Why would things be any different now?

He'd asked himself this question as he walked away from her, and had continued to ask it after he'd dashed around the side of the park and watched her leave, making sure she wouldn't catch up with him. He was still asking it as he watched the taxi's taillights disappear around the final bend and he ran to the Land Rover and hurried after her. At the main road he had to guess which way to go. There were two airports and two directions. She could've gone to the airport in Kingston by going either east or west. If she was heading to Ken Jones to catch a commuter plane, she would've gone west only. West had two possibilities and east only one, so he went west, honking his horn so the vehicles ahead of him would squeeze to the left and let him through. But west was wrong, it seemed. Because he didn't find them, and the people whom he'd questioned hadn't seen such a car.

If they were meant to be, he told himself now, about five miles from shore, wouldn't he have found her then? And wouldn't Pan Head have pulled off the road when he saw him flashing his headlights in his rearview mirror so that he could tell her that he wanted her to be with him and offer to give her time to end whatever she needed to end so they could begin anew? Fuck, man! He had tried for it and lost.

Feeling a swell beneath him he glanced over his shoulder and began to think about the task at hand. He would be stopping ten miles from shore in deep waters patrolled by sharks, and as he considered this, plus the fact that the beach was already invisible, he acknowledged that he was slightly afraid, for he was not a man of the sea. He'd gone out with Teego many times, but he was not accustomed to being on his own, especially at night in a vessel without a life vest. The fishermen did not carry them because doing so implied a lack of faith in Jah. Because he'd lost time in pursuing Sylvia, he never got a chance to eat, and he'd been too confused and melancholic to remember to carry food or water. He would be okay, though, he told himself; he'd learned to navigate by the stars, and there was a radio on board that he could use to call for help in case of difficulty. For a moment he thought of spreading the ashes closer to shore and turning around immediately. But he believed in the power and meaning of ritual, and understood the need for him to go on: this was not for Ian, but for him, because by forging ahead into the darkness he might meet and slay his own dragon—his fear that Sylvia would disappoint him.

The rise and fall of the boat on the swells evoked in him the recollection of making love to Sylvia on the common beneath the stars; then a smile creased his face as he thought about his victory over Blanche, who had almost broken his will at a moment of weakness. With the drone of the engine and the heave and crash of the hull as company, he began to feel connected in a new way to writers like Haley, Hemingway, Melville, and Conrad. They had loved the sea for its meditative power and its ability to bring out the best in men—for water, the giver of life, could also take it away. Was he prepared to die? he asked himself. And if he should die right now, what would be his greatest regret? In his head he heard Marvin Gaye singing "If I Should Die Tonight." He pondered this for the next few miles. His greatest regret? Was it his relationship with his father? Was it his failure to save Ian? Was it not winning the Booker? He stretched his mind across his skull, hoping to net the answer. But no answers were out this evening. His mind was pure water.

Up ahead the spotlight picked up fins. Were they sharks or dolphins? A pair swept by the bow. Sharks. He was cold now. Was it fear or hunger? he asked himself. He wasn't sure. He should've brought something to drink, he thought, as well as a sweater against the cold. He began to shiver, and he felt himself wobble once or twice in his seat. Looking around for the fins again, he dipped his hand in the water and wet his face. The salt burned his eyes. He shut them till the sting passed away and opened them to see the shark fins sailing off to his left. As he watched them disappear there was a sudden whooshing eruption and he whipped around to see a school of twenty dolphins, curling in and out of the waves. Arcing. Flapping. Splashing. Draining moonlight off their backs. Fire smiled. A half hour later, he'd cut the motor at the place where he would sprinkle Ian's ashes.

The dolphins were grouped in a circle toward the bow with

their heads above the water, chattering. They are spirits, Fire thought, coming forth to carry him home. Bracing himself against the thwart, he rose on his unsteady legs, holding the urn across his chest, and slipped. He ducked down to keep his balance and the boat tipped a bit, then settled. He rose again, much slower this time, gripping tightly with his toes, aware for the first time of the smell of blood and death that was soaked into the belly of the boat.

"Ian, my friend," he began. "Only you really know what you went through, and why you made certain choices. And as you go now, my brother, I want you to know that you are loved, that you are blessed, that you are remembered. How did life happen so fast? We were boys only yesterday. Little boys with a jawfulla sweetie and pocketloadsa marbles and a headfulla Anansi stories. And boom! here we are now, men . . . without the young boy's simple optimism or the elder's crystal wisdom. As I was coming out here, Ian, I thought about the sea, y'know, and great writers who loved the sea. Like theirs, my work is filled with heroic figures, people who fight on for their boon, who understand the cosmic truth that life is struggle. Life is struggle. One trial after another, and that is why we need heroes, for they remind us of how much we can endure. You are gone now, Ian, and I must go on. I must do what you did not do. I must learn from the errors of your ways. It is so easy to give up . . . and to give in. I must endure. How is it that we grew up listening to Marley without understanding this? What did we think the man was saying when he said: 'Everything's gonna be all right.' That he was wishing that fate would fix things? Naw, man . . . Bob was saying that things would be all right because Jah would give him the strength to make it all right. We have to ask for the strength sometimes, Ian, but the choice is ours—to fight or surrender. And I will not surrender. I have a whole life in fronta me. A whole life of struggle . . . struggle I will endure . . . because I have the blood of survivors in me. Today is a new day. We are born again."

* * *

A breeze picked up on the way back to shore. Thirsty and hungry on top of being cold, Fire tried to distract himself by singing and making lists of things—cars, books, countries, airlines, anything to stop thinking about the single knot of pain that had formed in his heart as he admitted to himself how deep the absence of Sylvia would be in his life. Even though he had grown to accept the notion of life as a series of struggles, he was still finding it difficult to return to the place where he had just lost her. As he began to feel depression claiming him, he willed himself to sleep, hoping he would dream of her. Cutting off the engine, he made a pallet out of rope and burlap sacks and lay there rocking in the bosom of the humming sea.

The stench of the blood in the wood and the searing memories of Sylvia's love prevented him from sleeping deeply, so when he heard Teego's anxious call, which came an hour after he'd decided to anchor and rest, it sounded like something supernatural.

"Yow, Fire! Yow, Fire! You deh-deh? You deh-deh?"

There was an insistence in the voice that told him that Teego had been trying for a while, so he made an effort to sound relaxed when he reached for the radio.

"Yow," he said. "You save any fish for me?"

"Everything awright?" Teego asked. "Cause people start get worried, y'know. And the next thing was gweh happen was a search party. A whole heapa people start worry if you dead or something. Whappen to you out deh?"

"Everything cool," Fire said, gripping the bench to keep his balance. "I was just out here meditating, y'know, on life and dem ting deh. As a rastaman you supposed to understand dem ting deh."

He heard Teego's voice relax as he asked where he was and he told him.

"Well," Teego said, "we might be able to see you from here, then. Flash the spotlight lemme see."

Fire flicked the toggle switch a few times. "You see dat?"

"No," he said. "Do it again."

After a few seconds, Teego said that all was well, that he could see him now.

"Okay then," Fire said, settling down to try and sleep again. "I'll just be another few minutes. Tell everybody to just gwaan enjoy themself."

"Anyway . . . is not only that I call you bout still. Somebody waah talk to you."

"Who?" Fire asked.

"Just cool," Teego said as Fire began to protest.

"If is I-nelik, tell him that I will deal with him tomorrow. I cyaah really deal with that now."

"Is not him," Teego said.

"If is my old man," Fire said, still feeling angry, "tell him it will just have to wait."

"You sure?"

"Yeah, man. I'm sure. Soon come."

"Ten-four."

He lay down again. Fucking Humphrey, he thought. Why does he feel he can talk to me that way?

He began to think of the time he'd asked his mother. She had just taken off from Tinson Pen in her Lockheed Electra and was leveling off over Kingston harbor. "He is jealous of you," she said. "He thinks I love you more than him." He asked her if she did. She didn't answer. Could that be it? he was thinking, as the radio squawked again.

"Fire!"

"Yes, Teego."

"I don't mean to pressure you but . . . I think you should take this call."

"Let it wait," Fire said. "You don't understand, Teego, I'm in a vibes right now where I just need some time to myself. I have things on my mind, Teego. Things that bigger than me or you."

"In other words, woman business," Teego said.

"Yeah," Fire said, hoping this concession would give Teego a sense of victory and make him leave him alone.

"I don't mean to pressure you, Fire, but chuss me . . . you should take this one. Seen."

"Okay," Fire grunted as he restarted the engine. The world had proven too insistent for sleep. As the boat nosed through the water, he said, "Gwaan."

Then there was a new voice, saying in a scolding tone, "Why are you making me worry that I'll never see you again?"

To which he could only reply, as a smile washed across his face, "I love you. I love you. I really, really do."

"Is that your smile or the reflection of mine?" she asked. The texture of her voice was soft now, like leather soaked in water, creating in him a momentary connection to her consciousness, enabling him to picture her as she was, standing barefoot, at the water's edge, her shoes in one hand, the radio at her ear, feeling the menthol coolness of the surf licking and lapping her toes. Behind her, beneath the thatch-roofed pavilions, the guests were skanking to old rock-steady choons and slamming dominoes on plastic tables and telling duppy stories and teaching the children old ring games.

"How do you know I'm smiling?" he asked.

"Because I can see you," she said. "I can see your beautiful face as clearly as I can hear your beautiful voice. And," she said jokingly, "what else could you be doing? Well, you could be laughing at me, because I got as far as the next parish over—St. Thomas—and decided to turn around. And I'm glad I did, because I can't think of calling any other place home, because people I've known for less than an hour have been calling me 'darling' and referring to me as 'friend' when they introduce me to other people who've been telling me I'm the 'dead stamp' of so-and-so from over, so, so we must be distant cousins. So, no, Fire, I'm not going to St. Lucia. I'm staying in this place. And Jamaica is only four thousand, four hundred and eleven square miles, and that's too small for the two of us. So what does that mean, buster?"

"That you are such a silly woman. Such a wonderfully missed and loved and needed silly woman."

"You forgot to add 'single.' "

"Did you say single?" he said, laughing as he gunned the engine, speeding toward her now. "Why didn't you tell me this before?"

"Why didn't you ask?"

"I just thought—"

"No, you didn't," she interjected. "If you'd thought you would've asked me."

"I'm asking now," he said. "So tell me again."

"I'm single . . . well, until you get here. So you better hurry."

"I came looking for you, y'know. After I watched you leave I dashed after you. But I went in the wrong direction."

"The story of our lives to this point."

"So there you go—we belong together."

"By the way, are you still smiling?"

"Yes, I'm smiling, Sylvia."

"Why are you smiling, Fire?"

"Because you are my woman, Sylvia. And I am your man. Tonight I will fall asleep inside you. And I want to take you to meet my father."

"I can see your light, by the way. Can you see me?"

From two miles away he couldn't make her out in the crowd on the beach; at half a mile he could see her waving; at fifty yards he could see her face; at twenty-five, where he anchored and rolled up his trouser legs to step into the water, he could see her smiling.

As the boat drew near, she wanted to rush out to meet him, to splash in the foam and wet up her clothes with girlish excitement. But she didn't. She couldn't move. She couldn't even breathe until he took her in his arms and hugged her, as the mourners began to nudge and whisper: "Is de girl dat, y'know." "She's a nice girl, man . . . we did really judge her wrong." "She look like she woulda make some pretty baby too." "From de way dem carrying on it might be nine months from now."

"So, single woman," he said as he held her chin. "You have a date tonight?"

"I'm not single anymore," she replied. "My man has come to claim me."

"So you'll have my eighteen children, I take it, and do the laundry by hand because I still don't have a washing machine."

Tears scrambled down her face. "Only if I get the chance to be the one to wash your hair."

"It all depends on how you behave," he said. "I don't give that privilege to any-and-everybody."

"Every day won't be like this, you know. Happy and sweet."

"I know that. But these will be the moments that we'll live for."

"I love you, Fire."

"I love you, Sylvia."

"By the way, is that your smile or the reflection of mine?"

acknowledgments

Mummy and Pearson, I love you both. Addis and Makonnen, you're the sweetest children a father could have. Marie Brown, you are more than an agent. You are mother, friend, nurturing spirit, and guiding force. Cheryl Woodruff, my first editor, every new author is a gamble. Thanks for taking a chance and working to make me deserve it. You are Pat Riley to my John Starks. Gary Brozek, Kristine Mills-Noble, Beverly Robinson, and the entire staff of One World/ Ballantine, thanks for your care and patience.

Many people took the time to read early drafts. Respect is due to you: Oliver Smith (yes, King Jammy), K. Maurice Jones, Donette Francis, David Pilgrim, David Eason, Susan Burrell, Paul Tulloch, Barbara Serlin, Gary Oates, Steve Elliot, Michael Bennett, Sherman Escoffery, Clinton Reynolds, Marlene Hanson, and Kim Barrajanos.

David Winn, my writing professor at Hunter College, thanks for raising the bar and forcing me to jump higher. Janet Fouche, my mother-in-law, your dal and curry sustained me through this. Ben Bailey, Danny Abelson, Jennifer Peerless, and the extended family at the Abelson Company, thanks for feeding my imagination and drawing me into that wonderful place of fun and learning. Kevin Powell, you opened your Rolodex to me. Now, that's class.

Patrick Synmoie . . . cho man. Monte Bartlett, you're a major part of this. Donna McKoy, nuff respect. Peter Tulloch, my bass teacher . . . Val Douglas the bass father, X-amounta vibes. Loris Crawford and Byrma Braham and the crew at the Savacou Gallery, you're such wonderful friends and godparents, and your knowledge of art informs so much of this work.

Rohan Preston, Kwame Dawes, and Geoffrey Philp . . . me haffe lef oonoo fe laas. Ro, you are my Coxsone Dodd. Thanks for allowing me to use your poem "Dreaming of Mango." Kwame, I am Gong to your Scratch. Thanks for writing all of Fire's poetry. Geoffrey Philp, the only person who can tell a funny narrative like you is Pluto Shervington. Thanks for allowing me to use your poem "Exile."

Special thanks to Bernardine Evaristo, George Harvey, and Dylan Powe.

John Updike, David Malouf, Caryl Phillips, and Derek Walcott, you humble and inspire me.

To the people of Jamaica at home and abroad . . . one love. I am one of you . . . a likkle yute from Hughenden.

Thanks be to God.

**Don't miss this sexy novel
by Colin Channer**

SATISFY MY SOUL

"A stunning novel of extraordinary power . . .
Highly recommended."
—*Quarterly Black Review*

Carey McCullough is haunted by a damaged past.
While in Jamaica, he crosses paths with a radiant
woman who attracts him like a flame. Their undeni-
able attraction is much more than chemistry. As
Carey soon discovers from a "reader" of the spirit
world, he and Frances share a history that has linked
their souls for more than four hundred years.
Though Carey views past lives with skepticism, he
cannot explain knowing the language of an ancient
African people—in particular the phrase: "Mulewe
anekoso kuduwe bana" ("I will search until I find
you"). Yet Frances conceals secrets of her own. And
while Carey visits his best friend, a bond that was
once thought to be unbreakable will be put to the
ultimate test as startling truths at last emerge. . . .

Published by One World/Ballantine Books.
Available wherever books are sold.